By Rachel Caine

The Weather Warden series

Ill Wind

Heat Stroke

Chill Factor

Windfall

Firestorm

Thin Air

Gale Force

Cape Storm

Total Eclipse

The Morganville Vampires series

Glass Houses

The Dead Girls' Dance

Midnight Alley

Feast of Fools

Lord of Misrule

Carpe Corpus

Fade Out

Kiss of Death

Ghost Town

Bite Club

Last Breath

Morganville Vampires Omnibus:
Glass Houses, The Dead Girls' Dance, Midnight Alley

Morganville Vampires Omnibus:
Feast of Fools, Lord of Misrule, Carpe Corpus

The Revivalist series

Working Stiff

Rachel Caine is the international bestselling author of over thirty novels, including the Morganville Vampires series. She was born at White Sands Missile Range, which people who know her say explains a lot. She has been an accountant, an insurance investigator and a professional musician, and has played with such musical legends as Henry Mancini, Peter Nero and John Williams. She and her husband, fantasy artist R. Cat Conrad, live in Texas with their iguanas, Pop-eye and Darwin, a *mali uromastyx* named (appropriately) O'Malley, and a leopard tortoise named Shelley (for the poet, of course).

www.rachelcaine.com

Thin Air

WEATHER WARDEN
BOOK SIX

RACHEL CAINE

Allison & Busby Limited
13 Charlotte Mews
London, W1T 4EJ
www.allisonandbusby.com

A CIP catalogue record for this book is available from
the British Library.

First published in the US in 2007.

This paperback edition first published by
Allison & Busby Ltd in 2009 (ISBN 978-0-7490-0781-2).
Reissued in 2011.

10 9 8 7 6 5 4 3 2 1

ISBN 978-0-7490-4064-2

Thin Air

The author wishes to thank:

Joe Bonamassa
(www.jbonamassa.com)

Josefine Corsten and Sondra Lehman, without whom
this book would not have been possible

The winners of the 2006 NaNoWriMo competition:

Janice Smith (1st place), Telaryn, Amanda M Hayes,
Rhienelleth, Carrie Miller, Mysticmoose, CKocher,
Tainry, Writerfangirl, Navah Wolfe, Kaylana-Nicole,
Laura Roman, Seeksadventure, Jenn Moffatt,
April Urbain, Karl F Hubert, Jennifer Carey,
Zoe Winters, Jennifer Kammerer-Pulley,
Jennifer Minnick, Katinka Espersen, Amanda Smith,
Alexa Silver, Brian A Crawford, Crystal Sarakas,
Charity Vandehey, Carla Lee, Larinzia, Andrea
Miccaver

My friends (especially PN Elrod, Kelley, Marla,
Claire, Becky, Katie, and Becky!) and my family
(especially my husband, Cat)

Grateful thanks to Donna Cummings, who fearlessly
waded in on short notice to give feedback...

Speaking of fearless, kudos to my fearless agents,
Lucienne Diver and Kevin Cleary

And most especially, thanks to my editor, Liz Scheier,
for her tremendous faith in me

To all the great people who have been so enthusiastic about the adventures of Joanne and David, and the world of the Wardens. It's been a long, strange trip, but you've made it the best ride of my life.

So far, anyway. ☺

Previously...

I was lying on something cold and wet, and I was naked and shivering. Afraid. Something was very, very wrong with me.

I reflexively curled in on myself, protecting as much of my body as I could, as awareness of the world washed over me in hot, pulsing waves.

Biting, frigid wind. Ice-cold sleet trailing languid fingers over my bare skin. I forced my eyes open and saw my arm lying on the ground in front of me, hand outstretched, and my skin was a pallid, blue-tinged white, red at the fingertips. Frostbite.

I ached all over, so fiercely that I felt tears well up in my eyes. And I felt *empty*, cored and thrown out like an old orange peel.

I forced myself to look beyond my own hand and saw that I was lying in a mound of cold, slimy leaf litter. Overhead, bare trees swayed and scratched the sky, and what little could be seen between the skeletal branches was grey, flocked with low clouds. The air tasted thin in my mouth.

I tried to think where I was, how I'd got here, but it was a blank. Worse, it terrified me to even try to think of it. I shuddered with more than the cold, gasping, and squeezed my eyes shut again.

Get up, I told myself. *Up.* I'd die if I stayed here, naked and freezing. But when I tried to uncurl myself from the embryonic position I'd assumed, I couldn't get anything to work right. My muscles jittered and spasmed and protested wildly, and the best I managed was to roll myself up to my hands and knees and not quite fall flat on my face again.

I heard a voice yelling somewhere off in the woods. Sticks cracking as something large moved through the underbrush. *Run!* something told me, and I was immediately drenched in cold terror. I lunged up to my feet, biting back a shriek of agony as muscles trembled and threatened to tear. I fell against the rough bark of a tree and clung to it as cramps rippled through my back and legs, like giant hands giving me the worst massage in the world. I saw sparks and stars, bit my lip until I tasted blood. My hair was blowing wildly in the wind where it wasn't stuck to my damp, cold skin or matted with mud and leaves.

I let go of the tree and lurched away. My legs didn't want to move, but I forced them, one step at a time. My arms were wrapped around my breasts to preserve a warmth that I couldn't find, either within me or without.

My feet were too cold to feel pain, but when I looked back I saw I was leaving smears of blood behind on the fallen leaves. Cuts had already opened on the soles.

I kept moving. It was more of a lurching not-quite-falling than running, but I was too frightened to wait for any kind of improvement. Had to keep going.

More shouting behind me. Voices, more than one. The hammer of blood in my ears kept me from focusing on the words. *Someone did this to me*, I thought. *Put me out here to die.* I didn't want them to find that they'd failed.

Not that they really *had* failed, yet.

Up ahead was a tangle of underbrush. My body was already covered with whip scratches and a lacework of blood against cold white skin. I needed a way around... I turned right, holding to a massive tree trunk for support, and clambered up a short rise.

Just as I reached the summit, a shadow appeared at the top of it. I gasped and started to fall backward, but the shadow reached down and grabbed my forearm, pulling me up the rest of the way and then wrapping me in sudden warmth as his arms closed around me.

I fought, startled and scared, but he was a big man, tall, and he managed to pin my arms to my sides in a bear hug. 'Jo!' he shouted in my ear.

'Joanne, stop! It's me! It's Lewis!'

He smelt like wood smoke and sweat, leaves and nylon, but he was warm, oh, God, warm as heaven itself, and against my own will I felt myself go limp and stop fighting. For the moment.

'Jo?' He slowly let his arms loosen and pulled back to look down at me. He was taller than I was by half a head, with shaggy-cut brown hair and a long patrician face with big, dark eyes. A three-day growth of beard was coming in heavy on his cheeks and chin. 'We've been looking for you for days. Are you—' He stopped himself with an impatient shake of his head. 'Never mind, stupid question. Obviously you're not OK or you'd have contacted us. Listen, we're in trouble. Bad trouble. We need you. Things have gone wrong.'

I realised, with a terrible sinking feeling, that I had no idea who he was. And then the sinking turned to free fall.

He must have known something was wrong, because he frowned at me and passed his hand in front of my eyes. 'Jo? Are you listening to me?'

I had no idea who I was.

Chapter One

There were worse things than being naked, freezing, and alone in a forest. For instance, there was being naked, freezing, not alone, and not sure of who the hell you were. And having people depending on you.

That was worse.

Lewis – the man who'd found me, the tall, ragged-looking specimen with the cheekbones – had put my silence down to shock, which was probably not far from the truth. When I just clung to him, shivering in the frigid wind, he finally stripped off his down jacket and draped it over my shoulders. I watched him, shivering and numb, clutching the down coat hard around me. It smelt of dirt and feathers and sweat.

'Say something,' he commanded. I didn't. I couldn't. All I could do was shake. What was that in his eyes? Anguish? Fury? Love? Hate? I had no frame of reference for him, or for what he was feeling. 'Jo, how'd you get here? Where have you been?'

Jo. I waited for some kind of internal recognition, some circuit to activate. I waited for some confirmation that Jo was my name.

Nothing.

When I kept silent, he finally shook his head and glanced around, then gathered up the backpack he'd dropped on the ground. 'Come with me.' I had no reason to, but I was too cold and too weak. Lewis steered me down the gentler slope of the far side of the hill, into a small clearing. Overhead it looked like twilight, everything masked into smooth grey cotton by low-hanging clouds. Virga draped from them, veiling the treetops. 'Sit,' he ordered, and I collapsed onto the cold ground in a huddle. I'd lost too much body heat; the coat couldn't warm me. Lewis turned away and grabbed handfuls of fallen wet wood from the underbrush – good-sized logs, some of them – and began putting together the makings of a fire. Within five minutes he had cleared a space, dug down to the dirt, created a fire pit, and ringed it with rough stones.

It wouldn't matter. The wood was way too wet to burn.

Lewis settled down next to the non-starting fire, glanced at me, and extended a hand, palm out, towards the inert pile of soaked wood.

It burst into immediate hot flame.

I jerked backward, startled, blinking in the sudden dazzle of light, and looked at him. He didn't seem to find anything odd about what had just happened; in fact, he barely paused before he began digging in his pack. He pulled out a rolled-up pair of blue jeans and a denim shirt. Thick thermal socks.

I started to edge away from him as discreetly as possible.

'Foot,' he said, and held out his hand. When I didn't move, he sighed. 'Jo, for God's sake, unless you want to lose some toes, let me help you.' I slowly extended my bare left foot. His large, long, blissfully hot fingers wrapped around my ankle and propped it on his knee. He frowned disapprovingly at the cuts on my foot. 'What the hell happened to you?' It was just a murmur and, by this time, obviously a rhetorical question. He was very intent on the cuts, not my face. 'OK, these are mostly superficial, but it's going to hurt like hell later if I don't do something about it. So please hold still.'

I expected him to reach for the first-aid kit I could see in the neatly organised backpack. Instead, he cupped my foot in both hands, and I felt a sudden pulsing warmth go through me, followed by a dull, shearing pain. In a second or two, the pain subsided and faded altogether. My foot felt deliciously warm. Tingling.

He let go and tugged one of the thermal socks on and up to my ankle, sealing in the warmth. I wanted to be grateful, but the truth was, I was scared. I didn't know this guy, although he claimed to know me, and he could start fires just by snapping his fingers. Not to mention whatever he'd done to my foot, which felt really good now, but clearly wasn't *natural*.

'Next,' he said, and held out his hands again. I hesitated, then gave him the right foot. I'd need those cuts sealed up if I had to make a run for it.

Maybe he's the one. The one who kidnapped you and knocked you over the head and dumped you out here to die. Maybe, but in that case, why was he doing magical first aid? He could have just let me go. I'd have died out here without help.

Wouldn't I?

When the right foot was healed and thermal-socked, he put the blue jeans and shirt on the ground between us, and looked up into my face.

I waited for some memory to make it past the big black wall. Anything. His name was Lewis; he acted like he knew me; I *should* know him.

I didn't.

He must have taken my long stare for something else, because he shrugged. 'Sorry. I don't know where he is.'

He? There was another one? I looked down, trying not to show how tentative I was. How confused and scared.

'Jo?' He sounded grim. 'Whoever took you... did they... Ah, dammit. I'm just going to ask it, all right? Were you raped?'

Had I been? The word made me feel sick and dizzy, and I had no idea how to reply. I didn't remember my clothes coming off. I must have fought, right? I must have tried to get away. I wouldn't have just ended up out here, naked and dying in the cold, without some kind of a reason.

Abducted and raped and left for dead. I tried it on as an explanation for the panic I felt inside, but it didn't feel right.

He was waiting for an answer. I didn't look up at him. 'I don't... I don't know.' My voice sounded shockingly cracked and small. 'I can't remember,' I whispered. 'Can't remember anything.' Tears suddenly boiled up hot in my eyes, and I couldn't get words out past the constriction in my throat. The panic hammering in my chest.

Abducted and raped and left for dead. Maybe it was true. Maybe it was just one of those sad stories that filled the daily newspapers and got the TV news industry good nightly ratings.

I felt so cold. If I kept shaking like this, pieces were going to start flying off.

'Ah, God, Jo. You're in shock,' he said. 'Look, I'm going to touch you, all right? We need to get these cuts closed up and this frostbite taken care of, and I can tell if there's...anything else wrong. Just...hold on. Don't fight me.' He reached out very carefully.

I flinched. I couldn't help it. I got hold of myself

somehow, and held still as his hands closed around both of mine. He moved to get on one knee in front of me.

'I have to... I have to get closer,' he said. 'I need you to lie down.'

Lie down. Lie down on this freezing ground.

Lie down, at his mercy.

Not easy. Not at all. I kept telling myself that if he could heal me – however he was doing it – then I should let him. I needed to be healthy. I needed to be able to run.

I slowly let myself sink back, holding on to his hands, until I was flat on my back. The coat didn't go very far down. The backs of my thighs felt instantly ice-cold in contact with the damp leaves, and although the fire was casting some warmth, I could barely feel it. My shaking was getting worse, not better.

'Easy,' he murmured, as if I were some wild thing he was out to tame. 'Try to relax.'

Yeah, sure. Relax. I couldn't watch what he was doing, and the darkness behind my eyelids was too frightening, too much of a reminder of everything I'd already lost. I looked up instead, at the clouds, and saw a ghost image of a vast wind flowing like a river, separated into layers. Every little eddy and swirl was suddenly visible to me. I stared, puzzled, entranced, and then gasped as I felt Lewis start in on me.

It *hurt*. Live-wire-on-the-tongue kind of hurt, every nerve in my body sensitising and responding and burning, and I made a moan of protest and tried to yank free, but he held on, leaning closer, on his knees in front of me with his head bent. It looked like prayer. It felt like torture.

Oh, God... He was inside of me. Not in a sexual way, although there was something in it that resonated along those nerves, inside those aching spaces; no, this was more invasive than that. I could feel him moving through every part of me, climbing the ladders of my nerve endings, searching...

Out. Get out! I was aware that I was panting, groaning, and trying to pull my hands free of his. *LET GO OF ME!* I was screaming it inside as I writhed on the ground, squirming, trying to suppress the terrible feelings welling up inside of me.

I got my wish with a vengeance as a pair of hands grabbed his shoulders and *threw* Lewis across the clearing to smash against a tree trunk. Lewis yelled and flopped, rolled over and came to his hands and knees, then slammed facedown into the leaves before getting up again, more slowly. His face was dirty grey with shock and rage.

'You asshole,' Lewis said shakily. 'I was trying to help her.'

I looked up at my rescuer.

For a moment my mind just didn't want to

acknowledge what it was seeing, because...he wasn't human. No man had skin like that, like living metal – flickering copper and bronze, cooling into something that was more like flesh, but still too burnished for anything outside of a special effect. His hair was longish, like Lewis's, a barely subdued blazing auburn. Although he was dressed like a regular guy, in blue jeans and a checked shirt, I had no sense of him being anything like normal.

His eyes were *illuminated*. Backlit, the way a cat's can seem in beamed light. A rich, scary colour like melting pennies.

He was staring straight down at me, riveted.

Expressionless.

Lewis spat blood and climbed painfully to his feet. 'Make up your mind, David. Do you want her to freeze to death? Or can I get back to healing her?'

David – should I know the name? Or was he a complete stranger? I couldn't tell, because he had absolutely no clues in his expression, in those crazy inhuman eyes, or in the tense, still set of his body.

Lewis must have taken his silence for assent, because he was coming back. He elbowed David aside and reached for my hands again. I yanked them free.

'No!'

'Don't be stupid. You've got frostbite. I'm restoring circulation.' Lewis made a frustrated sound and grabbed my wrists, hard, when I tried to pull away again. 'Dammit, quit fighting me!'

'Let her go,' David said very quietly. 'She doesn't recognise you. She doesn't understand.'

'What?'

'I can't see her,' he said. 'She's not on the aetheric.'

Lewis frowned at him and rocked back on his heels. 'That's impossible.'

'Look.'

Lewis turned the frown towards me, and his eyes unfocused. For a long few seconds, nothing happened, and then a very odd expression overtook his irritation, smoothed it out, and made it into a blank mask.

'Oh, shit,' he breathed. 'What the hell...?'

'I can't see her past,' David said. Which made no sense to me at all, but then, this was making less sense as it went along. 'Someone's taken it from her.'

'How is that even possible?'

'It isn't.' Suddenly David crouched down, startlingly graceful about it, and stared into my eyes. 'Joanne. Do you know me?'

I recoiled from him, crab-walking backward. Answer enough. For a long moment he didn't move again, and then he smoothly got back to his feet and stepped away. He crossed his arms across his chest and bowed his head, relieving me of the pressure of that stare, at least for a little while.

'Who *are* you people?' I blurted. 'He's got some kind of superpowers. And I don't know what the hell *you* are!' I pointed shakily at Lewis and then at David. I'd got farther from the fire, and I could already feel the chill biting hard on my exposed skin. 'No! Don't touch me!'

Lewis had started moving after me. He stopped, frowning again. 'What are you going to do?' he asked in a voice that sounded way too reasonable. 'Run around in socks and a coat in an ice storm? It's suicide. Let us help you.'

'Why? Why should I believe you?'

'Because you'll die without us,' David said. He hadn't looked up. 'We've been out here looking for you for days without rest.' He slowly raised his head, and I saw something that rocked me back as if he'd pushed me: tears. Very human tears, in those not-human eyes. 'Because we love you. Please.'

This time, when David came towards me, I forced myself to hold still for it. I still felt that nearly uncontrollable urge to run, to hide, and I couldn't stop the way I flinched when he slid his arms under my shoulder blades and my knees. Unlike Lewis, he didn't smell like a guy who'd been living rough. He smelt like fresh wind and sunlight and rain, and against my will I buried my face in the hollow where his neck flowed into strong shoulders. He felt solid and real, and he picked me up as if I weighed less than an empty plastic bottle. Heat cascaded out of him, crashed into me, flooded me in a drunken tsunami of warmth. Oh, so good. I clung to him, my hands fisted in the fabric of his shirt, and shuddered in sheer animal pleasure.

'I'm going to need to touch you,' Lewis said. I glanced up into David's face.

'I'll hold you,' he said. 'I won't let go.'

I nodded. Lewis's hands pressed against me, palms flat, this time against my shoulders, and jolts of electric fire began to flood through me. I might have resisted, but if I did, David was more than enough to keep me still.

When it was over, I felt nerves still firing in white-hot jerks, but as it passed a sense of numbing exhaustion took over, and I felt myself going limp.

'That'll do it,' I heard Lewis say in carefully colourless tones. 'Better get her dressed. It's going to get colder out here tonight, and she's still very weak.'

David's voice seemed to be moving away from me, growing thinner and fainter. 'Wait. What did you find?'

'Nothing,' came Lewis's faint, smeared whisper. 'Apart from nearly freezing to death, there's nothing wrong with her. Physically, anyway.'

'Then what happened?' David's question came as a ghost, lost in darkness, and then I was gone.

* * *

I didn't sleep for long, but when I woke up, I was dressed – blue jeans and a denim shirt over a thermal tee – and wrapped up in a sleeping bag next to the fire. I tried to figure out which one of them might have taken the liberty, but soon gave up. Either way, it was a deeply unsettling question.

'I can carry her,' David's low voice was saying from somewhere on the other side of the crackling fire. Night had fallen, and with it an absolutely deathly chill. Even in the sleeping bag, fully clothed, I could feel it nipping at me. 'I don't like keeping her out here longer than necessary.'

'I know,' Lewis replied. He sounded agitated. Exasperated. 'Dammit, I know! But it's more than a day's hike to the closest rendezvous point, and no matter what I do, the temperature just keeps falling. You think she's strong enough to make the trip? Like this?'

'She won't be any stronger tomorrow.'

'OK, I give. It's not just her I'm worried about. If I don't get some sleep, I could collapse on you, too.'

'You think I couldn't carry you both?' David asked. He sounded amused. 'All the way back, if necessary?'

'I'm pretty sure you could, but my pride's already taking a serious beating, and you know I love you, man, but I'm not ready for us to be quite that close.' Lewis's voice was as dry as old paper. 'And besides, if I start losing it, we start losing the weather. If you start messing with things, they'll find you, and us, and her.'

'Ah.' Evidently a convincing argument.

'I'll put up the tent,' Lewis said. 'Won't take long.'

I peered out from under half-closed eyelids and saw David walking towards me around the fire. Something different about him now – oh, he was wearing a coat. Not a modern hiking accessory; this one was a long olive-drab affair, like something out of the First World War, and it came down almost to his boots. He looked antique. Out of place.

Beautiful.

He noticed me. 'You're awake,' he said, and crouched down beside me. 'Thirsty?'

I nodded and pushed myself up on my elbows. He unscrewed a plastic bottle and handed it over. I guzzled cool, sterile water, almost moaning with ecstasy as the moisture flooded into me. I had no idea how long I'd been without a drink. Too long.

He leant forward to move hair back from my face, and I instinctively jerked back, putting air between us. He froze. *Oh, God*, I thought. *We're lovers*. There was no other explanation for the ease of his gesture, and the look on his face, as if I'd stuck a knife in his guts and broken it off. The expression came and went in a flicker, and then he was back to safely neutral.

I took another long drink to cover my confusion, to give myself time to breathe. Lewis glanced over his shoulder at us, and I wondered what the hell the dynamics were of this life I couldn't remember. David was – I was almost certain – my lover. And he wasn't human. Lewis was human, but not my lover – at least, I didn't think he was.

Not that Lewis was exactly the normal choice of the two. He could start fires with a snap of his fingers. And heal people. Whatever it was I couldn't remember about my life, it definitely wasn't what you could ever call boring.

David wasn't much for small talk, it appeared, which was a very good thing, given how confused I felt. He handed over a couple of trail bars, packed with sugar and protein, and I hungrily wolfed them down. Nearly dying takes a lot out of you. Eating served another purpose: It kept me from having to talk. I had a ton of questions, but I wasn't sure I was ready for any of the answers.

Lewis had the tent up in record time. Outdoorsy, clearly, though I guess I should have known that from his battered hiking boots and easy confidence and the neat, meticulously packed bag he was toting around. It wasn't a very big tent, barely large enough for two sleeping bags. We were all going to get very friendly.

At Lewis's orders, I clambered out of my warm nest, dragging my sleeping bag with me, and settled in. Claustrophobic, but at least it would be warm. I turned on my side and listened to the other two, who were still outside. Their fire-cast silhouettes flickered ghostly against the dark blue fabric of the tent.

'I have some MREs. Maximum calorie concentration,' Lewis said. 'So...does she like Stroganoff or meat loaf?' He was deliberately casual, but he sounded really, really tired.

'Ask her,' David said. 'But I doubt she'd have any idea. She remembers what they *are*, just nothing about how it relates to her directly.'

'How...'

'He took it from her.' David's voice had turned hard and brittle as metal. 'We have to get her back.'

'I'm not disagreeing, but...look, David, what if we can't get her back? We've got no idea at all what we're dealing with here. And the last thing we should do is get into this before we know—'

'*He's taken everything!*' David didn't shout it, but he might as well have; his voice ached. It bled. 'Djinn can see the history of things, and she has none. Do you understand? As if she never lived. The people who know her – we're all that's holding her here. Without us, without our memories of her, she disappears. Unmade from the world. Clearly that's what he meant to do. We *must* find a way to undo it.'

Lewis was quiet for a moment. I heard the fire

crackle, as if he'd thrown another log on. 'Then that's all the more reason not to go running off into the woods without a better idea of what we're doing,' he said. 'We've got problems beyond Joanne.'

'*I* don't.' David sounded fierce and furious.

'Yes, you do, David, and you know it. We're crippled. Both of us. Between the Djinn's withdrawal and the problems with the Wardens—'

'She's the only thing that matters to me now. If she's not the only thing that matters to you, then you shouldn't be here.'

'I'm just saying that we need to take our time. Be sure we understand what's happening here.'

'Use her as bait, you mean.'

'No. I didn't say that.'

'And yet I think that's what you mean. There's something out here – you know that. Something very wrong.' Silence, and a rustle of cloth. David's shadow lengthened as he stood up. 'She always thought you were a cold-blooded bastard at heart,' he said, and ducked into the tent.

I hastily squeezed my eyes shut, but there was no way he wouldn't know I was awake. I could just... sense that. He'd be a very hard man to fool.

He settled down next to my feet, his arms propped on his upraised knees. 'You heard,' he said. It wasn't a question. 'What do you want to know?'

I sighed, gave up, and opened my eyes. 'Where have I been? Do you know?'

Either my eyes were adjusting to the dark, or there was a dim, suffused illumination running through the walls of the tent. Moonlight. I could see a vague shadow of a smile on his face. It looked bitter. 'No,' he said. 'I don't. I'm sorry.'

'Well, tell me what you do know.'

'Beginning where?' he asked. 'With your birth? Your childhood? Your first love?'

Just how much did he know about me? 'How did we meet?' I asked.

'Ah. That's a good story. I guess you might say that I tried to kill you.' He paused, head cocked to one side. 'Technically, I guess you could say I succeeded.'

'What?'

'It's a long story. You sure you want to hear it?'

I felt a bubble of panic growing in my chest, making me short of breath. 'I want to know who I am. What's my name?'

'Joanne Baldwin,' he said. 'You're a Warden.'

'A what?'

'Warden,' he said. 'You're part of a small group of humans who have the ability to channel the elemental power of the world. Control fire, earth, or weather. You control the weather. And fire, these days, although you're still learning that skill.'

'I control the... Are you high?'

That drew a strange smile out of him. 'Try it,' he said. 'Reach out and feel the wind. Touch the sky.'

'You know, those lyrics must have been lame even back in the seventies.' But even while I was mocking him, I remembered that vivid ghost vision I'd had, of the wind running like a river in the sky. I'd been able to see curls and eddies in the flow.

Was that what he meant? But that wasn't controlling the weather; that was...X-ray vision. Or something.

'You're insane,' I declared. Which he found oddly amusing.

'I'm Djinn,' he said. 'So yes. At times, at least by your standards. Try, Jo. Try to reach out and touch the clouds. I'll help you.'

I bit my lip and thought about giving it a try. What was the worst thing that could happen? *No,* something told me inside, the same thing that had told me to get up and run, out there in the woods. *Don't do it. You have no idea what you're risking. What kind of attention you might draw.*

'How?' I asked.

David held out his hand. I slowly reached out to take it, and our fingers instinctively intermeshed.

Before I could even think about saying no – not that he was asking – he pulled me up and against him, body to body.

'Hey!' I yelled, panicked, and tried to push him

away. Not a chance. 'Get off, dammit!'

He put a hand over my mouth, stilling my protest – not demanding, more like a gentle caress. 'I'm not going to hurt you,' he murmured. 'If you allow yourself to feel for a second, you'll know that.'

I didn't. I didn't know. He terrified me in ways that I couldn't even begin to understand, starting with the too-bright, backlit colour of his eyes. I had pressed my hands flat against his chest, trying to hold him back from an assault he wasn't even contemplating, so far as I could tell. He took both of my hands in his and interlaced our fingers tightly again.

'Deep breath,' he murmured. He pushed me back to a distance, holding me there as if we were involved in a formal box dance. 'Not that deep,' he said, very softly, with a wry twist to his full lips. 'Bad for my discipline. Relax.'

Not a chance of that. I stared at his shadowed face, and I felt something beginning to unspool inside of me, as if he were drawing it out. 'What...? What are you doing to me?'

'Relax,' he said. 'Relax. Relax.'

And the world around me exploded into colour. Vivid, breathtaking colour, shimmering and trembling with fury and life. My skin glowed. David was a bonfire, glittering and dripping with raw power. Everything was so bright, so beautiful, so *complicated* – even the fabric of my shirt was composed of tiny pinpoints of light, woven from the fabric of the universe.

I felt David holding my hands, but they weren't really my hands anymore. I was drifting up, out of my body, and the world was moonstone and shadow and neon, a confusing, bewildering, amazing place.

I soared up, out of my body, and passed through the thin fabric of the tent as if it weren't even there.

Up, plunging into the sky as if gravity had reversed itself and I was falling up into infinity...

Stars like ice. Cold-shimmering clouds, held together with a crystalline structure that was brighter and more beautiful than diamonds, and oh, God, it was so *beautiful*...

I reached out and touched the bonds that held part of the cloud together, and made it rain.

Come back, I heard David whisper, and the thing that had unspooled inside of me like a kite string was suddenly reversing, tugging me back away from the wonder of the sky, and it felt as if I'd spilt wind from my wings.

I was falling out of control back towards the forest, the tent, the fire.

I slammed back into my body with a sickening jolt, gasped, and convulsively tightened my grip on David's hands. I heard the first cold patters of rain on the fabric overhead.

Outside, by the fire, Lewis cursed, and I felt a sudden hot snap of...correction. The rain stopped.

'Oh, my God,' I whispered. My hands were shaking, not with weakness but with sheer joy. 'Oh, my God, that was—'

'Nothing,' David said. 'Just a taste. You used to control more than rain, Jo. You will again.'

He pulled me into his arms, and his lips pressed gently on my forehead, my closed eyes...my lips. I didn't know if I should respond, but my body was already making the decision for me. The warm, damp pressure of his mouth on mine raised something wild inside of me, something deep and primal. I sank my fingers deep into the soft silk of his hair. He was a good kisser. Rapt, intense, focused, devouring my lips hungrily.

And then he broke free, sighed, and rested his forehead against mine. His fingers combed through the mud-caked tangle of my hair, leaving it straight and shining and clean.

'How long...' My voice wasn't quite steady. I licked my lips, nearly licked his as well. 'How long have we, you know, been...together?'

'A while,' he said.

'Years?'

I felt his smile. 'What do you think?' His lips brushed mine when he murmured that answer. *Keep talking*, I thought. Because I was tempted to do a lot more.

'Not years, maybe...um... I don't know.' All I knew was that whoever and whatever David was, he had the key to turn my engine. 'Then why don't I remember you? Remember *us*?' I was fairly sure, given the intensity of the kisses, that it was well worth remembering.

'You don't because you can't,' he said, and his fingers stroked through my hair again, gentle and soothing. 'Because someone took away your past.'

'Then...how come I can still talk? Remember how to dress myself – OK, not that I dressed myself, bad example...' I got lost on a side thought, and pulled back to look at him. 'Did you? Put my clothes on?'

'Do you seriously think I'd let Lewis do it?' David asked, raising his eyebrows. 'Of course.' He gave me a slow, wicked smile. 'Don't worry. I didn't take any liberties.'

I didn't know whether to be disappointed or relieved.

'In answer to the original question, certain kinds of memories are stored differently in the human mind. Memories – memories of events, of people, of conversations – these are more vulnerable. They can be taken away more easily.'

'Why? Why would anybody do that? Wait a minute – *how* could anybody do that?'

Outside, the fire suddenly died to a banked glow. The tent flap moved, and Lewis, crouched uncomfortably low, ducked inside. He gave the two of us an unreadable look, then crawled over to the other sleeping bag.

'Earth Wardens could have done it,' Lewis said. 'It's possible, if an Earth Warden had the right training and skill level, to remove selective memories. It's part of how Marion Bearheart's division drains away the powers of Wardens who have to be taken out of the organisation and returned to the regular human population. Only they don't just take memories; they take away the core of power inside.' He stretched out, put his hands under his head, and stared at the glow of moonlight on the tent fabric. 'But in your case it was done by a Djinn. His name is Ashan.'

'A Djinn,' I repeated. 'Like you?' I pointed at David, whose eyebrows rose.

'Not anymore. But yes, Ashan was Djinn, and he did this to you. He didn't want to kill you; he wanted you to have never existed at all. And he had the power to do it. He made a good start on it.'

'So what stopped him?'

David and Lewis exchanged looks. It was Lewis who answered. 'Let's get into that later.'

'Fine. General question.' I licked my lips and avoided staring directly at David. 'What exactly is a Djinn?'

Lewis sighed and closed his eyes. 'We've really got to get you fixed,' he said. 'The Djinn are another race of beings on this planet. They can be corporeal when they want to, but their real existence is energy. They're...spirits. Spirits of fire and will.'

'Poetic, but not exactly the whole story,' David said. 'We were once slaves to you. To the Wardens. You used us to amplify your powers.'

'Slaves?'

'Subject to your orders. And your whims.' He was watching me with half-closed eyes, and when I turned I saw sparks flying in them. 'We're free now.'

'So you're...all-powerful?' I had to laugh as I said it. 'Snap your fingers and make it so, or something like that?'

He smiled, but the sparks were still flying. 'Djinn move energy – that's all. We take it from point A to point B. Transform it. But we can't create, and we can't destroy, not at the primal levels. That's why I think we may be able to undo what was done to you – because at least on some level, the energy is never lost.'

'Great! So, just...' I snapped my fingers. 'You know. Make it so.'

'I can't,' David said, 'or I'd already have done it. Time was Ashan's specialty. I was never very good at manipulating it. Jonathan—' He stopped, and – if anything – looked even bleaker. 'You don't remember Jonathan.'

I shook my head.

'It would take a Jonathan or an Ashan to undo what was done.'

'Can't you just go get one of them?' I asked.

'Jonathan's dead,' David said, 'and Ashan's...not what he was. Besides, I can't find him. He's been very successful at hiding.'

'Too bad,' I said. 'I was going to offer to bear your children if you could get me out of this icebox and onto a nice, warm beach somewhere.'

I was kidding, but whatever I'd said hit him hard. It *hurt*. He got up and moved back to his original position at my feet, breaking the connection, breaking eye contact. There was a tension in his body now, as if I'd said something really terrible.

Lewis covered his eyes with the heels of his hands, digging deeply. 'She doesn't remember,' he said. 'David. She doesn't remember.'

'I know,' David said, and his voice scared me. Raw, anguished, fragile. 'But I thought...if anything...'

'She *can't*. You know that. It's not her fault.'

No answer. David said nothing. I opened my mouth a couple of times, but I couldn't think what to ask, what to say; I'd put my foot in it big-time, but I had no idea why.

No, I realised after a slow-dawning, horrified moment. I *did* know. Or at least, I guessed.

'Did you and I...do we have children?' I asked. Because I wasn't ready to be a mother. What could I possibly have to teach a child when I couldn't remember my own life, my own childhood? My own family?

The question I'd addressed aloud to David seemed to drop into a velvet black pool of silence. After a very long time he said tonelessly, 'No. We don't have any children.'

And *poof.* He was gone. Vanished into thin air.

'What the hell...?'

Lewis didn't answer. Not directly. He rolled over on his side, turning his back to me. 'Sleep,' he told me. 'We'll get into this tomorrow.'

I rolled over on my side, too, putting me back-to-back with Lewis with a blank view of a blue nylon tent wall. Uncomfortably close, close enough to be in the corona of his body heat. He needed a bath. So did I.

'Lewis?' I asked. 'Please tell me. Do I have a kid?'

A long, long silence. 'No,' he said. 'No, you don't.'

I didn't remember anything about my life. For all intents and purposes, I'd been born a few hours ago, on a bed of icy leaves and mud. I'd been dropped out of the sky into a bewildering world that wasn't what my instincts told me was normal...into the lives of two men who each had some agenda that I wasn't sure I could understand.

But one thing I knew for sure: Lewis was lying to me. I was certain of that. For good reasons, maybe...and maybe not. I didn't really know him. Lewis and David...they were just strangers. Strangers who'd helped me, yes, but still. I didn't know them. I didn't know what they wanted from me.

Deep down, I was scared that the next time I asked questions, they were going to start telling me the truth.

Chapter Two

We broke camp at dawn – well, Lewis broke camp, moving as if doing it were as normal as stumbling out of bed and making coffee. I mostly sat off to the side, huddled in his down jacket. Lewis had layered on all the clothes he had in the backpack – thermals next to his skin, and T-shirts, flannel, and sweaters over it.

He was going to die if he didn't have a coat. I was still shivering, and I was practically certified for the arctic in the down jacket.

I made a half-hearted attempt to give it back.

'No,' he said, not even pausing. 'Zip it up. You need to keep the core of your body warm.'

'But...you're—'

'I'll be fine. One thing about Earth Wardens: We're not likely to die of the cold.' Maybe not, but his lips looked a little blue, and so did his fingernails. As I stared at his hands, he noticed, frowned at them, and dug a pair of insulated gloves from a zippered pocket in the backpack.

He continued to break down the camp. I shovelled sand over the fire pit, smothering the embers, and looked around for something else to do. Nothing, really. I shoved my cold, aching fingers back into the pockets of the jacket.

There was still no sign of David. Lewis didn't refer to his absence. Neither did I. Lewis rolled the sleeping bags into tight little coils, tied them off, and then broke down the tent into a small pouch and some short telescoping rods. It all went into the backpack. He handed me a bottle of water and a granola bar – no coffee – and I frowned at the bottle and shook it.

Frozen solid. 'Um...'

'Melt it,' he said.

'What?'

'Melt the ice,' he said. 'You're a Weather Warden. Melt the ice.'

I had no idea what he was talking about. I remembered the world that David had shown me, but I couldn't think how to apply *that* to the simple, practical problem in my hand.

Lewis let out a growl of frustration, took the bottle and held it in his hand for about two seconds, then handed it back.

It sloshed.

'How did you—'

'We don't have time for lessons,' he interrupted. 'Let's move.'

'Um…shoes?'

He stopped in mid-stride and looked back at me. I was fully dressed down to the thermal socks, but those were rapidly getting muddy and damp.

'Shit,' he said, surprised. 'I forgot all about—'

'I didn't,' said a voice from behind me. I whirled to find David walking out of the trees, making a grand entrance that I instinctively knew must be standard procedure for a Djinn. He was holding a pair of hiking boots.

And a fresh pair of thermal socks.

And a backpack.

'Shopping,' he said, and handed everything over.

'Don't suppose you bought a Jeep while you were out,' Lewis said.

'I can do a lot of things, but rearranging forest trails without attracting attention on the aetheric…'

'Rhetorical question.' Lewis kept not quite watching David, who'd picked up a stick and was idly poking it into the damp ground. 'Any sign of trouble out there?' Which I supposed was a graceful way of asking if David had been off keeping watch, rather than brooding. Not that one precluded the other. I sat down on a fallen log, tugged off my muddied socks and put on fresh ones, then laced up the hiking boots. They fitted perfectly.

'There's snowfall two miles away,' David said. 'Heavy. You're keeping it to the south, I take it?'

'Trying,' Lewis said. 'This whole region's soaked with moisture. Sooner or later it's going to start coming down. There's only so far you can push the system before it starts pushing back, and the last thing I want is to start a winter storm while we're trying to get out of here. How's Mom, by the way?'

'Quiet.'

Mom? I debated it for a few seconds, then asked aloud. Both men turned to look at me as I tugged the laces tighter and knotted the right boot.

'Mother Earth,' Lewis said. 'The primal intelligence of the planet. Mom. She's been a little... unhappy lately.'

I tried to figure out if he was joking, and decided – rather grimly – that he wasn't. Great. Wardens who could control all kinds of things. Spooky disappearing Djinn. And now the ground I was walking on had some kind of hidden intelligence.

Losing my memory was turning out to be a real education.

I tied off my left boot and stood up, shouldering my pack. David had balanced it well; it seemed to ride nicely, with no extra strain.

'I can take it if you get tired,' David said, walking past me.

I snorted. 'I'm surprised you didn't try to take it in the first place.'

'I know better,' he said. 'When you want help, you'll ask for it.'

We'd left the campsite and gone about a mile before I broached the question again. David was in front of me, Lewis ahead of him. It was as private as this was likely to get. 'David? About last night... what I said...about children.'

No answer. He kept walking, long strides, following Lewis's progress. I had to hurry to keep up.

'Is there a child?' I asked. My heart was hammering, and I didn't think it was from the exercise. 'Mine, yours, ours? What's going on?'

'Not now.'

'Yeah, now. Look, the way you reacted—'

'I can't talk about it now.'

'But—'

He turned, and I stumbled to a halt, suddenly aware of just how tall he was. He wasn't especially broad, but I'd had my hands pressing against his chest, and I knew that there was muscle under that checked shirt. Plus, he'd thrown Lewis across the clearing like a plush toy.

'What do you want to know?' he asked, face taut, voice intense. 'That we had a child? We did. Her name was Imara. She was part of our souls, Jo, and how do you think it feels for me to know that you don't even recognise her *name*?'

He turned, olive coat belling in a gust of cold wind, and followed Lewis up the slope. Lewis had paused at the top, looking down at us.

He didn't say anything, just plunged down the other side. I saved my breath and concentrated on putting one foot in front of the other.

Imara. I kept repeating the name in my head, hoping for some kind of resonance, some spark of memory. I'd had a *daughter*, for God's sake. How could I remember the brand name of the shoes I was wearing and not remember my own child? Not remember carrying her, or holding her, or...

Or how she'd died. Because even though nobody had said it, that was what everybody meant. Imara had been born, and Imara had died, and I had no memory at all of any part of it.

And of everything I'd lost, that was the piece that made me feel desperately, horribly incomplete.

Lewis led us through what I could only guess was an old-growth forest of the Great Northwest. Oregon, Washington – somewhere in there. He set a brutal pace, moving fast to keep his body heat up. We didn't take breaks. When we finally stopped, I dropped my pack and staggered off into the woods to pee. When I came back, Lewis had another fire going, and he was wrapped in one of the unrolled sleeping bags, shivering.

His lips and eyelids had turned a delicate shade of lilac.

'Dammit, take the coat,' I demanded.

'No. I'll be fine.'

'Ask David to get you a jacket, then! Hell, he brought me shoes!'

Lewis's eyes flicked briefly past me, seeking out David, I was sure. 'When I need one.'

'Unless you're modelling the new fall line of lipstick, and this season's colour is Corpse Blue, you'd better damn well tell him to get you one now!'

'I didn't know you cared.' Shaky sarcasm. He was still strong enough to be putting up a good front, but it was all marshmallow and foam peanuts underneath.

'I don't. I care about getting stuck out here.' I didn't move my eyes away from Lewis. 'David, could you please get him a coat?' Out of the corner of my eyes, I saw David cross his arms and lean against a tree. The expression on his face might have been a smile.

'Of course,' he said, and misted away.

Lewis took in a deep breath, and coughed until I was afraid he was going to spit up a lung. I did what any medically inarticulate person would do; I rubbed and pounded his back. Which probably didn't help at all, but he didn't seem to mind. When he'd stopped coughing, he leant over, breathing in shallow gasps, face a dirty grey.

'What's wrong with you?' I asked. 'And don't tell me you're tired, or you've been up for three days, or whatever bullshit you've been shovelling at David.'

He pressed a hand to his ribs. 'Took a little fall. Maybe you saw it.'

Oh, shit. David had thrown him across the clearing. Since he'd climbed up again, I hadn't figured it was any big deal.

Wrong.

'Earth Wardens can't heal themselves real well,' he said. 'It's coming along. Couple of broken ribs. Bit of a punctured lung. Nothing to alert the National Guard over.'

'Can't David just, you know, swoop us out of here? To wherever he goes to buy retail?'

Lewis shook his head. His breathing was easing up a little. 'Free Djinn – well, I guess they're all Free Djinn now – can't take humans along with them when they do that. The times they've tried it, the results haven't been exactly encouraging.'

'Meaning?'

'Dead people.'

Great. So David could go in and out, but we had to hoof it. 'What about a helicopter? Some kind of rescue service?'

'We're still a pretty far hike from the closest place a helicopter can touch down. Believe me, I'll call for help as soon as I can.'

'Why the hell not now? We're stuck out here, you've got broken ribs, there's snow coming... Even if they can't land, maybe they can, you know, winch us up or something.'

'Trust me. We have to be very careful right now.' He looked vaguely apologetic. 'It's not about you. It's about me.'

Ah. I remembered what he'd blurted out when he'd first found me. *Listen, we're in trouble. Bad trouble. We need you. Things have gone wrong.* Like I was the go-to girl for that kind of thing. 'What's happened?' I asked.

'That's the issue,' he said. 'I don't know. I don't know if it's an isolated issue, somebody who just doesn't like me, or a genuine power grab within the Wardens' organisation. Until I know, you're just going to have to bear with me.'

'And you want me to trust you?' I shook my head in admiration. 'Unbelievable. So who's after you?'

'If I gave you a name, would you recognise it?' He sounded a little more snappy about that than was strictly necessary, really, and immediately looked sorry about it. 'I told you. Trust me.'

'If I didn't trust you, I'd be running like hell right now,' I pointed out. 'It's not like you could really stop me.'

'Don't kid yourself. I've got skills.'

'Apparently,' I said. 'Since you're not dead yet, which with your winning personality amazes me. *I* want to kill you, and I barely know you.'

'Funny. I've said the same thing about you, once upon a time.' He started to laugh. It turned into more coughing, alarmingly. 'Damn. You know, I never get hurt unless I'm hanging around with you.'

'If you'd just admitted you were hurt in the first place, maybe you wouldn't be this bad off right now. And what's that about, Mr I Don't Need a Coat Because I'm the Tough-assed Mountain Man? Is this some kind of pissing contest with David?' No answer. Lewis pretended to be concentrating on the fire. 'It is. David wasn't going to do you any favours unless you asked, and you weren't going to ask. Right? Jesus. *Men.*'

'Shhhh,' he said, and sat up.

'What?'

He shushed me again, urgently, and slipped the sleeping bag away from his shoulders. He reached in the backpack next to him and came up with the last thing, somehow, I expected to see in his hand.

Well, OK, not the *very* last. That would have been...a tulip or a Barbie doll or something. But a matte black semiautomatic pistol was pretty far down the list.

'What are you doing?' I kept it to an urgent hiss. He shushed me again, silently this time, and mimed for me to stay put while he got up. *Oh, no way.* I didn't remember anything about who I was, but I doubted it was in my general character to play it safe, especially when my currently assigned Sir Galahad had a punctured lung and a fifty-fifty chance of keeling over at any moment.

I got up, too, and whirled around at a sudden crash of brush to my right. If it was David, he was making an especially dramatic entrance this time...

It wasn't David.

There were two people stepping out of the underbrush. Naturally, I didn't recognise either one of them, but clearly Lewis did, because he turned and aimed the gun at the skinny, greasy young man first, then shifted his aim to split the distance between the boy and the blonde little Venus with him, dressed in blue jeans and a hot magenta sweater.

'Whoa,' the girl said, and her hands shot up above her shoulders. The boy just glared. 'Easy, Wyatt Earp.'

'Don't move,' Lewis said. He was absolutely steady, but I could see the sweat glistening on his face. 'What are you two doing here? How'd you get here?'

'We were looking for you,' the boy said. 'Obviously.'

'We're trying to help,' the girl put in. She tried a nervous smile, but she kept darting glances at me, as if she couldn't quite believe her eyes. 'Jo? You OK?'

She didn't look familiar, but I was getting used to that. I gave Lewis a doubtful look; he wasn't lowering the gun. 'I'm going to ask again,' he said.

'How'd you get here? Because the two of you were supposed to be in California, last I heard.'

'You need help.' The girl, again. She sounded young and earnest, and she looked it, too. Underdressed for the weather, and that bothered me. 'Lewis, man, put the gun down. You know us!'

'Tell me how you got here.' He cocked the gun with a cold *snick* of metal.

'You're crazy,' the boy said flatly. 'Yo, Joanne, a little help?'

'Jo,' Lewis said, with an unsettling amount of calm, 'he's right, I do you need your help. I need you to move two steps to your left so that when I shoot these two you don't slow down my bullets.'

I just stared at him, stunned. There was something cold and implacable in his eyes, and I just didn't get it. These two didn't look like dangerous desperadoes. The girl was just damn *cute*. Young, tanned, toned, beach-bunny perfect. If the boy was with her in a romantic sense, he was definitely dating outside of his weight class, because he was greasy, skinny, sullen, and generally unattractive, unless you went in for that sort of heroin-chic bad-boy vibe. Badass, but probably not bad.

Probably.

'Oh, come on. You really going to shoot me, Lewis?' the boy asked, and stuffed his hands into the pockets of the leather jacket he was wearing.

'Because I don't think you've got the stones.'

'Guess again.' Lewis's aim didn't waver.

The boy sneered. Really, openly sneered, which isn't easy to do with a serious weapon aimed at you. 'Please. I'm a Fire Warden. I can make sure that gun doesn't work.'

'You forget,' Lewis said, 'I'm a Fire Warden, too.' And he moved the gun about an inch to the left and pulled the trigger. The noise was deafening. I choked on the stench of burnt cordite that wafted over me and yelped.

The boy hadn't flinched. The bullet dug a fresh yellow hole into the tree next to him.

'Please don't do that,' the girl said, and deliberately stepped out in front of the boy. 'Look, we're just here to help, OK? There's no need for this.'

'Then tell me *how you got here.*'

She took a step towards him, hands outstretched. 'We don't have time for this.'

'Cherise, right?' he asked. 'Don't push it, Cherise. I *will* shoot you.'

'I think you would if you really thought I was dangerous,' she said. 'But look at me. How can I be—'

Lewis was totally not above shooting the pretty girl.

And he did, three times, right in the centre of her fluffy hot pink sweater.

Cherise rocked back, lips parting, and stared

down at the damage to her sweater for a few seconds, and then looked back up at Lewis. 'You *bastard*! That was *cashmere*!' She lunged at him. He grabbed her by the arm, swung her around her own axis of motion, and slammed her face-first into a tree.

Which did about as much damage as three bullets in the chest, apparently.

And she was my friend? That either kicked ass, or was a big, big problem.

The boy grabbed hold of Lewis, stripped away the gun, and the two of them got down to some serious fighting, only some of which was happening in the real world; I could feel the stinging force of powers being slung back and forth along with punches, but I couldn't tell who had the upper hand.

Cherise grabbed my arm, locked eyes with me, and panted, 'Run! Come on, we have to go, *now*!'

'But – you were shot—'

She waved that off impatiently. 'I'm OK. Come on!'

We ran. The trail was thin, and heavily clogged with debris, but Cherise was fast, and I moved as quickly as I dared, leaping over logs and branches and struggling to keep up. I was cold, very cold, and I couldn't believe she was this active without at least a coat. But I guessed that if she was bullet-resistant, being immune to the chill wasn't much of a stretch.

I felt a pulse of energy so strong it knocked me to my knees, and Cherise yelled and dropped flat, and a wave of heat rolled over us, thick and shocking.

A fireball erupted behind us.

'Kevin!' Cherise was up and running back towards the inferno, but she didn't get far before the flames drove her back. 'Kevin!'

She didn't need to worry. The boy plunged through the flames as if they weren't even there and doubled over, breathing hard. He wasn't even singed. 'Damn,' he gasped, and coughed. 'Ow. That hurt.'

Cherise immediately went to him. 'What happened?'

'He went for it,' Kevin said, and braced his hands on his knees. 'Damn. I'm sorry, I thought I could contain him, but he – he just—'

It dawned on me that Lewis wasn't coming out of the fire. 'You killed him,' I said numbly. 'You killed Lewis.'

Kevin glanced up at me. 'He did it himself. I just couldn't stop him. Look, the dude was going to kill you. We were lucky to get to you in time.'

I wished I'd picked up Lewis's gun. I felt hot, sick, disoriented, and oddly on the verge of tears. I didn't know the guy, not really, but... I couldn't believe what Kevin was saying. Lewis, going to kill me? No. That couldn't be true.

I needed to think, but I didn't have time. The fire was spreading. It had already jumped from one winter-dried treetop to another, and there were tendrils of flame and ash falling on us. Kevin might be fireproof, but I was pretty sure I wasn't.

Cherise yelped as a branch exploded from the heat, spraying us with burning splinters.

I didn't even plan what happened next. I don't even know *how* it happened. I just reached blindly for help, any kind of help.

And it came in a blinding, disorienting flash. Rain, driving down like a firehose to douse me to the skin. Cold water met hungry flames, and the resulting steam flooded the clearing in fog. The rain kept falling, a tap I didn't know how to turn off. Hell, maybe I'd broken off the knob. The underbrush was still smoking, but the flames were out, and they couldn't flare up again while the downpour continued.

Kevin looked like a stunned, drowned rat. He stared at me with narrowed eyes, measuring me, while rain beat down on his head and plastered his lank hair to his skull. 'You shouldn't be able to do that,' he said. 'How did you...?' Weirdly, I could almost hear another voice overlaying his, a *female* voice. Not Cherise's, who was just mutely staring at me.

'How'd you get here?' I yelled over the roar of the rain.

'Not that again!'

'It's a good question! How the hell did you two find me?' I backed away, and saw Cherise and Kevin exchange a glance. Not one that was particularly reassuring. Man, I wished I'd picked up the gun – not that it had done Lewis a lot of good. But I felt particularly vulnerable right now. 'Lewis was going to a lot of trouble because he thought somebody was following. He thought we were in danger.'

'Not from us,' Cherise said, and I almost believed her. She just had that kind of innocent trust-me face.

But I caught Kevin smiling, and my heart went cold.

I backed away a few more steps. Kevin's smile faded, and Cherise's blue eyes turned cool and expressionless.

'All right,' she said. 'I guess we do this the hard way.'

The downpour was localised around us, but as I reached the margins, fire suddenly flared up. Kevin. I could feel the energy pouring out of him. I held my ground, because running would be damn near suicidal; once I got outside of the downpour's zone, he could toast me up like a s'more. I wasn't sure I had a second trick up my wet, dripping sleeve.

Cherise and Kevin didn't make a move towards me. They just watched me, and I got the strangest feeling, like they were just...*there*. And not there. Like they weren't really present anymore.

And then I sensed something else. I couldn't even put a name to it – big, dark, wrong. Very, very wrong. It wasn't a real shadow, but I could feel it, spreading over the ground towards me.

And then there was a shadow in the trees, something flickering and indistinct.

Cherise blinked and said, 'There's nothing to be afraid of.'

But there was. There most definitely was. Whatever that was in the trees was *not right*, I could feel it like a sick black ache in my chest that was only getting worse with every breath.

The shadow seemed to be flickering in time with my heartbeat, and with every frantic beat it looked a little bit...darker. More real. More distinct.

I saw the curve of a pale face, dark hair.

I didn't want to see what came at the end, but I felt weak now, and bitterly cold. My knees threatened to fold up under me, and I thought, *This is it. I'm done.*

And then something inside me just refused, cold and furious, and I felt myself get steadier again.

'There's something to be afraid of,' I heard myself say to Cherise. 'Me.'

And I reached up into the sky and pulled at the air, pushing a whole wall of it like an invisible hard shield at them, driving her and Kevin backward.

Driving away the shadow.

I turned and ran, dodging blooming flames, barely managing to avoid slipping in the squelchy mud under my boots. Overhead, the downpour sputtered, let loose a final shower of ice-cold drops that froze into sleet as they hit the ground, and subsided. I kept running, and checked over my shoulder. I could see Cherise and Kevin standing there, dumb statues, and that shadow, that *shadow* was with them, and for a second...

For a second, in a flash of lightning, it looked just like me.

And then it just...vanished.

Cherise and Kevin toppled over facedown to the ground. Dead, stunned, I couldn't tell, but there was no way I could go back; I knew the shadow was still there, hoping to lure me in, and I couldn't fight it.

I hated myself for running, but I ran. It was survival instinct, nothing more, nothing I could be proud of, and tears streamed down my face, self-pitying and turning to ice in the cold, cold wind. *You should have tried*, something was screaming inside me, but I knew better. If I'd tried, I'd be dead.

I was alone, and I couldn't risk it.

I had no warning of another approach, but suddenly there were hands on my shoulders, and I was spun around, violently, slipping in the mud.

I instinctively raised my arms, trying to block a punch, trying to break free, but stopped when I recognised the stark pale face, dark eyes, and rough growth of beard.

Not dead, but definitely singed around the edges. There was a quarter-sized raw burn on his cheek, and bruises forming.

Lewis looked terrible, but he was alive.

'I thought you were dead!' I yelped, and his hand closed around my left wrist. He silently jerked me into a run. I barely had time to gasp, because we were running straight for a thicket of thorns and he *wasn't slowing down...*

And the thorns pulled right out of the way. I tripped, trying to twist around and stare, but Lewis's grip around my wrist was unforgiving.

'Wait,' I panted. 'We can't just—'

'Damn right we can. Run or die.' He sounded raw and exhausted, but he was outpacing me. I concentrated on not slowing him down; for some reason, having Lewis afraid and vulnerable was worse to me than my own terrors. The forest flew by in a blur of tree bark, flashing leaves, the occasional glimpse overhead of grey cotton sky.

It felt like we ran forever. I caught one glimpse of what might have been the shadow standing at the top of a hill, but it misted away like a bad dream.

We just kept on running. When I looked back

again, I didn't see anything. No sign at all, just the sullen smoke still rising from the place where Lewis and Kevin had combusted.

'Where's David?' I finally gasped. Lewis shook his head without answering, still struggling for breath. He was holding his side with his left hand as we ran, and I didn't like the colour of his face and lips. Or the bubbling sound when he took in air. 'You need to stop!'

'Not yet.'

'No, we have to stop *now!*' I insisted.

His effort to reply brought on a coughing fit, and when it was over he spat up blood. A lot of it. Enough to make my skin shrink all over.

We needed help. We needed it badly. And we needed it now.

And he must have known it, because he finally nodded. I could read the exhaustion in his face.

'Cave,' he said. 'Over there.'

Over there proved to be a long way off. I forced him to move more slowly, and I kept watch behind us for any telltale signs of a hot-pink sweater, or fire sprouting up around us. Nothing. The whole thing could have been a dream, except for the burnt patches in my clothes. We walked for a good half hour before an outcropping of rock came into sight – the end of the ridge. It commanded a good view of the valley floor below, and had a low shelf of rock that jutted out over the cliff. Below – *far* below – a shining ribbon of river glittered in the dull light. The trees, tall as they were, reached only about halfway up the cliff face.

'This way,' he said, and edged around the side of the hive-shaped rock formation. There was a crevasse that was larger than the others. Not what I'd call *large*, though. Big enough to squeeze through, if you didn't mind claustrophobic shock, and somebody was going to kill you if you didn't find a hiding place.

Lewis, without comment, wedged himself into the tiny space, wiggling his way through in grim silence. How that felt with broken ribs I didn't even want to imagine. I took a deep breath and then had to let half of it out – my chest was a little bit larger than Lewis's, and shoving my way through the opening in the rock was panic-inducing. I thought for a few seconds that I'd be stuck, but then my flailing right hand found something to hold, and I pulled myself all the way through...

...into fairyland.

'Careful,' Lewis said, and pointed up when I started to straighten. Stalactites, dripping frozen from the roof in needle-sharp limestone. I gulped and ducked, following him as he crouched against the wall. There was a pool of dark, perfectly still water in front of us, and the cave was cool and silent. Not warm, but not freezing, either. The only sounds were ones we made – shuffling on the rock, chattering teeth, the drips my soaked clothes made pattering on the floor.

'I can't make a fire,' Lewis said. 'Too dangerous in an enclosed space. Not sure I can manage the carbon monoxide.' He sounded mortally tired, but he opened the backpack he'd dumped on the floor – how the hell had he had the presence of mind to hang on to it through all that? – and dug out some packages. He threw two of them towards me, and I saw they were some kind of silvery thermal blankets. 'These work better if you get undressed. Your clothes are too wet. It'll just—'

If he was waiting for me to have an attack of modesty, he was sorely disappointed. 'Whatever,' I said, and began unbuttoning. The drag of wet clothes was making me nuts, and the cold had driven deep enough into me to make me uncaring about things like strangers watching me undress. Or maybe I was normally immune to that kind of thing. Hard to tell. I only knew that I didn't feel inhibited with him. Boy, and didn't *that* open up a ten-gallon drum of worms?

Lewis politely faced away while I skinned out of the sopping-wet pants. I decided to leave on the underwear, and wrapped myself up in crinkling silver foil. My skin felt like cold, wet plastic. 'So,' I said through chattering teeth. 'What the hell just happened?'

He glanced over his shoulder at me, saw I was

more or less decent, and fussed with his own crackling thermal sheets to avoid answering. Or at least, that was how it looked. I waited. Eventually Lewis said, 'Those two weren't right. They weren't themselves.'

'No kidding,' I said. I was feeling the cold now like sharp needles all over, and shivering violently. 'There was something else, too.'

'What else?' He paused, staring at me. 'What did you see?'

I didn't want to tell him, exactly. 'Nothing definite. Kind of a shadow.' *A shadow that kind of looked like me.* No, I didn't want to say that.

Lewis looked like he felt sicker than ever, but he nodded. 'I was afraid of that.'

'Afraid of what?'

His sigh echoed cool from the stone. 'There's a Demon after you. And we have no way to fight it.'

'Demon,' I repeated. 'OK. Sure. Right. Whatever.'

That definitely told me just exactly what was going on.

I was taking a walking tour of Hell, and my Virgil was insane.

I tried to avoid discussing the whole Demon thing under the grounds that, hey, keep your delusions to yourself, but Lewis kept on talking.

'They don't come from Hell,' he said very

earnestly, which only made him seem even nuttier. 'At least, not as I understand it. They're not from this plane of existence. They come from somewhere else. They're drawn here to our world because of power; they need to feed on the aetheric, and the best way they can do that is to grab hold of a Warden, because we're the equivalent of a straw to them – they can pull power through us. The more power they draw, the more dangerous they get.'

We'd been talking for a while. I wasn't exactly believing in the whole Demon idea, but he was scarily matter-of-fact about the whole thing, and besides, I'd seen a few impossible things in the past couple of days. Including, well, him.

But really. *Demons?* How was that right?

I took a deep breath, put my doubts aside, and said, 'So isn't there some kind of, I don't know, spell or something? Pentagrams? Holy water?'

'The only way we've ever found to stop a Demon, a full-grown Demon, is a Djinn,' Lewis said slowly. 'The Djinn and Demons are pretty evenly matched.'

Great. David was coming back, right? Problem solved. Lewis must have seen it in my face, because he shook his head. 'Not that easy,' he said. 'Any Djinn that engages with a Demon directly is probably going to die, and die horribly. The only thing we can do to contain the fight is seal the Djinn, and the Demon, into a bottle. It traps the

Demon so it can't do any more damage.'

My insides felt like they pulled together in a knotted ball. 'But what about the Djinn?'

'Like I said, they die horribly. And it takes some of them centuries.' Lewis's face was hard, his eyes bright. 'I didn't say I liked it.'

'That's – horrible.'

Lewis looked away. 'Yeah,' he said. 'Which is why we have a problem. Even if I wanted to, I couldn't let David—'

'Let David what?' said a voice from the shadows, startling me. David, of course, had arrived just in time to pick up his name being taken in vain. He stepped out of the shadows and stood there, watching us both, and whatever that was in his eyes, I couldn't read it. 'Let David make his own decisions? Thank you, Lewis. I thought the Wardens never let Djinn think for themselves.'

He was angry, and he was – I thought – scared. I didn't know how much he'd heard, but clearly enough to disturb him.

Lewis didn't answer. Probably a good move.

He dropped a thick forest green down jacket, complete with hood, on the floor next to Lewis. 'Here,' he said. 'Something to keep you warm. We don't need you dying on us.'

Lewis let out a slow breath and sat back, bracing himself against the wall. 'Thanks,' he said. 'Nice to know you still care.'

'To a point,' David said, and turned to me. 'Are you all right?'

I nodded, still shivering, but the last thing I wanted from him at this moment was a hug, which clearly he was thinking of offering, David slowly crouched, putting our eyes on a level. Not too close. He understood body language, at least, even if he wasn't human; I could feel the yearning in him, the frustration, the anxiety. I wondered if he could tell what I was thinking, and decided that he couldn't. He didn't look worried enough.

'Is there anything you can do for him?' I asked, and jerked my chin towards Lewis. 'Heal him?'

'He wouldn't welcome that,' David said. He edged just a bit closer. 'That is the stubbornest Warden I know, and considering I know you, that's saying something. Here. Put these on.' He reached behind him and retrieved my damp clothes from the floor – when I took them, they were soft and warm, like they'd come straight from a dryer. Something hardened in his eyes. 'Did you take these off yourself?'

Lewis laughed, a bitter sort of sound. 'David, if you think I'm in any shape to seduce her, you're giving me way too much credit,' he said. 'She was freezing, she was soaked, and I didn't even look. Can we move on to the next problem, which is a damn sight worse than your jealousy?'

'You think there's a Demon,' David said. 'I heard.'

'Worse than that,' Lewis replied. 'I think there's a Demon that's managing to control Wardens and walk them around like puppets. You got any idea how bad that is?'

David looked profoundly troubled. 'That means we can't trust the Wardens, either. Something's very wrong.'

I snorted. '*Wrong?* I'll tell you what's wrong. I saw Lewis put three bullets into one of them – a girl named Cherise – and she didn't go down. That's wrong. She's *little*!'

'Cherise?' David echoed, and looked to Lewis for confirmation. He nodded. 'The human girl? Why would a Demon be using her? Why would it bother? There's nothing in her to feed off of.'

'I don't know, but she was definitely in on it,' I said. I was tired now, though considerably warmer; pulling on the clean, dry clothes had definitely helped. I leant back to zip up the blue jeans and wrapped the tinfoil blanket around me again. 'So she's not a Warden?'

'Not remotely,' he said. 'The boy is, Kevin, but not her. She was just—'

'My friend,' I said slowly. 'She was my friend. That's what she said. God... Why is this happening to her? To all of us?'

Lewis didn't even try to answer. If David could have, he held back; I couldn't tell what he was thinking at all.

'There's got to be people we can turn to,' I said. 'Hell, if not the Wardens, what about the police? The army? The forestry service?' I was getting bothered by their shared silence. 'Dammit – David, you could bring help to us, right? Rescue?'

'If the Demon can puppet humans, it wouldn't be wise,' he said. 'It only adds more potential victims. The fewer we have to worry about, the better.'

'But we have to get *out of here*!'

'And we will,' Lewis said, and leant his head against the wall with his eyes shut. His skin was the colour of old, wet paper. 'But David's right. Bringing people into this is a bad idea, both for them and for us. We need to find our own way out, and to do that, we need rest.'

'But—' Lewis needed rest, that much was clear. I turned to David. 'Seriously, can't you see he's hurt? Can't you do anything for him?'

'If he'd let me,' David said. 'Which I doubt.'

'I'm fine,' Lewis growled.

'See?'

'*Lewis*,' I pleaded. 'Don't be a dick. OK, if you're going to be a dick, at least be smart. You'll slow us down. I need you in shape to get me out of here, right?'

Lewis didn't open his eyes, but after a long moment, he nodded. David stood up and walked to him, put a hand lightly on his shoulder, and then moved it to the back of his neck. He crouched down next to him, and his eyes burnt like lava in the darkness, nearly bright enough to read by.

Lewis made a sound. Not a happy one. His face went an even more alarming shade of grey. 'Sorry,' David said quietly. 'You should have let me do this sooner. There's damage to your lungs.'

Lewis just nodded, tight-lipped. He was sweating from the pain, and his hands were trembling where they gripped the foil blanket around him.

With a glance at me, David brushed his other hand across Lewis's forehead, and with a sigh, the man's long body relaxed against the wall.

Out like a light.

'He'll be better when he wakes.' David settled Lewis more comfortably, then turned back to me. 'He was afraid to let go. He didn't want to leave you alone with me.'

'What?' I couldn't quite believe what I was hearing. 'Why?'

David smiled slowly. 'Because like most Wardens right now, Lewis doesn't fully trust the Djinn. Even though I have more reason than anyone else to want to keep you safe.' David eased down on the rock next to me, not quite close enough to touch. 'He thinks my loyalties are divided. He's right, of course. And the Djinn certainly aren't making any of this easier.'

'What do the Djinn have against me?' Was there

anybody who didn't hate my guts?

'You, personally? Nothing, really. But many of them hate Wardens, and most of the rest have a kind of benign contempt for humankind in general. Our two species are not friends,' he said. 'We're barely neighbours.'

'What about you and me?' My eyebrows rose. 'I thought we were neighbourly.'

'We're different.'

'But Lewis is still worried about you. Because you're Djinn.'

'Exactly,' David said. His eyes met mine, and in the shadows they were dark, human, and very gentle. 'And as I said, he's right to be worried. I won't hurt you, Jo. I swear that. But I can't make that vow for other Djinn, not yet. There's too much anger. And – long-term, the future for us may not be bright.'

I sucked down a deep breath. 'I don't want to talk about relationships. Look, Lewis said the only way to stop a Demon was to throw a Djinn at it. Which I guess used to be an easier answer—'

'Try convenient,' David said. 'At least when the Wardens had plenty of Djinn as slaves. Now, they'll have to rely on our goodwill if they face a true crisis. Which, as I've said, isn't extensive.' He glanced sideways at me, then became very interested in the deep, still waters of the black pond. 'I wish I could tell you that I would sacrifice myself for you, if I had to. I would give anything to tell you that, and a few months ago I would have, without hesitation. But now – now I have to think of my people. I can't confront a Demon, not directly. Not even to save your life. I also can't order one of my people to do it. Lewis knows that.'

I could tell what saying that cost him, and I didn't quite know how to answer. It took me a few seconds to work it out, and when I spoke, my voice sounded soft and very tentative. 'You're ashamed of that, but you shouldn't be. It's OK, I'd never ask you to risk your life – or any Djinn's life – for me. I don't want Lewis to do it, either. If it comes down to it' – I swallowed, hard – 'I want you to promise me you won't throw yourself on any Demons for me. Because...I don't want anything to happen to you.'

He didn't speak, and he didn't move. I couldn't tell if that had helped or not, so I blundered on. 'I should have stayed back there earlier, to help Cherise and Kevin. They needed help, but I just – I just ran away. So I'm the last person to demand heroic sacrifices, here. I should have—'

'You should have done exactly as you did,' he interrupted. 'You should have run. You have to save yourself, Jo. Neither of your appointed guardians are all that capable of helping you now, no matter how much we—' His voice failed him for a second, and then he finished. 'No matter how much we want to.'

We sank into silence – not quite comfortable, but it mellowed out, and I felt tensed muscles easing. I don't know quite how it happened, but soon enough I was leaning against him, and his warmth felt so safe, so reassuring. After a while, he put an arm around my shoulders, and I let my head rest in the hollow of his neck.

'That girl, Cherise,' I said. 'Is she still alive? Did I leave her to die?'

His warm fingers stroked across my forehead, the same gentle gesture I'd seen him give Lewis.

'Sleep,' he murmured, and I felt the warm brush of his lips against my temple. 'Dream well.'

'I will,' I said faintly.

He kissed my hand, an old-world kind of gesture, full of tenderness, then got up with a grace that looked scarily sexy, and walked towards the opening of the cave. I didn't see him leave; it looked like he just misted away between one blink and the next.

I slept with that.

Yeah, and you know what? I had the distinct feeling that I'd probably enjoyed the holy hell out of it, too.

Chapter Three

I fell asleep, lulled by the gradual warming of my body and general exhaustion, and woke to find some trail bars and water sitting next to me. No sign of David. Lewis had draped his own thermal blanket over me, and clearly he'd gone out. Scouting, maybe. Foraging. Peeing. I had no idea.

I yawned, stretched, and got up to work out the wincing stiffness in my back and neck. Once I felt more or less human again, I folded up the foil blankets, replaced them in their little packets, and added them to the backpack leaning against the wall. I cautiously sniffed myself, to bad results, and wondered what the odds were of a nice, hot bath appearing if I wished really hard.

I squeezed through the opening and emerged in pre-dawn darkness – well, it could have been midday; it was hard to tell. The sky was a uniform grey, the colour of melted lead, and the clouds had a heavy, solid consistency that threatened real trouble. Somewhere way above, lightning flashed and was visible as a distant blue-white strobe. Thunder drummed, and it sounded just miles away.

It was *freezing*. I hadn't realised how accustomed I'd got to the relatively balmy temperatures inside the cave, but the first icy slice of wind reminded me. Convulsive shivering made me move faster, and in seconds I made the tree line, found an appropriately screened area, and took care of bladder issues. Once the immediate biological crisis was averted, I started back towards the cave…and then hesitated, because I could hear something.

Something like splashing.

I followed the sound over a low rise, down another steeper drop, and through a thick clumping of scrub trees.

I peeked through the branches and saw Lewis, naked, up to his waist in a small pond. And it was steaming with heat, like a natural thermal spring. Wisps of white curled up from the surface, drifting in a low layer of fog that obscured my view only a little.

Did I mention Lewis was naked?

I stayed where I was for a few seconds, getting quite a view of the lean strength of his body, water glistening as it ran in slow trickles down his abs. I felt guilty about it, but that didn't stop me. I wondered if there'd ever been anything between the two of us. If there had been, I clearly had some severe neural damage not to remember it. Vividly.

I had enough of a conscience-twinged epiphany to look away when he swam for the shore. Gawking I could justify. Actual *peeping* was something else.

When I looked back, Lewis was zipping up his blue jeans, water dripping from his brown hair to patter on his strong, tanned shoulders. Without looking up he said, in the most studiously normal tone I could imagine, 'The water's going to stay warm for the next half hour or so. Might as well use it. You need it.'

I hadn't made a sound; I was certain of that. But he wasn't shooting in the dark; after he'd towelled his hair dry with his T-shirt, Lewis lifted his head and focused his stare right on the scrubby trees that screened me from immediate view.

Busted.

I cleared my throat and pushed through, earning a few scrapes in the process. Apart from another distant mutter of thunder, the lead-coloured day was very quiet. Water lapped the shore. Lewis shook out his T-shirt and pulled it on, then a thermal top, then added one of those well-used flannel shirts on top, which he buttoned almost to the neck.

I took the plunge. 'Lewis, did we ever – you know...?

He concentrated on his shirt buttons, even though it wasn't like they took a lot of effort. I could see he was thinking about lying to me, and then he gave up and said, 'Once.'

'Wow.' I tried to smile. 'Was it that bad?'

'No, it was that good.' He kept his eyes fixed somewhere else, not on me, but I still felt a flash of heat and nerves. 'Look, I'm not in love with you,' he said. 'Maybe I used to be, but I'm not anymore. So you don't have to worry about any complications from me.'

I nodded. His gaze finally brushed over me, moving fast; even though his eyes didn't linger, I felt another wave of corresponding heat.

'I just want you to understand where I stand,' he said. 'You don't love me, I don't love you, and that's it. Right?'

'Right,' I said. My lips felt numb. 'I love David.'

'Yes. You do. You don't know it right now, but you do.' That warmth-inducing gaze came back to fix on me. With a vengeance. 'You'll remember.'

'What if I don't want to?'

He let out a breath, and it plumed white on the sharp-edged breeze. For a long, perilous second, it seemed like he had something to say to me, but I felt him give it up before he could make the leap. He looked away. 'Hurry up. We have to be on the trail in the next hour.' And with that he sat down on the shore, put on thick socks, laced up his hiking boots, and sauntered off.

I guess his ribs had healed. He wasn't favouring them, although there had been a spectacular multicoloured bruise on his left side.

On the one hand, it was good that my sole human ally and – to be fair – protector was back in top form.

On the other hand...the rib thing had been convenient for us to use as a shield between us. Now gone.

I watched, but he didn't glance back. The water was still steaming. I bit my lip, sniffed myself again, and stripped even though the bone-chilling wind made it torture.

I'd forgotten how *good* warm water felt. I guess I'd known intellectually, but the second I waded in and felt it immersing me, I could barely breathe for the pleasure of it. I sank down to my neck, then held my breath and slipped under the surface. I stayed under for at least thirty seconds, then broke through to take in a gulp of air. The bottom of the pond was slimy and the rocks were sharp, so even though I had no specific recollection, I was pretty sure I'd had better baths. It just didn't feel that way at the moment. This was the first real memory I had of one, and it was magical. I couldn't really relax, though. I kept watching the tree line, waiting for the bad guys to jump out.

Nothing. The day was silent, brooding, with a sharp smell of incoming rain or snow.

When the water began to chill I waded out, hastily dried off, dressed, and ran back to the cave.

My teeth were chattering by the time I arrived, and Lewis paused in the act of shouldering his pack to toss me a chemical heat pack.

'Open it, rub the pack, and put it in your shirt,' he said. 'It'll help keep your core temp up.'

I tore the package open and shook out what looked like a really big sachet, rubbed it between my palms, and was instantly rewarded with a burst of steady heat. I dropped it down my buttoned-up shirt, between shirt and undershirt, and gave Lewis a trembling good-to-go high sign. My fingernails were a little blue. I scrambled into my coat and gloves, and hefted my own backpack. It clunked with plastic water bottles.

'Enjoy your bath?' Lewis asked. His tone was about as neutral as you could get, so I couldn't read anything into it. I just nodded. 'Good. Let's move out.'

'What about Kevin and Cherise? Do you think they're still…?'

'David's scouting,' he said. 'He'll warn us if they come anywhere close.'

He took off. I had no choice but to follow.

I'll skip over the day from hell, which was spent scrambling through razor-edged brush, climbing steep hills of loose shale, falling, cursing, sweating, panting, and generally having the sort of outdoor experience most city girls dread. I had no affinity for this whole hiking thing, and while the outdoors looked pretty, as far as I was concerned it'd look even prettier seen from the window of a passing car.

When my road-show Daniel Boone finally called a permanent halt, it was because of the snow. Flakes had begun to drift silently out of the clouds just an hour after we'd started the trek, light and whispery and dry, brushing against my sweaty face like cool feathers. At first I'd been grateful for it, but that was before it started to stick to the cold ground. A few random flurries became a full-fledged blizzard within the next couple of hours, and what started out a nuisance became more of a hardship with every trudging step. Lewis held my hand, and sometimes the only thing real in the world seemed to be the pressure of his hold on me. I sometimes heard rumbles, as if miles up it was raining, and I supposed I ought to feel grateful that it wasn't sleeting. Sleet would have been a step down, circles-of-hell-wise.

No cave this time, but Lewis put up the tent and we crawled inside, into our sleeping bags, too tired to do more than murmur a couple of words before sleep sucked us down. I wanted to ask Lewis where we were going, but I didn't have the energy. I no longer cared all that much, frankly. *Just kill me and get it over with*, I thought. I ached all over, and I was still aching when, with the suddenness of a light switched off, I fell asleep.

It didn't even occur to me to wonder where David was, or why he hadn't joined us. The ways of the Djinn, I'd already guessed, were not necessarily easy to figure out, even if you were dating one.

I woke up alone. All alone. The tent was silent, not even a breeze rattling the fabric, and it was deeply dark. And very, very cold. The chemical pack I'd gone to sleep with was an inert, stiff, dead thing next to me in the bag, and my hands had taken on a waxy chill. I burrowed deeper in the sleeping bag, conserving warmth, and listened for some sign that Lewis was up and around and doing something useful, like making the weather balmy or at least making coffee.

It was quiet as a grave out there.

'Lewis?' I whispered it, because somehow it seemed like the time and place to whisper. No response. I contemplated staying where I was, but that didn't seem practical in the long term. Lewis's sleeping bag was neatly rolled up and attached to his pack, which was leaning where his body had been when I'd fallen asleep. I crept out, wrapped myself quickly in my coat, jammed gloves on my hands and a knit cap over my head, and ducked out of the tent into the night.

Only it wasn't night. It was full daylight, and the reason it had been so dark in the tent was that the tent was covered at least four inches deep with snow. It looked like an igloo. My first step sank almost knee-deep in pristine white powder: great for skiing, terrible for hiking.

Lewis's tracks went off in the direction of the tree line. One set, although midway through the unbroken snow another set of footprints joined him.

Had to be David, since the two of them had walked on without any obvious trouble.

So I was on my own, at least for a little while.

I swigged some water – on Lewis's advice, I'd taken a couple of bottles into the sleeping bag with me, to keep it sloshy – and tried to ignore a dull, throbbing headache. Caffeine withdrawal, pressure, general stress...who knew? I had no idea if I liked caffeine, but it seemed likely. I felt a surge of interest at the idea of hot coffee.

And then I heard something. Not Lewis, I was pretty sure of that; Lewis had that woodsy thing going on, and this sounded too heavy-footed for him. Bear? Something worse, maybe? I swallowed the water in my mouth in a choking gulp, screwed the cap back on the bottle, and hastily stowed it in my pack as I surveyed the underbrush. The lead-grey light seemed to bleach colour out of everything that wasn't already piled with snow, and all of a sudden the tent was looking quite cosy.

'Lewis?' I didn't say it loudly, because I felt stupid saying it at all. Obviously it wasn't Lewis.

There was another confused flurry of sound from the underbrush. *Bear,* I thought. *Definitely a bear. I am so dead.*

And then the underbrush parted, shedding snow, and a small woman pitched face-forward into the drift. Her skin was a sickly white, and her hair was matted and tangled with leaves and twigs and...was that blood? And she was definitely underdressed for the weather in a hot-pink sweater and blue jeans...

It was the girl who'd attacked us before. Cherise. She wasn't looking so tough anymore. In fact, she wasn't looking good at all, and as I hesitated, staring at her, she moaned and rolled over on her side and pulled her knees in towards her chest. Her half-frozen hair, now caked with snow, was covering her face, but I could see that her eyes were open.

She blinked slowly. 'Jo?' she whispered. 'Jo, help. Please help me.'

I wanted to. She looked pathetic, and she looked desperately in need...but I couldn't forget how she'd been earlier, when not even bullets could stop her. She certainly didn't look invulnerable anymore, though; she looked like she was in deep trouble.

The kind of trouble that kills you.

'Cherise,' I said, testing out the name. She was either nodding or shuddering with the cold. I didn't come closer, but I slowly crouched down, at least indicating a willingness to hang around. 'What happened?'

Lag time. A long, unresponsive second of it.

'D-d-d-d-don't know.' Her teeth were chattering like castanets, and her lips were an eerie shade of blue in her pale, pale face. Her eyes were huge, and they were the colour of her lips. 'Kevin... I remember Kevin was...he was trying to...'

'Was trying to what?'

'Jo, I'm so cold, *please*!' She didn't seem to have heard me at all. Her voice was faint. Her shuddering was lessening, and I wasn't so sure that was a good thing. 'Kevin was trying to show me how to fight the fire.'

'What fire?'

Another lag, as if she had to wait for the words to circle the globe a couple of times before comprehending. 'The one...' Cherise seemed confused by the question. 'You know the one. The one they sent him to fight.'

'They, who?'

She just stopped talking. Blinked at me, like she had no idea why I was being so cruel to her. And honestly, I was starting to wonder about that myself. She looked so helpless, so fragile, that I couldn't just *leave* her there. Not like some little match girl in the snow.

I looked around for Lewis, but he was a no-show, the fickle bastard. I could have used his ruthless practicality right now. Granted, he probably would have filled the poor kid full of bullet holes, but at least then she wouldn't have been *my* problem.

No sign of him. No sign of David, either. Just me, Cherise, and the falling snow.

'Hold on,' I said. I might have sounded angry, but the truth was that I was scared. My heart was pounding hard, and I wished to hell that I knew the rules of this world, which didn't seem to be the world I expected. Or knew. Or had known. Or maybe I was just going crazy; that would explain a lot.

I shook that idea off and focused back on Cherise. 'Can you get up?' I asked her. She nodded, or at least that was what I took the convulsive jerk of her head to be, and tried. She managed to get to her hands and knees, but seemed stuck at that point, trembling like some poor wounded bird. I stood up, reached down for her, then hesitated. If this was a trap...

Then you'll at least die with good intentions.

I sucked down a deep, cold breath, grabbed Cherise under her arm, and hauled her upright. It didn't take much effort, as small as she was. The fuzzy pink sweater rode up, revealing a tattoo on the small of her back. Some kind of little grey alien dude waving hello. That implied a sense of humour. Maybe she wasn't a bad kid, after all.

And maybe you're crazy, part of my brain reminded me. I didn't like that part. I wished to hell it would shut up.

I half dragged Cherise through the snow to the tent. She seemed barely capable of staying on her feet, even with me taking most of her weight, and I was glad I hadn't hesitated about it too much longer. She was hardly breathing.

Getting her through the narrow tent opening was an engineering problem, but I managed, and soon I had her settled, wrapped in two thermal blankets, with heat packs warming her core temperature. In the light of the battery-powered lantern, Cherise looked ghostly, like the living dead. Which, I thought, might not be far from the case.

She didn't say anything for a long time, and I didn't, either. I couldn't think what questions to ask, and obviously she wasn't compos mentis enough to be coming up with conversation on her own. When she finally did speak, it wasn't anything I expected her to say.

She asked, 'Where's Imara? I thought she'd be with you.'

Imara. I suddenly felt short of breath and I wished David were here. No, I didn't wish that, because I didn't want to think about what he'd be feeling at the sound of that name. This was all hard. It was hard not knowing, but it seemed to get worse the more I found out. Maybe ignorance really was bliss.

Cherise was shaking again, but I figured that

was good; shaking meant her body was trying to warm itself, which meant she was coming out of shutdown mode. 'Imara? Is she OK?'

I remembered the agony in David's eyes, and again I just knew there was something there it would be better if I never had to face. 'Where's Kevin?' I asked instead, because I figured that if he'd recovered from whatever crazy spell he'd been under, he was in the same boat as Cherise...freezing to death out there.

Cherise seemed to try to remember. One second. Two. Two and a half, and then I saw comprehension flood her expression. Then get driven out by fear. 'I...I don't know,' she said. Her voice was high-pitched with sudden panic. 'Jo, we were in the forest. He was showing me...showing me how he did the fire stuff, and it was really cool, you know. He was proud of himself, and he was saying we could help people...'

I nodded. Not that I really understood. 'And then what happened? Cherise, can you—'

'I don't remember!' she said. 'We were there, and everything was fine. We were doing fine, and...' Something darted through her expression like an electric shock, and her eyes widened. 'There was someone else. She came out of the forest. She was...there was something...' Her voice failed, or at least her vocabulary. She shook her head, sniffled, and wiped at her nose. I dug in the backpack for a travel pack of tissues and handed one over. It took her the now-familiar couple of seconds to see what was being held in front of her face, and then she clumsily grabbed it and honked. She sniffled some more, and seemed better. 'Something bad happened to us, didn't it?'

I had no idea, but it seemed pretty likely she was right. Something very bad indeed had happened to her and Kevin. The problem was, I had no idea if it was *still* happening, and if it was, what that meant for my own safety.

I watched her like a hawk, but Cherise didn't display any special powers, monomaniacal or otherwise. The lag time didn't go away. She napped for a while, lulled by the warmth returning to her body – yeah, I knew how that felt – and when she woke up I broke off some energy bar and shared it with her, washed down with plenty of water. I noticed her fingernails. She'd been out there scraping her way through the forest, but once upon a time she'd had a nice manicure. Her skin had that well-lotioned look, too. No wrinkles. A smooth, flawless complexion. She'd had better hair days, but I had the feeling she'd clean up fine.

So what was going on with her? What did her missing time signify, and how did that relate to *my* missing time, if at all? And why was she Time-lag Girl?

As if she were reading my thoughts – scary idea

– Cherise suddenly blurted, 'Do you think we were taken?'

'Taken?' I paused in the act of loading the water bottle back in the pack. Cherise looked nearly human again. Amazing what a little colour in the cheeks can do for a girl.

'You know. By *them*,' she said. She pointed upward with a trembling finger.

'They...?' And then I remembered the grey alien tattoo. 'Oh. Them. Right.' Not that I wanted to sound judgmental, and hey, I'd hooked up with a former boyfriend who was apparently made out of liquid metal and could disappear at will, so who was I to scoff? 'Uh, I don't think so, honey.'

She was staring at me as if she were waiting for my reply, and then, two seconds later, she looked agitated. 'But it makes sense! What if they...what if they did something to us!' Cherise suddenly threw off the thermal blankets in a crinkle of foil and began frantically groping at the back of her neck. She twisted the hair up and anxiously turned towards me. 'Is there a scar? Did they put the chip in my neck?'

'There's no chip.' I waited for her to grasp the fact that I was replying to her, and this time it seemed to take even longer. 'Cherise, get a grip. There's no scar, there's no chip, and I don't think you were abducted by little grey aliens. I don't think you were probed, experimented on, or beamed up. I don't think you went to the planet Bozbarr, either. Whatever happened, I think there's a different explanation.' Not necessarily one any less crazy.

Cherise frowned, then looked disappointed. 'But...it fits all the stories. We were away from people, and I don't remember what happened. There's missing time, and suddenly I'm back out here in the middle of nowhere...'

'This is something else.'

She was already talking over me by the time I got the words out. 'Unless it's something to do with the Wardens,' she said.

'You're sure you don't remember anything? Anything at all?' Cherise, after several seconds of silence, shook her head. I changed the subject. 'Do you remember anything about what happened to Kevin? Where he could be?'

The conversational train clickety-clacked along tracks for the required two heartbeats before she caught up. 'No. But...' A faint wave of colour bloomed in her cheeks. 'But if he could, he'd be here with me.'

So the beach bunny had a thing for skinny slacker boy? I'd thought they were just unrelated strangers, but clearly it wasn't even just a Mutt-and-Jeff partnership; it was a choice. Her choice, at least, and his, if he wasn't a total idiot.

I kept my voice low and quiet. 'How long have you been with him?'

That got me an odd look. 'You know. You were with me when I met him.'

Great. More big black hole to fill in. 'Pretend I don't know,' I said. 'When—'

There was a scratching at the tent, and I shot up to my feet, grabbing the nearest blunt object – which turned out to be a bottle of water – but my doubtful turf-defending skills weren't necessary. It was Lewis. He snaked through the narrow entrance, reached for his pack, and then he saw Cherise.

His stare fixed on her, and there was this sensation of something happening, something I couldn't see or control. Needles all over my skin. My hair blew back in a sudden gust of breathlessly cold wind, and I felt gravity give a funny little lurch, as if it were thinking of cancelling its regular appearance.

I blinked, and however I did it, I saw *things.* First of all: Lewis. He looked taller, stronger – not substantially different, just...more. He radiated some kind of aura for several feet around him, shifting like oil on water. And outside of that aura was a storm. Not literally, not with clouds and things, but still: a storm. There was no other way to think of it. It was sheer bloody power, sparking and gathering and flaring, coming from everywhere, out of the air, up from the ground, flowing into and out of him. And it was focused directly at Cherise.

I looked at her, and she almost vanished. Not totally, but she'd faded like some sepia-toned photograph, and her aura was weak and pale by comparison. There were broad, ugly, jagged streaks of pure black running through it, like claw marks. The tent around us glimmered with heat and power, and the light was getting stronger, so strong I could hardly stand to look at him.

'Lewis!' I turned back to him. 'Don't. She's OK.'

'No,' he said. 'She's not.'

Lewis wasn't letting down his guard. When Cherise looked at me, terrified, he held out a hand towards her, palm out, as if he were warning her to stay away.

'How'd she get in here?'

'I brought her. I know, that was probably stupid, but I couldn't just leave her!' Lewis transferred that X-ray stare to me. I got the impression that he was mortally worried about what he was going to see, but then it must have been better than he expected, because he blinked and seemed to back off from spiritual Defcon One.

'What's happening to her?' I asked.

'What we thought. The Demon used her, and now it's let her go. She's been badly hurt.'

'I didn't see any wounds...' There'd been blood on her sweater, but nothing wrong with her skin. As if the bullet holes Lewis had put in her had fully healed.

'This isn't the kind of damage you see outside,' he said. 'And it's not the kind that heals.'

I wasn't sure how much of this Cherise was following; she seemed confused, her eyes flickering back and forth between the two of us. Lewis kept staring at Cherise, frowning, tilting his head first one way, then the other.

'This makes no sense,' he muttered, and took a step closer to her. Then another one. 'No sense. Why would it go after her? She's not a Warden. No power, nothing like what they're usually drawn towards. She barely shows up on the aetheric even when she's not...' He didn't seem to find a word for it. 'Does she remember?'

'Ask her yourself. She's not deaf.'

He blinked, as if he'd forgotten she was something more than just a collection of interesting problems, and then hunkered down and started asking Cherise questions. It was a short conversation, since it didn't take too many repetitions of time-delayed 'I don't know' before Lewis began seeing the light. The light being, of course, more of a murky, indistinct confusion.

When he was finished, he cast a dark look in my direction and said, 'Outside. Now.'

I wasn't particularly fond of being ordered around, but I was willing to go along, for now. Seeing as he'd probably saved my life a couple of times already. We squirmed through the narrow tent aperture, I made a joke about birth canals that probably wasn't particularly appropriate, and then we were outside in the cutting, frosty wind. Little miniature tornadoes of blown snow whipped by, ruffling my hair and fanning it in a cold sheet across my face. I folded my arms, put my hands in my armpits, and said, 'What? What's wrong?'

Lewis was facing kind of towards me, but mostly away. Like he knew he had to have this conversation but didn't particularly want to. 'It's bad,' he said. 'She may seem OK now, but she's not.'

'Then do your voodoo and fix her up,' I said. 'Make her all—'

'She's dying,' he said.

I felt like he'd punched me in the stomach, and for a second or two I was at a loss for words before I rallied. 'No, she's not. She's getting better. Look, she nearly froze to death, but she's recovering, and—'

He met my eyes, and the bitter fury rolling in him cut me off cold. 'She's dying, Jo,' he said. 'The stuff that keeps her alive, the... I don't know, the soul, is gutted. Cored out. I can't save her. Once a Demon rips at someone like that, so completely, what's left after it leaves can't sustain itself. She'll just...slow down and die. You saw how hard it is for her to focus. That's only going to get worse. Fast.'

'I don't believe in Demons!'

'You should!' he shot back. 'You were killed by one!'

I had officially entered la-la land, and obviously it was no longer safe to be travelling on the crazy train with Lewis. Next stop: Lithium City. 'I'm not dead,' I pointed out to him.

'No, of course you're not...' He stopped himself with an effort, an overwhelming expression of frustration.

'There's got to be something we can do for her,' I said. 'Something. Anything.'

'No. Look, I've seen this before. She'll just fade. Quietly. She'll stop responding to us, and then she'll just...go.' For a second there was a sheen like tears in his eyes. I couldn't remember anything about him prior to his finding me in the woods, but I was fairly sure that crying wasn't his usual thing. He'd seen it before. I was guessing it was someone who'd meant something to him.

'So what do we do now?' I asked. Lewis crossed his arms.

'What we were going to do before she showed up,' he said. 'David and I scouted the route this morning. We hike to the rendezvous, make contact with Wardens we can trust, and find a place to hole up until David can lay his hands on Ashan and find out how to solve this thing.'

'Well, we can't just leave her!' I said. 'And I

don't think she's strong enough to hike it right now. Not in this weather.' Wasn't too sure I was, either.

'I'm sorry, but we can't wait. Kevin's still out there somewhere, and I have no reason to believe he can't find her. Or worse, he might know where she is already. We *have* to leave her. We can get David to lead a rescue party back for her. We'll leave her the tent, food, water, a supply of heat packs.'

'You think she'll last long enough to be rescued? Even with all the supplies?'

Silence. Lewis rocked back and forth, restless and weary, and shook his head.

'Then no,' I said. 'I'm not leaving her here to die alone.' Not because she was supposed to be my friend; it's hard to have friends when you don't remember the good times, not to mention the bad. But because it was just plain *wrong*.

Lewis looked like he wanted to argue with me, but I saw the torment in his face.

And the guilt.

'All right.' He sighed. 'We'll see how she is in the morning. But I still think it's a mistake.'

Cherise looked better when we went back in the tent, but one glance at Lewis told me that was deceptive; he wouldn't be that grim if her condition had improved. At least she didn't seem to be in pain. Certainly she was giving off no on-the-verge-of-death vibes. The only thing strange about her was the haunted, empty look in her eyes, and the fact that she seemed to have a longer and longer lag in responding to anything around her.

I tried to ignore it. The rest of the day was consumed with small talk, nothing very deep or probing. I didn't ask her much about my own life; I wasn't sure I was ready to hear how close we'd been. She volunteered details, though, mentioned people and places that I didn't and couldn't recognise. I was grateful when she fell asleep, finally, and zipped myself into my own sleeping bag next to her. Lewis sat cross-legged, crammed in the corner of the tiny shelter, lost in what looked like meditation but could have been a sitting-up nap for all I knew.

I was about to drift off to sleep when Cherise said dreamily, 'Jo?'

I sat up and did some unnecessary adjustments to her burrito-style wrapping. Her eyes seemed to take ages to focus on me, and she smiled slightly.

'You don't have to pretend. I know something's wrong,' she said. Her voice was soft. 'Look, if I did anything...said anything, you know, earlier...I didn't mean it. You know that, right? I didn't mean it. Don't be mad, OK?'

I didn't even know her, not really, but that hurt. I tried not to let it show. 'I'm not mad,' I said. My voice actually stayed mostly steady. 'You should sleep for a while. Rest.'

Another one of those eerie lags, like talking to someone in space. While she was waiting to get the message, she seemed to be just...vacant. Then she excavated a hand from the foil wrapping around her and took mine. She had a tattoo around the ring finger of her right hand, some kind of Celtic knot work. I figured, given the alien grey tat on her back, she probably had more body art, probably in places that only her boyfriends knew about. A normalish girl, one who loved her looks and devoted a lot of time to their enhancement. A girl who probably had the guys buzzing back home.

A girl who'd been my friend. Who still was, in ways that counted.

She said, 'Don't leave me here. Not by myself.'

'I wouldn't. I won't.'

'I'm scared.' She didn't seem to be hearing me, although her huge blue eyes were locked on mine. 'I can't just *die*, Jo. I didn't even do anything heroic yet. Not like you.'

I looked over at Lewis, whose eyes opened as soon as I focused on him. Serene as the Buddha. I took in a trembling breath. 'Isn't there *anything* you can do?' I snapped. I was displacing anger, I knew that, but it felt good to let a little of it out.

He sighed. 'I can try, but it won't be enough, and it will only prolong things. It can't stop the process.'

Cherise was visibly fading away now, panic in

those huge blue eyes. She tried to move but her arm barely twitched.

Trapped inside her own body.

'Help.' Her lips formed the word, but there was no breath behind it.

I was watching her die.

Sudden fury spiked through me. Not at Lewis – at *everything*. At the unfairness of the world. At losing someone I'd barely begun to know and like. 'No!' I said sharply. 'No, I'm not just going to sit here...'

I reached out and put my hands on her head. I had no idea at all what I was doing, but the frustration and fury inside left me no choice. I had to act. I had to *try*. It seemed like instinct, to put my hands where I did, but then I remembered David had used the same kind of placement when he'd healed Lewis.

'What the hell are you doing?' Lewis barked, scrambling up, but I wasn't listening to him. If this was magic, then I could do it, right? David had shown me how to reach for power...except that I had no idea what to do with it. I could grab the power and hold it, but handing a child a scalpel didn't make her a surgeon.

Show me, I begged. *Come on, somebody, show me what to do. SHOW ME!*

I felt a slow, warm, syrupy pulse come up through my body, flowing through my legs, up through my body's core, spilling out of my hands. Cherise dissolved into a sparkling network of tiny bright points of light, millions of them, layer upon layer upon layer, like a city at night. Some of the lights were bright white, some blue, some shading towards yellow and red.

And, ominously, a substantial part of her head was simply black. No lights at all.

And the black was spreading.

I heard Lewis shouting something at me, but I ignored him. I was expecting him to physically try to drag me away, but he must have had more sense than that.

Cherise's nervous system was an incredible design, mesmerising and intensely beautiful, and I found myself mapping the lines of colour and light in a kind of trace, my hands moving above her body just inches from skin.

I paused over the dead areas, both hands hovering uncertainly, and then I reached inside and touched one of the dead nodes.

Cherise screamed, both in my ears and – chillingly – inside my head.

'Stop!' Lewis was yelling in my ear now, but he wasn't touching me. I was radioactive, and he knew it. 'Jo, you're not an Earth Warden. Jesus, you're not meant to do this. *Stop!*'

I was hurting her, but I knew, somehow, that it had to hurt. There wasn't any choice, if I wanted to save her. The blackness was spreading across that network of lights, slowly consuming her, and if I didn't do something she'd be gone, this beautiful creation would be gone, and I couldn't let it happen.

I just couldn't.

Smells and sounds and chaos rolled over me, a huge vista of things I couldn't comprehend, a *presence* that guided my hands and my powers to touch *here* and *there* and *there*, a tiny spark of pure white power jumping from one burnt-out node to another, jump-starting and dying.

It's not working!

The presence inside wordlessly soothed me, and showed me again. And again. I was no longer seeing or hearing anything in the outside world; the world was what was under my hands and in my head.

And this time, the bridge sparked, flickered, and held, and the network of lights raced and flared and ignited through the dark.

I felt things shift into place. *Click.*

Cherise lit up with a blaze of power, and I heard her take in a whooping, gasping breath in the real world.

I did it.

Yeah. But now that the feverish desire to do it was passing…what exactly had I done?

'Let go!' Lewis was yelling at me, frantic. I

tried. Before I could get free, another spark jumped from my fingers, accessing a network of brilliance in Cherise's mind, and although I had no idea what I was doing...

I was suddenly inside her head.

Chapter Four

Being in Cherise's body took some adjustment. I felt dizzy, squeezed, *wrong*. I involuntarily tried to move something, but in the next instant I realised a couple of important things...

One, I wasn't Cherise. I was still me, but a silent observer sitting alongside Cherise in her body.

And two, this was the past.

This was memory.

It took me a second to absorb where Cherise was. Some kind of set. Movie? Television? I caught sight of the unmistakable configuration of a television news desk, and the call letters in red over it. Cameras. People milling around. There wasn't any easy way I could figure out what date this was, or even what city. I could sense Cherise thinking, but it was a random jumble of stuff, nothing I could make sense of – until it suddenly did.

Oh great, she thought. Time to make nice with the new girl.

And with a sense of having fallen completely

down the rabbit hole, I saw myself – Joanne – walking towards her. There was something so utterly wrong about seeing myself like this that I felt another surge of disorientation, and I wanted desperately to turn away.

But I couldn't. I was trapped, helpless, watching the memory play out before me. Trapped.

'Hi. I'm Joanne,' that other me said, and held out a long-fingered, strong hand with a halfway decent manicure. French nails. Not a great tan, but a pretty good one. She looked rested, but a little bit nervous. First day on the job, maybe? From Cherise's point of view Joanne was annoyingly tall, and most of it was leg. I sensed Cherise making an assessment. She was a cold and merciless judge of other women's looks – not unkind, but precise.

'You're Marvin's new assistant,' Cherise said. 'Right?'

God, did I really look that way when I smiled? My mouth looked funny. 'Assistant would be a kind way to put it,' Joanne said. I couldn't stand thinking of her as me. 'He just called me the weather girl.'

'Yeah, well, that's Marvin for you. Hey. I'm Cherise. I'm the dumbass who runs around in the bikini to give the surf forecast.' Cherise rolled her eyes to show it didn't really bother her. From this side of the conversation, I could tell that it wasn't an act; running around in a bikini really *didn't* bother her. She was pretty, and she knew it, and there wasn't much point in denying the fact that guys found her hot. She figured she had the rest of her life to use her brains. A fine body had a short shelf life, when it came to stripping down to a G-string. 'So how's it working with Marvin so far?'

I watched the former me make a face that I resolved I would never, ever make again. 'Oh, fabulous. Is he always that—?'

'Grabby? Always,' Cherise said, and leant forward. 'OK, time for the potential compatibility quiz. Who's the sexiest man alive?'

'Uh...' Joanne blinked. 'Probably...um... I have no idea.' Oddly, I couldn't answer it now, either. I only really knew two guys in the whole world, and they were both pretty damn sexy.

'Acceptable answers include David Duchovny, Johnny Depp, and James Spader. Sean Connery is always allowable. So – favourite TV show?'

'I don't watch a lot of television,' the other me confessed. Well, I consoled myself with the thought that losing my memory clearly hadn't made all that much difference in my conversational skills.

'Well, I watch a lot of television,' said Cherise. 'So you'll need to catch up. I'll give you a list of what you can start with, and yes, there will be quizzes later.'

Joanne laughed. She had a good laugh, one that made you want to get in on the joke – the first thing about her I couldn't quibble with. 'You always this take-charge, Cherise?'

'Pretty much. I'm little, but I'm fierce,' she said, and inspected Joanne's nail polish, giving it a nod of approval. 'Seriously, if we're going to be best friends, you really have to be able to intelligently discuss the relative hotness of television stars. It's a must. What do you think, too green?'

That would have thrown most people. It definitely threw me now, observing, but Joanne had followed the shift without trouble. She looked at Cherise's nail polish critically, tilted her head, and said, 'No, it's perfect. Picks up the colour in your shirt.' I felt Cherise's surge of satisfaction. 'But,' Joanne continued, 'you might want to consider pairing up that underlayer with a sheer teal instead of green. Make the colour really pop.'

Cherise blinked, looked at her nails, then at her shirt. 'Damn. You're *good*. Shopping,' she said. 'Tonight. Shopping and mojitos. Seriously, anybody who can one-up me on colour analysis must be worth my time.'

Then-me looked a little taken aback by that, searched for a reply, and then said, with a hilarious amount of consideration for Cherise's potentially bruised feelings; 'I'm not, you know, gay or anything.'

Cherise found that funny. 'You mean you wouldn't go gay for me? Sheesh. I'm not looking for a date. Nobody else here understands the power of Zen shopping. I think' – Cherise swept a look over her ensemble, then Joanne's, which actually was pretty cute – 'I think we can do some real credit card damage together. Somebody's got to keep the economy growing. It's almost patriotic.'

Joanne looked relieved. And then smiled. The smile still looked wrong to me, from this side.

'Deal,' she said.

It was a warm place to be, and I wanted to stay there, bask in that sensation of liking and being liked.

But I couldn't stay.

There was a blurring sensation, like being pushed hard from behind, and I jumped tracks, falling endlessly, falling, lost, and then there was a sudden burst of light.

Rapid-fire memories. Fragments of conversations. Ice cream on the couch, watching movies with Cherise. Shopping. Chatting.

Normal life. I'd had a normal life, once.

Another lurching sensation, a blur, and when I blinked it away, Cherise was pushing open a door from a dark hallway to the outside world. Time had passed, although I didn't have a good notion of how much. She looked over her shoulder, and I saw Joanne following her out of the building.

'So,' she was saying, 'What do you think? Hot Topic? And maybe some Abercrombie. Then lunch.'

'Girl, do you ever do *anything* but shop?' Joanne asked, but not as if she was really opposed to the idea. Cherise blew her a kiss.

'Well, I was thinking of dropping by the chess club, but you know how shallow those guys are...'

'Shut up.'

It was a bright, sunlit morning. The air was muggy and warm, with just a hint of salt air breeze. Joanne looked good: more tanned, more toned, wearing a pair of low-rise blue jeans and a teal blue sleeveless tee that rode up to reveal some firm abs.

Cherise, of course, looked even better. She was like orange sherbet, layered in pastels, all edible colours. She could have stepped out of a hair product commercial. The poster child for healthy and vibrant.

'Just for that, I'm adding Old Navy to the list,' Cherise said, and checked her purse. She frowned at a mirror and touched up her lipstick as they crossed a weedy picnic area behind the building they were exiting, towards a parking lot. 'And I'm going to make you eat sushi, too.'

'Hey,' Joanne said. Her tone had changed, turned quiet and dark. 'Cher. Heads up.'

Cherise looked up, alarmed, and focused on a man standing near the cars in the fenced-off parking area. I felt the surge of pure adrenalin go through her, sending her heart rate soaring. 'Dammit. I really thought that restraining order thing would work.'

Joanne's face had gone still and tense. She took her purse off her shoulder and handed it over to Cherise. 'Stay here.'

'Don't,' Cherise whispered, and grabbed her arm. 'Let's just go back in. We can call security – they've got his picture. They know to call the cops.'

'Yeah, that's done a hell of a lot of good so far,' Joanne said. 'This jerk isn't going away. How many times does this make that he's shown up here?'

Cherise sighed. I could feel the dread in her, honest and real. 'Six.'

'And phone calls?'

'God, I lost count. And don't even talk about the ugh-worthy letters.'

'Then this guy needs a stronger message,' Joanne said. 'Look, trust me. You just go back inside, OK?'

'But – Jo, you can't—'

Apparently, she certainly could. I watched myself walk purposefully towards the shifty-looking fellow standing near the red convertible. He was wearing an overcoat – a dead giveaway of weirdness in the current heat wave – and even from Cherise's distance looked like he needed not just a shower but a full-scale disinfection. Wild-eyed, wilder-haired.

Scary.

Joanne stopped just a couple of feet away from him. Cherise couldn't hear the conversation, because all of a sudden thunder rumbled overhead. Cherise looked up, startled, to see dark clouds moving in from the west – which, Cherise thought, was really strange, because she'd just been giggling about Marvin's out-of-the-box weather prediction about storms when the coast seemed clear, and all of the other stations were talking sunny skies.

Joanne must have wondered, too; she looked up at the sky with a frown, and it distracted her for a second from the guy in the trench coat.

Who suddenly lashed out at her with a fist.

I had to admit – this former version of me clearly had fantastic reflexes. She leant back, and his punch sailed cleanly past her chin. He snarled and reached in his pocket and pulled out...a knife.

'Call the cops!' Joanne yelled to Cherise, who dashed for the doorway. She dialled 911 on her cell while she ran, and yelled for help while it rang. Gaffers and techs came running from the studio – big strong guys, union guys. Tough guys. 'Jo's in trouble! Parking lot!'

They scrambled. Cherise blurted out the facts to the 911 operator and hurried back out to follow, terrified of what she'd find...

...only to find a ring of big, tough union guys standing around, and the stalker with the knife on the ground, flat on his face, with Joanne kneeling on his back. She had his left arm twisted up behind him, painfully far, and she looked calm and cool.

A passing gust of wind swirled through the parking lot, stirring sand and trash, and blew her hair over her face. She shook it back, and Cherise saw that Joanne was grinning.

'No problem,' Joanne said. 'One less stalker, Cher. That only leaves Brad Pitt, right?'

Cherise sucked in a shaky breath. 'He has *got* to stop calling me,' she said, in a brave attempt to make it look like she hadn't been terrified out of her mind that she'd find the other me dead on the ground. 'His wife's getting pissed.'

The stalker on the ground writhed and said some not very nice things. Joanne put her right hand on the back of his neck, and Cherise was almost sure she saw some kind of spark zap from her into her prisoner.

'Play nice,' Joanne said. 'Or you'll be waking up in a coma.'

Head electrician Sully, who was commonly acknowledged to be the hardest guy on the union team, clapped his hand over his heart. 'I think I'm in love,' he said.

All the union guys whistled in agreement.

Cherise held in a crazy urge to giggle as Joanne winked at her.

'All in a day's work for a weather girl,' she said, and the howl of sirens took over as the police arrived.

That, I realised, was the day Cherise had truly

thought of me as not just a friend, but *the* friend. Her best friend.

And that feeling...that was love.

I lost the thread of the memory, falling into a blur of sound and colour. A spiral of confusion. I felt a dull, leaden ache in my head, and wanted to get off the ride now. And never, ever get back on.

The next thing I caught was only a flash, a very brief one – I wasn't even in it, it was Cherise in a shoe store with a polished-looking blonde woman griping about her ex-husband.

And about her sister. From Cherise's sense of disgust, she just never shut up about her sister.

And she was still talking about her. 'I didn't like her much, you know. When I was younger. Joanne was a total bitch.'

Oh. *I* was the sister. So this was – who, exactly?

Cherise put a pair of shoes back and turned to face the other woman, frowning. Before she could open her mouth to defend me – if she was going to, which I couldn't actually be certain about – the blonde plunged ahead. 'Joanne was always *special*,' she said. 'Mom treated her like a little queen. I was always the one who had to work harder, you know? So we weren't close. Really, I wouldn't have come looking for her help if I hadn't been desperate.'

'No kidding, Sarah,' Cherise said. 'I guess it's nice that she's let you stay in her house, eat her food, and use her credit cards.' She put some emphasis on the credit cards, and I looked over the blonde with new interest. New dye job and haircut. Fancy designer outfit. The shoes she was trying on must have been a minimum of three hundred, and they didn't even look that cute on her.

Sarah didn't seem to take the rebuke all that well. 'Well, it's just temporary. So, do you have sisters?'

'Brothers,' Cherise said. 'Two.'

'Any of them rich?' Sarah was joking, only not really. Cherise gave her a flat stare. 'Oh, come on, don't be so judgmental. Marrying for money is a good career move. You're a nice-looking girl. You should take advantage.'

'I do,' Cherise said, and shrugged. 'I'm on television. That's shallow enough for me.'

'That's not what I mean. Surely you've met some rich, successful guys, especially in television.'

'Of course I have.' The feeling flooding through Cherise was annoyance, mixed in with a little toxic-feeling contempt. No, she didn't like my sister. At all.

'So with a little planning, you could really secure your future,' Sarah continued, clearly not seeing the stop sign Cherise's expression had to be flashing. 'Girls like Jo, they don't really understand the world. In the end, she's going to end up with some loser, if she can get a guy at all, and she'll never be happy. Strong women end up alone, that's just the way things are. I, on the other hand, plan to end up in the Diamond Club surrounded by a huge circle of friends.'

'Yeah, well, didn't you already try that?' Cherise asked blandly. 'You know, marrying for money. Wasn't your ex loaded?'

'My ex was a bastard,' Sarah said. 'And he was a criminal, too.'

'But you stayed married.'

Sarah shrugged. 'Until I didn't.'

Cherise was busy foreseeing a future for Sarah, one of bitter martini-fed binges, debt, and multiple divorce. She was kind of having fun at it, too.

'I don't think you know Joanne at all. Your sister kind of rules,' Cherise said. 'And the next time you say anything bad about her, I'm going to smack you so hard the rocks in your head will rattle.'

Sarah's mouth opened, then closed.

Then she laughed, because she assumed that Cherise was kidding.

Only I knew Cherise hadn't been, really, and that warmed my heart.

Blur.

Things flashed through my mind faster and faster, memories that didn't belong, things I didn't want to know, things I never wanted to know, and I needed it to just stop, stop, *stop.*

Cherise and Not-me in a car, racing ahead of a

storm. A fight on a deserted road. Kevin holding Cherise while Lewis and I fought off enemies. Cherise behind the wheel, whispering prayers under her breath as we drove into a storm.

I couldn't take it all in. Overload. *Stop!*

I tried to pull out, and somehow the connection began to fail, but in the last instant I saw a face.

My own face, with eyes that weren't human – incandescent, glowing eyes. Eyes like David's. I watched her lips part and heard her say, 'Mom?'

Chapter Five

Chapter Five

I screamed and sat up, lost my balance, fell, and ended up sobbing and gasping for breath. The air around me was still and cool, and there was grit under my palms where we'd tracked snow and dirt into the tent from outside. It smelt like unwashed blankets and sweat and fear.

Back to reality.

I felt an overwhelming surge of sickness, fought it down, and slowly sat up. My breath came hot and ragged, and I wasn't sure if my head would ever stop throbbing. Oh, God, it hurt.

Lewis's hand pressed warmly and silently on my shoulder, and then he went past me to kneel beside Cherise. Her eyes were closed, and she was very still.

Too still.

'Is she OK?' I asked. My voice sounded raw and ragged, and I didn't like the way it seemed to quaver at the edges. My head felt as if someone had stuffed it, mounted it, and used it for batting practice.

Mom, the image in Cherise's memory had said. Mom. David had said that we had a child. I hadn't expected her to be…adult. And look so much like me.

Imara.

'She's alive,' he said, and for a crazy second I thought he meant Imara, but he was focused on Cherise. 'Christ, Jo. How did you do that? How could you do it? You're not an Earth Warden; you've never…' He turned to me, and I saw his eyes flare into colours, like the Djinn, but no, that was on the aetheric; I was seeing it superimposed over the real world and it was disorienting, sickening. I tried to get up, and fell down. Hard.

'Jo!' He grabbed me and held me, and I could feel his whole body trembling, a wire-fine vibration. He was so bright, I couldn't see. I squeezed my eyes shut. '*Focus.* God, what did you do to yourself?'

I could barely breathe. Nothing was right. Too much colour, too much sound, every heartbeat thundering from him was like a roar, his voice echoed in my head and deafened me, even the smells were too raw and immediate…

His touch was the only thing that soothed me, stroking through my sweaty hair, over my skin, grounding me gently back in the world.

'Shhhh,' he whispered in my ear, barely a breath. 'Shhhh, now. Breathe. Breathe.'

He was rocking me in his arms, and I could feel

my heart hammering wildly. My body felt too tight to contain me; I was bursting out of it; I was... I was...

Oh, God.

I exploded with light, convulsing in his embrace, trying to scream but my throat was locked tight, sealing in sound.

And Lewis held me until the waves subsided and left me empty and broken, trembling with reaction.

I'd dug my fingernails into his skin, and when I let go I saw blood welling up in the wounds.

He didn't speak. I don't know if he could. His face...his face was full of an indescribable mixture of wonder and horror.

Cherise sat up as suddenly as if somebody had jerked her upright by the hair, and blinked at the two of us in surprise. 'What just happened?' she asked. 'I feel better. Am I better?'

Lewis let out a slow, unsteady breath. 'Yeah,' he said. 'You're better.' And he looked at me. Wordless, again.

'And me?' I whispered. 'What am I?'

He was looking at me with unfocused eyes. With the eyes of a Warden.

'I don't know,' he confessed. 'But whatever you are now, you're damn strong.'

'Yeah, like *that's* news,' Cherise said, then blinked and stretched. 'Man, I'm hungry. What's for dinner?'

I was looking into Lewis's face, and he was staring right back at me. It felt intimate, but not in a sexual kind of way – this was something else. Frank and appraising and a little frightening. My heart rate was slowing, not speeding up. My body was cooling down from overdrive.

'Prime rib,' Lewis said, and broke the stare to turn to smile at her. 'Baked potato. Fresh hot bread with whipped butter.'

'Food tease,' she said, and unzipped herself from the sleeping bag. 'What's really for dinner?'

'Trail bar.' He fished in his backpack, found one, and handed it over.

'Comes with champagne, right?' Cherise's smile was brave, but still scared. He offered a bottle of water with the gravity of a sommelier.

'Only the finest vintage,' he said, and cast another wary, strangely impartial glance at me. 'You'd better eat something, too.'

I didn't want to. The trail bar tasted like...trail dust. Even the chocolate chips seemed bitter and wrong, but I doggedly chewed and swallowed. The water seemed all right, and I chugged it until I burped. It all stayed down, and after I'd finished the brief meal I felt full and more than a little exhausted. Lewis watched me without seeming to, looking for any sign I was about to come apart at the seams, I guessed, but he didn't ask me any questions. He quizzed Cherise lightly about what she remembered – which was very little, just what she'd told me before – and how she was feeling, which was apparently great. And sleepy, because she kept yawning and finally curled up into the warm nest of the sleeping bag and fell asleep.

I was just as tired, if not even more so, and gravity dragged my eyelids down one remorseless fraction of an inch at a time. Lewis didn't say anything, just took my empty bottle and set it aside and helped me climb into my own sleeping bag. It felt amazing being warm and horizontal.

Lewis's hand smoothed hair back from my brow, and his eyes were at once wary and concerned. 'Do you know what you did?' he asked.

I mutely shook my head.

He leant over and kissed me very gently. 'You did the impossible,' he said. 'And that worries me.'

It worried me, too.

But not quite enough to keep me awake.

'Rise and shine, ladies.' That was Lewis's voice, too loud and too cheerful. I groaned and tried to burrow into the warmth of my blankets, because the chill outside was sharp, but he robbed me of that pleasure by unzipping the sleeping bag and flipping it open, exposing me to the cold. 'Right now. We're breaking camp. We've got a lot of ground to cover if we're going to make it to the rendezvous.'

I didn't want to think about it. My calves and ankles and thighs were stiff and sore, and my neck felt like it had been locked in an iron vice all night. I had a headache, and every bruise I'd collected over the past few days was making itself loudly known.

But yes, I got up. Mainly because Cherise was already moving, and it would have looked pretty bad to be outdone by the girl who'd been on the verge of death.

Lewis jerked his head towards me and exited the tent. I squeezed out after him and groaned softly as the brutal cold closed in around me. I was surprised my breath didn't freeze and fall to the ground.

Lewis wasn't even wearing his goddamn *coat*.

'How are you?' he asked.

'Sore,' I said. 'Tired. Fine.'

He looked at me, and I was sure he was examining me in more than the normal way. After a few seconds he gave me a grudging nod. 'You look all right,' he said. 'But, Jo, understand: What happened with you yesterday, that wasn't natural. It wasn't right. You're a Weather and Fire Warden. You are not an Earth Warden. There's only one person alive right now with all three powers, and that's me.'

'Is that what this is about? You're *jealous*?'

He barked out a laugh that hung white in the still air. 'No. God, no. If you were truly a triple-threat Warden, I'd be completely relieved. But, Jo, I don't see it. I don't see it in you today, and I never saw it in you before. So what the hell happened? After... You seemed...' He looked honestly uncertain how to phrase it. I saved him the trouble.

'Orgasmic? Yeah. Kinda.' He looked away. 'Not normal, huh?'

'There's no *normal* when you talk about a thing like this, Jo. Did you access Cherise's memories?'

I nodded.

'Did they make sense to you?'

'At first. It got more confusing the further I went.'

'Because your brain was overstimulated,' he said. 'Which in turn must have triggered the—'

'Big O,' I supplied. 'Honestly, Lewis, you're not *twelve*; you can say what you mean. Come on!'

He ignored that. 'That means you were channelling power through neural paths that normally carry sexual energy,' he said, half to himself. 'Which would fit, because some of the Earth Wardens are wired that way, too. But why can't I see it now? Your aura is just showing normal strength, in the normal range for you. Weather and Fire, and the Fire's not that strong.'

I shrugged. 'Does it matter?'

'It might, yeah.'

'Does it matter enough to *freeze our asses off* talking about it right now?' I demanded. 'Because in case you hadn't noticed, you're shivering again.'

'Am I?' He looked honestly surprised, and reached into the tent to grab his coat, which he draped around his shoulders. 'There. Happy?'

'Thrilled, man.'

Lewis quickly moved on to other, more practical things, like breaking camp, which Cherise and I didn't do all that efficiently, and then leading us on the second half of the Winter Wonderland Death March. Cherise asked questions, some of which I could answer and a lot of which I couldn't. Lewis rescued me on the biggest one, which had to do with what had happened to Cherise and Kevin.

'You remember being sent out by the Wardens,' he said. 'To fight the fire in California?'

'Yeah.' Cherise was flushed and breathless, but on her it looked good. Lewis wasn't exactly immune to it, either, even if it wasn't conscious attraction on his part; he was simply lagging back, paying more attention to her than mercilessly slave-driving us through the snow like a pack of sled dogs. 'He was showing me how he did some stuff. Like creating firebreaks. It was cool.'

'Do you remember what happened then?'

She was silent for a few seconds, blue eyes far away, and then she nodded. 'This woman came out of the trees. At least, I think it was a woman.' She frowned. 'Why can't I remember what she looked like?'

Lewis sent me a look that clearly said, *Demon*. I didn't disagree. Once you're already off the cliff, you might as well pretend you're flying.

'What happened after that?' Lewis asked as we puffed our way down another treacherous hillside, feeling for good footholds beneath a cruelly smooth blanket of snow. I nearly slipped on a rock that turned under my foot, and grabbed wildly. Lewis caught my arm and steadied me.

Cherise took her time answering. 'Um... I remember falling, and there was – I don't know. Pain, maybe. I mostly remember passing out. And waking up out here, in the snow. Freezing.'

Eerily similar to my experience, in fact, except that she'd managed to hang on to her clothes. Lewis and I traded another long look.

'Could I have been—'

'No,' he said, definitely. 'What happened to her was clear. What happened to you isn't.'

He tested the featureless snow ahead of us with a long twisted branch, then nodded for us to come ahead. We trudged in silence for a while.

'I do remember something,' Cherise said suddenly. 'I remember – hey, did you shoot me?' She frowned and unzipped her coat to peer at her sweater. 'Oh, man. You really did. But I'm not—'

'We'll talk later,' Lewis promised. 'Save your strength. We've got a way to go.'

No kidding. Hours of it, breathlessly scrambling

over cold, slippery terrain. Not my best time ever. But I had to laugh when Cherise, clearly tiring, accepted Lewis's help across a narrow frozen stream. His big hands spanned her waist and he lifted her easily over. 'Oooooh, *nice hands*. You know, I could get to like you, mister.'

'Ditto.' Lewis grinned briefly, and then turned his attention back to the trail.

'Hey, Lewis?' Cherise's cheer had faded almost instantly, and she grabbed his sleeve to drag him to a halt. 'You haven't said, about Kevin. Do you think… Did whatever happened to me happen to him, too? Was he out there looking for help?'

Lewis glanced over at me, then focused on the snow. 'Not likely,' he said. 'If what I think is true, Kevin would have lasted longer. Been of more use. For all I know, he could still be under her control.'

'Her, who?' We reached the bottom of the long icy hillside and started the tiring trek up the next one, hauling ourselves by grabbing icy branches when the going got too tough. 'Come on, you guys are like superheroes or something! There's got to be something we can do for him!'

Lewis looked at her for a second, and his eyes looked dark and cold. 'If there was,' he said, 'I'd be damn well doing it. But I can't take chances. Not with the two of you.'

Cherise's foothold broke loose, and she began to slide. I gripped a handy branch, reached down, and grabbed her by the coat sleeve, hauling her upright again. Lewis helped me get her to the top of the hill, where we paused for breath. The view might have been gorgeous, except for the low clouds obscuring the mountains and pressing down like dirty cotton on the treetops. Snow continued to fall in a steady, soft, relentless assault.

I wanted to ask how far we had left to go, but it wasn't worth wasting my breath. I didn't think it would help if I knew. My legs were burning, sore in the calf muscles, and I had scrapes and bruises and my headache hadn't gone away. My acquired memory of Cherise's experiences had settled into an uneasy, slippery state that felt like I could have imagined them or dreamt them. But at least I had a memory of me, of the television station, of Cherise, of Sarah, of...

Of the girl calling me Mom.

'Lewis,' I said. He hesitated in the act of stabbing the branch through the snow, then took two or three more steps. 'I saw Imara. In Cherise's memories.'

He didn't answer. He took another step. I followed in his wake, puffing for breath. The air felt icy and wet around us, and sleet burnt my face. The sky was an unbroken grey bowl, and it felt oppressive, as if it were slowly lowering down onto my head. Nature. Who needed it?

'You going to talk to me about her?' I demanded.

It came out sharper than I intended.

'No,' he said. 'It's one complication you don't need right now. One thing at a time, Jo. Let's get ourselves safe before—'

'Before we talk about my dead *kid*?' I shot back. 'Well, if you're worried about me breaking down, don't. I can't even remember her. All I have is a name and a face.' That wasn't true, but I didn't want him to know how raw and bloody that simple vision had left me.

Cherise stopped in her tracks, puffing hard. 'She's *dead*?' she blurted, and made a gesture as if she were going to reach out towards me, but then thought better of it. 'Oh, my God. What happened?'

'I don't know,' I snapped. 'I don't know anything. That's the problem.'

Lewis poked the stick into the snow with unnecessary violence.

'I want to know how she died,' I said.

'If wishes were horses, you'd be doing one fifty in a cherry red Mustang on the autobahn.' He sounded bleak and cool. 'No.'

'You son of a bitch.'

'Probably.' He gave me a smile that was equal parts apology and sadness. 'But I've always been like that. You've just forgotten about—'

He stopped in his tracks, straightened, and held up a hand for silence. Cherise and I both froze, too.

Wind swirled across the clearing, picking up snow crystals and peppering me in the face with them, but I didn't move.

In the distance I heard a faint chopping sound. 'What is that?' I whispered, and then I recognised it. That was the sound of a helicopter. 'Trouble?'

'No,' Lewis said. 'That's what I was hoping for. We just arrived here a little early, that's all.'

'Here?' Cherise turned a slow circle. 'Where's here, exactly?'

Lewis held up his GPS device, which had a blinking red light. 'Rendezvous point. That's our ride out of here.'

That suddenly. *Wow.* Except that even though that had to be good news – right? – Lewis didn't look any less tense. He shrugged out of his backpack and unzipped pockets, moving quickly and competently.

'So what's the problem?' I asked. 'Because there's a problem, right?' There was always a problem.

'I think we're being followed,' he said. 'Head for the tree line,' he said. 'Both of you. Move it.' Cherise took off instantly, plunging through the snow as quickly as possible. When I didn't immediately snap to obey, Lewis yelled it at me, full throat: 'Move!' A drill sergeant couldn't have put more menace into it. I galloped clumsily along, my feet sinking deep into the snow. I prayed I wouldn't hit a sinkhole, because a broken leg right now would be inconvenient.

When I looked back, Lewis was standing in the middle of the clearing, looking up at the grey sky. His backpack was at his side, and in his hand was a black, angular shape – the gun he'd fired at Cherise.

He scanned the far side of the clearing, but it was obvious it was a useless effort; he might have sensed trouble coming, but he wasn't sure which direction it was heading. He saw me hesitating, caught in the open, and motioned for me to keep running. Cherise had already made it to the trees; I saw a flash of pink as she found cover and stayed there.

And I would have followed her, really, but I caught sight of motion to Lewis's left, out in the deep forest shadows, and I sensed a blurring, as if someone were trying to avoid notice.

'Lewis!' I yelled it, but the increasingly loud churning of the rotors drowned me out. 'Lewis! Over there!' I waved my arms frantically, trying to catch his eye, and just as I did something hot ignited in the tree line where the blur had been, incandescent and round, and it shot straight towards me.

I didn't even think; I just hit the snow face-first. The fireball sizzled over my head right where my midsection would have been had I been caught flat-footed, and rolled away, hissing into open snow, where it quickly melted drifts in a five-foot radius to the bare dirt.

That caught Lewis's attention. He whirled just as Kevin stepped out of the trees. The teen looked grimy and scraped, but there was a burning light in his eyes, and as I wondered what to do he held up his hand, palm up, and formed another ball of fire in it.

Apparently my dive-for-it tactic was Warden-Approved, because Lewis did the same thing; he waited until Kevin threw the fireball, and then threw himself flat in the snow. Kevin's fireball streaked through the air and exploded like a bottle of napalm against a tree on the far side of the clearing – he'd thrown that one with a lot more fury. Lewis rolled, brought up the gun, aimed...

And didn't pull the trigger. I held my breath, horrified, because Kevin was already reloading, forming fire in his hands and snarling in rage.

No. Dammit, why didn't Lewis shoot?

Kevin threw the plasma straight at Lewis, who was helpless and prone on the ground, and Lewis still didn't pull the trigger.

He also didn't try to avoid the impact of the flame.

It hit and erupted in white-hot fury, sizzling the snow around him into an instant spring thaw, and then Lewis was *on fire*. I screamed and started towards him, then stopped, because Lewis – burning all over, fire clinging to him like a second skin – calmly pushed himself up to his feet, brushed a hand over his chest like a man flicking away dust, and the flames just…died.

Not a mark on him.

Kevin's eyes went wider, but then he shut down, went hard and cold. 'You cold-blooded son of a bitch,' he spat at Lewis. 'I'm going to kill you.'

'Good luck with that,' Lewis said. 'I think the waiting list is into double digits by now.'

'Where's Cherise? What did you do to her?'

Lewis took a step towards him. He was still holding the gun, but carefully, at his side. I doubted Kevin could even see it. 'Kevin, relax. She's all right.'

'No. No, she's not, or she'd be here. She'd be with me.' Kevin's fingers, consciously or not, were dripping with fire. 'You're lying. You hurt her.'

'I've got no reason to lie to you,' Lewis said. His voice was still and quiet, very gentle, and he continued moving towards the boy without seeming to be in any hurry at all. 'She was hurt, Kevin, but she's better now. You're hurt, too. I need you to stop fighting me. Can you do that?'

'No!' Kevin screamed, and extended both hands towards Lewis. Fire erupted in a hot, incandescent wall that swept towards Lewis at a frightening rate, searing the snow into instant steam, leaving everything dead and smoking behind it...

And I caught a flash of pink, and Cherise ran out in front of the advancing flames, and stopped just in front of Lewis.

'No!' I screamed, and lunged up. 'Cherise, no! He can't see you!'

Kevin's view was blocked by the flames. Maybe he could see Lewis, I didn't know, but he couldn't possibly have seen Cherise, and he was going to kill her.

And she wasn't going to move.

Lewis put out one hand, palm out, and stopped the wall of fire cold. His fingers curled down, and so did the blaze, collapsing into a confusion of hot streamers and flickering out of existence a bare two feet from Cherise's pale, terrified face.

When he saw her, Kevin's mouth opened, a dark O of horror, and he lurched forward at the same time she started towards him. I climbed up to my feet, brushing away the snow, as the two of them collided to form a frantic pile of arms and legs.

Kevin was talking as he kissed her, but the words were only for Cherise, and besides, the noise of the approaching helicopter was rattling around the valley like thunder. I moved back towards Lewis, feeling tired and achy and even more anxious than before. What if Kevin was still possessed? What if we had to kill him? *Oh, God.*

Lewis was ready for that; I could see it in the

way he was standing, watching the two of them. Nothing but calculation in his eyes. If he thought it was adorable, the slacker and the beach bunny reuniting, he kept it well hidden behind a blank, empty expression.

'Stay behind me,' he said as I approached. I nodded and obeyed. 'Watch for the helicopter. Signal it when you see it.'

I risked a glance over his shoulder and saw that Cherise had taken Kevin's hand and was leading him over towards us. 'Cherise,' Lewis called. 'Let go and step aside.'

'But—'

'Do it.'

I'd have done what he said, too; that tone didn't leave any room for negotiation. I scanned the skies – still nothing but low, grey clouds – and peeked again. Cherise let go of Kevin's hand and moved away – not far, but far enough for Lewis's purposes, apparently.

Kevin glared at him. The kid looked ill, pale, frostbitten, and on his last legs. As Lewis took a step forward, fire began dripping from Kevin's fingers.

'Stop fighting me,' Lewis said, his voice dropping low. He was using some kind of power, something that made me feel sleepy even in the corona effect; I saw Cherise yawn and stagger. 'Cherise is fine. Let us take care of you now. I know what happened.

You have to stop fighting, Kevin. I'm not your enemy.'

Kevin swayed. His hands fell to dangle at his sides, and fire dripped and smoked from his fingertips, hissing into the snow. 'Don't,' he said. 'Don't touch me. You shouldn't touch me. In case.'

'I know,' Lewis said. He was nearly within grabbing range. 'It's OK. It's gone now. You're going to be all right.'

Kevin staggered and collapsed to his knees in the snow. Where his hands met the white powder, the snow sizzled into steam. 'I tried,' he mumbled, and shook his head angrily. Fire flew like drops of sweat. 'I tried to stop it. It came out of the forest fire; I'd never seen anything like that before; I didn't know what to... I couldn't protect her. I thought I could, but—'

Lewis was there by then, and without any hesitation at all he grabbed Kevin and pulled him upright. 'It's not your fault,' he said. 'There's not a Warden alive who could have done any better. Including me. You survived. That's the important thing.'

Kevin was barely conscious, and Cherise moved to help support him, casting looks at Lewis that silently pleaded for him to make things right. I heard the *thump-thump-thump* of rotors overhead growing clearer, and finally spotted a shadow moving through the mist.

I started scissoring my arms. The colour of my down jacket – green – might not be enough for them to pick us out, but I did some jumping up and down and yelling, even though I knew the yelling was useless. The helicopter headed towards us, hovered overhead, and started circling in for a landing.

As I lowered my arms to shield my eyes from blowing snow, I saw someone standing in the shadows across the clearing. She was tall, and she had long, dark hair that blew in a silken sheet on the wind. She wasn't wearing a coat, just a pair of blue jeans, some not-very-practical boots, and a baby-doll tee in aqua blue. I had that disorientation again, the same as when I'd been watching myself through Cherise's eyes, but this was different. For one thing, it wasn't a memory. She was there, facing me, in real time.

It took exactly one second for the full implications to hit me, hard, and run me down like a speeding train.

'Imara?' I whispered. Or tried. My voice was locked tight in my throat. I glanced desperately at Lewis, but he was occupied with the kids, and besides, he couldn't possibly have heard me over the roar of the descending machine. 'Oh, God. Imara, is it you?' Because it had to be my daughter, didn't it? She looked just like me – the same height, the same curves, the same black hair, although hers looked better cared for at the moment.

And the wind blew her hair back, revealing her face fully. She smiled, and my whole skin shivered into goose-flesh, because that smile was *wrong*. I felt the dark impact of it all the way across the open snowy space. She was *not* my daughter. There was a crawling, sticky sense of *evil* to it. There was also an overwhelming feeling of danger, even though she wasn't making any overt moves in my direction.

She was...*me*.

'Lewis!' I said, startled into a yell.

He can't help you, she said, as clearly as if she were standing at normal conversational distance. It wasn't a voice, though. Not really. *If he does, I'll have to take action. Do you want me to destroy him? And the children? I will. It means nothing to me, really.*

She wasn't my daughter.

She was the *Demon*.

Walk towards me, she said. *Walk towards me, and no more have to be harmed. That's what you want, isn't it? I promise you, I will make it painless.*

'Lewis,' I said, louder. 'Lewis, dammit, *look*!'

You'll only make this harder in the end.

She turned and walked back into the trees. Gone, I couldn't even see tracks where she'd been standing.

'What?' Lewis shouted to me, suddenly at

my side and bending his head close to mine to be heard over the noise. The dull blunt-force thud of helicopter blades was very loud now. 'What's wrong?'

Would he believe me if I told him? Or would he think I'd just finally lost my last screw? There was nothing to see there now, and as I extended the senses that Lewis and David had been showing me how to use, I got...nothing. Nothing but whispering trees and a slow, sleeping presence that I assumed was how I now perceived the Earth.

'Nothing,' I said. 'Never mind.'

I watched as the helicopter began its descent. I held my hair back against the harsh, ice-edged wind it kicked up, and backed up with Lewis to give it room to land. The helicopter touched down, and the rotors slowed but didn't stop. The emblem on the side was some kind of seal, and nothing I recognised.

A burly shape, well muffled in winter gear, hopped out of the passenger door, ducked the way people instinctively do when there's sharp metal chopping the air just about head level, and hurried towards me through the snow. He shouted something to me that sounded like, *Need a ride?* which was fine with me.

I helped Lewis load Cherise and Kevin into the helicopter, and belted myself in for the rattling, noisy ride.

You're safe now, I told myself. *It's all OK.*
But I didn't really believe it.

If I'd ever been in a helicopter before, I didn't know it, but one thing was for certain: I sure didn't like it. The dull roar of the rotors never let me forget that those fragile blades were all that stood between this clanking metal insect and a catastrophic crash, and I shuddered to think about all of the things that could happen to all those very breakable parts involved, including my own.

It was also a rough trip, full of bounces, jounces, drops, sideways lurches, and other exciting contraventions of gravity. I kept my eyes squeezed shut, clung to the handhold strap, and pretended not to be scared out of my mind.

Lewis, next to me, was so relaxed I thought he might actually drop off into a nap. He held my hand – not a romantic gesture, and he must have regretted it when I periodically dug my nails into his skin in sheer terror. A gentleman born, he didn't pull away. On his other side perched Kevin, hunched in on himself like someone nursing a gut wound. His face was tight and looked years older than it had just minutes ago, even though Cherise was pressed against him like a winter coat. I felt inarticulately guilty, as if there were something I might have done.

The Demon looks like me.

Yeah, that made me feel guilty as hell, and there was nothing to be done about it. I had no idea what I'd say to any of them, when the decibel levels dropped enough to allow me to say anything at all.

A paramedic wrapped each of us in warm blankets, but since none of us had obvious bleeding wounds, that was the extent of our medical treatment. They gave us coffee, though, hot and strong out of a steel thermos. I was right. I did like coffee. Even black.

The helicopter, for pretty much the entire journey, was enveloped by low, dingy clouds, and updrafts and downdrafts battered us from side to side, up and down, until I felt as though the damn metal monster were a toy on a stretchy string. I don't know how long we were in the air; constant heart-crushing panic made it seem like forever, but it couldn't have been too long. When we dropped down below the clouds, right on top of a cleared landing area, I was weak-kneed with gratitude.

There were people waiting at the edge of the rotor backwash, holding their hats on if they had them. I didn't recognise anyone. I was getting used to that, but it didn't make me feel any more secure. My eyes skipped over them, looking for David, but he wasn't there.

And then my eyes moved back, because while I didn't recognise the tall black woman standing with her arms folded, staring at me, there was something familiar about her. She was striking. Her features were sharply patrician, her hair worn in a multitude of small braids, each one fastened by colourful beads. She wasn't trying to hide; that was obvious. She was wearing neon yellow, even down to the long, polished fingernails.

She disdained coats.

And her eyes, even at the distance of fifteen feet, flashed with a colour that didn't look real, or human.

So, she was like David. A Djinn.

As we disembarked I poked Lewis in the side, avoiding his sore ribs, and nodded towards her. He looked a little less angry. 'Rahel,' he said. 'She's—'

'Djinn,' I said. 'Yeah, I figured that. Friend or foe?'

'Depends on her mood.'

'Wonderful.'

Lewis turned to face me, blocking my path. 'Jo... be careful,' he said. 'I wanted to keep you safe and out of the way until we were sure we understood what was going on. I can't do that now.' He nodded towards the assembled people. 'Most of them are Wardens. That doesn't necessarily make them on your side,' he said. 'That's Paul; he's a friend. When we get to the group, stick with him if I have to take off for any reason. Paul will look after you.'

I nodded. 'Anyone else I can trust?'

'That's Marion.' He nodded towards a woman

in a wheelchair with long, grey-streaked blue-black hair worn in a thick braid. 'I'd trust her with my life. In fact, I have. I'm going to hand Kevin off to her for—'

'No,' Kevin said flatly. His face was chalk-pale, but his eyes were angry. 'No way. I'm not going anywhere.'

Lewis sighed. 'You're not in any shape to—'

'I'm not some baby,' Kevin said. 'I'm not gonna drop dead because I find out it's a cold, hard world out here. Fuck off, man. Nobody messes with my head. Especially not *her*.'

'Sure, big guy. Only if you can stand on your own,' Lewis said, and stepped away from him.

Kevin wavered, stumbled a little, glared, and stood on his own two feet.

Barely. But he managed.

'Well, guess you're stuck with him now,' I murmured. Lewis snorted, with a sharp edge of annoyance. 'Couple of things before this gets crazy. First: Have you ever seen a Demon?'

'Yes,' Lewis said. His eyes went distant and dark. 'Why?'

'What should I be looking for?' *And does it just automatically look like the person who's seen it? Please tell me that's the case.*

'Usually they look like smears, dark shadows, but they can appear to be anything.'

'Human?' I hazarded.

He frowned. 'Doubt it,' he said. 'They can inhabit a human, but if they can assume a semblance, I've never heard of it. Why?'

I shrugged. Shrugs were fine things for avoiding issues. 'Second thing: Do you think I can do what I did with Cherise – that memory thing – with other people?'

Lewis looked towards me sharply. 'From them to you? I wouldn't try it. What you did was... wrong, Jo. You shouldn't have been able to, in the first place, and I've got no idea how it happened. Earth Warden skills take years of training, even for the basics. What you're trying to do...no. I wouldn't.'

We didn't have time for anything else. The Wardens, tired of waiting for us to come to them, were heading our way.

I was about to meet the family, and I was pretty sure I wasn't ready.

'Joanne's OK,' Lewis said loudly. A pre-emptive strike that halted at least four of them who had opened their mouths to comment or ask questions. 'She's been through some trauma, and her memory's a little shaky right now, but she's going to be fine. So give her some room, guys.'

At least half of them looked irritated, and I wondered why. Maybe they hadn't wanted me to be found at all, or if so, maybe they'd expected me to be up to full strength and ready to dive right in to pull my share of the load. Hard to tell.

The Djinn, Rahel, had moved closer, too, and now those eyes were just plain eerie. A hot, metallic gold, with flecks of brass. Predatory eyes. She slowly drummed her neon-coloured talons along her folded arms, and I couldn't tell what she was thinking.

Marion, in the wheelchair, was easier to read. She looked worried. And contemplative. And from the unfocused way she was examining me, she was doing that aetheric vision thing.

'Joanne,' she said. She was the first to smile at me. 'It's so good to see you safe.' She held out her hand, and I shot Lewis a nervous glance. He nodded, so I took it and shook. Her skin felt warm, her grip firm. Her dark eyes held mine steadily. 'I see you've had some hard times, but so have we all. It's good you're back with us again. We can use your strength.'

It was, at the very least, a public endorsement. Probably more than I could reasonably ask for. 'Thanks,' I said. I had the feeling that I might not have been a friend, but at least there was respect between us. Respect, I could return. The others standing around were regarding me with varying expressions of wariness or hope, neither of which made me feel any too secure.

Marion's attention slid past me to focus on Kevin, and her expression changed to concern. 'My

God, Lewis, what happened to the boy? No, never mind. Not here. Let's get him to the clinic.' Her eyes passed over Cherise, then came back, and she frowned, puzzled. She looked sharply at Lewis, an open question on her face, and he shook his head.

'Later,' he said.

She pressed controls and wheeled the chair in a tight circle, leading the way to a small parked caravan of plain black sedans and vans. I started to follow.

The guy Lewis had pointed out as Paul caught my arm in a big, square hand and dragged me to a stop. 'Not so fast, babe,' he rumbled. He had an East Coast accent, maybe Jersey, if I had to guess. Olive-toned skin, dark hair with flecks of grey, dark stubble showing even though I was sure he'd freshly shaved. 'No welcome for me?'

'Paul,' I said, and he hugged me. Full-body. 'Um, hi.' I resisted an urge to struggle, because he seemed to want to hold on a little too long for comfort.

'Kid, I thought you were gone,' he murmured, lips close to my ear. 'Don't do that again, all right? You've given me plenty enough heart attacks already.' And then he pecked me on the cheek and backed away. The way he looked at me, I wondered... No, surely not. Surely I hadn't slept with *every* guy I knew.

'I-I'll try to be more careful,' I said. Awkward. I didn't know where I stood with this guy – kissing-close, obviously, but not much else. He was a little intimidating up close, which was funny, since I'd been spending time with Lewis and David, guys who defined intimidating. I swallowed and forced a smile. 'I need to go with...' I mimed following Lewis. Paul studied me for a second, brows pulling together in a frown, and let go.

'Yeah,' he said quietly. 'I was hoping... Yeah. You probably should get yourself looked at, too. Call when you're done, OK? We got to talk. Things to work out.'

I nodded, kept the smile going, and walked quickly after Lewis, who was helping Kevin and Cherise into the black cargo van, the one with the Handi-Lift on the back that was already lowering for Marion's wheelchair.

I didn't make it to join them. Another person stepped into my way, and I felt whatever nerves hadn't already been alarmed wake up and start screaming.

'A moment,' Rahel said softly, holding up one graceful, long-taloned hand between us. She looked at me, close range, and yes, Djinn eyes were frightening. Her expression stayed blank and still, and I hesitated, wondering whether or not to yell for help. Her eyes flicked past me, focusing on the Wardens behind me, and she reached out and took hold of my shoulder. 'A moment of your time, my friend. I have been so concerned for you.' She didn't wait for agreement. She steered me sideways, away from the Wardens but also away from any potential rescue from Lewis. When I tried to pull back, her fingers dug deeper, and I hissed in pain. 'Sistah, you come whether you like it or not,' she warned in a very low tone. 'I have news for you, from David.'

The use of his name got me at least willing to listen. She kept hold of my shoulder, but loosened her grip so I wasn't in danger of deep-tissue bruising.

'I don't remember you,' I said. Seemed best to get it out of the way. 'I'm sorry. It's...this problem I have.'

'I'm well aware,' she said. No smile at all, and her tone was dry and cool. 'You shouldn't be here, Snow White. Not as you are, neither here nor there, living nor dead, human nor Warden. They think to bring you back. I think it is a foolish concept. It opens doors that are dangerous for us all.'

'Gee, thanks,' I said with no sincerity. 'That's the news?'

She snorted. 'Opinion. At least you haven't lost your sense of the absurd. David wishes me to tell you that he is on Ashan's trail, and for you to stay with Lewis.' Rahel smiled. She had pointed teeth. I mean, seriously. *Pointed.* 'You know what happens to little lambs who wander from their herd.'

I yanked myself free this time. 'Hey, Creep Show, save it for the cheap seats. Aren't you supposed to be on my side or something?'

She blinked, and I had the satisfaction of seeing a Djinn thrown just a half step off balance. It didn't last. 'I am,' she said. 'As your kind is measured, you're not insufferable, only infuriating. And...you loved the child. I count that in your favour.'

'Imara,' I said. 'You're talking about Imara, right?'

Her expression composed itself to instant formality, and she tilted her head. Beads clicked as the braids slithered over her shoulders with a sound like dry paper shifting. 'Ashan was fortunate the Oracle took him before we could reach him. Had he been in my hands, he'd still be screaming.'

Which was supposed to be comforting or something.

'Great,' I said faintly.

That made Rahel look up again, sharply. 'You don't remember the child, either,' she said. 'Do you?'

I started to lie about it, then shook my head. To my surprise, Rahel put her hand to my cheek in a gesture that was almost human. Almost affectionate.

'I can pity you for that. You will remember, though,' she said. 'Such emptiness must be filled.'

And in a weird sort of way I suppose she *did* comfort me. A little. 'Thanks,' I said. 'I... Will you tell David I'll be with Lewis?'

'I will.' She stepped back. 'Ashan is lucky once again. David would have hunted him and ripped him into nothing by now, had he not been distracted by concern for you. It appears he needs Ashan alive and functioning to try to fix what was done to you.' A slow, cool smile revealed even, white teeth. Non-pointed. 'After his usefulness comes to an end, well, maybe David will organise an entertainment. We haven't had one of those for ages.' I was sure she meant it literally. The ages part, anyway. I shuddered to think what *entertainment* might mean.

'So David's OK, then,' I said.

She shrugged. 'David's obsession with you puts his leadership of us in some doubt. But he remains the conduit to the Mother, and so may not be easily challenged. Still, he is not secure. His insistence on repairing what was done to you has been taken badly in some quarters.'

'Including your quarter?' I asked her, looking her right in the eerie eyes.

It was very quiet. I could hear the whine of the rotors powering down on the helicopter, the hiss of blowing snow, the engines starting in various SUVs around the landing area. I could hear my own heartbeat pounding fast.

'For my part,' Rahel finally said, 'I should think the world less interesting without you, sistah. Take that as you wish.'

And she turned and walked away, misted into nothing, and was gone.

Wow. Not sure how I felt about her, but I couldn't dislike her. Fear her, sure. Dislike her...no.

I hurried over to the black van, which was starting its engine, and piled into the back with Lewis, Kevin, Cherise, and Marion. Lewis slid the door shut with a solid thump, and whoever was driving – just a black silhouette against the dim grey sky – turned the van in a tight circle and headed out, bumping over uneven ground.

Marion let out a slow sigh. 'That was about as civil as we might have expected,' she said. 'Lewis, be careful. They're going to pull you aside and talk politics.'

'Politics? We've got time for politics?'

'There's always time for politics,' she said. 'Something you never could grasp, I'm afraid.'

'What a load of bullshit. How's the rehab?' He gestured at the wheelchair.

'You know that Earth Wardens are always slower to heal themselves, and besides, there haven't been any shortage of victims to tend.' She shrugged. 'I'll be all right. Another month, maybe two. I'd have been walking already if I'd had the time to devote to it, but we've been a little busy. As you've probably heard.'

'Guessed,' Lewis said. 'Between the remnants of the California fire, the earthquake in Kansas City, and the hurricane in North Carolina—'

'We've been stretched thin,' Marion agreed.

'Not just here in the US, of course. Latin America's having a hell of a time. Even Canada's being pummelled. Europe's an icebox, Africa's an out-of-season swamp, Asia's got all of the above, and Australia and New Zealand keep flipping from summer to winter from one day to the next.'

'Great. Anybody *not* having a climate shift?'

'Middle East,' she said. 'But they have other problems. So. You going to explain to me what I'm looking at here?'

'What do you think you're looking at?' Lewis asked.

Marion gave him a hard look. 'Save the rhetorical method; I'm not in the mood. Him – that's Demon damage, obviously. Fixable, but we need to get him to a clinic for treatment.'

'No such things as Demons,' Lewis said. Which confused me, until she smiled.

'Indeed not. And so we're still telling people. So, you believe this one has hatched out? Is an adult?'

'Yes.'

'Any idea where it could be?'

'Back where we came from, most likely, but specifically? No.'

Marion shook her head and frowned absently at the rolling forest scenery beyond the van's windows. 'Not good. We don't have a way to detect or track it.'

'What about Garson?' Lewis asked. 'He's the best at—'

'Garson's dead,' she interrupted. 'Killed by his own Djinn during the initial attack. Every adept we had who was capable of tracking or identifying Demons, or Demon Marks, is dead or incapacitated, except me. And believe me, I'm being damn careful.'

'Specifically targeted?'

'Well, it's worse than our usual rotten luck,' Marion said. 'You can't detect them, can you?'

Lewis shook his head. 'If I'd been able to, maybe we wouldn't be in this mess in the first place,' he said. 'I'd have smelt it on Star when she first came after me two years ago.'

Marion's dark almond-shaped eyes narrowed, 'Estrella? I never got the full story from you about that.'

'And you won't now,' he said easily. 'Old news. Let's talk about what we're going to do about this.'

'Well, the Djinn aren't of any practical use anymore. A few might help us out, if they're feeling generous and we're feeling lucky. But I wouldn't count on them.' She looked deeply troubled about that. 'I never liked the servile system they operated under, but it's going to take some time to get used to their freedom. Time for us, as well as them.'

'The Ma'at can help out with that,' Lewis said. 'Their system is based on cooperation, not the coercion the Wardens used in dealing with the Djinn. I'll get them in touch with you.' To me, he said, 'Separate organisation, the Ma'at. They've been working to create balance between Wardens, humans, and the world around us.'

'Trust me, it sounds more high-minded than it is in practice,' Marion said. She seemed annoyed. 'I always meant to ask, are the Ma'at your creation? Because their manifesto has that just-out-of-school, disillusioned, fight-the-power feel to it, and only someone young could come up with something so idealistic. And base it in *Las Vegas*.'

Lewis shrugged. 'Doesn't matter who formed it, or how. What matters is that it works.'

'Sometimes,' she shot back. 'Guess what? The Wardens work sometimes, too.'

'Less and less often. You have to admit that.'

The van reached a freeway, and the ride turned smooth as glass. The van rocked slightly in wind gusts, but for the most part we sped along so easily we might have been flying. I began to feel just a little safer. *Safer?* some part of me mocked. *You think a little thing like distance is going to matter? When are you going to mention that the Demon looks like you?*

Later, apparently.

'I'll talk to them,' Marion was reluctantly saying. 'It's possible the Ma'at have Demon trackers. I'll see what we can horse-trade for the privilege.'

'One other thing,' Lewis said. 'I want you to

check Joanne over thoroughly when we get to the clinic.'

Marion raised an eyebrow and glanced at me, as if she'd forgotten I was there, clinging to a handhold and swaying to the hiss of the van's tyres. 'For?'

'Anything. Everything.' His face was closed and suddenly unreadable. 'I found her in the forest, half-dead from the cold. Naked.'

'Naked,' Marion repeated. 'Any injuries?'

'Nothing frostbite couldn't explain.'

'You checked—'

'Of course I checked. But you're better at that kind of thing.' He shrugged slightly, shoulders hunched. 'Maybe I don't know what to look for. Or I didn't want to find it. I was under a little bit of pressure. And she's displayed some...unusual effects.'

His voice was as dry as sand on that one, and I remembered David bouncing him like a basketball. Yeah, a little bit of pressure. And unusual effects didn't much cover what I'd been able to do to bring Cherise back from the nearly dead.

'I'll do a thorough scan,' Marion said. 'Anything else?'

Lewis raised his head to lock eyes with me for a second, then said, 'Yeah, actually. I'd like you to test her for the emergence of Earth abilities.'

'Thought you might,' Marion said, and leant

back in her wheelchair. Her smile was full and yet not very comforting. 'I can feel some change in her latent abilities. One of you was bad enough. I have no idea what we'll do with two of you.'

The clinic was a modest-sized place up a winding road in the hills, and I'd have frankly mistaken it for anything but a medical facility. It looked rustic, but industrial in its square shape. Couldn't have been intended for long-term care, at least, not for many patients.

The faded, paint-chipped sign on the building said, WARDEN HEALTH INSTITUTE, EXTENSION 12. There were four cars in the small parking lot, and the van made it five as the still-unseen driver pulled in and parked under the whispering shade of a large pine. It was cold outside – my breath fogged on the window – but the overcast sky was breaking up, and the snow had stopped. I saw wisps of blue through the clouds.

'Need help?' Lewis asked Marion. She shook her head as the rear doors popped open, and the Handi-Lift's operation was engaged to move her and the wheelchair safely out and down. The rest of us disembarked the old-fashioned way. The snow here was only a couple of inches deep, and melting fast on the parking lot's warmth-hoarding surface. My face stung from the icy wind, and I thought wistfully about being warm again, really warm, but somehow the building that was ahead of us didn't seem that inviting, centrally heated or not.

I glanced over at Kevin. He looked sullen and shaky. 'It'll be OK,' I said. He shot me a filthy look.

'Shut up, Pollyanna,' he said. 'In my world, every time I let anybody else get me under lock and key, I get fucked.'

I shut up. Clearly, comforting people wasn't my calling.

Once Marion's chair was down and moving, Lewis was the one who made sure the path was clear and ice-free on the ramp. I didn't even think about it, and Kevin obviously couldn't have cared less about doing public service. Lewis held the door, too, as Marion's chair powered inside, and kept holding it for me and Cherise, then Kevin.

So Lewis was the last one inside before the lock engaged behind us. I heard the metallic clank and turned, startled; so did Kevin, white-faced with fury. Lewis held up a calming hand. 'Secured facility,' he said, and rapped the glass with his knuckles. 'Bullet-resistant glass, too. Come on, Kevin, it's not meant to keep you in; it's meant to keep things out. Security's still high in Warden facilities worldwide.'

Evidently, because there were two armed guards standing in the lobby, wearing cheap polyester blazers and expensive shoulder holsters. They didn't look like they were in the mood to take crap from anyone, either, and all four of us got the instant laser stare. I expected Marion and Lewis to dig for credentials, but instead they held up their right hands, palm out. I blinked, then hesitantly did the same when even Kevin followed suit. I expected... Hell, I don't know what I expected. Some kind of scanner ray? But I didn't see anything, and nothing happened, and after the security guys' gazes moved from one hand to the next, each in turn, they both nodded and stepped back, letting us have access to another closed door beyond.

They blocked Cherise. 'Hey!' she protested, and looked beseechingly at Lewis. 'I'm with them! Just ask!'

'Nobody but Wardens in the secured area,' one of the guards said.

Kevin was looking dangerously angry, but Lewis solved the whole thing by moving the guard back, taking Cherise's hand, and saying, 'She comes with us. No arguments.'

The guard looked at Marion, who shrugged. 'Technically, he's still the boss,' she said. 'I'd make an exception.'

I blinked at Lewis. 'You're the boss?'

'Pretty much,' he said. 'Long story. Believe me, I hate the job as much as they hate me having it. We're working through succession planning.'

Lewis held the door open for me. Kevin had already stalked through it, following the low whine of Marion's power chair. Cherise followed, glancing back at me with mute appeals to stay close. This door shut behind us, too. This time it was positively disquieting. I hung back, let Lewis go ahead of me, and pretended to need to adjust my shoe. While I was doing that, I leant back and tried the doorknob.

It didn't open.

Who's being protected here? I wondered. *And from what, exactly?*

Lewis glanced back. I gave my sock another token pull and hurried to catch up.

It was a short, narrow hallway, and it had an antiseptic smell. Even if you have your past and memory damaged, you don't forget that smell, and you can't avoid its giving you a little unpleasant tingle somewhere in the back of your brain. Something was telling me to get the hell out, but I didn't know if that was good instinct or bad. We passed three closed doors with plastic folder bins on the outside – none of them occupied, apparently, as there were no charts in the bins – and the hallway opened into a large, warm sitting area. The furniture looked industrial, but comfortable, and I sank gratefully down in a chair when Marion nodded at me. Someone in a lab coat came in from another entrance, head down, checking over something on a clipboard, and looked up to smile at Marion with an impartial welcome. 'Ma'am,' he said, and extended his hand. He was a small man, neatly groomed, with ebony hair and eyes and a golden tint to his skin. 'Dr Lee. I wasn't informed you were dropping in today.'

'Unscheduled visit,' she said. 'Hope that isn't a problem, Doctor. We have some urgent needs.'

'Not at all. We have a light caseload today – most of those who were injured during the fires have been rotated out to other facilities. We were strictly serving as triage here. I have two Wardens in critical condition who haven't been moved, back in ICU – Leclerq and Minetti. You here to visit?'

'I'll be happy to drop in,' she said. 'Meanwhile, if you could have a look at the boy, I'd really appreciate your help.'

Dr Lee turned his attention to Kevin, and those large, dark eyes widened. 'I see,' he said in a much quieter voice. 'Your name?'

'Kevin,' he snapped, but he directed it towards the carpet.

'Would you mind coming with me, Kevin?'

'Yes. I'm not going anywhere with you.'

Marion sighed. 'I see the boy hasn't changed. Kevin, no one is going to harm you. I swear it.'

He glared at her. 'No drugs.'

'Don't worry. We wouldn't waste them on you.'

Kevin shot Lewis an utterly mistrustful look, then made it a group thing, because it was the same look he gave Marion, then me. Me, he seemed to trust least of all.

'Can I go with him?' Cherise asked in a small voice. She'd slipped her hand in his. 'Please?'

'I don't see why not,' Dr Lee said. 'We'll see about getting you food as well. And some fresh clothing.'

I don't know if Kevin would have gone on his own, but Cherise's presence gave him an excuse to conform. He took her hand and followed Dr Lee through the door and into what I presumed was a treatment area.

Leaving me with Lewis and Marion, who weren't saying much.

'Well?' I asked. 'What now?'

'Now,' Marion said, 'we see if we can determine the extent of your damage.'

'Here?'

'Here's fine. I don't need you to wear a funny open-back dress for this.'

Lewis walked away. I stared at Marion for a few seconds, frowning, and then nodded. 'All right. What do you need me to do?'

'Relax and let me drive,' she said. 'Eyes closed. I want you to focus on a sound.'

'What sound?' I closed my eyes and immediately felt drowned by darkness. I fought the urge to open them again.

'This one.'

For a brief second I didn't hear anything, but then I did, a low musical tone, steady and unchanging. Like the sound a deep-note chime makes. A sustained ringing.

'Do you hear it?' Marion asked. Her voice was soft and slow, blending with the sound of the chime. I nodded. 'Concentrate on the sound. Only on the sound.'

It got louder, and the more I focused, the purer it seemed. It made me imagine things...a bright crystal, turning and reflecting rainbows. A flower slowly unfurling its petals. A chair rocking on a porch on a fresh, cool morning.

I could feel something moving through my body like a warm wave, but it wasn't alarming, and somehow I wasn't afraid of it. The sound compelled me to stay quiet, stay still, suspended in time...

'Hey,' said a new voice. I opened my eyes, or some part of me did; I could tell that my actual, physical eyes were still closed tight.

But part of me was somewhere else entirely. In another reality.

'Hey,' I replied blankly. I felt like I should know the man who was sitting across from me – there was definitely something familiar about him. Tall, lean, athletic; a little bit like Lewis, but more compact and certainly just as dangerous, if not more so. A greying brush of light brown hair cut aggressively short. A face that seemed harsh one moment, and amused the next. When he smiled, it seemed kind, but also mocking.

'You don't know me,' he said. 'My name's Jonathan.'

'Um…hi?' It felt like the real world, but somehow, I knew it wasn't. Illusion, most definitely. So what was this guy? He smiled even wider, not giving me a clue.

'We don't have a lot of time for this little drop-in, so I'm going to be brief. You just acquired some skills that you're not ready for. Wasn't my choice, but hey, done is done.' He shrugged. 'You're going to need them, no doubt about that, but your adjustment's going to be a little rocky. Just thought somebody should warn you.'

'Who *are* you?'

He laughed. Chuckled, really. 'Used to be a lot of things. Human, then Djinn. Now – well, there's not really a word for what I am. But there's a word for what you are, kid. Trouble.'

This made no sense. It had to be a dream. I was sitting on a couch in a living room – stone fireplace, clean lines, masculine furniture. Warm throw rugs on the wood floor. A big picture window overlooking a field of nodding yellow sunflowers in full bloom, which was wrong, wasn't it? It should have been fall at least, or full winter. But here… here, it was summer. Bright, cloudless summer.

'Stay with me, Joanne. I'm going to bounce you back in a second, but first I have to tell you something.'

'What?' I asked.

'What's happening to you has never happened before. Never. That's a big word, in my world – it was big enough to make a whole lot of forces pay attention. David's right to look for Ashan, but you're going to have to do your part, too. If you screw this thing up, I can't help you. Nobody can.'

'Could you be a little less vague?'

'Yeah,' he said. He leant back on the leather sofa to take a pull on the beer in his hand. Cold, frosty beer. It made me thirsty, and I didn't even know if I liked beer. 'Do not, under any circumstances, think about throwing your life away. If you die – if you let her kill you – you have no idea what kind of hell will come calling.'

'So that's your big message? Stay alive?' I felt like pounding my head against the wall, only I wasn't sure the wall was real enough. 'Great. Great advice.'

'Hey, don't blame me. Most people wouldn't have to be told, but you? You seem to want to martyr up when you lose a quarter in the soda machine.'

I didn't know Jonathan, but I wasn't liking him much. 'Funny.'

'Not really, because it's true. My job is to take the long view, kid. And right now, the long view is that you need to be selfish and stay alive. Got it?'

I didn't, and he could see it. He shook his head,

tipped the bottle up and drained it dry.

'Crap, you really are always a pain in my ass, Joanne. Not to mention the fact that if you keep on dragging David down, he's going to lose everything, up to and including his life,' he said. 'You see that, right?'

'I – what? No! I'm not—' But I was. Lewis had said as much. Even David had hinted around at it. Which of course made me defensive. 'David's free to do whatever he needs to do. I'm not stopping him. I never asked for any of this!'

Jonathan looked amused. Impatient, but amused. 'Don't whine to me about it. I have nothing to do with it, not anymore. I'm just here to tell you to use your head for once.'

Which had the effect of completely pissing me off, even though I was pretty sure he was supernatural, powerful, and could crush me like a bug if he wanted. And besides, hadn't David said he was dead? I was pretty sure.

So of course I blurted out, 'Great. You told me. If you don't have anything better than that to offer, butt the hell out!'

Jonathan's dark eyes met mine, and they weren't human eyes. Not at all. Not even *close*. I was pretty sure that even the Djinn would flinch from that stare; it froze me like liquid nitrogen, held me utterly still. There was something vast and chilly behind it, only remotely concerned with me and my problems.

'I will,' he said. 'Too bad. If you'd been a little bit more on the ball, you could have avoided all the heartbreak that's coming.'

And then he opened his hand, dropped his bottle to the floor, and it shattered. The noise became a tone, a steady, ringing tone that grew in my ears until it was a shriek, and I jack-knifed forward in my chair, hands pressed to my ears...

And then I was in the waiting room of the Wardens Health Institute Extension 12, gasping for breath, and there was no sound at all.

Until Marion put her wheelchair in gear and backed up a couple of feet. Fast. I looked up. She was staring at me, and her expression was distraught. 'Oh,' she said faintly. 'I see. I think I understand.'

'Understand what?' Something inside my head hurt, badly. I clenched my teeth against the pain and pressed my fingers to my temples, trying to massage it out. 'What did you do to me? Who was that?'

She avoided that by simply wheeling the chair around and leaving me. I tried to get up, but I felt unexpectedly weak and strange.

A blanket settled warm over me. Lewis, my hero. 'Stay there,' he said, and pressed a hand on my shoulder for a second before going after Marion. They talked in low tones on the far side of the room, careful to keep it under my radar. I didn't really care at the moment. Pain has a way of making you selfish that way, and this headache was a killer.

When they came back, Lewis looked as grim and strained as Marion. Which surely couldn't be a good thing. He stopped, but Marion continued forward, almost within touching range, and her dark almond-shaped eyes assessed me with ruthless purpose.

'How long have you had Earth powers?' she asked. I blinked.

'I don't know what you—'

'Don't,' she interrupted. 'When did you first feel them emerge? Be specific.'

'I can't! I don't know! Look, I barely understand any of this, and—'

She reached out and put her hand on my head, and this time it wasn't a gentle, healing touch. It was a fast, brutal search, like someone rifling through my head, and I automatically slammed the door on it.

Whatever I did, it knocked her back in her chair, gasping.

'She's strong,' Marion said to Lewis. 'But this didn't come naturally. Somebody put it in her.'

'I figured that. Who? How?'

'I don't know.' Marion visibly steeled herself. 'I'll try to find out.' They were both acting like I wasn't even there. Like I didn't have any choice in the matter.

This time, when she reached out for me, I caught her wrist. 'Hey,' I said. 'At least buy me dinner first. I don't even know you.'

'Lewis, hold her.'

'No!' I shot to my feet, but Lewis was moving to block me, and he was bigger than I was, and stronger in a whole lot of ways. His hands closed over my shoulders and forced me back into the chair, and then touched my forehead. I felt an irresistible drag of sleep. 'No, I'm not... You can't do this... I... Lewis, *stop*!'

But he didn't, and Marion didn't, either.

And out of sheer desperation, something came alive inside of me and struck, sinking deep inside Marion's mind, and then I couldn't control it as the world exploded into the map of points of light, beauty, order.

I couldn't help it at all. It was sheer, bloody instinct.

I began to greedily grab for memories.

Chapter Six

I'm going to have to kill her, Marion was thinking as she watched a much younger version of me walk out of a conference room. I was defiant, I was gawky, I was just out of adolescence, and she thought I was the most dangerous thing she'd ever seen.

'This is a mistake,' said the old man sitting next to her. He had fine white hair, a barrel chest, fair skin with red blotches that spoke of a fondness for the whiskey barrel. 'That bitch is trouble.'

'Bob,' Marion said, 'give it a rest. The voting's over. You lost.' She said that not because she disagreed with him, but because she simply disliked the man. *Bad Bob*, her memories named him. There was something about him that set her teeth on edge, always had. He was, without a doubt, one of the best of the Weather Wardens in terms of skill, but in terms of personality...

He was staring at the door through which the earlier version of me had exited. He and

Marion weren't the only ones in the room; there were three others involved in a separate side conversation, muttering to one another and casting glances towards Bad Bob that made me think he wasn't exactly well loved, though obviously he commanded respect. Or fear. 'I'm telling you, she's trouble,' he said. 'We haven't heard the last of her. One of these days you'll be hunting her down.'

It was eerily like what Marion herself had just thought, and not for the first time she found herself wondering if Bad Bob had some latent Earth powers. But she'd never seen any trace of it, and she'd looked.

It was her job, looking. And it was a job she hated, and loved, and realised was perhaps the most important job of all.

'Maybe,' she said quietly, 'someday I'll be hunting you, Bob. It could happen.'

He turned towards her and met her eyes, and she couldn't suppress a shiver. There was something about his eyes, she decided. Cold, arctic blue, soulless eyes. He had charm, she supposed, but she'd never felt it herself. She'd seen its effect on others. She knew how much loyalty he inspired in those he commanded, and so she was cautious, very cautious indeed.

She'd gone against him on this vote, to save Joanne Baldwin's young life, and she knew he wouldn't forget.

He smiled. 'That'll be a treat, won't it? You and me?'

She said nothing, and she didn't break the stare. It was a gift of her genetic heritage that she could look so utterly impassive when her emotions inside were roiling. She knew he saw nothing in her dark brown eyes or in her face. No fear. No anticipation. Nothing to feed from.

Bad Bob Biringanine shook his head, smiled, and walked away, and Marion took in a slow, steadying breath. She was aware, on some level, that she had just passed a test nearly as dangerous as the one the young girl had almost failed. Would have failed, had it not been for the strong support of one or two others on the intake committee.

Marion gathered her paperwork and walked out to her car, in the parking lot of the hotel. It was another oppressively warm day in Florida, one she had not dressed for, as she'd flown in from the cooler Northwest; she was wearing a black silk shirt under a leather jacket stitched with Lakota beadwork. A gift from a friend who produced materials for the tourist trade, but saved the best for her fellow tribal leaders. Marion had recently been in the mood to emphasise her heritage.

She started her rental car and did not bother with the air-conditioning; it was a simple matter to adjust her own internal body temperature down to make herself comfortable. She waved to Paul and two of the other Wardens, who stood locked in conversation near Paul's sporty gold convertible. No sign of the girl in the parking lot; maybe she'd already left.

'So,' Marion's Djinn said, misting into reality in the passenger seat next to her. 'Are you on vacation now?'

'Do I ever get vacation?' she asked, and smiled slightly. 'I assume you're here for a reason.' Her Djinn's name was Cetan Nagin, or Shadow Hawk in English. She'd given him the Lakota name, since he'd refused to admit to one of his own. Proud, this one, and not above trickery. Djinn appeared as the subconscious of their owners dictated, and it had disturbed her a great deal that Cetan Nagin had taken the form of a Native American man, with long braided hair and secretive black eyes. His skin was darker than her own, and it shimmered with a phantom copper tint that did not seem quite... human.

And she had realised for quite some time that she was falling in love with him. No doubt he realised it as well. They did not speak of it.

'A reason,' he repeated, and looked at her directly. 'You asked to be informed if any of the Wardens violated protocol.'

'Substantial violations, yes.'

'Define substantial.'

Ah, the Djinn. They did love specificity. 'Use of

powers for personal gratification or gain. Use of powers without adequate provision for balancing of the reactive effects.'

'How very scientific,' Cetan Nagin said, and slouched against the seat at an angle. He was wearing blue jeans and a long black leather coat, and he must have known how good he looked to her. His eyes were half-closed, and she knew he could feel the sparks burning inside her. It was as if he fed on it at times. 'Thank you.'

'Did you have something to report?' she asked. Her heart was hammering, and she concentrated on driving, on the feel of the steering wheel beneath her palms, the vibration of the road. The cars around her on the busy street. *Real world.* Sometimes she felt only half in it.

'The Warden you dislike,' Cetan Nagin said. 'He crosses those lines regularly. Did you know?'

Bad Bob. Of course he did. She had no proof, but Cetan Nagin could provide it, of course. He could provide whatever she required, but then it would be her own responsibility to bring the case before the senior leadership of the Wardens, and Bad Bob had many friends and allies there.

'I know,' she said quietly. 'I choose battles I can win.'

Cetan Nagin shrugged and looked away. 'The girl you were testing today.'

'What about her?' Surely she was too young to be corrupted already.

'He hates her,' the Djinn said. 'Perhaps she's a way to entrap him. If he kills her, you will have a case to bring forth, won't you?'

As much as she felt heat for Cetan Nagin, as much as she wanted him, she feared him at moments like this. The Djinn were game players, politicians, and even at the best of times it was never clear whose side they were on. *If they ever get free...* It was a thought she didn't want to linger over.

'If that happened, I would have a case,' she agreed.

'Then all you have to do is wait,' he said, and smiled. 'Now. As to that vacation...'

She glanced at him, and his smile grew warmer.

And so, reluctantly, did hers.

'I was thinking I might go with you,' Cetan Nagin said. 'If you're willing.'

She tried not to be, but there were some things that were simply meant to happen.

Blur.

I lost my hold on the memory; Marion was fighting me, trying to keep her private life private. I released and sped past other memories. It wasn't just the cold calculation of her leaving me as a stalking horse for Bad Bob that chilled me; it was more than that. Marion had hunted me at the behest of the Wardens. She'd trapped me and tried to kill me more than once.

Lewis had let me believe she could be trusted, but she couldn't. Marion was a zealot. She would follow her ethics past any personal considerations, past likes or dislikes.

Still, there was something more. *Cetan Nagin.* Her Djinn had been taken from her, and I'd got him back. And she hadn't forgotten that I'd saved his life.

The richness of Marion's inner self was mesmerising, and I wanted to experience it, know more, know *everything.* The soft touch of her Djinn's hand down her back. The white-hot presence of the Earth filling her like liquid light. The cold fear that drove her when she was forced to destroy other Wardens who'd misused their powers, or couldn't be trusted...

I wanted it all. I wanted a *life.* Even someone else's.

Something knocked me out of Marion's head with the force of a car crash, and I slammed back into my own body. I jack-knifed forward in the chair, cradling my throbbing head. The pain was crushing. Every sensation felt more intense; every sound rang louder. I curled up in a ball in the chair, gasping for breath.

'Marion!' Lewis was shouting, his voice as loud as a bell in my head. 'Oh, God. God, no. Lee! Get your ass back here *now*!'

When I tried to run, Lewis grabbed me, slammed me down on the floor, and tried to restrain me. And all of a sudden I felt a surge of utter terror.

I couldn't let this happen to me. Not again.

So I lashed out, the whole world dissolved in chaos, screaming, and pain, and then I was gone.

I woke up alone, in a cell.

Technically, maybe not so much a cell as a hospital room, but it might as well have been a cell. There were bars on the narrow window, plain ugly walls, and I was cuffed with leather restraints to the metal bars on the bed. They'd stripped me and put me into a nasty-coloured hospital gown.

I was all alone.

'Hey!' My voice came out a frightened croak. 'Hey, anybody! Help?'

There was a button next to my hand. I pressed it, and kept frantically pressing it until I heard a buzzing sound, and the cell door clicked open.

It admitted the doctor who'd gone off with Kevin earlier – Dr Lee. He came back up with not one but *two* security guards, along with a small flying wedge of nurses.

No sign of Marion or Lewis.

The crowd stayed well out of reach, even though I was restrained.

'Hello,' Dr Lee said. He sounded like he was

making an effort to be cheerful. 'Feeling better?'

'Peachy,' I said, and swallowed. My mouth felt like it had been upholstered in fur. 'Water?'

A nurse poured me a cup, added a sippy straw, and held it for me. The effort of lifting my head seemed exhausting. I drained the cup and collapsed back to the pillow, gasping for air.

'You're lucky,' Lee said. 'You nearly fried your entire central nervous system. If Lewis hadn't been here, you'd be hooked up to a ventilator right now, and we'd be transferring you to permanent care.'

I let that sink in for a second, then asked, 'Marion?'

Silence. Lee stared at me for a long moment, then checked the monitors. 'She's in a coma,' he said. 'We can't wake her up.'

Oh, crap. *Crap!*

'I didn't mean—'

'It doesn't matter,' he cut me off, but I could hear the anger under his veneer of calm. 'I need you to rest. Your scans are still far from normal. We'll talk about all this later.'

I jerked at the restraints. 'Can you take these off?'

'No,' he said. 'As soon as you're able to be moved, you'll be transferred to a facility where you can be properly examined and controlled.'

Meaning I was under arrest. The security guards, grim and well-armed, more than confirmed that. I didn't like it, but there was really nothing I could do about it.

And really nothing I *should* do about it.

'Can I talk to Lewis?' I asked, very respectfully. Lee shot a glance towards the security people.

'I'll let him know you're asking for him,' Lee said. 'I'm going to give you a sedative now, all right? Just something to help you sleep.'

He used drugs instead of the Earth Warden-patented hand-on-forehead; I wanted to do something to stop him, but I controlled the impulse. Clearly, it wasn't going to be a good idea for me to start fighting, not with the odds as they were.

David, I thought. *David will help me.*

I wondered where the hell he was, but before I could do more than wonder, the fog swept in, rendered my mind cool and blank, and I drifted away.

When I woke up, it was dark, and there was someone sitting in the chair next to me, snoring. I blinked and tried to rub my eyes, and remembered the restraints only when they clicked and rattled the bars.

Which cut off the snoring. A light clicked on, and I saw Lewis's tired but freshly shaved face in the pale glow.

'Hey,' he said, and reached out to wrap his fingers around mine. 'How do you feel?'

'Pissed,' I said. 'I'm tied to a bed, in case you hadn't noticed.'

'I noticed,' he said, and yawned. 'Trust me, the restraints are there for a reason.'

'What reason?'

'Your protection,' he said. 'I know you. If you had half a chance of breaking out, you'd already be blowing the door and running for the exit, and that will get you killed right now. I'm trying to help you, Jo, but you've got to help yourself.'

'Fine,' I said. 'What exactly did I do?'

He blinked a couple of times. 'You don't know?'

'Look, I know that Marion's in a coma, but—'

'You screwed around with things that you weren't ready for, and you put her in that coma. Then you went after me.'

'I – I what?'

Lewis didn't change his expression, not at all. 'You heard me. If I hadn't put you down, hard, you'd have ripped my brain apart like a piñata.'

'But – why would I do that?' I felt bewildered, alien in my own skin.

'Post-traumatic stress, I'm guessing. The point is, you were a danger to everybody around you.'

'But...not now.' I said it like I believed it. Lewis didn't grace me with agreement, but he didn't disagree, either. He just sat, gently providing reassurance through the contact of our hands. 'Lewis, I don't want to hurt anybody. Really. You have to believe that.'

'I do,' he said. 'But the best thing right now is

for you to rest and get your strength back. I had to put you down pretty hard. Harder than I'd have preferred. You need to heal.'

'Lee said I'd be moved somewhere else,' I said. 'It sounded like prison.'

Lewis's thumb stopped stroking my fingers. I wasn't sure I liked that.

'It's not prison,' he said. 'But it's a medical facility, and it's run by people from Marion's division. If they can't find a way to stop you from misusing your Earth powers, they're going to have to block the channels to stop it from happening. I don't want to see that happen, so you need to concentrate on staying calm and steady, OK? No overreactions. No attacking people. And quit trying to eat peoples' brains.'

I laughed, but it was shaky, and so was his smile. 'I swear, I'll try,' I said. 'Has David been here?'

Lewis looked away. 'Not yet,' he said.

'Is it normal, him being gone this long?'

'You know it isn't. But there's no way we can check on him, so we'll just have to wait.'

There was a discreet knock at the door, and it did the buzz thing. Lewis leant back as a security guard leant in. 'You're wanted on the phone, sir,' the guard said. 'Conference call.'

Lewis nodded, then gave me a distracted kind of grin. 'Politics,' he said. 'Marion was right. There's always time for politics. Rest, OK? I'll come back.'

I didn't trust myself to say anything. He left without a backward glance, and I tried to close my eyes and damp down the panic inside.

I'm trapped. They're taking me to prison. No, worse – they were taking me to screw around with my head, to keep me from hurting people.

I was, in Warden terms, mentally ill. Crazy with a capital K. Except somehow, I knew that I wasn't – and that if I let them mess with my head, that would be bad. Very, very bad.

A monitor beeped somewhere near my head. My heart rate was up, and getting faster. Some other electronic alarm joined the chorus – blood pressure? I felt sick all of a sudden, almost dizzy. There was a hissing sound in my head, like interference, and this terrible pressure inside my chest...

In the corner of the room, a shadow stirred. I couldn't see who it was for a second, and then once my bleary eyes focused I felt a jolt of sheer terror driving away what was left of my drugged sleep.

I had a visitor, and the visitor was me.

No...the visitor *looked like me*, right down to the nasty hospital gown and unkempt hair. But there was something cold and inhuman behind her blue eyes, something that wasn't me at all.

It just stood there, looking at me, and I could feel space warping between us, see the air shimmering and turning dark and thick.

We were drawing each other closer, but at the same time, I could feel the sickening drain on my life.

'Help!' I tried to scream it – Lewis hadn't gone far, he couldn't have – but my voice was a weak, choked squeak in my throat. *Oh God*. It took a step towards me, and I felt a corresponding surge of dizzying weakness sweep over me.

'Quiet,' the Demon whispered, and moved even closer. I gasped for breath, but it was like breathing at the bottom of the ocean. I was drowning in the dark. 'We're nearly there. Nearly there. You need to let go, let go and give me what I need.'

I knew in a flash that this was why Jonathan had come to warn me. Right now, the Demon was missing something, something vital. Something I had.

And against all odds, I needed to hang onto it.

I needed to fight for my life, because I was the only one who could.

Of course, I was also drugged and tied to a bed, but nobody promised it was going to be easy.

David. God, David, please.

If he could hear me, he couldn't respond. Maybe he was hurt, or imprisoned, or just cut off and unable to get to me. I could almost feel him out there, feel his frustration and fear, but...

Look inside.

It was a whisper, and I didn't know where it was

coming from, but it steadied me. I got my breath and reached deep within, reached in for something I didn't even know I had.

Power flowed up through me, thick and honey-sweet, slow as the heartbeat of the Earth herself.

Yes. There. Just like that.

The restraints were leather and metal, both things that Earth Wardens could manipulate and control. I dissolved them into sand, pulled my wrists free of the gritty pile, and rolled painfully up to my knees to face the Demon.

She stopped moving, staring at me. If I scared her at all, I couldn't tell it from her expression.

'Back off,' I panted. 'Right now.' As a threat, it was pretty empty... I didn't have a clue how to hurt this thing. But she was standing there, waiting, frowning just a little. Maybe she didn't know much about me, either.

Maybe she was just a little bit afraid.

She said, with an eerie flatness, 'There you are. I've been searching for you. It's time to finish this.' She held out a hand towards me, and I felt the shimmering, sickening blackness sink deeper into me. 'Do you know who I am?'

My voice was barely a whisper. 'Demon.' I didn't doubt that, not at all. There was something so utterly wrong about her...

'No.' Something changed in her expression – no longer doll-blank, but a glimmer of something else.

Life. Personality. *My* personality. 'Not anymore. I'm becoming something else. I'm becoming you.'

I swayed on my knees, too sick to move, too terrified to do anything. She came closer, and with every step, she was...more *me*. Expression, body language, confidence. Even the smile.

'Why are you doing this?' I managed to whisper. Her fingers were moving towards me, and I knew, knew without the shadow of a doubt, that if she touched me, it was all over.

'No choice,' she said. 'Your memories changed me. I have to complete the process. Only one of us in this world, and it will be me. You're weak. I'm the stronger.'

'No.' My breath felt thick and stale in my lungs already, as if I was gone and didn't know it. 'David—'

That smile was definitely mine, right down to the lopsided twist at the corner of her lips. 'He won't know. Nobody will know, because I won't be pretending – I'll be you. Completely.'

I fell backward as her fingers moved towards me; I rolled over and used the cold metal bars of the hospital bed to pull myself to a sitting position. I lashed out with Earth powers, feeling for the cold, solid structure and heating it at the atomic level; the metal sagged, turned liquid, and hit the floor with a hiss.

I rolled off the edge of the bed, avoided the

molten mess, and backed away. I was in a corner, and the Demon was between me and the door. My head felt like I'd slammed it in a door a couple of times, and my whole body seemed cold, on the verge of giving up.

The building was made of concrete and metal and wood, and under normal circumstances that might have posed a problem, but I was beyond panic, and I was beyond controlling the surging, deadly flow of the Earth power in my body. I lashed out and felt the concrete soften. I liquefied the metal struts in the wall, and blew a hole in it with a compressed ram of air that manifested so suddenly it made my ears pop from the pressure.

The wall collapsed in a hail of debris and sparks, and I stumbled over it, barefoot and dazed. All I wanted was to get away, to get to Lewis and find some kind of protection if nothing else...

Lewis wasn't in the next room. Only Dr Lee, two nurses, and one security guard who fumbled for his sidearm at the sight of me. I must have been pretty scary; he took his time.

And then the *other* me stepped through the rubble behind me, and I saw Dr Lee and the others perceive, if not comprehend, the impossible.

My double made an annoyed sound. 'Now you've done it.'

I didn't know what she was going to do before I felt the balance of power in the room tilt – tilt drastically – and before I could even try to grab for it everybody in the next room exploded into flames, screaming. Dr Lee. The nurses. The armed security guard, who whirled in a confused blur of combustion, trying to smother the blaze. I stared numbly at them, unable to react for a second, and then grabbed the oxygen from around their bodies to smother the fire. They dropped, but only one was still screaming. Even though I'd reacted, it hadn't been fast enough; they were badly burnt, maybe dying.

I whirled to look at the Demon, but there was no sign of her. I could feel her, though. She was here, somewhere just out of sight. I felt the sick surge in my chest, and knew she was very close.

I couldn't do anything for the victims. I ran for the door, sobbing for breath, and clawed it open. Beyond was the waiting room, empty of everyone. I heard alarms screaming, and as I got my bearings I heard a door open to my right.

Kevin looked out.

'Inside!' I screamed, and reached out with a blast of hardened air to push him back, grab the door, and slam it shut. I melted the lock, too. 'Don't come near me!' I kept replaying it in my head, those startled people turning towards me, then the flames...that had been my fault. I hadn't realised how ruthless she was.

I couldn't take the chance that she'd hurt someone else.

I heard Lewis's voice, and the temptation to run towards him was very strong, but I thought about what could happen. *I can't. I can't risk him. I need to get out of here, now.*

I felt the blackness pressing in again, close and thick, and stumbled drunkenly against a coffee table. I looked down at it, picked it up on a cushion of air, and hurled it full force against the plate glass window on the other side of the room.

It bounced off. Hardened glass.

I forced myself to think. Even hardened glass was silica, and silica was something Earth Wardens could manipulate. I started to unravel its chemical structure, returning it to its base elements. Given time, I'd have just dissolved it into a pile of sand, but that wasn't fast enough. As soon as I got the process fully started, I launched the coffee table at it again with the force of a battering ram, and this time, the whole window shattered with a tremendous crash.

I scrambled up, heedless of the broken shards, and was just about to jump when something hit me with tremendous force, right in the back, and slammed me face-first into the ground outside. I tried to roll over, but it felt like a freight train was parked on my back.

That was it. I was about to die. I decided to commemorate it by cursing the Demon's heritage, its hygiene, its sexual habits...

And then a very soft, high-pitched voice, right next to my ear, said, 'I'm trying to save your life. Please shut up now.'

I stopped, astonished, and realised that the way I was lying, I ought to be able to see my right hand. It was lying right in front of my face...but it wasn't there. I wiggled my fingers experimentally and clenched my fist. I could feel the play of muscle, but there was nothing there.

I'd gone invisible.

'What the hell...?' That earned me a thump on the back of the head. 'Ow! Who the hell are you?' Someone, obviously, with the ability to turn me completely invisible. The scary thing was that it didn't really narrow down my choices.

'*Quiet!*' the voice hissed, and I obeyed, because I felt the Demon close, very close. The blackness swept over me like gravity, as if I were going to be pulled into her and destroyed, smashed apart at the cellular level.

And then it faded again, slowly, leaving me weak and sick and somehow...less.

I found myself being yanked upright by some tremendous force, and held there when my knees wobbled. I couldn't see anything near me, but then, when I looked down, I couldn't see myself, either.

'Hold on,' the voice said. 'This is going to hurt.'

She wasn't kidding. Heat swept over me, and then a feeling of being instantly flash-frozen, and then every nerve in my body screamed as one...

...and then I was on my knees in deep, soft carpeting the exact colour of caramel.

I pitched forward, face-first, and tried to scream, because whatever had just happened to me was wrong even by the considerably liberal standards of wrongness I was getting used to.

I couldn't make a sound.

I watched as my body started to come out of its invisibility, growing shadows first, then a kind of translucent reality, and then I was flesh and blood again.

And I could scream, but this time, I managed to lock it in my throat and moderate it to a helpless sort of whimper.

My benefactor – if you could call her that – walked around to face me. I looked up. Not far up, because she was only about four feet tall, cute as a button, a perfect little blonde girl with inhumanly blue eyes and an outfit straight out of *Alice in Wonderland*, complete with patent leather Mary Janes.

'You can get up now,' she said. 'I don't think you're hurt.'

Not hurt? She had to be kidding. I rolled slowly on my side and worked my way up to a sitting position, bracing myself with my arms. Standing up was not on the menu, not yet.

'What—' My voice was a hoarse croak; I cleared

my throat and tried again. 'What the hell did you do to me? Who—?'

'My name is Venna,' she said. 'I'm Djinn.'

No freakin' kidding. I stared at her mutely, and she folded her hands over the front of her white pinafore and stared right back without blinking.

'You don't remember me,' she said. Not a question. 'You used to call me Alice. You could call me that again, if you like.' She said it with the generosity of a noble dispensing a penny to a peasant. I just kept on staring. Why I'd know her as Alice was pretty self-evident, given her appearance. I was waiting for the Red Queen and the Mad Hatter to join the party. 'I had to take you away. You couldn't fight her. She was taking you apart, and if I hadn't stopped you, you'd be dead now.'

I finally found my voice. 'Did David send you?'

Venna's blue eyes didn't blink, and her expression didn't shift, but I sensed that she was choosing her next words too carefully. 'David cannot *send me* anywhere,' she said. I wanted for her to get around to a further explanation. It wasn't forthcoming.

'I need to go back,' I said. 'She'll kill everybody back there.'

'No,' Venna said. 'She killed the ones who saw you together. Now she's convincing the rest that she is you.'

'She – wait, *what*?'

'She's given herself up. She will tell them that she has recovered her memories – and that will be true, because the Demon already had them. She will tell them that she's you, and...' Venna shrugged. 'They will believe her.'

'But – that can't happen. *That can't happen!*' She just looked at me. Obviously, it could. 'They'll know. Lewis will know.'

She was already shaking her head. 'Any doubts can be explained away. She's been through a great trauma. Any of them can tell that, and they won't disbelieve her story.'

I grasped at my last straw. 'David! David will figure it out. Hello, mother of his child! Surely he knows me better than—'

'He would know if she could be perceived as a Demon. She's different now. He also has no reason not to accept her.' Venna's eyes seemed to get deeper, darker, and scarier. She looked twelve, and twelve hundred. Twelve *thousand*. 'You can't win this by going against her. It will only destroy you, and everyone who believes you.'

I found I was able to get up, and staggered across the carpet to a king-sized bed, where I collapsed in an untidy sprawl. 'So what am I supposed to do? What if she follows me?'

Venna cocked her head at me, interested as a robin with a worm. 'Do as I say,' she said. 'You will be safe here, so long as you don't go out or talk to

anyone. She can only find you when she's close –
the same way you can sense her. As long as you
avoid attracting attention, you'll be fine. I am going
to retrieve someone who can help you.'

I had just enough spark left to ask, 'Who?'

'Ashan,' she said.

'David was looking for him.'

'I know.' Venna smiled slowly. Not a comforting
kind of smile. 'I've been keeping him safe; David
would have killed him. And now we need him, so
it's good that I got him, don't you think?'

I had no idea what to say to that. Venna
smoothed down her dress, nodded to me gravely,
and walked off into…thin air. Just…gone.

She came back, silent as a ghost, for a few
seconds, to say, 'You understand…don't go out.
Don't talk to anyone. I've put clothing in the closet
for you. *Don't go out.*'

I nodded. I might not understand much of this,
but that part, I got. And hey, not a bad place, as
hideouts went. I was in a big, well-appointed hotel
room, immaculately clean, with a big plasma TV
on the wall, a comfy bed, and – visible through the
open door – a gigantic whirlpool tub.

Venna gave me one last doubtful look, then
vanished. I waited, but she didn't come back to
check. So I got up, went to the window, and pulled
the brocade curtains.

Below, a whole city stretched out, a dizzying

array of architectural marvels, fountains, people, lights, cars, dazzling sunlight. There was a gigantic Sphinx's rear end pointed towards my room, about seven stories down. The window sloped, and when I craned out for a look, I saw the building itself was sloped, like the side of a pyramid.

A hospitality book on the desk identified the hotel as the MGM Grand, Las Vegas.

That seemed weirdly familiar to me, but staring out at the landscape didn't seem helpful.

I went to try out the tub instead.

Chapter Seven

I was up to my neck in suds and blessedly warm water, experimenting with the various controls for the water jets, when I heard the door to the room open and close. I'd shut the bathroom door, so I couldn't hear or see anything else. I waited, but Venna didn't knock, and the last thing I wanted was to face her naked and dripping, anyway. I scrambled up, towelled off, and put on the underwear, blue jeans, black shirt and plain flat shoes that had been Venna's idea of appropriate costume.

I walked out, prepared to find out what kind of trouble I was in *now*, but it wasn't Venna.

And the two people I walked in on didn't even know I was there, at least not at first. I had to give them credit, they were very fast off the blocks – the clothing trail started at the door, with his tie, and finished in a heap at the foot of the bed. They were definitely *not* paying attention to me, quite, um, vigorously.

I tried tiptoeing to the door, and didn't quite get halfway there before the woman – leggy, redheaded, with a model's perfect ass, which had been on major display – caught sight of me and shrieked, falling off of her boyfriend, who thrashed around like a wounded seal in a shark tank. I held up my hands and backed towards the door.

'What the hell are you doing in our room?' he yelled, and came off the bed at me, still stark naked. I backed away, faster.

'Um…sorry, room inspector, I was just…making sure you had toilet paper, and…so, you like the bed? Brand-new bed. Very bouncy.' I was babbling, shaking, and I kept fierce eye contact with him because the temptation for my gaze to wander was…overwhelming. I felt the handle of the door dig into my back, reached behind me, and twisted it open. 'Sorry, sir, ma'am. Please, enjoy your stay…'

I barely made it into the hall before he slammed the door on me. I leant there, puffing for breath, trembling with reaction, and had to put both hands over my mouth to keep from screaming with laughter.

Don't go out. Yeah, thanks, Venna. Thanks a lot.

And you know, it would all have been just fine, if Romeo hadn't got on the house phone and reported me, but by the time I'd got in the elevators the security machine was already in motion.

When the elevator dinged to a halt at the ground floor, I was wondering where the hell I ought to go, and how I was going to get word to Venna.

I didn't have to wonder about that first part, not anymore. Facing me, blocking my path, were two guys in matching sports jackets, with logos on the pockets. They were the size of minivans, and they didn't look happy.

'Come with us,' one of them said. Not that I had a choice, because before the third word of the phrase was out, there were hands around my upper arms, and I was being marched off to the side, away from the busy foot traffic and ringing slot machines, to a discreet unmarked door with a key card entrance.

They sat me down at a table and stared at me in silence.

'So,' I said. 'Guys, this is all just a...mistake. OK? I was looking for my...my niece, she's about twelve, cute kid, blonde hair, blue eyes, looks like Alice in Wonderland...'

They kept on staring at me. One of them finally demanded my name. I lied. They kept staring.

After about two eternities, a woman came in and bent over to whisper in one of the guards' ears. He nodded. She left.

I waited for someone to explain to me what was going on. That was about as successful as you'd expect; these were *not* chatty fellows. I kept offering conversational olive branches, and they kept snapping them off.

Thirty minutes later, give or take, two uniformed police officers entered the room, escorted by the woman I'd seen earlier. I felt a real, serious chill spread over me.

'Joanne Baldwin?'

I didn't nod. It didn't matter.

'Joanne Baldwin, I need you to stand up and put your hands behind your back,' the older of the two cops said. 'Are you armed?'

'Armed? No! What's going on?' I stood up, mainly because there wasn't any point in not complying. More than enough muscle in the room to enforce the request.

'There's a warrant out for your arrest,' he said, and spun me around as he grabbed my right wrist. I felt the cold metal pinch of handcuffs on that side, then the other hand, and it was done before I could even react. 'I'm going to need you to stay calm, ma'am. I'm sure if there's a mistake you can work it out, but we have to take you in now.'

'But – what kind of warrant?' I asked. Because this seemed pretty excessive for accidental Peeping Tom-age. Or even accidental breaking and entering.

'You're under arrest for the murder of a police officer,' he said. 'You have the right to remain silent…'

I didn't remember the words of the Miranda warning. It's possible I'd never even heard them before, at least not directed at me. *Murder of a police officer?*

Man, you'd think that somebody would have mentioned it to me if I was a cop killer.

I didn't remember the guy I was supposed to have killed, although they showed me pictures. I suppose that didn't exactly come as a shock, but what disturbed me was more the fact that I had no idea – none at all – whether or not I'd actually committed the crime. Nothing seemed clear-cut anymore, since I'd done whatever it was I'd done to Marion.

The dead guy's name was Detective Thomas Quinn, and they had surveillance footage of me with him – or someone who looked exactly like me, who used my name. Like, say, a Demon. How long had she been impersonating me? Could she have been responsible? It didn't really matter, because as far as the police were concerned it wasn't exactly a viable defence.

So I went with the truth as I knew it. I didn't remember. No, I couldn't recall being in Las Vegas before. No, I didn't know Detective Quinn. No, I had no idea what had happened to him.

They showed me photos of a blown-up truck in a deserted area to prove that I'd killed him, but all I came up with was a feeling...a bad one. If I *had* killed the guy, it would have been in some sense necessary, right? Justified? God, I hoped so.

The two detectives interrogating me seemed interchangeable – not physically, but in every other way. No personality to speak of, and all they wanted from me was a confession, which I couldn't properly give. I asked for an attorney, because at least that would give me time, and the questioning ended for a while.

Which left me stranded in a hot, airless interrogation room that smelt of sweat and desperation, old coffee and vomit. Charming. I fidgeted with the coffee cup they'd given me – it was paper, of course; accused murderers didn't rate the good china – and tried not to think about the consequences of what was going on.

Look on the bright side, I thought. *You don't have to worry about not having any cash. Free food and lodging.*

The door rattled, and a new man came in. I didn't know him, either. He moved slowly, like he might be in pain. He had a badge showing, so he was another detective, maybe their secret weapon pinch hitter who was known for extracting confessions. Was he going to beat me? I didn't think so; he didn't look like he was in any physical shape for hand-to-hand, even though I was handcuffed to the table. I looked at him silently and sipped my coffee as he sank into the chair across the table from me.

And then he waited. I took the opportunity to study him. He was in his mid- to late forties, Hispanic, with greying hair and large, dark eyes as hard as obsidian. I couldn't tell what he was thinking, and my feeling of stunned, low-level fear that had been with me for the past few hours, since they'd dragged me in here, was gradually ratcheting up to full-fledged panic.

He finally said, 'I'm fine; thanks for asking.'

Great. Another person I was supposed to recognise. *Wonderful.* 'Glad to hear it,' I said. I sounded tired. I felt exhausted, wrung dry by all the uncertainty.

'Your friend left me by the side of the road,' he said. 'I was lucky someone found me in time. Twenty-two stitches. Nearly lost my spleen.'

OK, I was definitely in over my head now. 'Do I know you?' I asked slowly. And he actually blinked. His eyes revealed something at last, but nothing that was very comforting to me.

'Hard to believe you'd forget a thing like that,' he said. Not a question. His lips curled, but there was nothing remotely smile-like about the expression other than the muscles controlling it.

'Sir, I'm sorry, but like I told the other detectives, I can't remember—'

'Amnesia. Yeah, they told me.' He sat back, studying me, arms folded across his chest. 'You know how many we get in here a year who claim to have amnesia? Dozens. You know how many actually have it? I've never met one. Not even one.'

'Well,' I said, 'I'm busting your streak, because I really don't know you. I don't know *anyone*. If you tell me I killed this detective, this Quinn, then maybe...I don't know. But I *don't remember*!' I heard the hard, cutting edge in my voice, and closed my eyes and fisted my hands and fought for internal calm. 'Sorry,' I said. The chains fastening me to the table clanked softly when I shifted position. 'It's been a tough day.'

He leant forward, staring. 'Let me get this straight. You're telling me that you don't remember me.'

'No, sir.'

'And you don't remember Thomas Quinn.'

I bent over and rested my forehead against my fists. 'I have no idea,' I said. 'Did I know him?'

He didn't tell me, not directly. He said, 'My name is Detective Armando Rodriguez. I met you in Florida. I followed you. You remember any of that?'

I didn't bother to do more than shake my head this time.

'You told me things. Showed me...' He gave a quick glance towards the corner, where I was sure audio and video were being recorded. 'Showed me things that I didn't know were possible. And you convinced me that maybe Thomas Quinn wasn't the guy I'd believed he was.'

The frustration boiled inside me, hot as lava, and I had no place to let it loose. Why couldn't I remember? I had no idea how to play this, what to say, whether or not he was trying to trap me or even help me. There was simply no way to tell.

So I made it a direct question, looking him straight in the eye. 'When I talked to you about Quinn, did I tell you that I killed him?'

Detective Rodriguez was quiet for a few seconds, and then he shook his head. 'No. You said you didn't.'

'Did you believe me?'

'I didn't drag you back here in handcuffs.' His lips stretched in a thin, hard smile. 'But then, I was on vacation. And out of my jurisdiction.'

'*Did you believe me?*' My fingernails were digging painfully into the palms of my hands, and I leant forward across the table, willing him to tell me the truth. Or at least the truth as he saw it.

'Yes,' he said softly. 'I believed you.'

I let out a slow, careful breath and felt tears sting my eyes. 'Then can you help me?' I sounded pathetic. I felt pretty pathetic, too. He seemed genuinely saddened by that.

'No. I can't.' He stared at me for another dark second before he said, 'This isn't my case, Baldwin. They don't let detectives who have personal connections work murder cases, so whether I believe you or not, it really doesn't matter.'

'But you could tell them—'

'I already did,' he interrupted. 'I'm sorry. It probably won't do any good, whatever I say about you. So I'd advise you to start thinking about confessing, if you want a lighter sentence. Make this easy on yourself.'

'I'm not going to confess to a murder I didn't even commit!'

'I thought you said you didn't know,' he said. 'Didn't remember.'

'I don't,' I said. 'If I had a clue, I'd tell you. All I know is that I woke up a couple of days ago freezing to death in the forest, and things went downhill from there. Believe me, as bad as this is, I don't think going to prison is exactly the worst of my problems.'

He gave me a strange smile. 'I see. Then it's more or less the usual for you.'

'Is it? Great. My life *sucks*.'

He chuckled. I drank coffee. He silently joined me, sipping from his own ceramic mug embossed with PROPERTY OF LVPD. 'So what are you doing here?' I asked him. 'Minding the store while they decide how to crack me?'

'Somebody's got to. Watch you, I mean.'

'And they picked you.'

'I volunteered. Look, don't you want to call anyone? Your friends? What about your sister?'

I'd love to have called Lewis, but I had zero idea how to go about it. I had no idea where my sister was, or if I wanted to have anything to do with her. Though jail was certainly making me feel a lot more familial. 'I'd call my sister if I had a number for her.' I left it open-ended, hoping that maybe he'd have more resources than I could think of. Well, of course he did; he was a detective. Finding people was more or less his job description.

He shrugged. 'I'll see what I can do. The way your sister lived, she shouldn't be hard to track down.' Someone knocked at the one-way glass, and he nodded towards it. 'Looks like our time is up. Nice to see you, Joanne.'

'Same here,' I said faintly. He got up slowly, favouring his side, and I saw the lines of pain groove deeper into his face as he took a shallow, careful breath. 'Detective? You going to be all right?'

'Yeah. Better every day. You hang in there.'

I watched him head for the door. As he opened it, I said, 'You believed me awful fast about the amnesia.' Not that it was going to help me one way or another, but I found that curious. Cops weren't the most credulous of people, and he had reasons to distrust me, obviously. 'Why?'

Rodriguez raised his eyebrows just a bit. 'Maybe I like you, Ms Baldwin. Maybe I think you're the real thing.'

'The real thing.'

'Innocent.'

'Oh,' I said softly. 'I doubt that. I really do. Come on, tell me. Why do you believe me?'

'Quinn,' he said. 'I know how you felt about him, and there's no way you could say his name like that if you remembered him at all, especially after what he did to you. You're good. Nobody's *that* good.'

Rodriguez didn't go into detail, and I didn't ask. I was almost certain that was yet another memory I was better off not having in the total-recall file. He nodded once to me, a kind of comrade's salute if not actual friendship, and stepped outside. There was a murmur of conversation in the hall, and then the door opened again and the first two detectives came back inside and shut the door. They took up seats on the other side of the table, facing me.

'Detective Rodriguez,' I said. 'Mind if I ask what happened to him?'

'Stabbed,' Tweedledee said. 'Dumped in a ditch, left to die. He's a tough bastard, though. Wouldn't want to be the guy who shivved him in the long run.' He studied me closely. 'You seemed chummy, considering.'

'Considering what?'

'Considering he was partners with the guy you killed. Thomas Quinn.'

* * *

My lawyer arrived, some recent law school graduate with the ink still wet on her diploma. We chatted. I explained patiently about the memory thing. She didn't seem optimistic. Well, she probably didn't have reason to be, and she certainly wasn't being paid to be, since she was court-appointed.

And then they took me to arraignment, which was an efficient sort of in-and-out procedure. I barely had time to draw breath between when my case was called, I was shuffled up to the dock, and my attorney filed a not-guilty plea. There was bail, but I didn't hear the amount, and it didn't much matter anyway. Nobody was going to be rushing to my rescue, I figured. If Venna did, she wouldn't need collateral.

I was right about that. I went to jail. Long process, humiliating and nerve-racking, but in the end the cell wasn't so horrible, if you could get over the lack of privacy. My roommate was a big girl named Samantha – the strong, silent type, which was fine with me. I just wanted to lie still and let my head stop aching for a while.

David, where are you? I couldn't believe this was happening to me. I was some kind of supernatural weather agent. Supernatural weather agents didn't get arrested and dressed in tacky bright orange jumpsuits. Supernatural weather agents kicked ass and took names, and they did not, ever, end up with a criminal record and a jail-house address.

I was leery of falling asleep, but staying awake was too much of a struggle. I was exhausted, and even if the cot was no feather bed, it was at least horizontal. The pillow smelt of industrial soap, but it was clean. Even Samantha's snoring seemed less like a disruption and more like a white-noise generator to lull me into a coma.

I woke to a clank of metal, and opened my eyes to see that it was still artificially dark out in the hall, but a guard was opening up my cell. I sat up when she gestured at me. 'Let's go,' the guard, said. 'Baldwin. You've made bail.'

'I have? How?'

'No idea,' she said. 'Maybe somebody got you confused with one of those actor people; we've had one in here before.'

I tried to get my head around that, but not for long. Bail sounded like a great idea, even if it seemed suspiciously miraculous. I followed the guard out, and we marched down the centre of the prison hallway. On both sides of the hallway were rows of bars and dimly lit rooms. Snoring. Mumbling. Crying. The guard was short, round, and jingled with keys. Her name tag said, ELLISON. 'Who posted for me?' I asked as we arrived at the sally port gate. She gave a high sign to the guard on the other side, and we were buzzed through.

'Don't know,' she said. 'Let's go, honey; you

may have all night, but my shift's over in twenty.'

Processing me out took nearly as much time as it had spent to lock me up – the wonders of bureaucracy – and it gave me plenty of opportunity to wonder who, why, and how. I tried to decipher the forms they had me sign, but the light was poor, I was tired, my head hurt, and those things were complicated anyway.

So by the time I'd changed back into street clothes, it was getting near morning. Or at least, the indigo horizon was turning more of a milky turquoise. I'd hardly been in the big house long enough to get nostalgic about freedom, but still, that breath of cool, fresh air was sweet. Even if I still had to go through two more gates, some steely-eyed guards, and a final intrusive pat-down on my way out of the yard.

Beyond, there were a couple of taxis parked, complete with sleeping drivers. I wondered at the desperation involved in ferrying around criminals for cash, but remembered just in time that not all of us were, in fact, criminals. Some of us were just *alleged* criminals.

I looked around, wondering who would bother to bail me out and then leave me standing by the side of the road. I didn't have to wonder long. A sleek black car pulled out from behind one of the taxicabs and ghosted up next to me. The passenger window power-rolled down, revealing a pale, tired face. I didn't recognise her for a second, and started automatically cataloguing features. Like blonde hair that needed a root touch-up. Like an inexpert, hastily applied makeup job that didn't conceal the discoloured bags under her eyes.

Like eyes that seemed a lot like my own blue shade.

I blinked. 'Sarah?' I asked, and took a tentative step closer. It was the woman from Cherise's memories, rode hard, put away wet.

She gave me a thin, tired smile. 'Jo,' she said. 'Need a lift?'

I nodded and opened the back door of the car. No surprises lurking back there, just clean dark upholstery. My sister rolled up her window, and the driver – I couldn't see him – accelerated the car smoothly away from the jail into traffic. No matter what time of the day or night, there was traffic in Las Vegas, at least near downtown, where we were. I saw a confusing blare of neon up ahead, and had a strong, wrenching sense of déjà vu.

'How'd you find out I was here?' I asked.

'A detective called me, and Eamon and I pulled together the bail money.' She looked kind of defiant. 'Can't say we don't care, can you?' Like I was going to?

'Of course we care,' said the driver, in a low, musical accent that I could only vaguely identify as British. I saw his eyes in the rear-view mirror, couldn't tell what colour they were in the glare of passing headlights and ambient neon. He was watching me as much as he was watching the road. 'You're looking better than I expected – a hell of a lot better than the last time I saw you. Feeling all right?'

I opened my mouth to reply, something polite and non-confrontational, because I had no idea what my relationship was to this new guy. I didn't get a chance to be evasive.

'Before you start,' Sarah said, 'Eamon wants to apologise. So let him, please. He's the one who insisted we come and get you. You owe him, Jo. Give him a chance.'

Who was Eamon, and what did he have to apologise for? What was I holding against him? *God*. Welcome to Brain Damage Theatre. I was tired of confessing ignorance; I decided that maybe dignified silence was the best defence. They must have taken it for assent.

'I know you told me to stay away from Sarah, but I couldn't do it,' the driver – Eamon – said. 'I won't apologise for that; whatever she and I do is between the two of us. But I do apologise for making that promise to you in the first place.'

OK, so whoever Eamon was – and nice voice, by the way – I hadn't approved. But since I had no idea why I hadn't, and Eamon and Sarah weren't likely to give me an unvarnished explanation, I just nodded. 'Water under the bridge,' I said. Aphorisms were made for moments like these. Saved me from saying anything that might be proven wrong. 'Are you two OK?'

Eamon's eyes focused on me in the rear-view for so long that I thought he might drive over a curb. Or another car. He was one of those avoidance drivers, though – either great peripheral vision or awesome luck. *Or something else. Maybe he's a Djinn.* Except I didn't get any Djinn vibe from him.

'Us?' Eamon said, and raised his eyebrows. 'Of course we're all right. Sarah, tell your sister you're fine.'

'I'm fine,' Sarah said. She didn't look it. She looked tired and puffy and not in the best possible state. Hung-over, maybe. Or worse. The way she said it sounded hollow, but not as if she were really scared of him. Just...submissive. Wonderful. I had a wet rag for a sister. 'Jo, you need to understand, I love Eamon. I know you didn't want us to stay together, but...'

Oh, God. The last thing I needed was to be the relationship police for a sister I'd barely met and – based on Cherise's memories – hadn't had much in common with to begin with. 'I'm over it,' I said. 'Eamon and Sarah, sitting in a tree. True love. Trust me, I'm more worried about the fact that I was sitting in jail for a murder that I didn't commit.' I left it there. I wanted to see what they'd have to say. Which was nothing, apparently. Eamon braked for the light at Fremont Street, and we all stared at the explosion of dancing lights during the pause. 'Thanks for bailing me out.'

'It seemed the thing to do.' Eamon was being just as uninformative as I was. Not helpful. 'Did you speak with the good Detective Rodriguez while you were in the precinct house?'

So he knew my friendly – or, at least, not adversarial – cop. 'Yeah, I saw him.'

'Ah. How is he?'

'Healing up. He had some kind of accident.'

Eamon nodded. He kept watching me, and there was a tight frown grooved now between his eyebrows. 'Did he say anything about what happened?'

'No.' I felt a weird surge of alarm. 'Why?' *Please don't tell me that I'm responsible for that, too.*

Was I crazy, or did he look oddly startled for a second before smiling? 'No, nothing, don't worry. Listen, love, are you all right? You don't seem... quite yourself.' His voice was low and rich with concern, and man, that was seductive. I wanted somebody to care whether or not I was OK, and obviously that wasn't going to be my sister. Disappointing, but there it was.

Sarah twisted in her seat again to look at me. Her pupils were huge. Bigger than they should have been, even in the dark. I wondered if she was on some kind of pain medication. 'Well, she *did* just get out of jail,' she said. 'Of course she's not quite herself. She's scared, and there's nothing wrong with that. God, what are you doing in Vegas, Jo? You came looking for me, didn't you? I told you I didn't need your help. I told *her*, too.'

'Her?' I repeated blankly.

Sarah's pointed chin lifted so she could look down her thin, patrician nose at me. 'You know who. *Imara*.'

My heart thudded hard against my rib cage, rattling to be free. Oh, that hurt. My sister had seen Imara. Imara had been part of my life. Had tried to help Sarah, evidently, for all the good that did. 'When did you last see her?' I asked. Because if Sarah had seen her recently, maybe everybody was wrong about Imara. Wrong about her being...gone. *Come on, Joanne, say it*. Wrong about her being dead.

What, even David? some part of me mocked, more gently than the question deserved. Surely David would know if his child was alive. I didn't have to know a lot about the Djinn to understand that much.

Sarah avoided my gaze this time, turning back to stare out the windshield as Eamon navigated the car through the neon pinball machine of the Strip. 'I haven't seen her since I told her to leave me in Reno,' she said. 'I know you both meant well, but honestly, Jo, she was getting on my nerves. And besides, she was worried about you. She wanted to get back and check on you, even though I told her you'd be OK. You're *always* OK.'

Ouch. That stung, especially delivered in a tone so bitter it could have stripped paint. Apparently having a superhero wizard for a sister wasn't the party-in-a-box that you'd assume. Well, I wasn't finding it all clowns and puppies on this side, either.

'Jo,' Eamon said, drawing my attention back to him. 'I'm guessing that perhaps in this instance your sister might not have been exactly correct. Right? Things haven't gone as planned?'

'No,' I said, and turned to look out the window at passing strangers who didn't notice me, or care. 'Not exactly. Where are we going?'

'It's best if we don't tempt fate and stay in the city,' he said. 'Sarah and I have a small place a couple of hours down the road. If you don't mind?'

I shrugged. I had no money, no transportation, and no real alternatives; seemed like I was stuck with Sarah and Eamon. At least Eamon seemed like a decent kind of guy.

A better person than my sister, anyway.

I wondered if maybe I was internalising the dislike Cherise had felt for Sarah; probably I was. After all, I didn't have the normal family bonds and memories, nothing that would let me overlook

Sarah's flaws and love her anyway. I didn't know her, except on the surface, and the surface wasn't looking very pretty.

Besides, it was fairly clear how she felt about me.

But she bailed you out.

Interesting.

Chapter Eight

Two hours and a boring number of minutes later, we entered a dry, sun-faded little town called Ares, Nevada. Population 318, and no doubt declining. It wasn't a garden spot, unless you liked your garden with lots of thorns and spikes. I remembered – actually, Cherise had remembered – my sister as being impeccably groomed, focused on polish and presentation. I doubted that would get her very far in the social scene of Ares, which probably revolved around the local Dairy Queen we'd passed, and possibly a strip club.

There was one stoplight in town, and Eamon obeyed it at the corner of Main and Robbins, then turned right. Nothing after the next block but some emptied-out stores with soaped windows, and the ruins of a few buildings that hadn't been so lucky or durable. We kept driving. About a mile on, Eamon turned the car off on a bumpy, unpaved side road, and I saw that we were heading for a mobile home community.

As trailer parks went, it tried to rise above the clichés. There were a few struggling bushes, some attempt at landscaping at the front entrance. Not much clutter. The trailers were mostly in decent shape, although a few showed the ravages of time and weather. There were a couple of retirees walking small, fat dogs along the roadside, and one of them waved. Eamon waved back.

'I hate this place,' Sarah said. She sounded like she meant it.

'It's temporary, Sarah. You know that.' Eamon must have been tired of explaining it; his tone was more than a little sharp. 'Just until the funds come through on the international transfer.'

'Meanwhile, we're living in a *trailer park*. With crack-heads! I used to live in the same zip code with Mel Gibson, for God's sake!' I wondered if the trailer park had its fringe benefits for her, like being a good place to score drugs. Heroin? Meth? Coke? Something that made her pupils so inordinately wide. Eamon seemed sober as a judge, though, so it wasn't likely he was the one supplying her habits. I wasn't sure he even knew, which made me think that he was wilfully blind to her problems. Or he knew, and he'd given up trying to fix her.

'It's only temporary,' Eamon said again. 'I'm sorry, love; I know it's not what you're used to. Things will get better. You'll bear with me, won't you?'

There was a kind of wistful longing in his voice, and Sarah softened. She stretched out a hand towards him, and he took it and held it. He had amazing hands – long, elegant, beautifully cared for. His fingers overlapped hers by inches. 'I'm sorry,' she said. 'I didn't mean it that way. Of course I'll put up with whatever I have to for us to be together.' She threw me a look in the rear-view mirror. A defiant one. 'No matter what other people think.'

I'd thought *Eamon* was bad for her? *Wow.* I really hadn't had a clue about my sister if I'd thought that a slick English guy who would put up with her bullshit was a bad deal for her. 'Other people meaning me?' I asked, and let a little of my frustration out. Sarah glared.

'Of *course*, meaning you,' she snapped. 'What other controlling, know-it-all relative do I have in the backseat? Is Mom in your pocket?'

Eamon pulled the car to a stop before I could think of a suitably acid reply to any of that. Probably for the best. The sedan wasn't big enough for a real girl fight, and the bloodstains would never come out of the upholstery.

'Home sweet home,' he said with just the right touch of irony. 'Sorry, I've given the staff the day off. Do forgive the mess.'

It was a trailer. Not a very big one – not one of the kingly double-wides, like the one across the road. And it was dented, faded, and run-down. There were some cheerful window boxes, but they were full of dead plants; what a shock. I couldn't see Sarah as the getting-her-hands-dirty gardener. Apart from the bold landscaping choice of a chain-link fence around some struggling, sun-blasted grass, there wasn't much to recommend the place.

'Nice,' I said noncommittally, and got out to follow Eamon towards the aluminium Taj Mahal.

It wasn't any better on the inside, although it was darker. The smell was a little strange – a combination of unwashed towels and old fried fish, with a little stale cat litter thrown in – and as I blinked to adjust my eyes I saw that the place must have been bought fully furnished. Matted, ancient gold shag carpet. Heavy, dark furniture that had gone out of style twenty years ago, at least. Clunky, vegetable-coloured appliances in the small kitchen. There were dips in the carpet that I suspected meant rotting floors.

Still, they'd made an attempt. The place was mostly clean, and it was also mostly impersonal, with only a few personal items – Sarah's – in view. A trashy candy-coloured book on the coffee table, facedown. A wineglass with some sticky residue in the bottom next to it. A fleece robe flung over one end of the couch, and I hoped it didn't belong to Eamon, because pale pink wasn't really his colour.

Eamon swept the place with a look, tossed

his keys on the counter, and turned to face me. It was my first good look at him, and I wasn't disappointed. My sister *did* have good taste in exteriors, at least. He wasn't gorgeous, but he was nice-looking, with a clever face and a sweet smile. The only thing that bothered me about him were the dark, steady eyes that didn't quite match the rest of his expression.

'Jo,' he said, and opened his arms. I took the cue and hugged him. He had a strong, flat body, vividly warm, and he didn't hang on an inappropriately long time, though he gave good value for his five seconds. When we parted again, his eyes were bright, almost feverish. 'I'll tell you the honest truth: It's good to see you again,' he said. 'I know I speak for Sarah when I say that we were worried when you dropped out of sight. Where have you been?'

I had no idea what span of time that covered, of course, not that I was going to tell him that. 'Around,' I said, and smiled back. 'I'm parched. Can I get something to drink?'

'Of course. Sarah.' He said it as if she were his servant, and I saw her frown work its way deeper into her forehead. Couldn't blame her on that one. I wouldn't have appreciated it, either. Still, she wandered into the kitchen and started rooting through cabinets, assembling me a drink. She didn't ask what I liked. I guessed either she already knew or didn't care. 'Please, sit down. Tell me what happened to get you into this problem.'

'Mistaken identity,' I said, but I obeyed the graceful wave of his hand towards the couch. Eamon took a chair next to it. 'Nothing to tell, really. They think I killed a cop.'

'Ah. Which cop would this be?'

'Detective Quinn.'

'I see. And did you?' he asked, not looking at me. He needed a haircut; his brown, silky shag was starting to take on a retro-seventies look that made him look a little dangerous.

'I can't believe you asked me that,' I said, which was a nice non-answer. 'What do you think?'

'I think that they're talking about Orry, aren't they?'

'Thomas Quinn,' I said. 'They didn't mention anyone named Orry.'

He shot me a quick, unreadable glance. 'Oh,' he said. 'I see. Not the same person, then.'

I covered with a noncommittal shrug. Eamon smiled slightly, and then moved back in his chair as Sarah came towards us with drinks. Eamon's was clearly alcohol – something amber, on the rocks – and mine was just as clearly not. It bubbled with carbonation. I sipped carefully, but it was just Coca-Cola. No rum, no whiskey. It was even diet.

And yes, it was delicious. My body went into spasms of ecstasy over the faux-sugar rush, and it was all I could do not to chug the entire thing in one long gulp.

Sarah perched on the arm of Eamon's chair, her own glass clutched in one long-fingernailed hand. She needed a manicure, and she didn't need to be drinking whatever was in that glass, which wasn't likely to be as innocuous as my Diet Coke. 'What were you talking about?' she asked. Eamon raised his eyebrows at me.

'Water under the bridge,' he said. 'Now. Just so we understand each other, Jo, I did put up your bail money. It wasn't purely because I like you, although I do...or because I love your sister, although I do love her, obviously. It's because I have a business proposition for you, and I thought this might be an opportunity to have your full and undivided attention while we discuss the details.'

What kind of business did I have with Sarah's boyfriend? I felt a growing sense of disquiet, and it wasn't anything I could put my finger on... Eamon's body language was kind, gentle, unaggressive. His eyes were bright and his smile a bit too sharp, but that might have been my own paranoia. Yes, the trailer wasn't a Malibu beach house, but it wasn't exactly a horrifying dump, either. Sarah was on drugs – I was nearly sure of that – but that didn't mean danger to me, only to her.

And yet. And yet.

'A business proposition,' I repeated, locking

gazes with Eamon. 'Go on. I'm all ears. Anybody who puts up bail money gets that much.'

His smile got wider. 'You might not recall, but I had a small business venture under way in Florida when you arrived back there and took up residence. I was investing in construction with some silent partners. I was hoping to revive that effort, maybe do something on the West Coast for a change. I'd like to have your commitment to be involved.'

'I'm not really up for investing,' I said. 'What with the murder charge, and the fact that I seem to be running a little short of cash. Nothing personal.'

Something flashed in his eyes, and I had no idea why he'd find that funny. 'No indeed,' he agreed. 'Not personal in the least. Well, to be blunt, you do owe me, Joanne. Not just for the bail, although obviously I have to consider that. No, before you left Florida, you promised to locate something very rare and very special for me – something I needed a great deal. As it turned out, you had a bit of a problem delivering on your promise, which was very disappointing for me, and caused me to lose something that I really wasn't planning to give up. But as you said, water under the bridge, and that's certainly far downstream at this point. Both our circumstances have changed – perhaps not, in your case, for the better. So please consider my offer as being a way for you to get back on your feet, in a sense, as well as a way to repay your debts to me.'

'I see.'

'It's either that or, regretfully, I'll have to ask you to immediately pay back the money. As you heard, I'm waiting on a funds transfer from Asia, but various political problems in that part of the world are causing delays. And, of course, I had to sink some of my capital into providing for your temporary freedom, pending trial. So perhaps you'd like to contact your bank and have them wire me about five thousand dollars. That should tide us over.'

In a trailer like this, in Ares, Nevada? I imagined that five thousand would probably tide them over for months on end. In style. Even if Sarah's drug habit was worse than I thought. 'I'm sorry,' I said. 'Even if I wanted to, I can't. I don't have any cash. No wallet, no credit cards, no cheques. Nothing. I can't even go to a bank and draw out cash with no identification. If it makes you feel any better, I'm just as pissed about that as you are.'

'Ah,' Eamon said, and sat back, eyes going half-lidded and remote. 'Well. How ever are you planning to pay me back for your bail money, then, if you're not interested in the investment and you can't provide the cash?'

'It's a temporary situation. It'll all—'

'Work out?' he supplied dryly. 'Yes. I'm sure it will. Things do seem to do that for you. The favoured, fortunate child, aren't you just?' Eamon suddenly came up with a lovely, charming smile, which he turned on my sister like a cannon, with about the same effect. 'Sweets, why don't you give us a moment alone?'

Sarah clouded over, but it was a foregone conclusion that she'd obey. I ignored the intervening whines and concentrated on Eamon and on my environment. What kind of trouble was I in? And what could I do about it?

Sarah finally left the room, went to the bedroom, and slammed the thin, scratched door behind her.

He watched her go, his eyes intent and strangely fond, and without any change in his expression Eamon said, 'I don't want to alarm your sister, but I'll warn you, if you try to pull any of your magical shit with me, I'll make both of you pay for it. Are we clear, then?'

It felt like he'd kicked me in the stomach. I opened my mouth but didn't quite know what to say. What the hell had just happened?

'Right,' he said. 'Enough of our little dance, my dear. You're a puzzle to me at the moment – a not entirely unattractive one, but I have issues of my own to overcome, so I'm not terribly concerned about yours. Although you certainly can't believe some of the things you've been telling me, and I wonder what kind of mad plan you have in mind if you're lying about so much, and so blatantly.

Nothing to my benefit, I'm sure. Well, let's be blunt, then: I need to get out of this town before I either go mad or do something quite unpleasant to your dear sister. Neither of us wants that, and I'm sure you'd like to help me out in this.'

'Are you threatening Sarah?' I asked. I stood up – not because I meant to, just because my muscles tensed so badly I couldn't sit still. I stared at him, and he smiled, still entirely at ease.

'Oh, yes,' he said. 'Come, now, don't act surprised. You knew it was coming, love; it was just foreplay to get there. Now we're down to the sweaty parts.'

'Watch it.'

'Well, you know that I do enjoy that as well,' he said, and grinned like a wolf. It made my skin crawl. Who *was* this guy? Why couldn't I get a decent read on him?

'Why'd you really bail me out?' I demanded. Eamon shrugged and tossed back the rest of his drink in one neat mouthful.

'I suppose because Sarah felt it was the thing to do, and I was curious about what you'd do and say; besides, I thought you might be useful. You had to know that I had her sometime, and it seemed to be a good time to press my advantage in that area. Tell the truth. Did you know I'd be with her? I know you were very serious about the threats you delivered last time, and I don't underestimate your ability to carry through...except that you do seem to be more alone than ever. What's wrong, love? Finally drive away the last few people who cared about you?'

I felt a buzzing in my head and a build-up of power along my spine. *You can fry him like an egg,* I thought. *Erase any trace of this asshole. It'd be a public service.* Except that I wasn't a murderer, and I didn't aspire to become one, either. I controlled my anger and directed it in less mutilating ways. 'So tell me, was Sarah already an addict when you brought her to this little paradise, or did you start her on that once you got her here, just to keep her occupied?' I asked. 'And don't give me any you-didn't-know bullshit. *I* know, and—' *And I just met her.* I didn't want to say that, though. One thing about Eamon: He was inspiring me to keep my cards close to my chest. 'And I don't live with her.'

I thought I saw a deep flash of something in his eyes, quickly hidden. Anger? Appreciation? No idea. He was pretty hard to read, all around. His physical cues – a relaxed posture, friendly smile, graceful and gentle gestures – were all completely at odds with what I sensed was going on inside of him. Tightly controlled, this guy. And dangerous. I was sure of that part.

'Hardly my master plan. Sarah was bored,' he said. 'I didn't encourage her, but no, I didn't stop her, either. It keeps her...relatively content. And I'm sure you know that Sarah can be demanding. She's always going on about how much she misses her old life, with all her country club friends and shopping sprees. And while I'd love to give her that life...well. It's not possible, given what I do.'

'And what is it you do?' I asked.

'Oh, love,' he said. 'You know exactly what I do. I'm a criminal. I'm a very bad man, and if you don't remember that, well, there's something very wrong with you, isn't there? And that can only work to my advantage.'

The trailer was starting to close in on me. I was thinking wistfully of open forest, cold, sharp air, the company of David and Lewis. Good times, even if I'd thought I'd been suffering. *This* was suffering, right here. What my sister was going through with this asshole was real suffering, and he had every intention of spreading the joy to me, too.

'What do you want?' It came out harsher than I intended. My hands were curled into fists, and I forced my aching fingers to straighten out.

Eamon smiled at me, the same blindingly charming smile he'd used on Sarah. Luckily I was wearing my cynical sunglasses. 'You don't remember, do you? None of it. Not Quinn. Not what happened in Florida. No wonder you're so careful when you say something to me. Couple of critical mistakes along the way, though: First,

Thomas Quinn and Orry are one and the same, and you of all people should have remembered that, if you remembered anything. It was a bit important to you, that piece of information.'

'What do you *want*?'

'Almost nothing, really. I just want you to change the weather,' he said. 'See? Couldn't be easier. Do that, and I'll forget the money you owe me, the favours you failed to perform, *and* I'll put your sister into rehab and part ways with her for good. I'll leave you and yours strictly alone in the future. In short, I'll give you everything you want, Joanne.'

'In exchange for changing the weather.'

'Exactly.'

'Where?'

'Ah.' His teeth flashed, white and slightly crooked, just enough to give him character. I could see how Sarah got sucked into this guy's orbit; she didn't strike me as especially strong, and Eamon just radiated competence. *Bad* competence, sure, but... 'I'll show you, but not until we have an agreement. Do we?'

'No. We don't.'

'Damn. I was hoping I wouldn't have to raise the stakes, but you really leave me very little choice.' The warmth drained out of his smile. 'Things can happen to your sister. Terrible things. I'm not saying that I would personally do them, but such things can be outsourced these days, and it's such a cold, cruel world for a sensitive woman with a drug problem, yeah?'

I was almost speechless with fury. 'You—'

'Ah!' He held up a long finger and waggled it gently from side to side. 'Let's not insult each other. We both understand that Sarah's a dependent personality; if I want her to stay with me, she'll stay, no matter how I treat her. No matter how much I hurt her. If you want to ensure your sister's future safety and happiness, you're going to have to pay me off. And that means this one simple favour.'

'Fine,' I snapped. He raised his eyebrows. 'What, you want me to sign it in blood? You've made your fucking point!'

Eamon sniffed the air. 'Is that brimstone I smell? Love, I'm not the devil. I don't require signatures, and I wouldn't want your grimy, well-used soul, either. Don't play the innocent with me; I've seen you without your airs and social graces.' His eyes focused in on me like laser guidance systems for a bomb. 'And by the way, I know what Orry did to you that day in the desert. I don't blame you for killing him. It did put me to a spot of inconvenience, but no one can debate that he deserved what happened to him out there.'

That spoke volumes about things I didn't remember, and was glad I couldn't. I shuddered, but I did it inside, where he couldn't see. 'Let's leave the past out of it,' I said. 'So I do this thing for you, and you're out of my life? Out of my sister's life?'

'Once and for all,' he said. 'Truthfully, I'm a bit sorry I ever came back into it. She's…difficult. But I did – and do – care about her. Please believe that. It's not all about leverage. If it had been, I'd have kicked her to the curb weeks ago, when she ceased to be amusing.'

Strangely, I did believe that. Or wanted to, anyway. 'I wish you had,' I said. 'She'd be better off.'

He gave me a pitying look. 'When I take the trash to the curb, I put it out in plastic bags,' he said. 'Think, love. I never claimed I was a good catch. But in my own way, I have tried to do my best for her.'

'Just not enough to keep her off of drugs,' I said.

He shrugged. 'The only person who can keep Sarah clean is Sarah. You know that.'

Eamon's philosophy of personal responsibility was convenient, to say the least. I got up and paced the trailer's worn carpet. The floor creaked. Eamon watched me without appearing worried about anything I might do; I stopped near a lopsided scattering of framed photographs and stared.

There I was, with my arm around Sarah. Happier times, clearly; I had a smug grin, and she looked rosy and glowing with happiness. Younger, both of us. There was another photo next to it of an older woman sitting on a beach, looking out to sea. There was a contemplative air to the picture, and a kind of sadness. I reached, out and touched the face with a fingertip.

'I haven't seen this in years,' I said. I was taking a guess that Eamon wouldn't bother with family photos – if he had, and I was pointing at a picture of his dear old mum from Manchester or wherever, I was probably screwed. He already knew my memory was faulty; I just, didn't want him to know the extent of it. He'd probably assume it was confined to a specific period – hell, I'd have assumed that, in his place. The alternative would have seemed ridiculously unlikely.

Whatever he thought, he just said, 'Sarah loves that photograph. She said it was your mother's favourite, as well. You took it, didn't you?'

I decided the safest course was not to answer. I picked up the picture and stared at it, trying to read its secrets. *My mother.* What had she been like? Had she been protective? Proud? Absent? Abusive? So many questions, and I knew I wouldn't get the answers here. Not out of Eamon, anyway.

'Not that I'm unsympathetic to your current stroll down Memory Lane, love, but there's a deal on the table,' Eamon said. 'And you know how much I like to close deals.'

Some dark, velvet tone of amusement in that made me put the picture down and turn to look at him. I hadn't, right? Oh, *tell* me I hadn't slept with my sister's skanky, possibly homicidal boyfriend.

Man, I was changing my ways if that was the case. Possibly joining a nunnery.

'You show me where you want the weather changed,' I said, 'and I'll make it happen.'

He smiled slowly. 'I know you will. Because you're not stupid enough to double-cross me twice.'

I wasn't too surprised to find that while Eamon and I had been trading threats and barely concealed attacks, Sarah had taken the opportunity of self-medicating herself into oblivion. Not surprised, but sad. I found out what her poison of choice was, because it was in plain sight on the nightstand...an orange-brown prescription bottle of OxyContin. At least, I thought, it wasn't meth. But Sarah would have found meth too low class, no doubt. To me, high was high; it didn't really matter whether you blissed out from prescription drugs or something a toothless wonder cooked up in a pot on his stove. The problem was the same.

I got her out of bed. She opened her eyes, and the pupils were hugely dilated. She yawned as I tossed clothes at her. There were bruises on her arms and legs, and I felt a newly sick sensation bubbling deep in my stomach. Those were not exactly the signs of a loving relationship, but then, what had I really expected? Consideration? *Dependent personality*, he said, and although I hated him for it, Eamon was right. Sarah had hooked up with a guy who'd treat her like crap, because deep down that was what she expected to get. And maybe he was what she needed to continue eroding her own nonexistent self-worth.

How could two sisters be so damn different?

'Where are we going?' she mumbled. I helped her put on a floral shirt with ruffles down the front; it would have looked like crap on me, but on her it looked fresh and pretty. It offset the haggard lines in her face, anyway. She needed sleep, and not the kind induced by chemicals. And an environment where she could find out just how powerful she could be, if given the chance.

'We're going on a little trip,' I said. 'Sarah, look at me. *Look at me*. You recognise me, right?'

Her wandering eyes focused on me. I was eerily reminded of Cherise's time-delayed attention, but this was different; Sarah had at least chosen this. 'Of course I know who you are,' Sarah said, and put a hand to my cheek. Her skin felt cool and clammy. 'You're my sister. You're all I've got. Sometimes I hate you, though. But mostly I love you.'

I felt that artlessly cruel statement lodge between my ribs, sharp and cold, and felt tears sting my eyes. I loved her. I had no reason to, but I loved her anyway.

And now I'd made myself responsible for her, and right now I wasn't sure that was such a great idea... I could hardly take care of myself. But I couldn't exactly leave her with Eamon.

'That's right,' I said, and managed a smile. I put my hand over hers, holding it to my cheek. 'I love you, too. You and me against the world, Sarah. But I'm going to need your help now.' I reached for the prescription bottle and checked the label. Unless her name was Mabel Thornton, they weren't her pills. I rattled them in front of her until she focused on them. 'You're going to have to stop taking these.'

She blinked, and then she grabbed for them. I easily pulled them out of reach. 'Those are mine!' she said, and set that sharp chin of hers in a hard, stubborn line. 'Jo, give them back! I only take them when I need them! I take them for pain!'

Her life was full of that right now, starting with being in a relationship with the asshole in the other room, and ending with the fact she was living in a trailer in Ares, Nevada, with nothing to look forward to but more abuse. But it could all be fixed. It *would* all be fixed.

'I'll hang onto them for you,' I said, and slipped them into the pocket of my jeans with a mental promise to ditch them in the first trash can I passed. 'Up and at 'em, kid.'

She giggled drunkenly. 'I'm not the kid! You're the kid!'

Not at the moment, I wasn't.

Getting Sarah dressed was an effort. While she figured out the complexities of pants, I ransacked her closet, shoved what passed for her wardrobe into a bag – Louis Vuitton, evidently a souvenir of better days – and added the few personal touches she had around the trailer. Especially the photographs. I lingered over the one of our mother, and I ached to ask...but I didn't dare. So far, I thought I'd danced around the subject of memory pretty well with her, but one false move and everything could fall apart.

It was depressingly easy to remove all traces of Sarah from what was supposed to be her home. I supposed it was possible to look on it as freewheeling independence, but it just seemed really creepy as hell. A reminder of just how easily a life could be erased from the world.

Eamon didn't help, literally or figuratively. When I ushered Sarah back out into the living room and got her sitting on the couch, weaving and blinking, Eamon was finishing off a fresh glass of whiskey. 'Ah,' he said with that slow, all-knowing smile. 'I see you're ready.'

'Yes,' I said, and thumped the suitcase down next to the door. 'Where are we going?'

'California,' he said. 'Land of fruits and nuts, they say. You ought to be right at home.'

I thought, somehow, that Sarah would have

looked pleased – after all, pretty much anywhere in California had to be an improvement over the current situation, and she'd talked about living in the same zip code with Mel Gibson. But instead she looked mortified. Scared, even. 'No,' she said. 'No, I don't want to go to California. Jo, why can't we go back to Florida? I liked Florida. It was nice, and—'

Eamon interrupted as if she hadn't even opened her mouth. 'I suppose you could do this from anywhere, but I'd like to actually be there to see it, if you don't mind. Not that I don't trust you, but... well, I don't trust you.'

'Ditto,' I said grimly. 'Oh, and you're not driving, jerk. Give me the keys.'

'But I don't *want* to go to California!' Sarah repeated, half a wail.

'OK,' I said. 'Want to stay here? Alone?'

She looked from me to Eamon, back to me. Eyes wide and still medically dilated.

And she burst into an addict's helpless tears.

'I'll take that as a no,' I said, and got her under the arm to help her up. 'So let's get moving.'

The instant I banged open the rickety front door of the trailer and stepped down onto the cinder-block steps, Louis Vuitton suitcase in hand, I knew something was wrong out there. There was a sense of stillness, of the world not quite breathing. No birds in the sky, no wind. It was the weightless moment before the ground crumbles under your feet, and you fall, screaming.

I froze. Maybe the old me would have known what to do, but the new, not-so-improved me had no earthly idea what the right move might be. I just waited for the hammer to fall.

She's looking for me. I held myself completely still, completely silent, until I felt the shadow drift away. Maybe this was how the rabbit felt when the shadow of the hawk moved overhead. It was humbling and horrifying, and I had no idea how I was supposed to react except that I had a deep, burning desire to get the hell *out. Come on, Venna,* I thought. *If you're not too busy braiding your hair.*

I finally let myself draw in a breath, blinked, and came down the two unstable steps to the soft, sandy ground. It still felt strange, but maybe it was just me. Maybe I was just paranoid.

You're not paranoid. Somebody's out to get you, remember? Several somebodies, maybe, but certainly including that evil doppelgänger back at the clinic. And if the Joanne back at the clinic had her way – somehow I was almost sure she was managing it – she'd have convinced Lewis of her sincerity by now. And, though it turned my stomach to think about it, she might have even fooled David. In which case it wouldn't be her getting her hands dirty, coming after me. She'd have plenty of shock troops available, and all the eyes and ears of the Wardens.

A breath of wind touched me from the west. It blew hair across my eyes, and I reached up to push it away. In the half second of partial vision, something flickered across my line of sight, and was gone.

'David?' I whispered. I felt nothing, and if it was David, he didn't show himself. I don't know why I wanted it to be him; he was trouble, and nothing but. Especially now.

And I still missed him, as stupid and shallow as that might be.

I stalked out the gate, dragging the designer luggage ruthlessly across gravel and sand, and popped the trunk of the black sedan. I heaved the suitcase up to dump it inside, and staggered backward, off balance, in shock. Because the trunk was already occupied.

Dead guy. Dead guy in the luggage area, and recently dead, too. There was very little blood, and just one neat hole in the centre of his forehead and a thin trickle, but I didn't want to examine the exit wound, which was luckily facing away from me.

I didn't recognise him, naturally.

I was still staring at the body, frozen in shock, when Eamon reached over and slammed the trunk lid closed. 'Full up. Suitcase in the backseat,' he said. 'There's a love.'

I dropped the suitcase and backed away from him. He looked surprised. Well, not really surprised, but as if he *wanted* to look surprised. Eamon was a master at putting on emotions like outfits.

'Something wrong?' he asked. 'You're not one to shy away from violence; I know that for a fact.'

'You killed him,' I said. 'Who is he?'

'You don't know?' He studied my face, and I felt naked. Way too exposed. 'I know you're not generally popular with your peers, but I'm surprised you don't at least know the ones who want you dead.'

'This isn't about me. This is about the *dead man in your trunk.*' I was clenching my teeth now, and wishing I had a weapon. A big one. Large-calibre. 'What the hell is going on?'

'No idea,' Eamon said. 'He was waiting for you outside of the prison with a rather nice three-eighty, which would have put a large and bloody hole in your back, shredded your lungs, and blown your heart halfway to hell. I say your back because of where he'd stationed himself. Because of the angle.'

I felt sick, and a little bit relieved. *OK, so it's a bad guy dead in the trunk. That's better, right?* Of course it wasn't, and just because the psychopath went after other villains didn't make him any less of a psychopath, did it? Besides, I had no idea if Eamon was telling the truth. He seemed sincere, but he seemed a lot of things he wasn't – nothing if not facile.

'Oh, don't look so worried,' Eamon said, and opened the back door of the car for Sarah. She moved as if she were missing some bones, folding like wet cardboard when she was finally in the seat. I opened the other side and put her suitcase inside. She promptly used it as a pillow, and went right to sleep. 'I doubt he'll be missed. Contract killers rarely have what you might call an extensive social circle.'

Eamon had brought out a cheap-looking velour blanket. He spread it over Sarah as he spoke. It was an odd gesture of kindness from a guy who thought nothing of loading up the trunk with corpses, and his contradictions were starting to make my head hurt.

'What are you going to do with him?' I asked.

'Let's just say he won't be accompanying us all the way to California,' Eamon replied. 'There's plenty of desert between here and there.'

'Do you know who he is?' I asked.

'Not a fucking clue,' he said, and reached in his pocket. He took out a slim black wallet, which he flipped over the car's roof to me. I caught it, startled. 'Perhaps you'll see something that rings a bell, eh?'

I opened it and checked for ID. There was a driver's license for a guy named John T. Hunter.

I wondered if that was a joke of some kind: *John The Hunter.* Like, assassin. But why would I have a professional assassin on my case? Then again, why wouldn't I? Given the gigantic mountain of nothing that I knew about my life, I supposed I couldn't rule it out.

Other than the license, his wallet was empty except for a fat stash of cash, which I felt sick about taking, but hey, I needed it.

'Well?' Eamon asked, staring at me over the top of the black car. 'His chances of recovery aren't improving, I assure you. So I'd suggest we roll along.'

'What if I just walk away?' I asked. 'What if I go to the police?' I darted a look into the backseat. Sarah slept on peacefully.

'Well, two things will happen. First, you'll be arrested, because of course I'll have to give a statement that *you* shot this poor man and stole his money. Second, your sister will be dead, and it'll look as if you had quite a bit to do with it. Did you know that statistically most murders are committed by a person close to the victim? Shocking.' He said it flatly, without any emphasis, but I believed him. 'All right, even if you've lost your memory, you know exactly who I am and what I can do, because there's ample evidence in the trunk with a bullet in his head. So let's stop dancing around the proprieties and get on with it, shall we? I need your particular talents for one thing and one thing only, and then, as far as I'm concerned, you can go to hell and take Sarah with you. Are we clear?'

His eyes glittered. There was something feral in him, something pushed into a corner. I didn't doubt he'd kill. He was right. The body in the trunk was proof enough of that.

I didn't answer him. I held his stare long enough to promise him a whole lot of things, most of them violent, and then I opened the front driver's-side door, got in, and started the engine. I considered gunning it and leaving him there in the dust, but all he had to do was make a phone call, and I was a wanted felon with a body in the trunk.

Play along. Find an opportunity. Wait for Venna.

It was risky, but it was the only card in my hand at the moment.

Chapter Nine

We buried Mr Hunter, whatever his name might have actually been, in a shallow, sandy grave six miles from Ares, in a stretch of desert that probably hadn't had human visitors for ten years, and wouldn't again for ten more. Eamon and I buried him, that is; Sarah slept on in the backseat, the sleep of the OxyContin-coddled innocent. By the time it was done I felt sick, angry, filthy, and gritty with sweat and sand. I wanted to kill Eamon, in a figurative if not literal sense. He *had*, apparently, saved my life, even though he'd shot someone to do it. Once again, the sticky grey centre with him. I wanted to be able to hate him with a whole heart.

Well, of course, there was the threat against my sister. That helped keep me from doing anything stupid.

We didn't talk, except that he directed me along Highway 95 to 160, where we turned west. He wasn't telling me the final destination.

I hated the car about as much as I hated him.

The pedal was sluggish, the steering was loose, and it shimmied through curves. Looked good on the outside, rotten on the inside, just like Eamon himself.

I didn't draw Eamon's attention to it, but somewhere outside of Pahrump we picked up a tail. Of course, it was hard to be sure – highways by definition had a lot of people travelling the same direction, especially in the boonies – but I did some experimenting with speed, and the white panel van stayed right with me, whether I sped up, changed lanes, or slowed down. He was hanging back, and he was covering up with other traffic, but he was a fixture in my rear-view mirror.

He hadn't been there when we'd dumped the body, though. That had been a clear road for miles, and no chance of being spotted by anything but a high-flying eagle. So if he was hoping to catch us red-handed, literally, he was out of luck. No doubt the trunk would sink us with forensics, if it came to that, and of course I was driving, wasn't I? And Eamon had made sure that my fingerprints had stayed on the wallet, which was safely in his coat pocket. Insurance.

The weather was shifting. I felt it rather than saw it, a sensation like pressure in my head. I tried to focus on it as I drove, and before I knew what I was doing, I was looking at the world through the lenses that David had shown me. Oversight, he and

Lewis had called it. And the world was different when you knew how to interpret the clues.

The car I was driving, in Oversight, was a rust bucket, tainted by indifference. Past the hood, the road glimmered flat black, sparking with little explosions of light – tiny creatures, maybe, living and dying in their own little dramas? – and in the distance the sky was a rolling, strange landscape of greys and blues and orange streaks. More like fluid than air. The orange was pushing its way through. I had no idea if orange indicated heat; if so, that was some kind of warm front, and it was creating all kinds of swirls and eddies and muted flashing chains of energy. Those showed as black streaks, like oil dropped in water.

I'd become so engrossed in the strange view that I'd backed off on speed. Eamon growled in frustration. 'Are we on a sightseeing tour, pet, or do you actually want to *get there*?' he snapped. I jammed the accelerator down and checked the rear-view mirror. It made me light-headed to look at the world this way, but it was weirdly compelling. The van behind me looked like a scarred battlewagon. Whoever was driving that thing had an intimate knowledge of being in the thick of things. I couldn't get more than a shadowy glimpse of the interior.

Sarah sat up and yawned, and I nearly yelped. In Oversight she looked horribly distorted – puffy, sick, surrounded by a flickering black cloud edged in red.

I didn't dare look at Eamon. Some things I just didn't want to know.

I blinked, and the visions were gone. It was just a road, and those were just cars, and in the mirror my sister looked grumpy, tired, and ill. 'I need a bathroom,' she said.

'You'll have to hold it,' Eamon said. 'Nothing out here, love. Nothing but sand and things that sting.'

He wasn't wrong. We'd taken the 372 out of Pahrump, and although there was some traffic, there were no towns. A few clusters of sun-rotted buildings, but nothing that deserved the name of *town*. We'd seen one Nevada state trooper cruising slowly in the opposite direction, but I'd held our speed to just under the legal limit. No sense in tempting fate, when fate included jail time and possibly even a death sentence.

Clouds boiled up in the west by the time we'd crossed the border into California. Sarah had whined periodically about a need for bathroom, water, and food; I felt the same needs, but I knew better than to encourage her. We raided the polyunsaturated goodness of the snack aisle of a Quik Stop on the outskirts of Tecopa, which was more or less the last call for calories, gas, and restroom facilities.

Night closed in early, and with it came rain. Blinding, silvery waves of it, glittering in the car's headlights like a downpour of diamonds. In a strange way it felt comforting. *I've done this before*, I thought. I could sense that, although I couldn't really touch the memory of it. I could sense the energy up there in the sky, feel it rippling through me in ways that I couldn't begin to understand or explain. It was soothing.

Eamon fell asleep. I kept driving.

And the white van stayed in the rear-view mirror all night.

Ever driven all night through a rainstorm?

Tiring.

I stopped the car about dawn, or what would have been dawn if the sun had been able to pierce the cloud cover, and switched places with Eamon. We ate convenience store food, drank stale coffee, and after a while I dropped off to sleep, or at least an uneasy approximation of it, lulled by the steady drum of raindrops on the roof of the car.

I dreamt there was something staring at me from outside of the car window, something that looked like me but wasn't me, something with my smile and eyes as black and empty as space. *I can see you*, she mouthed, and grinned with razor-edged teeth. *You can't run. You don't belong here.* I woke up feeling sick and afraid and lost, and it didn't get any better when reality set in. I *was* sick and afraid and lost. I couldn't trust Eamon. I couldn't trust my sister. And I had no way of contacting anyone who might have had my best interests at heart.

Sometimes you've got to save yourself, I told myself. It didn't make me any less afraid, but I did feel a significant improvement in my ability to keep a stiff upper lip about it.

'Where are we?' I asked. We were in the burbs of a major metropolitan area, and the landscape had definitely changed from flat desert to hilly desert. The rain had stopped, but the weather was still cloudy and – by the feel of my window glass – blood-warm. Eamon, still driving, looked tired and annoyed. Sarah was asleep again. I felt in the pocket of my jeans to be sure I still had possession of her Oxy. She was whimpering quietly to herself – bad dreams or withdrawal, I couldn't be sure.

'Doesn't matter where we are; we're not where we're going,' Eamon snapped. 'Someone's following us.'

No kidding. Well, I hadn't thought he'd miss it. 'White van?'

'Yes.' He glanced at me with hard, shiny eyes like wet pebbles. 'You knew.'

I shrugged and stretched. 'Didn't matter,' I said. 'Right? Plus, I didn't want you solving the problem with a bullet.'

'The first problem I solved for you with a bullet is buried back there in the desert, love, and if I hadn't, we'd be identifying you on a cold steel slab,' he said. I was ominously afraid he was right. 'We need to find out who might have an interest in tailing us. One of your Warden friends, perhaps. Or someone from the police.'

'It's not the police. At least, not official. They wouldn't be following us across state lines. Besides, I think it's probably about you, not me. You don't strike me as the kind of guy who makes a lot of friends, Eamon.'

He evidently found that logic to be slightly persuasive. He even looked a little thoughtful. 'They do tend to have a short shelf life,' he admitted. 'Friends, lovers, relationships of any sort. I've often regretted that.'

Just when I thought it was possible to really work up a decent hate for him, he had to disarm me with self-deprecation. *Dead guy,* I reminded myself. *Shot in the head. Remember who you're talking to.*

'Speaking of short shelf lives,' he continued in a far too casual tone, 'I'm surprised you're not travelling with your beau.'

'Beau,' I repeated. Was he talking about Lewis? David? Somebody else altogether?

'How soon they forget. And I thought it was true love.' Eamon's smile became positively predatory. 'Oh, come now. You *do* remember him, don't you? I wouldn't think amnesia could wipe out *that.*'

'Just because I don't want to talk about it with you doesn't mean I don't remember,' I said hotly. 'Back off.'

'He made quite a production of telling me to stay away from you, once upon a time,' Eamon said. 'I've got the scars to prove it. Thoughtful of him to leave them – although to be fair, he did keep me from bleeding to death. So, shall I worry about your somewhat supernatural boyfriend charging to your rescue?'

'Maybe,' I said, and smiled back at him. One good menacing pseudo-grin deserved another. 'Nervous?'

'Terrified,' he said, in a way that indicated he wasn't. But I wondered. 'What about the girl?'

I stayed quiet. *Girl* covered quite a lot of territory.

'Don't tell me you don't remember your own daughter.'

Imara. He was talking about... How did he know her? What had happened between the two of them? I glared at him, trying to find a way to phrase questions that wouldn't reveal my ignorance, and failing miserably.

'Let's agree to stay off the subject of my personal life,' I said, 'because I swear to God, if you mention either of them again, I'll rip your tongue out and use it for a toilet brush. *Please* tell me we're getting close to wherever it is we're going.'

'Yes,' he said. 'We're getting close.'

'Then explain to me what it is you want me to do.'

'Nothing too terribly exciting,' Eamon said. 'I'd like a building destroyed.'

I gaped at him. Honestly. *Gaped*. He *what?* 'Are you insane?' I asked. 'No, strike that; the answer's pretty obvious. What makes you think I'd do a thing like that?'

'For one thing, you've done it before – and, of course, so have more than a few of the Weather Wardens, for fun and profit. I told you I had a construction investment in Florida – it was more of a construction investment designed to experience catastrophic failure during some natural disaster or other. Florida's quite prone to them, but California...well. It's the mecca for that sort of thing, isn't it?'

'Eamon—'

'It's perfectly simple. I know you can do it without even breaking a sweat. I won't bother threatening your life, Joanne. You've amply demonstrated to me how little your own survival means to you.' Eamon shrugged slightly. 'I'd almost admire that, if I didn't find it ridiculous. Sacrificing your life for others is nothing but a socially accepted version of suicide. It's just as bloody selfish.'

'You're one to talk about selfish,' I said. 'You

want me to *bring down a building*?'

'A small one,' he clarified. 'Hardly the apocalypse you're imagining. Seven stories. An office building.'

'Why?'

'Why is not your business,' he said. 'Suffice to say, money.'

'No. I'm not doing it.'

'I promise you, there will be no casualties. It'll be deserted. No chance of murder hanging heavy on your conscience.' He said it with irony, as if I already had a lot to worry about. Which I was starting to think wasn't far from the truth. 'A small price to pay for your sister's life and ultimate well-being, isn't it? Not to mention your own, as little as that means to you?'

Eamon was almost – *almost* – begging. Interesting. I stared at him for a few seconds, read nothing in him but what he wanted me to read, and turned my attention outward, to the passing cars, the landscape, the weather, as Eamon kept us moving relentlessly onwards. Clouds hovered close. Gray mist swept the tops of hills, and as we passed a small stock pond just off the road, I saw it was giving up wisps of vapour.

It was an eerie sort of mood out there. And I didn't think it was just me.

'Nobody in the building,' I said. 'Right?'

'Cross my heart and hope to fry,' he said.

'There's exactly one security guard. I'll make sure he's off the premises.'

'And how exactly do you expect me to bring down a building without destroying everything around it?'

'You're joking, surely,' he said. 'I don't care, so long as it appears to be a natural phenomenon. A storm, a tornado, freak winds...use your imagination.'

'All of those are going to do more damage than just the one building.' And I wasn't capable of handling that kind of thing, anyway, not that I'd be admitting it to him anytime soon. 'Unless it's an isolated location.'

'Well, if you can't do it, or won't, then I'll have to resort to my alternate plan. Sadly, that involves a quantity of C-4 explosive and a daytime terrorist attack, which will cost lives and no doubt inconvenience everyone in the world for at least a few days. There's a day care facility in the building, I understand. It would be quite the tragedy.'

I blinked. 'You're bluffing.'

'Am I? Can you really be completely sure of that? Because if you're not, love, I'd suggest you weigh your own moral values against the lives of the six hundred people who work in that building during the week. And the fourteen preschoolers who could end up tragic statistics.'

It wasn't possible, was it? He wouldn't really

be willing to bomb a building, especially when it was full of people. Especially with kids inside. My hands ached where I was gripping the dashboard, braced against the tense panic in my stomach. Eamon glanced over at me, but wisely said nothing. He just let me think about it in silence.

Oh, Christ. How was I supposed to know whether he'd do a thing like that or not? I didn't know him. I didn't *remember* him. The best I could do was go by my impressions, and my impression was that Eamon was nobody to screw around with. He *might* do it. And *might*, right now, was more than good enough, given the stakes.

'Pull over,' I said.

'Why?'

'Pull over *now*.'

He did, bumping onto the rough shoulder and activating emergency flashers. I opened the door and stepped out into the humid air, gasping for breath. If he thought I was about to barf all over his leather interior, fine. I just wanted to get away from him for a couple of minutes. His company was toxic.

The wind whipped around me, caressing and cloying. I looked around for the white van, but it hadn't slowed and it hadn't stopped; it blew right by us without a pause, and was receding in the distance.

So much for my paranoid tail theory. And

Eamon's. Unless the driver was very, very good, and had overshot us to pick us up later on the road. It was a good strategy, if he had it in mind; the road was pretty straightforward, and we weren't likely to turn off quite yet.

I heard the crunch of gravel behind me. Eamon had got out of the car.

'Jo,' he said quietly. I stiffened at the sound of my name on his lips. 'Let's do this in a businesslike fashion. It doesn't have to be so ridiculously dramatic. Just do the job, and we're finished, the two of us. I think it would be best for us all.'

He wasn't wrong about that. I fought back a powerful desire to turn and knee him in the balls.

'How much farther?' I asked. I managed to keep most of the fury out of my voice.

'Two hours,' he said. 'Give or take. If it'll make you feel any better I'll let you drive.'

The target building Eamon wanted to destroy was in San Diego, within sight of the ocean. It was built in the shelter of a large ridge, but that wouldn't pose much of a problem. At least, I didn't think it would. Hard to know how difficult this was going to be, when I couldn't remember ever trying anything like it before.

I did some reconnaissance, taking my time, sipping a Mexican mocha from a coffee vendor and enjoying the warm, velvety evening. It was, the outdoor barista told me, unseasonably warm even for SoCal.

Eamon came with me. Not like I could really stop him.

We walked in silence the four square blocks around the building, which was at the outer edge of an industrial park. Its proximity to the beach would make things easy, I sensed. Two floors of it were still under construction, and that would help; any instability would work in my favour.

'Just tell me one thing. Why do you want it done?' I asked Eamon, as we came around the back side of the building. He shot me a glance. 'Insurance money?' I asked.

He looked bored with my questions. 'Can you do it or not?'

'Destroy the building?' I shrugged. 'Probably. But weather's a funny thing. It's not exactly a precision instrument.'

'I don't care about precision. I care about results.' He stared for a second at the building. 'It's a weekend, and I've already made inquiries – there's nobody working today, and the guard's been called away. Building's locked up and unattended for the next six hours. How long will it take?'

I had no earthly idea. I was winging it. 'Two hours,' I said.

'What do you need?'

I waggled the Mexican mocha. 'Another one of

these, and you out of my face.'

He left. I wasn't stupid enough to assume he'd let me out of his sight, and, of course, there was Sarah holding me hostage for good behaviour. I sat down on a boulder on the beach, watching the dark tide roll in. Point Loma Lighthouse glowed not far away, and from somewhere back towards town I heard bells tolling. The night air smelt of sea and rain.

I had an irresistible, self-pitying urge to weep.

'So, are you going to do it?'

Venna's voice. I turned. She was standing just a couple of feet away, perfectly turned out in a sky blue dress, white pinafore apron, white ankle socks, black patent-leather shoes. Straight blonde hair, held back with a blue band. Huge cornflower eyes. Looking absolutely the same as she had back in Las Vegas, when she'd left me.

'Are you going to do it?' she asked me again. 'You know he only wants it done for the money. I didn't think you approved of that.'

'*Now* you show up?'

'Well, I was busy,' she replied. She came and sat down next to me, neat and tidy, hands folded in her lap. The sea air blew her fine blonde hair back over her shoulders, and her black shoes dangled several inches off the sand. 'Why did you leave?'

'Leave?'

'Where I put you,' she said patiently. 'It was a

perfectly nice place. I even checked with other people to be sure it was all right.'

'Did you actually rent the room?'

She looked at me like I'd grown a second head. 'Why would I do that?'

'Because hotels have a funny habit of *renting them out if they're empty*? Like, I got arrested for being a trespasser?'

'Oh.' She contemplated that with a slight frown. 'I can never keep you people's rules straight.'

I gave up. 'Why didn't you just find me and poof me away again?'

'It's dangerous,' she said. 'It could kill you.'

I stared at her, struck dumb for a few seconds. Lewis had told me something about this, but honestly, I'd thought he'd been exaggerating. 'You mean teleporting me out of the hospital could have killed me? And you were going to tell me this when, exactly?'

She seemed offended. 'Most Djinn kill people every time they try it. I do a lot better.'

'Well, that makes all the difference.'

Another largely indifferent shrug. 'You're all right, aren't you? I didn't remember the police would want you, too. It's hard to remember things like that.' She shook her head as if it was amazing anyone would bother with something as trivial as arrests for murder. 'You were supposed to stay. I didn't know you'd leave.'

'I didn't *leave*. I was *arrested*!'

'If you say so.' Alice – Venna – sat there looking for all the world like a surly ten-year-old girl. Maybe twelve. Not a well-developed twelve. 'Are you going to do what he wants? Bring down the building?'

'Not a clue,' I said. 'I guess I'll have to try. He's going to hurt my sister if I don't. Unless—'

'I could kill him.' She meant it. And seriously – I considered it, too.

'No,' I said, reluctantly. 'I don't think so. Besides – and don't take this the wrong way – how do I know you wouldn't just skip off and leave me with a dead guy and no explanation?'

Alice considered that very gravely. 'I suppose you don't really have any reason to trust me,' she acknowledged. 'That's a problem, isn't it? I'm sorry. I'm not used to being mistrusted. It's inconvenient.' Her eyes suddenly focused back on the ocean. 'There's a low pressure system pushing in from Mexico. You can use that. Do you remember how?'

'No.'

She shrugged. 'I can show you. Oh, and I've thought of a reason you should trust me.'

'Do tell.'

'I could kill you anytime I wanted.' It was a cool, measured observation. Creepy in the extreme. 'I'm Djinn. You're really not very important to me. If that's true, why would I lie to you? What would be the point?'

I swallowed hard. 'Maybe you're having fun lying to me.'

'Maybe I am. But I'd have more fun doing something else.' She sighed. 'I can help you with this, though.'

'You can help me destroy the building. Like Eamon wants.'

'Of course,' she said, as though it were about as easy as scuffing over an anthill. Which, for her, might very well be true. 'And then we can kill him.'

Creep. Eeeeee. 'No,' I said. 'No, we won't be killing anybody.'

'Why not?' She looked surprised. 'Don't you want him to go away? He scares you, you know.' Yeah, like that was news to me. She must have read that in my expression, because she looked contrite. 'I'm sorry. I don't do this very often. Talk to people. I'm not doing it very well.'

This was turning into pretty much the ultimate in surrealism, I thought. I was having a conversation with Alice in Wonderland about destroying buildings and killing people, and she was worried about her communication skills. We sat in silence for a few seconds, watching people strolling the beach in the distance. It was getting late, so the place was more or less deserted.

I wondered if Eamon was watching us. Probably. I could almost feel the oily slime of his regard.

Venna turned her attention to the dark, rolling

ocean, and I felt a stronger puff of breeze. 'I can show you what to do,' she said. 'But we need to make the rest of these people go away first.' She was talking about the few hardy souls out strolling the beach in the moonlight. I was going to ask how she planned to do that, but I didn't have to.

The skies opened up, and the rain began to fall like silver knives.

'There,' Venna said, and smiled. 'That's better.'

I should have known that we wouldn't go unnoticed, but somehow I just wasn't prepared for the cops to show up.

Not the actual cops, the handcuffs-and-truncheon patrol; these were the *other* kind. The kind who radiated competence and power, and they showed up after Venna had been demonstrating how to curl the strands of storm one on top of another, building the tightly controlled fury of a tornado.

Two of them. I didn't know them, but they clearly knew me. The smaller one, female and prone to piercings, circled around to face me, while her partner, the tall, dark, and silent type, shadowed Venna. Not that Venna was paying the slightest bit of attention to him.

'Warden Baldwin?' the woman shouted over the wind and pounding surf, and held out her hand, palm out. Lightning flashed, hard and white, and illuminated something like a stylised sun on her palm. 'I need you to cease what you're doing!'

'Hi,' I said. 'I can't do that.'

'Warden, I'm not messing around with you. I know who you are, and there's a warrant out for your detention and return to the headquarters in New York. So, please, let's not make this hard, OK? Nobody has to get hurt!'

I sighed. I felt grimy, tired, and angry. Too much had been taken away from me, and if Venna was right, I was in real jeopardy of losing whatever was left. To a Demon, wearing my face. 'What's your name?' I asked.

'Jamie,' she yelled. 'Jamie Rae King.'

'Weather?'

'Yes, ma'am.' She looked cautious, and she kept flicking looks at her partner. 'That's Stan. He's Earth.'

'Hey, Stan,' I said.

'Hey.' He nodded, and the wet sand suddenly went soft under my feet and dragged me down to my knees, trapping me. 'Sorry, ma'am. But we've got orders.'

Venna, who'd been oblivious to that point, turned to face him, and I saw Stan gulp. I was busy trying to pull my legs out of the sand, but it was no good; the stuff was like cement, set around my feet to hold me in place. He was good at this kind of thing, obviously. 'Stan,' Venna purred. Not a drop of rain had touched her, of course; it just slid off in a silvery curtain about four inches from her body. 'You don't want to do that.'

'No,' he panted. 'Probably don't. But I don't have a lot of choices. You're Djinn, right?'

She didn't answer, but then again, she didn't really have to. She walked up to him, a force of nature packaged in a pinafore, and put her small hand flat on his chest.

She blew him twenty feet. Stan impacted the wet beach, rolled, and flopped to a limp stop. He groaned and tried to get up, but she held up a finger.

One finger.

And he shuddered and went flat.

'Hey!' I yelled at her over the boom of thunder. I was soaked to the skin, shivering, and more than a little scared by the fact that Jamie Rae was standing there looking from me to Venna as if trying to decide which of us to put the smackdown on first. 'Leave him alone!'

'Oh, relax; he's not dead,' Venna said impatiently. 'I didn't break him.' She turned to Jamie Rae. 'You want to stop trying to do that.'

Whatever Jamie was doing – and in the chaos of the storm that was quickly getting worse, I couldn't tell – she kept doing it, because Venna looked frustrated and annoyed, and flicked her fingers in Jamie Rae's direction.

Bang. She went down, coldcocked. I felt bad about that. She and Stan didn't seem like bad types, comparatively speaking.

At least they weren't trying to bring down a building.

'We should hurry,' Venna said, and glanced at the sand where I was buried knee-deep. It let loose, spilling me to my hands and knees, and I climbed out of the resulting hole. 'Focus now. You know what to do?'

I nodded, and followed her into the aetheric. In Oversight the storm was a glittering layered network of tight-spinning forces. I couldn't see Venna clearly, but I could see what she was doing, and it was amazing. My attempts to help were clumsy by comparison; I could see her reaching to slightly alter the magnetic force of one part of the storm, and what that did to the direction and speed of the wind. See it...not necessarily *do* it. Or even control it. But I could feel it coursing through me like a continuous warm pulse, pounding harder and louder with every beat.

It was intoxicating. Freeing. I heard myself laugh, and reached out to touch a glittering chain of molecules. Lightning sparked through the net and flashed in my eyes down in the real world.

It was like playing God. Beautiful and terrifying.

The first lightning strike hit the roof, and the

concussion was so intense at this close range that I went temporarily deaf and blind, and every hair follicle on my body seemed to rise in the electrical aura. When it passed, I barely had time to draw a breath before the next bolt hit steel, and then a third. Hammer of the gods.

When the wind hit the smoking, glowing structure, spinning down in a dark spiral from the low-hanging clouds, the metal just collapsed in on itself like a dropped Tinkertoy model, and the whole beach seemed to vibrate from the impact. Fire licked and hissed as some of the more flammable components caught, but it wasn't likely to spread; the rain was intense, and concentrated right on the worst of it.

Venna hadn't moved. She was smiling slightly, and when she looked at me she said, 'Now you have to balance it.'

'What?' I yelled over the roar of thunder and pounding, wind-driven surf. I stumbled towards her and swiped wet hair back from my face. 'Balance what?'

'The scales,' Venna said. 'Make it all go away, but don't let the energy bleed over into more storms.'

'You mean it's not *over*?'

Venna shook her head. She'd let the funnel cloud dissipate, its purpose completed, and the rain was slacking off from a monsoon to a downpour.

'You'd better hurry,' she said. 'The Wardens will be screwing it up if you don't hurry. They never can get it right.'

I had no idea what she meant, but Venna was notably not helping me. She crossed her arms and stood there, Zen Alice, untouched by the chaos she'd helped unleash.

I turned my attention to the storm.

'The Wardens teach you to do this from science,' she said very softly; I didn't know how it was possible to hear her over the wind, but she came through as if it were a still, silent day. 'Science can fail you. Learn to listen to it. Sing to it. It doesn't have to be your enemy. Even predators can be pets.'

I struggled to make sense out of what I was seeing. So much detail, so much *data*, all in spectra the human eye wasn't meant to see, much less understand. *I can't do this. It's too big. It's too much.*

I took a deep breath, stretched my hands out to either side, and stepped into the heart of the storm.

It *hurt*. Not only physically, though the windblown sand and debris lashed at me like a dozen whips. It got inside my head, and howled, and I flailed blindly for something I could touch, could control, could stop...

And then, when I opened my eyes on the aetheric, it all made sense. The swirling chaos became a shifting puzzle of infinite intricacy, and where the pieces met, sparks hissed through the dark, bright as New Year's fireworks lighting the sky. I reached out and moved two of the pieces apart; the spark leapt and died in midair. I tried it again and again, until the grand, gorgeous pattern of the air was whisper-quiet, glowing in peaceful shifting colours.

When I blinked and fell back into the real world, I could see the stars.

Venna gave a very quiet sigh. 'Yes,' she said. 'Exactly like that. Now you are Ma'at.'

So now I was guilty of some kind of supernatural sabotage, at the very least, but I figured it probably boiled down to plain old insurance fraud. Something simple and skanky, something with an immediate financial benefit for Eamon, of course.

But hey, at least I'd learnt a useful skill.

'Astonishing,' Eamon murmured, looking at the wreckage and all of the emergency crews swarming around the scene in the predawn light. We were sitting on the low rock wall – Eamon, Venna, me, and Sarah, with the two Wardens asleep behind the rocks, held in that state by Venna. I didn't think Eamon could see Venna at all, because he hadn't asked about her, and she didn't exactly fit in.

Didn't seem prudent to mention her.

'Complete destruction,' Eamon said, and seemed utterly satisfied. 'You are a one-woman wrecking crew, love.'

'Thanks,' I said with an ice edge of chill. 'We done now?'

'Done?' His eyes were preoccupied, and it took him a second to pull his attention away from the human aftermath on the beach to focus on me completely. 'Ah, yes. I did say that I wanted only this one thing from you, didn't I?'

Bad feeling bad feeling bad feeling. 'That's what you said.'

'I don't think that will be possible after all,' Eamon said, and smiled just a bit. Just enough to keep me from killing him. 'This is the start of a beautiful and very profitable relationship, Jo. After I marry your sister—'

'After you *what*?' I blurted. 'Time-out! Nobody's getting married. Especially not to *you*.'

Sarah didn't even look up to meet my fierce stare. Haggard and strung out, but my sister, dammit. My family. 'You can't tell me what to do,' she said.

'Sarah, wake up! He's a criminal! And he's a *murderer*!'

'Yeah, well, what about you?' she flung back. 'You think you're not guilty of things? You think you aren't just as bad? Don't you dare lecture me!'

'Keep your voice down!'

'Or what? You'll call the cops? Go right ahead, Jo; they're right over there!'

Sure enough, two uniformed cops standing next

to their cruiser were looking in our direction. I swallowed and tried to moderate my own voice to something in the range of reasonable. 'Sarah, you do not want to jump into this. Really. You don't know this man. You don't know what he's capable of doing.'

Eamon took her hand. His long, lovely fingers curled around hers, and then he kissed her fingers, staring at me with bright, challenging eyes the whole time. 'She's not jumping into anything,' he murmured. 'And really, Joanne, you're making far too big an issue out of this. I only want to make her happy.'

'You want to use her,' I said. 'You want to threaten her to get me to do whatever you want. Trust *you* to find a way to make money off of disaster.'

He made a *tsk*ing sound. 'Construction companies, insurance companies, cleanup crews, police, fire, ambulance, paramedics, hospitals, doctors, funeral parlours, coffin makers...all those people make money off of disaster. And thousands more. I'm merely a novice.'

'You want to *cause* them!'

'Don't be so negative,' he said. 'Freak accidents happen. No reason not to arrange them to our benefit once in a while.'

Venna hadn't moved. She continued sitting on the wall, neat and prim, kicking her black patent-leather shoes like a kid, watching the emergency crews with every evidence of total fascination. I shot her an exasperated look. 'Help me out here.'

'It's human stuff. I can't,' she said serenely. 'Besides, they can't see or hear me. I'm a figment of your imagination, Joanne.'

Hardly. My imagination would have conjured up a hunky, half-naked guy Djinn, preferably one who looked like David. I glared at her.

'Do you want me to kill him?' Venna asked, and met my eyes. It was a shock, seeing the complete flat disinterest in them. 'I can, you know. I can kill anyone I want. Any human, anyway. Then you don't have to worry about him anymore. I could make it fast. He wouldn't even feel it.'

I stared at her for a long, silent second, and then shook my head. No, I wasn't prepared to do that. Not even to Eamon.

Venna sighed again, jumped down off the wall, and looked up into my face. 'It's been long enough,' she said. 'We should think about going now. Do you want their memories before we go?'

'Do I...what?' I was aware it looked to Eamon and Sarah like I was talking to empty child-sized space, because they were exchanging a look. The she's-lost-her-mind kind of look.

'Like what you did before, although you didn't do it very well,' Venna said. 'I can take their memories and give them to you. If you want. But you may not like it. Decide now, because we can't stay here much longer.'

Memories. Sarah was the key to a lot of my childhood, wasn't she? Who else would I get that kind of thing from?

I nodded.

'Oh, you don't want hers,' Venna said. 'Hers won't be very good for you. You want *his*.'

Venna didn't even bother touching me. She just turned those incandescent blue eyes on Eamon, and I was sucked into a different world.

Chapter Ten

Eamon was thinking about murder, in an abstract kind of way. He had no real objection to killing, but he did dislike complications, and he was, at that moment, royally pissed about just how complicated a perfectly simple scheme had become.

'All you had to do was pay her off,' he said, staring at his business associate. Thomas Orenthal Quinn – Orry to his less than savoury friends – shrugged. They were sitting at a café near the Las Vegas Strip, surrounded by noise and colour, an island of calm in a sea of frantic activity. Eamon was sipping tea. Whatever Orry was drinking, it wasn't quite that English.

'Look at it this way,' Orry said, and stirred the thick, dark drink in front of him. 'She was badass enough to kill poor old Chaz. You should've seen what was left of him; Christ, it was disgusting. I couldn't take the chance she might come back for more. Dead is simple, right?'

'Generally,' Eamon agreed. 'Dead Wardens, not

so simple. They'll investigate. I don't want them finding any link to you, forensically or otherwise.' He glanced around – habit – although he was certain nobody was within earshot. Amazing what people would ignore. 'You're sure she's out of the picture?'

'I'm sure.' Orry gave him a tight, unpleasant smile. He was a nondescript man, and few who met him seemed to understand what lay underneath that unremarkable exterior. Eamon knew, and respected it. He might have been insane, but he was definitely not insane enough to cross Thomas Quinn without cause. 'Unless she can breathe underwater, she's not bothering us again.'

'You need to be sure.'

Orry shrugged. 'Let's go. I'll show you.'

I felt that slippery fast-forward sensation, and fought to hold on to the memory. Eamon's filthy, cold mind made me shiver, but at the same time it was real, it was *life*, and I wanted more.

Even though I felt a sick sensation of dread at what he was heading towards on this particular trip down memory lane.

I watched as Eamon and Orry drove into the desert, taking unfamiliar roads deeper into the wilderness. When Orry finally pulled the car off the road, Eamon was bored, thirsty, and regretting the idea, but he followed Orry up the hill and into the darkness of a cave.

It stank, but it wasn't the stink of decomposition. Orry switched on a flashlight and led him through a series of narrow passages. Boxes stacked against the wall – *Product*, Eamon thought, and made a mental note to move it when this was done. It was a filthy place to store anything. He heard a cold chatter of bats overhead, and thought again about murder. Orry, dead, would solve so many of his issues.

'Fuck,' Orry said tonelessly. His flashlight played over a milky pool of water, its surface placid and undisturbed. 'She was right here. Right here.'

Eamon hated being right. 'And you were certain she was dead.'

'Yeah. Christ, I strangled her before I drowned her. What is she, a goddamn superhero?'

If she was, Eamon thought, they were in for a great deal of trouble. 'Anything else?'

'Such as?' Orry was poker-faced, but Eamon knew his weaknesses too well.

'Have a little fun before you did her in? Or tried?'

Orry didn't answer, which was answer enough. *Perfect*, Eamon thought in disgust. *Probably DNA evidence as well.* 'Did she see you? See your face?'

'No.'

'You're certain.'

'Yes, dammit, I'm sure. She can't identify me.'

'Even if that's so, we have very little time,' Eamon said. 'We need to clear everything out and clean up as much of the forensic evidence as possible, in case she's able to lead them back here.'

'Eamon...' Orry turned towards him, looking at him oddly. It took Eamon a second to realise that it was an expression of apology. 'I really thought she was dead.'

Murder would be *such* an easy answer. But in all his travels, Eamon had met only two other people in the world who could match him for ferocity and ruthlessness, and it would be a shame to lose a partner over something so essentially trivial. If she couldn't identify him, they could simply avoid the entire issue.

Still. Killing Orry sounded very tempting, and for an unblinking moment Eamon imagined how he'd do it. The knife concealed in his jacket, most likely, driven up under the ribs and twisted. Fast, relatively painless, not a huge amount of blood. Or he could snap his neck, though Orry was a wiry bastard and, as a cop, fully trained to prevent harm to himself.

No, the knife was better, far better.

'You going to stare at me or move the fucking boxes?' Orry snapped. 'I've got things to do.'

Eamon smiled slightly. 'By all means,' he said. 'Let's move boxes. It's easier than moving bodies.'

Blur. This time we jumped years.

Eamon, in a car, parked outside of an apartment building. Watching someone with field glasses.

As with Cherise, I could feel what he was feeling. Unlike Cherise, what Eamon was feeling was completely alien to me.

I didn't know people *could* feel that way. Dark, cold, detached. Mildly annoyed at the inconveniences.

He was thinking about ways to hurt the woman he was watching. I didn't want to see any of that, but Venna wasn't discriminating; if it was in Eamon's head, it spread into mine like a sick, fatal virus.

Eamon was not a normal man. Not at all.

The woman he was watching, visible through the open sliding door of her apartment balcony, turned, sipping a glass of wine. Red wine.

It was me.

Pretty enough, he was thinking. *She'd do, for a while*. He liked fair skin. Fair skin showed bruises better.

It took me a breathless moment to realise that however sick I might feel about what he was thinking, Eamon didn't plan to carry out any of his fantasies. They were just entertainment for him, a cold way to amuse himself during a boring job.

'You're sure she's the one,' he said, and I realised there was someone sitting in the passenger seat of the car next to him. A matronly woman, middle-aged, with a nice face and quick, friendly smile. 'She's the one who killed Quinn in Las Vegas.'

The woman shrugged. 'That's what they say. Doesn't look too likely to me; just look at her. Not exactly Quinn's level, is she?'

'Looks can be deceptive,' Eamon said, and lowered the glasses. 'You're sure Quinn's dead.'

'As sure as I can be,' the woman said. 'Cops found his SUV blown all to hell out in the middle of nowhere, no sign of Quinn's body, but they found a lot of blood. Too much for him to have survived. They figure coyotes scavenged his corpse, or else the flood got it. There was a storm around that time, a real gully-washer. Could have carried his body for miles if he fell into the arroyo. Anyway, he's dead for sure if he didn't contact me by now. I'm holding some stuff for him.'

'Anything good?' Eamon asked, and looked through the field glasses again. Not-me looked polished and glossy, tanned and toned. Contemplative, as she gazed out over the horizon. She had an ocean view, apparently. Nice.

'A package from our friend Mr Velez. Nothing too unusual this time. I was thinking of moving it through the East Coast channels, unless you had a better idea.'

'No, Cynthia, that's fine. You do as you think best.' Eamon stretched, sighed, and put the glasses down. 'She's one of them, though. You're certain.'

'She's one of them,' the unknown Cynthia said. 'I'd stake my life on it.'

Eamon started the car. 'You are staking your life on it, love.'

Joanne Baldwin was, Eamon knew, the one Quinn had failed to kill all those years ago in the cave. How very interesting that it would come to this.

Blood would tell.

Blur.

Eamon with my sister. Eamon gaining my trust and betraying it in the most shocking way. I couldn't possibly have hated anyone more after I saw what he was up to, but the betrayals just kept on coming.

Mine, as well as his.

Eamon trading me Sarah for what he supposed was a Djinn bottle – which it was, just a booby-trapped one that let loose an insane Djinn who couldn't be controlled. Eamon fighting his way through a terrifying hurricane to cut me and Sarah loose from a tree, where the wind and debris would have killed us in a matter of minutes.

Eamon running away with my sister. And Sarah *wanted to go.*

Eamon coming back to me afterward, threatening Sarah again, but realising that he'd lost his leverage. Not giving up, though. He was nothing if not persistent.

Imara was in the memories, too. Helping me.

Guarding me. Terrified for me, as Eamon calculated how far he could push me – and her – to get what he wanted.

And David. *That* memory was crystal clear in Eamon's mind. David had come out of nowhere, *nowhere*, picked up a fallen knife, and – *The second you disappoint me, little man, the instant I think that you're mocking me or even thinking about harm to my family that ends. I watch you bleed your life away in less than a dozen heartbeats.*

We'd left him, the three of us – mother, father, child. We'd been a family once. And David had loved us both with such intensity that it burnt through to even a self-absorbed predator like Eamon.

Eamon respected him. And he liked me – in the same way he'd once liked Thomas Orenthal Quinn.

That turned my stomach.

What was worse, far worse, was that even as sick and horrifying as Eamon was, as far from human as I thought he was, when I looked at him with that dizzying rush of power, when his body dissolved into multilayered lights and networks of flowing energy, he was beautiful. Unique and beautiful and impossible not to somehow love for his damage and his brilliance and his fierce, unflinching intelligence...

I couldn't help but go back for more. So many memories, every colour, every flavour filling my empty spaces. His memories weren't like Marion's; hers had been astringent, like dry white wine. Eamon's were red, blood-red, thick and salty and choking in their intensity. Horrors and wonders. Things that even in that state I tried not to see.

Venna yanked me out with her hand on the back of my neck, and her eyes were wide and very strange. The world lurched around me, tilted, and Eamon slid bonelessly off of the wall to collapse in a heap. Sarah cried out and knelt beside him.

'Oh,' Venna whispered. She didn't spare any attention for Eamon, but she stared holes through me. 'I didn't know you could do that. You shouldn't have, you know.'

When Venna let me go I staggered off, fighting nausea, not fighting tears. I needed a shower, a wire scrub brush, and bleach to feel clean again. *Oh, God.*

I found myself sitting limply in the sand, tinted with flashing red and blue lights. Shaking.

'Jo?' It was Sarah, looking so much older and harder than in the memories. He'd had her for only a few months, right? And already she was destroying herself. 'Eamon passed out. I think he's sick, but he's breathing, would you please—'

I reached out to her and grabbed hold and hugged her. Hard. I dragged her down to a kneeling position. 'I had a daughter,' I said. My voice didn't sound at all right. 'I had a daughter and she's gone,

Sarah, she's gone...' More than anything else in Eamon's memories, seeing Imara had hurt me. A sound welled up out of me, a helpless tearing sound, and I couldn't stop shaking. Sarah held on somehow. My sister. Selfish, shallow, wilfully deluded...but deep inside, still my sister.

'Oh, Jo,' she said, and kissed my hair. 'I'm sorry. You mean Imara? Something happened to Imara?'

'Something...' I didn't even know the details. I hoped I wouldn't. 'She's gone.'

Sarah hugged me again, harder. 'I'm so sorry. She wasn't...well, she wasn't human, but she was sweet. Like the best parts of you. She...she tried to keep me safe, like you told her, but I wasn't... I didn't want to be safe. I sent her away.' I felt her hitch a damp, unsteady breath. 'Oh, God. Was it because I did that? Did she get hurt because of that?'

'I...don't know,' I said slowly. *God.* That couldn't be true, could it? That somehow my own sister had been a part of... No. I couldn't think that way.

'Sarah,' I said, and pulled back to stare into her eyes. 'You need to listen to me. Just this once. Promise?'

She nodded. I took in a deep breath.

'Eamon will hurt you,' I said. 'He's toxic. Maybe he doesn't mean to hurt you, I don't know, but he won't be able to help it. It's what he does.

He can't do anything else. You need to walk away from him, and stay away. Get clean. Find out who you are without him or me or anyone else.'

She tried to pull away, but I held her where she was. 'Sarah,' I said. 'I'm not kidding. *You have to leave.*'

Her eyes filled up with tears. 'I know,' she said. 'I know all that's true. But I love him.'

'He used you to get me to do this,' I said, and nodded at the wrecked building. 'Nobody got hurt this time. What happens next time? What happens when he has cash sunk into some hotel or resort or something, and he wants a nice big tsunami to wash it away? How many people do you think he'll kill who stand between him and a payday? You say you love him, Sarah, but do you love him that much?'

The tears spilt over.

'I want you to go,' I said. 'Get in the car and go. It doesn't matter where, just away, and don't call him. Don't contact him. Do you have any money?'

She nodded numbly. There were more tears where the first ones came from. 'There's a suitcase in the trunk,' she said. 'It has cash in it. He doesn't think I know about it.'

I'd expected that. Eamon wouldn't go anywhere without an emergency flight kit. He was too good a criminal. 'Are there drugs in it?' She didn't answer, which was as good as a yes. 'Sarah, I want you to promise me that you'll stop. Take the drugs and pills and flush them. Will you?' I played the only card I had, the guilt card. 'For Imara, if you won't do it for yourself?'

She just stared at me, face gone blank and lifeless with fear and uncertainty. And then she said, 'He'll come after me. Jo, I can't say no to him. I just can't.'

'You'll have to learn.'

'But—'

'Just go.'

Venna turned and watched my sister staggering away. She put her hands primly behind her back and rocked back and forth. 'Do you still want her memories?' she asked.

'No.' An image of something from Eamon's filthy, diseased brain rose up in my head, and I almost gagged. I didn't want to live that nightmare from my sister's point of view, too. 'You were right. I've seen enough for now.'

Venna shrugged and turned towards Eamon, who was stirring where he sat slumped against the rock wall. He didn't look like a monster. He looked like a nice enough man, attractive if you went in for the lean and hungry look with a bit of scruff thrown in. He'd taken in my sister. He'd even taken me in, for a while, until he wanted me to know his real self.

He was waking up, and I didn't know if I could face him again.

'Venna,' I said in a normal tone of voice, and set my feet in the sand. 'Does he have the keys to the car?'

'Yes.'

'Can you get them?'

She extended her hand, and a set of keys appeared in her tiny palm.

'Can you give them to Sarah?'

She didn't even have to move to do it, just shrugged and the keys faded out and disappeared. A few seconds later I heard the black car start up with a rumble.

I didn't turn to watch. I didn't take my eyes off of Eamon as he moaned, clutched his head, and staggered to his feet. He looked quite mad. His eyes were fiercely bloodshot, and there were trickles of blood coming from his nostrils. I'd done that to him.

The sound of the car faded into the distance before he managed to straighten up. Sarah was gone.

Now it was just the three of us.

Well, two of us, because without warning Venna skipped away, kicking at the sand in her patent-leather shoes, just like a regular kid. I wasn't dumb enough to think it made any difference in the amount of concentration she had on the situation.

Eamon sniffed, wiped at the blood on his face, and glared at me. 'What the hell did you do to me?' he growled.

'You'll be all right.' I had no idea if he would or not, actually, but right at the moment if his brain exploded like a pumpkin in a microwave, I couldn't really care less. 'Don't.'

He took a couple of steps in my direction. His body language was attack-dog stiff.

'*Stop.*'

'Where's Sarah?' he spat at me, all Cockney edges and sharp angles, and I held out my hand towards him, palm out.

A wall of wind hit him and shoved him back, hard. Knocked him on his ass.

He got up and lunged. I knocked him back again, and this time he took out a knife.

'Oh, come on, Eamon, look around!' I said, and jerked my head at the police cars, the firefighters, the onlookers all still staring at the wrecked building. The news crews. 'You really want to do this? Here?'

'*Where is she?*' he yelled, and paced from side to side. His eyes were almost crimson from the burst blood vessels, and the expression in them was just one breath away from complete insanity. He held the knife concealed at his side, but he was clearly on the verge of violence. 'You stupid, interfering *bitch*. Do you think you're saving her? She'll kill herself! She's already tried! I'm trying to save her!'

'You're the reason she's dying inside,' I said. 'And damned if I'm going to let you do that to her. Sarah's strong. She'll be fine.'

'*She won't*! For Christ's sake, woman, who do you think your sister is, exactly? She's not some helpless, stupid waif! Her ex-husband didn't get wealthy by keeping his hands clean, and she was neck-deep in it, too. Taking up with me wasn't a sign of her weakness; it was a sign she recognised an opportunity, that's all. You think I don't *know* that's wrong? *I know what I am!*' I didn't want to buy it, but there was an undeniable desperation to what he was saying. 'I did this for *her*!'

I blinked. 'What?' I hadn't got that far in his memories before Venna had yanked me out. Eamon made a raw sound of frustration.

'The building, you twit! *Sarah owns it!* She'll be making a fortune from the insurance. This was her idea, you bloody fool.'

I didn't believe him. I couldn't. Not...not that. 'You're a lying, crazy bastard.'

'No, I'm a *fool*. So are you. She used you.'

'You're a liar. Sarah had nothing to do with any of it.' I was shaking, I was so angry. 'I told her to go ahead and spend your suitcase full of money. That's for being an asshole, Eamon.'

Something flashed in his expression, and I braced myself. 'Just one problem, love,' he said. 'I don't *have* a suitcase of money. Sarah does, and she got it by selling you far, far down the river. She's driving off with cash and a car, and leaving the two of us to finish each other. Not bad for a helpless little drug-addled waif, eh?'

I felt stunned, and a little sick. *The hit man*, I thought. *The hit man who'd been waiting outside the jail.* Was that possible? Would she really sell my life like that? For *money*?

Eamon took another step towards me, and I snapped my attention back to the present. 'Put down the knife, Eamon.'

He looked at it, turning it in his long, sensitive fingers like he'd never seen it before. 'Ah,' he said. 'But that would mean I wouldn't have any fun at all. And I'd so hate to disappoint dear Sarah by not living down to her expectations. She does need to understand that there are limits to my patience, and you're just the way to show her.'

And he lunged for me, knife out.

I blew him backward, and I didn't even know how I'd done it, except that I'd reached for *something*, and *something* had responded.

I didn't blow him far, and he snarled, and he came back for me, and I knew if he came within slashing distance my ass was dead.

So I made the sand melt under his feet, like the Wardens had done to me when they'd been trying to trap me, and Eamon plunged without a sound below the surface.

Venna, who'd been ignoring me through all this, whirled around, lips parted, eyes blazing. 'Look at you,' she said. '*Look at you*. So pretty. So bright. So *strange*.'

I had no idea what she was talking about, because I was trying to figure out what I'd *done*. I'd meant to trap Eamon's legs, the way I'd been restrained, but instead... Where the hell was he? 'Eamon?' I asked, and took a step forward. 'Eamon, are you all right?'

The sand eroded under my feet. I yelped and jumped back.

Whatever I'd done, it was still spreading.

The sand sagged where I was standing, and I continued a slow, uncertain retreat. 'Um...Venna? What's happening?'

She was still staring at me, with a light in her eyes that was creepily close to rapture. 'It's you,' she said. 'You're happening.'

'*Not helpful!*' I tried to figure out how to make sand sticky again. That seemed to be not quite as instinctual as making it slippery and talcum powdery. 'How do I stop this?'

'Let him die,' she said. 'It's the best thing, really.'

And she skipped away.

What the hell...?

I had bigger issues: Namely, I was killing a guy, probably, and whatever chain reaction I'd set in motion looked likely to collapse the entire beach, the cliff, maybe the whole California coastline before I could get it under control. And I had no idea what I was doing.

But somebody did.

I circled around the spreading pit of quicksand and vaulted over the low rocks. Jamie Rae and Stan, my friendly neighbourhood Warden cops, were stretched out on the sand, carefully arranged to look like they were napping. Jamie Rae murmured something in her sleep and burrowed closer to Stan. Cosy.

'Hey!' I said, and grabbed Stan's arm, hauling him up. His eyes tried to open, then fluttered shut. He wasn't quite deadweight, but damn close. 'Stan, wake up. *Wake up!* Warden emergency! Yo!'

I slapped him. That made his eyelids flutter some more, and when I went to hit him again he clumsily parried. My third attempt was met with a fairly precise interception, and Stan finally focused on me.

'You,' he mumbled. He sounded drugged and loopy. *Great.* Just what I didn't need. 'Thought you were going to kill us. Dangerous.'

'Yeah, well, you're right about the dangerous part,' I said. 'Hurry.'

I dragged him to his feet, leaving Jamie Rae to whimper in dreamy frustration at the loss of his warm, solid body, and pulled him around the rocks. It had been less than a minute, but the sinkhole was growing. Fast. It was already at least ten feet in diameter, and as I watched, part of the rock wall sagged with a groaning sound.

'Oh, crap,' Stan said. 'What did you do?'

'Hell if I know. Do something!'

He tried. I could feel the surges of energy radiating out of him, plunging deep into the earth. Trying to reinforce the erosion. Trying to stop what was spreading like some virulent plague through the beach.

'There's a guy in there!' I said, and pointed at the centre of the depression. 'Can you get him out?'

Stan cast me a wordless look of horror.

'Please?' I asked, because even if it was Eamon, there was something far too horrible about choking to death in a pit of talcum powder. Maybe he deserved it. No, I'd been in his head – I *knew* he deserved it – but I didn't want to be the one dispensing justice.

'I'll need your help,' he said. 'Just relax. I'll show you.' He put a hand on the back of my neck, and through the connection I felt something warm moving through my body. I remembered what it had felt like when Lewis had healed me – not too different. I held still for it, tried to relax as instructed, and concentrated all my energy on the idea of saving Eamon's life.

The pit of sand rolled, as if a miniature fault line had shifted beneath it, and began to fill in, or rise up – it was hard to identify what was happening. But it was happening quietly. Nobody on the beach, not even the news crews, had paid any attention to us so far.

That changed when Eamon emerged from the sand, a limp body lying curled in on himself and flour white with fine dust. His eyes were tightly shut.

He wasn't breathing.

I exchanged a quick glance with Stan; he let go of me and nodded, as if he understood what I intended to do. I stepped out onto the treacherous sand. It shifted – more than it should have – more like tiny balls of slick ice than gritty grains. I fought for balance, windmilling my arms like a tightrope walker, and slowly moved forward. My shoes kept sinking – not enough to stop me, but enough to make me sweat. Stan hadn't fixed things so much as temporarily stopped their disintegration, and I wasn't at all sure how long he could hold on. A look over my shoulder told me that he was sweating bullets and trembling – not exactly a vote of confidence. 'Hurry?' he not quite begged. I took a deep breath and crossed in four quick, sinking steps to Eamon, grabbed him by the shoulders, and started dragging.

One problem. With every backward step my feet went deeper into the sand. 'Stan!' I snapped. I took a firmer grip under Eamon's limp arms and heaved hard, fighting my way through the rapidly softening sand. *'Hold it together!'*

Which wasn't really fair. It wasn't his fault in the first place; he was just trying to clean up my mess. But right at the moment the price of failure would be a little out of my budget.

The news crews were paying attention now, running towards us with lights and cameras, shouting questions. That drew the attention of some firefighters and cops.

The term *media circus* doesn't really do justice to that moment when the clowns start rolling out of the tiny little car, does it?

Chapter Eleven

Luckily I didn't have to decide whether or not I had the ethical strength to give Eamon the kiss of life. After the firefighters formed a human chain and pulled us out of the mysteriously formed pit of dry quicksand, the paramedics pounced, did some paramedic-y things, and got him breathing, choking, and swearing again. He looked like he'd taken a bath in flour – dusty white except for his bloodshot, furious eyes and the blood caking his mouth and nose. He started raving, but he shut up quickly enough when he realised our little feud was no longer private.

Stan was sweating bullets. I stood next to him, shaking a little myself, as the cops formed a cordon around the sinkhole and the news crews swarmed in frustration near the barrier, camera lenses and microphones pointed our way.

'Oh, man, this is bad,' Stan whispered.

'You've got some kind of system for handling these things, right? Right? This can't be the first time in the history of the Wardens that people saw something happen...'

'Well, it's the first time for *me*!' he shot back. 'Jesus, I'm not even allowed out on my own yet. I'm still on probation! I'm not equipped to handle this!'

'And you think I am?'

'Well...you're the most senior, right?' He looked puppy-dog hopeful.

We didn't have time to do any more plotting; one of the cops – a detective in civilian clothes with a badge hung on his shirt pocket – came over and herded us away, behind a crime scene van parked a little way down the beach. 'Names?' he barked. He looked more stressed than me and Stan put together.

Oh, crap. I was supposed to be out on bail in Nevada, and I was pretty sure it was a violation to be out here in California...and maybe there was more that I didn't remember that could jump up and bite me when he entered my name in the system. So I gave him my best, shiniest smile and said, 'Jo Monaghan.' Where it came from, I have no idea. He wrote it down and pointed a pen at Stan, who said, 'Stanley Waterman.'

Waterman? For an Earth Warden? Funny.

'ID,' the cop demanded. Man of few words. I was about to fumble around for an excuse when I felt a tug on my sleeve and looked down to see Venna.

Kind of Venna, anyway. Not blonde Alice in Wonderland anymore; she'd ditched the telltale blue dress and pinafore in favour of blue jeans and a cute pink shirt with kittens on the front. 'Mommy?' she said, and held up a purse. 'You dropped it.'

I blinked at her, trying to take it all in, and smiled. 'Thank you, honey,' I said, and accepted the purse as naturally as I could, under the circumstances, I glanced at the cop; he was smiling at Venna, so evidently she'd gone with a total-reality appearance this time. The purse was Kate Spade, and not a knockoff, either; Venna's little joke, I guessed. Inside, there were a few random things that she must have thought I'd need, like a travel-sized deodorant (trying to tell me something, Venna?), a small bottle of hand cream, a compact black shape that it took me a few seconds to recognise...

A Taser. She'd handed me a purse with a Taser in it.

I shot her a look. She kept smiling at me in sunny innocence.

The wallet was red faux alligator. I opened it, and there was a California driver's license in the name of Jo Monaghan, with my wide-eyed mug shot picture next to it. Unflatteringly realistic. I passed the plastic-coated card over, and the cop inspected it for a few seconds, noted down the address that appeared on the card – I wondered whose address it was – and then gave it back. Stan had produced his own ID. The cop followed the same process. Not a chatterbox, this guy. He hadn't even offered his name.

'OK,' he finally said, and looked at each of us in turn. 'Somebody start talking.'

Stan looked at me with mute desperation on his face. I controlled the urge to thwack him on the back of the head, and summoned as much charm as I could. (Not a lot. It had been a long day.) 'I don't know what we can tell you, sir. My daughter and I were just walking on the beach – we saw the lights and sirens, and we thought we'd take a look.'

'Your address isn't anywhere near the beach.'

Venna looked chagrined. Of course, a Djinn wouldn't think about things like that.

'No,' I agreed. 'We were out sightseeing, and I didn't realise how late it had become. We were still driving around when the storm hit. Some storm, huh?'

The detective grunted. 'So after that you decided to come looky-loo?'

'Yes.' I pointed at the rock wall, dangerously sagging now. 'We were sitting there on the rock wall, with a couple of other people – I didn't know them. There was a British man; I think he might have been a little...' I made the international symbol for crazy at my temple. 'He was rambling, you know? And he sounded really angry. I was

going to take my daughter home when he got up
and ran out there and started yelling. He started to
come back at us, and he started sinking.'

The knife, I remembered, just as the detective
turned his chilly X-ray eyes on me and said,
'Somebody said he had a knife.'

'Oh,' I said faintly. 'Did he? Oh, my God.'

'Any reason this man might want to hurt you?'

I shook my head. Venna shook hers, too.

'So when he started sinking, you...what? Tried
to save him?'

It didn't take a lot of work to look guilty. 'Not
right at first. I was afraid,' I said. 'I ran for help. I
found this guy' – I nodded at Stan – 'and he came
with me. We managed to pull the other man out,
but—'

'Yeah, yeah, I know the rest,' the cop said. 'So
you, Waterman, you never saw Miz Monaghan
before?'

'Never saw her before today,' Stan said. He
sounded utterly confident on that score. 'She saved
his life, though.'

The detective was looking faintly disappointed
with the whole thing. 'Either of you here when the
building came down? See anything either before or
after I should know about?'

'Wasn't it an earthquake?' I asked, and tried to
sound anxious about it. 'The building collapsing, I
mean? It wasn't bombs or anything?'

'We're still looking, but yeah, so far it looks like bad luck and bad weather. Still, we like to ask.' He demanded phone numbers. I made Stan go first, then made mine up, hoping that his area code would work for mine as well. It must have, because the detective snapped his notebook shut. 'OK, I've got your statements. If anything comes up that I need clarification about, I'll call.' He unbent enough to give Venna another smile. 'Better get the kid home,' he told me. Venna looked up with a grave expression, and I wondered just how funny she was finding all this. Hilarious, I was willing to bet. The Djinn seemed to have a very strange sense of humour.

I had no car. I was about to say something to Stan about that, but Venna shook her head minutely, pulled on my hand, and led me across the sand in the opposite direction from where all the crazy news media was gathered. Stan trotted to keep up. 'Hey!' he said. 'You can't leave!'

'Bet I can,' I said. 'Bet you can't stop me, Stanley. In fact, I'll bet you don't even want to try.'

'What about Jamie Rae?' he challenged, and got in my way. Venna looked like she might be tempted to say or do something; I squeezed her hand in warning. 'What am I supposed to tell the Wardens?'

'Tell them you were overmatched,' Venna said sweetly. 'They'll believe that.' She smiled. I was glad I wasn't on the receiving end of that particular expression. 'Your friend is waking up,' she said. 'You'd better go get her and leave now.'

'But...the sinkhole...'

'You stopped it from growing,' she said. 'Someone else will fix it. We have to go now.'

'But...the newspeople – they'll have tape!'

'Then I suppose the Wardens will have to handle that,' Venna said serenely. 'I can't be bothered. Move.'

He did, skipping out of her way as she advanced. I trailed along, shrugging to indicate that I didn't have much choice, either; I was pretty sure Stan believed it. There was a hill beyond him, and we trudged up, avoiding the scrub brush and sharp-edged grasses. Stan didn't follow. He stood there, hands on his hips, looking lost, and then he turned and went back to get Jamie Rae and, I presumed, make a full report to the Wardens.

Venna was right: We needed to get the hell out of here.

'I hope you have a bus schedule in your bag of tricks,' I said, and glanced back down the hill. Some of the news crews had spotted us, and a couple of athletic Emmy-seeking types were pounding sand next to the road, curving around the cordoned-off area and heading our way. 'Oh, boy.'

She tugged my hand harder, and we climbed faster. The poststorm air felt clean and soft, the sand under our feet damp and firm. It would have been a nice day, except for all the chaos and mayhem.

'Eamon?' I asked, as we achieved the top of the hill. 'He's alive?'

'Oh, yes,' Venna said. 'You saved him. I suppose that makes you happy.' She sounded mystified about it. Well, I was a little mystified about it, too. 'It was good you told them he was crazy. That'll take time for him to convince them he's not, but then they'll be looking for you.'

'So, bus?' I asked. A well-dressed anchorwoman – well dressed from the waist up, anyway, wearing blue jeans and sneakers below – was sprinting up the road, with her heavy set cameraman puffing behind her. 'Anytime would be good.'

'You don't need a bus.' She pointed. 'That's your car.'

Parked next to the side of the road sat...a gleaming, midnight blue dream of a car. I blinked. 'What the hell is that?'

'It's a Camaro,' she said. 'Nineteen sixty-nine. V-eight with an all-aluminium ZL-one four twenty-seven.' She said it as if she were reciting it out of a book. 'Lewis gave it to you.'

I turned to stare at her. '*Lewis* gave me this. *Lewis* gave me a car.' She nodded. 'And...I took it?' She nodded again. 'Oh, boy.'

'You needed a car,' she said. 'He just thought you should have a nice one.'

'When did this happen?'

'Just before—' She stopped herself, frowned, and edited. 'Before you lost your memory. You drove it on the East Coast. You took a plane from there to Arizona, so it's been sitting in a parking lot, waiting for you.'

'And you...had it driven here?' We were at the car now, and I ran my hand lightly over the immaculate, polished finish. Not so much as a bug splatter on its surface anywhere. 'You get it detailed, too?'

Venna shrugged and opened the passenger-side door to climb in. She looked more little-girl than ever once she was inside, with her feet dangling off the floor. Somebody had installed after-market seat belts; she gravely hooked hers, although I figured there was little chance of a Djinn being injured in a collision. Still playing the daughter role, evidently.

I wondered if my real daughter had ever been in this car. I could almost imagine her sitting there...

'Better hurry,' Venna said. I blinked, looked back, and saw that the newsanchor was hauling ass towards the car, already shouting breathless questions.

I got in and turned the key that was already in the ignition.

Peeling out and spraying gravel wasn't a skill I'd lost with my memory.

It didn't give me much comfort when I looked

in my rear-view mirror and found a white van pulling out of a parking lot and quietly, tenaciously following.

'I need a plan,' I said to Venna. She stared out the window, kicking her feet, and didn't respond. 'Venna, I need to get my memory back. No more screwing around. Tell me how I can do that.'

'You can't,' she said simply. 'Your memory belongs to *her* now. And you don't want to try to get it back. She'll kill you. The only way to make this right is to get Ashan to go back to the Oracle.'

We were about fifteen minutes out from the beach, and I was just driving, with no clear idea of where we were heading. The steady rumble of the car gave me a feeling of being in control at last, and I thought that I might be happy if I could just drive forever. Or at least, until my problems went away.

The white van, for instance. It didn't seem inclined to vanish on my say-so, however. It kept a steady three-car distance from me, not really hiding, but not really making itself known, either. Too far back for me to catch sight of the driver.

'Ashan has my memories.'

'No. He...' Venna searched for words for a second. 'He tore them from you. Threw them away, made them excess energy. It put you adrift in the universe, and when the Demon found your memories, it knocked things out of balance. I think only Ashan can fix that.'

'But Ashan...he's not a Djinn, right?'

'No,' she said. 'Not anymore.' For a brief second Venna's expression revealed something that physically hurt, a kind of anguish that I could barely comprehend. 'He was one of the first, you know. One of the oldest. But he just couldn't understand that the Mother loves you, too.'

'Me?' I asked, startled.

'Humans. Maybe not as much as she loves us, because she understands us a little better. But she's fond of you, too, in a way.' She shrugged. 'He blames you. You made her understand that humans weren't intending to hurt her.'

'*I* did.'

'Yes. You.'

'And by Mother, you mean...'

'Earth,' she said. 'Mother Earth, of course.'

I decided to stick to driving. 'Where am I going?' I asked. 'If we're heading for Ashan?'

'I have him safe.' Venna took a map out of the glove compartment, unfolded it, and traced a line with her fingertip. Where she touched it, a route lit up. I glanced over. We were going to take I-8 to Arizona, apparently. 'It's about eight hours. Well, the way you drive, six.'

'Was that a joke?'

Venna shook her head. Apparently it was an expectation.

'What do we do when we get there?' I asked. 'I'm not killing anybody, Venna.'

'I wouldn't let you,' she said. 'Although if you knew Ashan, you'd probably want to... What do you want me to do about the man following us?'

'You noticed.' She gave a little snort of agreement. I supposed it wasn't exactly beyond her capabilities. 'Do you know who it is?'

'Yes,' she said. I waited. She waited right back.

I gave her a hard look. Which was just a little bit hilarious, admittedly; I was giving *her* a hard look? As far as I could tell, Venna could pretty much destroy me any day of the week, and twice at matinees. 'Just tell me!'

'I don't have to,' she said. 'You'll have to stop soon. When you do, you'll find out.'

She seemed smug about it. I gave her another completely ineffective glare, and checked my gas gauge. Still nearly full. Why in the world would I have to stop...?

The back left tyre blew out with a jolt and a sound like a brick slapping the undercarriage of the car, and I cursed, fought the wheel, and limped the Camaro over to the shoulder of the road. The uneven *thump thump thump* made it clear that we weren't going to make any quick getaways.

'Fix it,' I said to Venna. She smoothed her palms

over her blue jeans. Was there a way to be beyond smug? 'Come on, Venna. Be a pal.'

'You have a spare tyre,' she said. 'I'll wait here.'

I cursed under my breath, opened the door, popped the trunk, and unloaded the jack, spare tyre, and other various roadside disaster tools. I was evidently no stranger to mechanical work, but I wasn't in the mood, dammit. I had the lug nuts loosened in record time, but as I was jacking up the car with vicious jerks of the handle, I saw a sparkle of glass behind us, and the white van glided over the hill...slowing down.

Shit.

'Hey, Venna?' I said. She looked out of the window at me. 'Little help?'

She rolled up the window.

'Perfect.' I sighed. 'Just perfect.' I went back to cranking the jack, grimly focused on the job at hand but keeping at least half of my attention – the paranoid half – on the van as it crawled and crunched its way slowly towards me. The brakes squealed slightly as it stopped.

I couldn't see a damn thing through the tinted windows, and I was suddenly very glad of the tyre iron in my hand.

And then the doors on both sides of the van opened at once, and people got out. The woman was young, toned, and well coiffed. She had a microphone. Behind her, in a flying wedge, came a fat guy with a camera and a skinny guy with a boom microphone.

'You've *got* to be kidding me,' I said, and stared, paralyzed, while they moved purposefully in my direction. 'Holy crap.'

'Joanne Baldwin?' The reporter got out in front, framed the two-shot, and made sure her best side was to the camera. 'My name is Sylvia Simons, and I'm an investigative reporter for—'

My paralysis snapped, replaced by a quivering all-over tremor. *She knew my name.*

'I don't care who you're with,' I interrupted, and started pumping the jack again. The tyre crept upward, cleared the asphalt, and I repurposed the jack to start removing the lugs. 'Get lost.'

'Ma'am, do you have any comment about what happened back there on the beach?'

'I don't know what you're talking about,' I said. 'And I don't know any Joanne Baldwin. You've got the wrong—'

'I interviewed your sister a few weeks ago. She gave us a photo,' Sylvia Simons interrupted, and held out a picture of me and Sarah, which had been removed from its frame. We looked happy and stupid. I still felt stupid, but I certainly wasn't very happy. 'She told us that you're a member of an organisation called the Wardens. Can you tell me something about that?'

'No,' I said. Four lug nuts off. I kept moving,

careless of the grease and grime on my hands or what was getting on my clothes.

'My understanding is that you have some kind of responsibility for protecting the general public from natural disasters,' Simons continued. Lug nut five came off, then six, and I slid the tyre free with a screech of metal and let it thump down on the road between us. I wiped sweat from my forehead and ignored her as she leant closer. 'She claimed it was magic. Care to tell us exactly what that means? We'll get the information some other way if you don't, but this is your chance to tell your side of the story...'

Crap. I put the other tyre on and began replacing lug nuts. 'I don't have a side,' I said, 'and there isn't any story. Leave me alone.'

I could tell they weren't going to. They'd been digging, and struck gold. Sarah had dropped the dime and taken the money after ensuring that the white van and the reporters knew to keep on my trail. And maybe she'd called somebody else, too. Somebody who'd dispatched a killer to silence me before I could talk. That way she'd have the money from the reporters free and clear, and no Wardens after her.

'Tell you what,' I said, spinning lug nuts down with both hands. I didn't look at the reporter directly, wary of being even more on-camera. 'If you turn around and leave now, nothing's going to happen to your nice digital equipment.'

Simons made a surprised face, and looked at the camera as if she wanted to be sure it caught her amazement. 'Are you threatening us, Ms Baldwin?'

'Nope.' I finished finger-tightening the nuts, and released the jack to let the car settle back on four tyres. I began applying the tyre iron to finish the job of making the wheel road ready. 'But things do happen.'

And right then, things did happen. The camera guy said, 'What the...?' and a whisper of smoke suddenly oozed out of three or four places in his equipment. I heard a cooking sound from inside the electronics.

Nice. I sure did enjoy some things about being a Fire Warden.

'What's wrong?' Simons asked, and moved towards him. Together, with the sound guy craning in for a look, they reviewed the damage. Which, I could have told them, was catastrophic. Yay, me.

I shoved the old flat tyre and all the equipment in the trunk, slammed it, and said, 'I think the phrase I'm searching for here is "no comment".'

Simons stared at me with a grim, set expression as I got in the Camaro and headed off down the road.

When the van tried to follow, its engine blew in a spectacular white cloud of steam.

'I should be ashamed. That,' I said to Venna,

'was really low. Then again, blowing out my tyre was pretty low in the first place, Venna. Shame on you.'

'Perhaps,' she said. 'But you needed to know. So you won't trust your sister again.'

'No,' I said grimly. 'I don't think I will.'

Driving is therapy for me. Interesting thing to discover about yourself... There was something hypnotic about the road, the freedom, the feeling of being in control and having a direction. I drove fast, but not recklessly, and if Venna had anything to say, she said it to herself.

I had a lot of time to think. After a couple of hours of that, I said, 'Venna. Why haven't you given me *your* memories?'

She raised her eyebrows. Pint-sized haughtiness. She was still wearing the blue jeans and pink shirt; I was getting used to the less formal look, but I didn't let it fool me. There was nothing informal about Venna.

'You couldn't handle it,' she said. 'Djinn memory isn't the same as human. We see things differently. We see time differently. It wouldn't make sense to you, the way human memories do.'

'But...you can become human, right?'

'We can take human form. That doesn't mean we become human. Not really.'

So even though David had fathered a child

with me, he hadn't been...human. Not inside. Comforting thought.

I edged a bit more speed out of the accelerator. 'You said David would be on her side, not mine. Are you guessing, or do you know that?'

She didn't answer me.

In a way, I supposed, that was answer enough.

The countryside began feeling weirdly familiar. If I'd put together the pieces properly, Sedona had been the last place I'd been seen before my absence from the world, followed by my appearance, naked and memory-free, in the forest. I felt like I *ought* to remember it.

I was, quite simply, too tired. Sedona had motels, and I had cash, and although Venna was contemptuous of the whole idea, I checked myself in for the day, took a long, hot bath, and crawled into a clean bed for eight blissful hours. When I got up, the sun had already set.

Venna was watching a game show, something loud that seemed to involve people shouting at briefcases. She was cross-legged on the end of the bed, her chin resting on her fists, and she was absolutely enraptured.

'Well,' I said as I zipped up my black jeans, 'I guess now I know who the target audience is for reality TV.'

If I hadn't known better, I'd have thought she

was embarrassed. She slid off the bed, and the TV flicked off without her hand coming anywhere near a remote control. She folded her arms. 'Are you done sleeping?' she asked.

'Obviously, yes.'

'Good. It's such a waste of good time.' She moved the curtain aside and looked out. 'We should go.'

We pulled out of the parking lot and cruised slowly through town. Venna navigated, my very own supernatural GPS, pointing me through the streets until I was thoroughly lost. Sedona looked pretty much like any other town – maybe a little funkier, with more New Age shops and Southwest architecture, but McDonald's looked the same. So did Starbucks.

'Are we close?' I asked. I was still tired, but it was a pleasant kind of tired, and for the first time in a long time I felt like I was going into trouble with a clear mind. The road vibration was almost as good as a massage.

'That way.' Venna pointed. I didn't ask questions. We made turns, crawled along a road that led into the hills, and eventually stopped in a parking lot at the foot of a bluff whose definitions were lost in the growing darkness.

The sign said, CHAPEL OF THE HOLY CROSS.

Venna said, very quietly, 'We're here.'

'Where's Ashan?'

'Safe,' she said. 'I'll bring him here when we're ready. If he panics, he can be hard to control.'

A Djinn – well, former Djinn – who had panic attacks. That was a new one. I parked the Camaro in a convenient spot, killed the engine, and sat listening to the metal tick as it cooled. Outside, there was a living silence that pressed heavily against the car windows.

I didn't like it here.

'This is hard for you,' Venna said. 'Yes?'

'Yes.'

She turned those blue, blue eyes on me and said, 'Do you know why?'

I silently shook my head. I didn't think I wanted to know.

We got out of the car and walked to a steep set of concrete stairs leading up into the dark. Motion-sensitive lights bathed the steps dusty white, a startling contrast to the reddish rocks. I put my foot on the first one, and suddenly I couldn't breathe. Couldn't move.

Venna took my hand. 'I know,' she said quietly. 'This place remembers. It remembers everything.' She put her head down, as if there were things she didn't want to see. I could understand that. I could feel it brushing at the edges of my consciousness, and without meaning to I drifted up into the aetheric...

And I saw chaos.

Raw fury. Horror. Anguish. An abiding, keening grief that had reduced this place, on the aetheric level, to a black hole of emotion.

'My God,' I whispered numbly. 'What did this?'

Venna glanced up at me, then back down. 'You did,' she said. 'David did. We all did. When she died—'

She shut up, fast, but not before I put the pieces together. 'Imara,' I said. 'Imara died here.'

'I'm sorry,' she whispered. 'We didn't know what to do. She was part human, and that part couldn't be saved. He tried, after you were...after you disappeared.'

'David tried to save her.'

Venna bit her lip and nodded. She looked genuinely distressed. No wonder there was so much pain here, so much grief. David's agony, staining this place like ink.

Maybe mine, too.

'We'd better go,' she said, and took my hand. Hers felt warm, childlike, human. 'It'll be better at the top.'

It wasn't exactly easy ascending those stairs; I felt as if I were moving through the same quicksand I'd fought through back on the beach. The handrail felt sticky. I looked at my hand, almost sure I'd see bloodstains, but no...nothing. Up above, stars were twinkling in the dark blue sky; there was still a band of pale blue towards the horizon, shot through with threads of red and gold. Beautiful.

There seemed to be a thousand steps, and every one of them a sacrifice.

When we made it to the landing I was gasping for breath and shaking; Venna let go of my hand and moved to the door of the chapel, which was closed and had a sign on the front that gave the hours it was open – which didn't include the hour of now.

That didn't seem to matter to Venna, who simply pulled, and the door opened with a faint *snick*. The puff of air from the darkened interior smelt of incense and cedar, a timeless scent that carried none of the horror present outside.

Except for the flicker of a couple of red candles here and there, it was quite dark inside; the dim, fading sunset showed a small chamber, inked in shadow at the corners, with a few plain wood pews facing the huge expanse of glass windows. It was breathtaking, and it was, without a doubt, a holy kind of place.

Venna held the door for me, and locked it once we were inside. The place looked empty.

'I thought you said—'

'I said I'd bring him,' she said, and I felt a massive energy surge sweep over my body, staggering me, and I almost saw the golden arc of it blow past.

It seemed to outline a human body, glowing hot,

and then the glow vanished and there was only a man standing there, unsteady and pale as a dead man.

He pitched forward to the floor, retching.

I knew *exactly* how that felt, actually. I'd felt it when I'd flown Air Venna from the Great Northwest to Las Vegas, non-stop.

'I thought you said teleporting could kill people,' I said.

'It didn't.'

Even though I knew it was a mistake, I took a step towards them and heard that he was gasping for breath in helpless, hopeless sobs. He looked up, and the dim light gilded a pale face, pale hair.

'I shouldn't be here,' he said. 'I can't be here—' And then he just...stopped, staring at me.

'Ashan?' I asked. He should have rung some recognition bells, I knew that, but...nothing. A frustrating lack of context. 'You know who I am?'

He licked pale lips and wiped away his tears with shaking hands. 'You're gone,' he said. 'I killed you. I killed both of you.'

He lunged at me, and slammed the heel of his hand into my shoulder. He seemed as surprised as I was – apparently, he'd been expecting a ghost, not flesh and blood. And I hadn't expected him to move quite that fast. 'Whoa!' I said, and skipped back out of reach. 'Watch the hands!'

Ashan didn't exactly look well. He was wearing

some kind of a grey suit, but it was dirty, smudged, and torn, and he smelt. I mean, *really* smelt. His hair was greasy, and all in all, he looked like somebody who'd never discovered the basics of hygiene. Which I suppose would follow, if he'd been busted from near-angelic status to the merely human. Venna clearly hadn't taken the time to clean him up, or maybe she hadn't been able to convince him to even try.

He kept looking at me like he wasn't sure he was sane. Well...actually, he looked like he'd blown past the borders of actual sanity some time ago. I glanced over my shoulder. Venna was still there, watching with unnervingly bright eyes.

'You have to be dead,' he said. 'I watched you die. I *felt* you die. And I paid the price.'

'Sorry to disappoint you,' I said. 'Guess what? Good news. You get to make amends and help me get my life back.'

He was *fast*. Faster than he ought to have been, and I hadn't moved far enough. He crossed the space, grabbed me by the throat, and slammed me down to the floor with such violence that I could barely comprehend it, much less react.

Upside down, Venna's face was still inscrutable. Great. No help from that quarter.

My instincts reached for power...and failed.

There was no access to the powers I'd started to get accustomed to, not here. This was like a bubble, cut off from the outside. Cut off from the aetheric.

'Get off!' I squeaked, and twisted, trying to throw Ashan's weight to one side. He wasn't heavy, but he was wiry, and he had an unholy amount of strength. I had no leverage. I grabbed a handful of his greasy hair and yanked, and he howled and used his free hand to grab my wrist. I bucked, got him off balance, and we rolled down the aisle of the chapel, spitting curses, and this time *I* ended up on top, *my* hands on *his* throat. Holding him down.

'Go on,' he spat at me. 'Break my neck. Kill me like I killed your child. Put me out of my misery, you pathetic bag of meat!'

I went very still. I must have looked like a crazy woman, my hair sticking to my sweaty face, my eyes wide, my lips parted on a truth I didn't want to speak.

He'd killed my *child*.

That was what Venna hadn't wanted to tell me. I was facing Imara's murderer, with his life in my hands.

This time, Venna did react. She stepped forward and said, very quietly, 'You can't. You can't kill him.'

Oh, I was pretty sure I could. And *should*.

Didn't the daughter I couldn't remember, whose pain had soaked into the very stones outside of this place, demand that much?

Chapter Twelve

It wasn't so much the moral quandary that stopped me as the fact that something changed in the room, right at that moment. Not Ashan – he was a stinky, horrifying excuse for a human being, and right at that moment I had no reason in the world not to hurt him as badly as he'd hurt my daughter. I didn't figure that Venna would really be able to stop me.

What changed was that the three of us were no longer alone.

Venna took in a deep, gasping breath – more reaction than I'd ever heard from her – and moved slowly back, until her shoulders fetched up against the polished wood of the side of a pew.

And then she slipped down to her knees, put her hands in her lap, and bowed her head.

'Oh,' she said faintly. 'I see now. I'm sorry. I shouldn't have brought them here.'

And there was someone sitting in the blackest shadows of the room, an outline of a person, nothing more, but a sense of presence and power sent little shocks up and down my spine.

I hesitated, staring at that dark shape, and then I sat up, grabbed Ashan by his filthy collar, and yanked him to a sitting position. 'Who is it?' I asked Venna.

She didn't answer.

'Venna!'

Whoever it was, Ashan looked destroyed. The expression on his face was horrifying in its vulnerability. His eyes filled with tears, and his whole body trembled with the force of something like grief, something like rage, more toxic than either one of those. I let go, because he didn't even know I was there, and he crawled away from me, *crawled*, to kneel at the end of the pew where the shadow figure sat.

'You can't be here,' he said. 'You can't.'

But whatever the shape was, it didn't move, didn't speak, and didn't seem to notice him at all. I got slowly to my feet and watched Ashan tremble, and suddenly killing him didn't seem like a priority. He was suffering, all right. Suffering in ways I couldn't begin to understand.

Good.

All around the chapel, candles came alight – one after another, a racing circle of warm flame.

And I saw who was sitting in the pew. I guess I should have known, from Venna's reaction, and from Ashan's, but I still wasn't prepared.

She looked human, but there was no way she was anything like it; she had a stillness to her that not even Tibetan monks could attain. She was wearing a full brick-red dress, shifting and sheer in some places, solid in others; it fluttered in a breeze I couldn't feel, and her full lips were parted on what looked like a gasp of delight, as if she'd seen something truly wonderful that none of the rest of us could grasp.

And then her eyes, a brilliant shade of hot gold, shifted to fix on me.

Ashan pressed himself down on the floor, totally abasing himself, and I thought, *No, this can't be true. This can't be happening.*

Because it was my daughter. My Imara, the Imara of the memories I'd got from Cherise and Eamon. And yet...not her at all.

Not until she smiled, and shattered my heart into a million pieces.

'Oh,' I whispered, and felt my knees go weak. 'Oh, my God...' I didn't know what to say, how to feel. There was this storm of emotion inside of me, overwhelming in its pressure, and I wanted to laugh and cry and scream and, like Ashan, get down on my knees in gratitude and supplication. But I wasn't Ashan, and I didn't. I braced myself with both hands on the back of a pew and stared at her until my eyes burnt.

She didn't speak.

'Imara?' I asked. My throat felt raw, and I could barely recognise my own voice. 'Are you...?' *Alive? All right?* I didn't even know what to ask.

Venna said, 'The old Oracle was dying after the Demon wounded her. The Mother made a new Oracle in her place from the energy that was lost. I didn't know it would be Imara.' Venna sounded very quiet, very small. 'Does it help?'

Help? My daughter was there, smiling at me. How could it not help? I swallowed. 'Can she...can she hear me?'

'Not the way you think. She hears who you are, though. And she knows.'

'Knows what?' I felt a bizarre mixture of pain and grief and anger fizzing up inside, overwhelming the relief.

'Everything,' Venna said soberly. 'She knows you still love her.'

There was something about Imara that kept me from rushing to her, touching her, babbling out everything I felt. Something...other.

But that look, that smile...those were pure love.

'It's why you could do what you did on the beach, when you made the Earth obey you,' Venna said. 'And how you can touch people's memories. Because through her, you touch the Earth. You've got all three channels now. Earth, Fire, Weather. You're like Lewis.'

She didn't look particularly happy about it.

Imara's smile faded, and she looked down at Ashan, cowering near her feet. Her eyes shifted colour to a molten bronze.

I didn't need words to understand that look, and it chilled me.

If Venna noticed, she didn't mention it. She was frowning now, looking as disturbed as I'd ever seen her. 'This isn't going to work.'

'What? What do you mean?' For a terrifying second I thought she was talking about Imara, that there was something wrong, but no; Venna looked too calm, too still.

'She's new,' Venna said, and rested her hands, palm down, on her thighs. 'She hasn't come into her full power yet. And that means she can't help Ashan – even if she wants to.'

I doubted sincerely that what Imara had on her mind for Ashan could go by the description of help.

'So that's it?' I asked. 'We just give up?'

Venna threw me an all-too-human look of exasperation. 'No,' she said. 'We take him to another Oracle, that's all. I'll take him out of here.'

I didn't watch how she did it, but I heard Ashan scrambling, and heard him cry out, once. Then they were gone, and the door shut behind them.

I didn't take my eyes off my daughter, the Oracle.

'Can you hear me?' I asked. 'Imara?'

Her eyes slowly swirled back to that lovely shade

of gold, but she didn't smile this time.

I waited, but the candles began to dim, slowly winking out one by one. While I could still see her, I said, 'Please say something. Please, baby. I need to know that you're OK.'

She was just a dim shadow against the deeper shadows, a glimmer of gold eyes in the dark, when she whispered, 'Hang in there, Mom. I love you.'

And then she was gone.

I sat down hard on the pew, put my face in my hands, and prayed. Not to my daughter. Not to the Earth, whoever that was.

I prayed to God, whose chapel it was. Who'd built this glittering, beautiful, hurtful world with all its magic and deadly sharp edges. I needed a higher power to get me through the rest of this, because I didn't think I could do it by myself.

I don't know if He answered, exactly, but after a few minutes I felt a kind of peace inside, a stillness, and an acceptance.

My child wasn't suffering, and she wasn't totally beyond my reach.

Maybe that was enough.

I scrubbed my face clean of tears, got up, and went to find Venna.

Venna had Ashan – actually, he was on his knees, and she had one hand on his shoulder. It didn't look like restraint, exactly, but I was sure it was.

He looked worse in the merciless glare of the motion-activated spotlights on the concrete stairs – bleached, grimy, with an unpleasant light of madness lurking in those blue eyes.

He'd killed my daughter. And if he'd got his way, she'd have been completely dead, not sitting in there in the chapel, elevated to some level I couldn't understand. In a very real way, he'd still taken her away; Imara the Oracle wasn't Imara at all, not the way I'd known her.

You never knew her at all, some cold part of me said. *You never had a past; you never had a daughter. Remember?*

That was the point. I didn't remember. And Ashan had done that to me.

Miles to go before I could see that put right.

'So,' I said. 'Where now?'

I'd expected her to hesitate, but instead, Venna promptly said, 'Seacasket.'

'Pardon?'

'It's in New Jersey.'

I hadn't forgotten geography. New Jersey was a long way from Arizona. A long, long way.

'We should go,' Venna said. 'I can drive when you get tired.'

Yeah, like I was going to let a kid behind the wheel of *that* car. Even a many-centuries-old kid. 'One other thing,' I said, and pointed a thumb at Ashan. '*He* needs a bath. I'm not smelling him all the way to the East Coast.'

Ashan shot to his feet, running like a rabbit for the rocks, not the stairs. 'Hey!'

He slammed face-first into an invisible wall, staggered back, and whirled to face us. Venna had broken his nose, and it was streaming blood. Not a good look for him. When he tried to come at me, Venna stopped him again with just as much force.

'Ashan,' she said to him. 'You know you can't fight me. I'll just keep on hurting you.'

He tried it again, as if he hadn't heard her, and I winced this time at the sound of flesh and bone hitting the barrier. 'He's *trying* to make you hurt him,' I said. 'He wants you to kill him.'

Venna blinked. 'That's odd.'

'That's human. And kind of crazy.'

'I will *never* understand mortals,' she said, sounding aggrieved. 'How do I stop him without hurting him?'

'Let me handle it.'

This time, when he lunged at us, I took the Taser out of my purse, switched it on, and zapped the holy living shit out of him. Ashan convulsed and went down. I crouched next to him. His eyes were unfocused, and there was blood dripping from his chin in a gory mess. 'Ashan. Can you hear me?'

He could. He just didn't answer. I could tell from the immediate flicker of rage in him that I had his attention. The shock had incapacitated him, but it hadn't done much to make him like me any better.

'Venna's going to keep you from doing any damage to me, or yourself,' I said. 'Right, Ven?' She gave me a look that could have doubled as a crematorium. 'Sorry. Venna.'

'Yes.' She wasn't forgiving me anytime soon for an attempt at a pet name; that was clear from her tone. 'Up, Ashan.'

At first he couldn't get up, and then it was clear he didn't want to. The smile Venna gave him was evil enough to haunt a serial killer's nightmares.

'If you don't,' she said, 'then I'll make you, brother.'

Brother? I didn't know if that was literal or figurative, but either way, it worked; Ashan climbed silently to his feet and walked down the steps without trying to run, pitch headlong to his death, or take me with him. I looked back up at the Chapel of the Holy Cross; it was quiet, no signs of life. No sign of my daughter haunting its warm, incense-scented shadows.

I wanted to run back up the steps and throw my arms around her, but somehow I knew that it wasn't the time. Not here. Not now.

Not until this was over.

Venna saw me looking, and said, 'We should go.'

Ashan coughed, and spat a mouthful of blood

at Venna's feet. She raised one eyebrow and made it disappear. Just like that.

I raised the Taser and activated it, letting him get a good look at the jumping spark. 'Get in the car, Ashan.'

He slid into the backseat. I pointed a finger at Venna. 'Watch him,' I said.

'Of course.' She gave me a cool raise of her eyebrows, as if I were being completely stupid, and climbed in the passenger seat.

I stood there for a few seconds with my hand on the car door, looking up at the chapel. For a second, I thought I saw...something. A flicker of red, a dress fluttering in the wind.

A smile.

'I'll see you soon,' I promised her, and got in the driver's seat.

We drove out towards the main road, and when I reached an intersection I idled and waited for traffic. Venna seemed lost in thought, but she finally said, 'I can conceal us from most, but he is going to be a problem.'

'Venna, could you ever once in a while use a *name*? Would it kill you? He, who? Ashan?'

'David,' she said, with a little too much enunciative precision. 'He's been looking for you. I can keep him from finding us for now, but I'm not sure I can do it for long. He's very smart.'

'He's looking for me?' I felt a surge of gratitude

and relief, and then I remembered that it wasn't a good thing. 'Oh. Looking for me because he thinks I'm the wrong one. The fake Joanne.'

'Yes.'

'And where is he?'

She shrugged. 'I said I could hide us from him, not keep track of him. It's not that simple. You'd better get going.'

'Do you think this is going to work?'

Venna looked suddenly very young, and very uncertain. 'I don't know,' she said. 'It's never been done before. And I didn't expect that the Earth Oracle would be Imara. That complicates things.'

I swallowed, suddenly very cold. 'What if it doesn't work?'

'Eventually,' Venna said, 'the Demon will win. And I don't know what will happen then. I really don't.'

We looked at each other in silence for a second.

'Go east,' she said. 'We've got a lot of ground to cover.'

I love to drive, but this wasn't driving, it was being trapped in a car with a crazy man (who kept muttering things in a language that I didn't understand), a Djinn who was by turns cute and creepy, and constantly operating under the threat of impending, though non-specific, doom. It was the Paranoia Ride, which I was sure wasn't going to catch on at Disney World. Venna wasn't exactly comforting company, and Ashan...I hadn't liked him at first sight, I'd begun to hate him when I'd realised what he'd done, and now I outright loathed him. Venna had, at my request, dumped him into a shower at a roadside motel, and I'd bought him some fresh clothes to replace the filthy suit he'd been wearing. Clean, he looked and smelt better.

It didn't help his attitude at all. Venna's calm, menacing presence kept him from trying to bash my head in, but there was nothing she could do to make him any less of an asshole. I couldn't keep him in the trunk; that would be emotionally satisfying, but morally questionable. Still, keeping him in the backseat was no picnic. Every muscle in my body ached with tension, and when I managed to pull over to sleep (catnaps, at best) I woke up more tired than ever. Ashan never stopped watching me. He was crazy as a rat on LSD, and I thought I could understand why; having spent time with Venna, seen how different she was from human, I could imagine the shock of being busted from Djinn back to merely mortal. Be enough to drive anybody mad – and I wasn't convinced that he hadn't been a little mad to start with. If what he'd done to me was, in fact, forbidden, he'd been playing with fire. When the old commercials said, 'It's not nice to fool with Mother Nature,' they hadn't exactly been kidding around.

I wondered what he'd been like before. Maybe Venna inferred that from my frequent, nervous glances in the rear-view mirror, because she said about fourteen hours into the drive, 'He didn't hate you at first, you know. You weren't more than an annoyance to him. It was all because of David – Ashan was jealous, and he wanted to be Jonathan's heir. You were David's weakness, so Ashan exploited that, because he wanted to destroy David before he got too powerful.'

All politics. 'Funny,' I said. 'It feels personal now.'

'Now it is,' she agreed. 'You're like a virus, you humans. You get under our skins.'

'Flattering.'

She frowned. 'Was it? I didn't mean it to be.'

I resisted the urge to explain sarcasm to her. Barely. 'What about memories? Are you going to give me his since he's human?'

She looked away. 'Do you think you want them?'

'Just the ones about me.'

This time, she looked at me straight on. 'Do you really want them?'

I realised then what I was asking for. Not just memories of me as Ashan saw me, but the things Ashan might have done to me. To other people I loved.

To my daughter.

I cleared my throat. 'Let me think about it.'

She nodded. From the backseat Ashan said, in a low, harsh voice that didn't sound like it got much use, 'You can't be saved, you know. Whether you die today or in fifty years, you still die.'

Cheery little fella. 'I'll take surviving the fifty years, if I have a choice.'

He smiled thinly. 'You don't.' His eyes were bright – not Djinn bright, which was a whole order of magnitude weirder, but plenty bright enough to indicate crazy. 'I'll freely give you my memories, meat. I want you to know everything. It would please me if you went to your death remembering every painful second of what I did to her.'

I thought longingly about the Taser, then deliberately relaxed. 'Can't you shut him up?' I asked Venna.

She glanced over the seat at Ashan. 'I don't like to keep him unconscious all the time. It's not good for him.'

'Like I care.'

Venna giggled. I nearly drove off the road. 'Sorry,' she immediately said, subdued. 'Was that wrong? I don't usually try to laugh. I never was human, you know. I never learnt.'

'Really? What a shock, you seem like such a regular kid.' I checked the map. We were making good time, and the lodge that Venna had indicated was our stopping point for the day was only about an hour's drive down the road.

I was starting to feel pretty good about the possibilities when I felt the engine give the tiniest little hitch.

'No,' I whispered.

There it was again. Stronger. It sent a shudder through the car.

'No!'

The third time, the whole engine seized up with a clatter of valves. *Great.* 'Venna! Little help!'

But she wasn't looking at me. I wasn't even sure if she'd realised we were coasting to a stop at the side of the road.

'She's found you,' said Ashan, and smiled coldly. 'They may kill me, but I think they'll kill you, too. And that would be worth my death.'

'Venna!' I pumped my foot on the gas, but it was stupid; the car wasn't going anywhere, not without supernatural repairs. 'Dammit—'

'He's right,' Venna said. Her voice sounded colourless, emotionless, but there was a bright spark of fear in her eyes. 'David broke my shields. He must know I was hiding you. They're coming, and they'll kill Ashan. I can't risk that.'

I couldn't help but think that it was the threat to *Ashan* that got her interested, but I didn't have time to think about it; something happened to the car's engine, and it choked, growled, and caught fire again. The car leapt forward. I hastily shifted gears to accommodate.

'Maybe we should talk—' I began.

'No! Drive!' Some invisible force slammed the gas pedal down, and I struggled with the steering wheel as the tyres screamed, propelling us down the road at a terrifying rate of speed. 'Don't slow down!'

'I'm sorry,' Ashan was saying. I had no idea if he was sorry he was in the car, sorry we were all going to die, sorry that he'd done what he'd done to Imara, and to me. Or just a sorry excuse for a human being. It didn't really matter, and I could barely hear him over the shriek of tyres on the curve. The Camaro was drifting over the line. I fought the wheel and got her straight by sheer force. *Come on, baby. Work with me.*

I didn't know what was chasing us, but whatever it was, it was scary enough to panic one badass Djinn, and one who at least used to be.

Sounded good enough for me to panic, too.

I loved driving fast, but this was a little *too* fast, on a road that snaked like a car commercial and featured oncoming tractor trailers loaded down with raw lumber and giant tree trunks. Venna didn't enhance my ability to keep my cool; she continued to put the mystical hammer down on the Camaro while looking steadily out the rear of the car.

Leaving me with the not very enviable task of steering in overdrive.

'Slow down!' I yelled at her, and tried to downshift. The gear knob didn't budge. I yanked at it anyway. The clutch pedal didn't respond, either, even when I jammed it to the floor. Ditto, brakes. In desperation I yanked the emergency brake, but it flopped uselessly.

'If we slow down, you die,' Venna said. She sounded unnaturally calm. I was glad I was too busy to see her face. 'So does Ashan.'

'News flash: If we *don't* slow down I'm going to die, and ruin a perfectly beautiful car!' I shot back. I nearly bit my tongue off as the Camaro hit a patch of ice, tyres broke traction, and the whole thing started going sideways with a vengeance. '*Shit!*' I'd heard somewhere that these days, that was most often a person's last word. I didn't want it to be mine, and I fought the skid, begging the car to find some traction.

It did. The tyres caught, squealed, bit, and slewed us back in the opposite direction just in time to avoid an oncoming RV. I kept the Camaro off of the steep, narrow shoulder, sprayed gravel, and managed to point it in the right direction.

Another truck barrelled past us, buffeting us in its wake. Busy road.

'Venna!' I yelled. 'Plan B! Because plan A's *not working*!'

The engine seized up again. It was catastrophic, a crunching grind of metal followed by the sound of parts coming off, breaking loose, and ripping apart everything in their path. Steam erupted in a white cloud from beneath the hood, and no amount of magical gas pedal pressing was going to get us moving again. Not unless Venna was one hell of a roadside mechanic.

The car lurched, clunking metal, and slowed drastically.

We coasted, moving more and more slowly, and I found a slightly wider spot on the shoulder that would double as an emergency breakdown lane, flipped the hazard lights, and hit the brakes – which, finally, worked.

The road, which had been choked with traffic a few seconds ago, seemed quiet now. The last eighteen-wheeler was disappearing over the ridge, grinding gears, and there didn't seem to be anybody else in view. I was having trouble getting my breath, and I was shaking in reaction to the adrenalin rush.

'Venna, what the *hell*—' I began, but I didn't even make it to the end of the sentence.

'Get down!' She reached over, grabbed my head, and forced me sideways across the seat, with the safety belt digging into my neck nearly to choking point.

I forgot to complain about the discomfort of that, though, because I started to feel it, too. A disturbance in the aetheric, one even somebody like me, who was all but a novice, could feel.

There was a *sound*. I'm not sure what it was like, because there was nothing in my mind I could equate it to; it was a chaos of sharp snapping sounds, thunderous crashes, howls, screams...

Venna threw herself on top of me just before a wall of wind hit the car and flipped it, end over end, through the air.

I blacked out when the car slammed into the ground, which was probably lucky. When I woke up I was out of the wreck, lying on the cold gravel shoulder of the road, and there was a smoking heap of metal a dozen feet away that wasn't immediately recognisable as anything like a motorised vehicle. Certainly not the lovely, gleaming car that I'd been driving. But I saw a glint of unblemished midnight blue paint, and felt a mournful stab of anguish. The poor Camaro wasn't coming back from that with a little body work, even if there'd been a way to save the engine.

When I focused past the wreckage, I forgot to breathe, because the Camaro hadn't taken the brunt of the brute-force attack...and it hadn't exactly been a surgical strike. It was like a bomb made of air had exploded, and the Camaro had been ground zero. The indescribable sound I'd heard had been the howling wind slamming into old-growth trees and snapping them off their bases, or uprooting them completely to crash into their neighbours.

It was a veritable crop circle of downed trees.

I tried to sit up, and something in my back lodged a loud protest. I groaned, told it to shut up, and compromised by rolling over on my side. No sign of Venna or Ashan. No sign of anybody, actually. Just me, a bunch of killed trees, and the dead Camaro puffing black smoke into the empty sky.

'Venna?' My voice sounded thin. I tried again, but it didn't work any better. Mindful of my back pain, I rolled to my hands and knees, then got to my feet. *Gonna be sore in the morning*, I thought crazily.

Somebody had destroyed almost a quarter mile of forest to try to kill me. Being sore was the least of my problems, and if Venna hadn't acted as my Djinn air bag...

I wondered if Ashan was still in the twisted wreckage of the car.

'Venna?'

A car topped the ridge, heading towards the devastated area. No, a truck, an SUV, and there was another one behind it. It was moving slowly because of the debris, but steadily enough. I didn't want any Good Samaritans right now; I wasn't sure I could protect them against whatever had just put the unholy smackdown on me. No, actually I was sure... I was sure I couldn't. My heart sank as I saw it was a family, and they slowed radically as they got close to the crash scene.

'Keep going!' I yelled as the father rolled down his window. I forced myself to get up to my hands and knees, then to my feet. I managed not to black out doing it. 'I'm fine! Don't stop; it's not safe!'

He seemed like a nice enough guy, but he had kids in the back of his truck, and a wife who looked hugely pregnant, and I did *not* want their lives on my conscience. 'I'll call nine-one-one!' he yelled. I waved frantically, trying to shoo them on by sheer force of will, and it seemed to work.

He negotiated his way around the maze of downed trees and got the hell out.

I remembered there'd been a second SUV behind it, and turned to look.

It had stopped about fifty feet away – a large black SUV, tinted windows, very classy. I thought I saw something shimmer on the paint, and blinked, then went into the aetheric and saw a stylised sun symbol on the door not visible to the naked human eye. It was where an official seal would have been for a government vehicle.

Wardens.

I backed up out of the centre of the road and looked around for some kind of cover, but of course there wasn't any. I didn't feel like cowering in a ditch, especially when they'd undoubtedly already spotted me. *Maybe they're friendly*, I thought.

Yeah, and maybe the next Djinn I met was

going to look just like Brad Pitt and grant me three wishes, too.

The SUV eased forward very slowly. It crunched to a stop a few dozen feet away and idled its engine. Nobody got out. I couldn't see inside. I felt an odd sensation, as if every hair on my body were stirring – static electricity, maybe.

'Let's get this over with,' I muttered. 'What're you going to do, stare me to death?'

The driver's side of the SUV opened, and David got out. He looked fantastically good to me in that moment, and I let out a sigh of relief and took a step towards him...

And stopped, because there was no welcome in his face. Nothing but blank fury.

'David?'

I felt the energy gathering above me, and flung up a hand to catch it before it could form itself into a deadly strike. I wasn't sure what he'd intended, but the devastation around me was proof that somebody had removed the safety switches on this game. I let the power bleed harmlessly off in a thousand smaller tendrils that manifested in gusts of wind, blowing my hair across my face, then switching directions and streaming it back like a flag.

'Give up,' David said flatly. 'You don't have a choice.'

'David, you don't understand—'

This time I wasn't quick enough to stop him. The aftermath of the lightning strike left me blinking, half-blind, concussed, and with an ache on my right side that felt suspiciously like first-degree burns. I smelt something burning, feared it was me, and rolled, trying to smother the flames.

When I writhed around to try to spot what David was doing, he was just...standing there. Watching me. I couldn't read his expression, but he wasn't exactly racing to my rescue.

There were other people climbing out of the SUV. I recognised only one of them: Lewis. My onetime saviour looked like he was badly regretting that decision. I stared at him, trying to guess what he was thinking, but like David, he'd closed himself off.

Neither of them liked being here; that was all I could tell.

And both of them were more than prepared to kill.

Chapter Thirteen

'Guys,' I said, and held out my hands, palms open and out, showing that I had nothing up my tattered, smoking sleeves. 'There's no need for this. I was coming to you, OK? I wasn't running. I'm not going to run. And by the way, you owe me for a really nice car.'

I was standing up to them because, hey, not like I had a choice, anyway. There were four Wardens and one Djinn, and any one of them could have probably taken me down without breaking a nail, even if I hadn't been knocked half-silly by the crash and the lightning bolt.

'Down on your knees,' Lewis said. 'Do it. If I have to ask again, we'll kill you and get it over with.'

Lewis had a gun in his hand. Not one to neglect the merely mortal advantages, apparently, and that just gave them another way to bring me down if all the mystical mojo failed to work. If Venna was biding her time, she was biding a little too long. I had to choose.

I held up my hands in an attitude of surrender and, wincing, got down on my knees. I laced my hands behind my head.

Lewis exchanged a glance with David. Clearly they were the two alphas in the pack; the other Wardens were along for the ride. Although it wouldn't do me any favours to assume they weren't capable in their own right, especially since they'd taken up positions surrounding me. 'Facedown,' Lewis said. 'Hands behind your back.'

'Dammit, road oil is never coming out of these pants,' I said. 'Lewis, it's me. Joanne. What the hell are you doing?'

'Correcting a mistake,' he said. 'Down or die. Your choice.'

Well, when he put it that way... I pitched forward to my hands and knees, lowered myself to the gritty, oily road, and put my hands behind my back.

Somebody – not Lewis and not David – was on me instantly, digging a sharp knee into the small of my back and ignoring my yelp of protest. Plastic zip-ties slipped around my wrists and hissed tight.

'You didn't make a mistake,' I said. I couldn't see Lewis or David. I couldn't see anybody, since my hair had fallen across my eyes. I was blind and helpless, and I could feel something closing in around me on the aetheric, something like a smothering coating of plastic, scaling me off from access to the powers that I was about to be driven to use. 'No! Wait, listen to me! You didn't make a mistake, Lewis; it's *me*! She's lying to you; don't you understand? She's...'

The wind blew my hair away from my eyes, and I saw her. The other me. She'd left the SUV, and she was standing next to David like she belonged there.

It was a good thing I'd had a lot of recent experience seeing myself from the outside, because it allowed me to get over the shock fast. Yeah, that was me, down to the last well-dressed detail. David, or someone who'd cared, had got her a nice flare-legged pantsuit with a fitted jacket, something that hugged her body and made her look tall, lean, elegant, and businesslike. In short, she looked like she belonged. Like she was more than capable of handling whatever needed to be handled.

Me, I was a cheap fax copy, grubby and soiled with road dirt and smoke. And I'd lost a shoe.

'I can't believe you got her,' she said. 'She must be planning something. She shouldn't be this easy to catch.'

David *took her hand*. The Demon exchanged a look with him and smiled. It was *my* smile, dammit. And *my* love in her eyes. She'd taken it. She was using me just as much as she was using him.

'We got lucky,' David said. 'We're even luckier that Venna decided to cut her losses. Although why she'd be helping a Demon...'

'She wasn't!' I yelled. They ignored me.

'I want you out of here,' David said to the other me. 'I'm not taking any chances. Not again.' I hated the way he leant into her space, the way his lips brushed the shining curtain of her hair. The way his hands curled around hers, so gently and protectively. 'Take the truck back to the lodge and wait there.'

'David, she's a *liar*!' I said. 'So, Fake Joanne, what's next? You can't control David, can you? He's too powerful. So maybe you find a way to hurt him so badly one of the other Djinn has to take over, one you *can* subvert. Got to be a weak one in the bunch, right?'

She watched me with steady, familiar eyes. She looked completely real. Completely *me*. 'I'd never hurt David. The fact you think I would just proves who you are.'

'You'd never hurt David unless you knew you could get away with it.' I panted. 'Look, what do you really want? My life? Well, you can't have it, so just hand over the clothes and stop using my face and *move on*.' Towards the end I sounded – and felt – savage. Like I could rip her head off with my bare hands for what she was doing to me. All I wanted to do was *live*, and she'd taken that away.

She stared at me for a few more seconds, and there was something like pity in her face. *There but for the grace of God...* I knew what she was thinking. It made my stomach hurt with the intensity of my fury. 'Say something,' I said.

'Why?' she asked. 'What's to say? You tried to steal my life away, and you've failed. Game over.'

I turned to David, willing him to believe me. 'David, if you kill me, she wins. The Demon wins.'

She laughed. 'Nice. I was waiting for her to pull the old "You're the bad twin" on us. Come on. Who do you think's going to believe you this time? *I've got my memories back.* You're nothing but a cheap copy.'

That was an echo of what I'd been thinking. I blinked, startled. Either she could read my thoughts – icky, but possible – or her mind simply worked the same way. If she'd taken on my memories, my experiences that completely, if she could fool David and Lewis, then maybe she really had become me, as much as a Demon could.

That made my job a hell of a lot harder, because she wasn't faking. As Venna had warned, she really was me, in all the ways that would count.

I looked desperately at Lewis, at David. 'Guys. What if you've got the evil twin standing right there? What if I'm the one she stole everything away from? Kill me, and you'll never be able to fix that; it'll be too late—'

Evil Twin snorted, exchanged a wry look with David, and walked away, arms folded. Heading calmly back for the SUV.

'Wait!' I yelled. 'David, *you know me*! You have to know that's not me!'

That earned me nothing. Evil Twin opened the passenger-side door of the truck and climbed in, then slammed the door. Lewis and David exchanged another one of those unreadable looks. God, I'd never realised how scary it was from this end, faced with these extremely competent people. How desperate it was to be on the losing side.

She's going to pull it off. She's going to have David, live my life, and be happy until she pulls off whatever evil plan she's concocted, and there's not a goddamn thing I can do about it.

I hated losing.

Wind whipped across me, blinding me with grit and a mouthful of black smoke from the still-smouldering wreck of my car. 'Then just get it over with,' I choked. 'If you've got the guts, just do it.'

The SUV's engine started up, and it drove away, slowly winding around the trees. Taking my future with it.

'We're not going to kill you,' Lewis said with an eerie amount of calm. 'We couldn't, could we? If you're a Demon, you'd just assume another form. The only way to destroy a Demon without sacrificing a Djinn is with another Demon.'

'Guess you don't have one of those handy,' I said, and closed my eyes in exhausted relief.

When I opened them, David, expressionless, was

taking a sealed bottle out of his coat. There was red wax around the stopper, and an ancient-looking seal dangling from a complicated knot of ribbons.

The knee in my back dug in harder when I tried to raise up, driving me flat and helpless. I struggled to reach for power, but whatever they'd done to me up on the aetheric was holding fast. I couldn't move the weather, or fire, and when I tried to grab for the slow throb of energy in the earth, something slapped me back with stunning force.

Lewis. I'd recognised the handprint of the slap.

'No,' I said quietly. 'You can't. David, you can't. *I'm not a Demon! David, no!*'

He walked towards me, put a hand in between my shoulder blades, and nodded to Lewis to let go. The relief of the pressure coming off my back didn't last, because David's hand might not have been as heavy, but it was just as effective in restraining me.

'This bottle contains a Djinn,' he said. 'A Djinn infected with a Demon. Under normal circumstances the Demon wouldn't migrate back to a human, but you're different. Demons will destroy each other by preference. If there's any good news, it's that by destroying you, we're going to save a Djinn's life.'

'David, *no! I'm not a Demon!*'

It was no good. He was going to do it. I could see it in his eyes, in the fierce, focused determination on his face. 'Please,' I said. I dropped all my defences, and let him see me as vulnerable as I really was. 'Please don't do this to us.'

His lips thinned, and he flinched a little. 'I wish you didn't look so much like her.'

'I *am* her, and if you open that bottle you're going to find that out, because the Demon *won't* migrate, and then you'll have a much bigger problem! *David!*' He wasn't listening to me. I heard the crackle of the wax seal breaking. 'David, God, *stop it! Our daughter isn't dead!*'

It seemed like, for one second, time stopped. Even the wind ceased to blow. Then it all snapped back with a vengeance, as David snarled and grabbed a handful of my hair and yanked it painfully back, staring into my face with terrifying fury.

'You,' he said, 'don't talk about my daughter. *Ever.*'

It hurt to talk, but I had no choice. 'David, if you open that bottle, you're making a huge mistake. Imara's alive. She's become the Earth Oracle. Go check if you don't believe me.' I tried to swallow, but the painful angle at which he was holding my head made it almost impossible. 'Go on. I'm not going anywhere.'

He was about one second from killing me. Or popping the cork on that sealed bottle. I didn't know what that would do, but it wouldn't be good.

I got support from an entirely unexpected

quarter: Lewis. He said quietly, 'It couldn't hurt to check.'

'Stay out of it,' David hissed at him.

'What if we're wrong? Look, I'm the first one to want to believe in miracles, but Joanne's memories came back too fast; we both said so. What if...' Lewis looked at me, then at David. 'What if this one's telling the truth? If you're wrong and you open that bottle, we can't make that right without a lot of death and destruction.'

'She's lying!' David's grip on my hair tightened. I squeaked faintly, sure my neck was on the verge of separating from my shoulders. That would be a real mess.

'Then go and check.' Lewis sounded *awfully* calm. Almost offhand about it. 'She's not going anywhere. It's a short trip for you to Sedona and back.'

The pressure on my head relaxed so suddenly it was all I could do to keep my face from bouncing off the road. The push of his hand on my back went away at the same time. I struggled up to my knees, trying to put my shoulders at some angle that didn't hurt like hell, trying to ignore the cutting ache of the zip-ties on my wrists, and looked around. The other Wardens were standing silently around. Nobody was shifting attention, including Lewis.

David vanished with an audible *pop* of air.

I let my head drop. Sweat ran down my cheeks,

funnelled to the point of my chin, and pattered on the stained fabric of my blue jeans.

I had no idea what he was going to find, or believe. But at least I had five minutes.

'If you try anything—' Lewis began.

'Yeah, yeah, you'll kill me,' I finished in a tired mumble. 'Save your breath.' What if Imara didn't appear to David? I hadn't even considered that maybe he wouldn't be able to see her, or that she might not want to see him. It had seemed like my only shot, and now that I thought about it, it was thinner than a Hollywood starlet on diuretics. 'I am *so* kicking your ass later, Lewis.'

He smiled. Cynically. 'Always possible,' he said. 'Shut up before I seal your mouth.'

He could do it, too. I shut up and concentrated on breathing, and wondering where the *hell* my Djinn cavalry had ridden off to. Venna had just left me. Cut her losses and skipped. I didn't know if Ashan was dead in the wreck, or if she'd taken him with her; either way, nobody was stepping up for me when I needed it.

My fingers were tingling. I tried adjusting my wrists, and to my shock I found that the zip-ties were softening. Stretching like rubber bands. I stopped moving after the first second, holding my breath and praying that Lewis – or the other Wardens – hadn't noticed. It didn't look like they had. 'How's Marion?' I asked. 'I didn't hurt her, did I?'

'Marion's fine.' Lewis's tone said the subject was not only closed but locked. 'Last warning. Shut up.'

I'd blurted out the question only to keep him from noticing that I was working my hands free, but the Warden behind me, some young brown-haired surfer dude, yelled a warning. 'She's getting loose!'

Narc.

I abandoned any pretence of trying to keep it low-key, snapped the zip-ties, pushed myself up from the road, and ran for the nearest fallen tree. I dove behind it just as a firebolt zipped towards me, and the wood exploded into splinters and flame. I didn't stop. I crawled, frantic to find some way, *any* way, to defend myself, but it was a useless effort. Lewis was blocking me on the aetheric. The other Wardens weren't as powerful, but they were competent enough, and when I rolled for the shelter of another pile of brush it went up in flame, driving me back. A gust of wind hit me full in the chest and knocked me back, staggering, and I tripped over a sudden profusion of wildly growing tree roots erupting out of the ground to wrap around my feet.

It was over that fast.

The Earth Warden – the young girl of Chinese ancestry, I guessed, who was standing nearest to me – fastened me down with more whipping roots, saw-edged grasses, vines...anything that would hold. I wrestled futilely, then relaxed as a vine wrapped three times around my throat and squeezed.

'Right,' I choked out, and shut my eyes. 'I'll wait here, then.'

The minutes ticked by, each one both torturously slow and unbelievably fast. I could almost see the sand running out in the hourglass – or, more appropriately, the blood dripping out of my veins.

I wondered whether I was going to end up dead at David's hands, or some crazed, Demon-infected Djinn's. Either way, my prospects looked none too shiny.

I sensed the disturbance of air that accompanied David's arrival, and opened my eyes as he formed, already striding out of the air. He was wearing his coat again, the long olive-drab military coat, and under it his shirt was black, as were his pants. He looked ready for battle, and the look on his face was fierce and focused.

Shit. I'd thrown my last set of dice, and I'd lost.

'Well?' Lewis asked. David didn't pause, and he didn't answer. He kept walking, past Lewis, right to me.

Then he ripped the roots out of the ground that held me down, unwrapped the vine from around my neck, and collapsed to a kneeling position to gather me in his arms and rock me slowly back and forth. His hands stroked my back, up and down, then moved up to cup the back of my head. I felt a burst of heat move through me, sealing cuts, healing strained and herniated muscles, infusing me with a warm glow of safety.

He felt so incredibly warm, real, and solid against me.

'Oh,' I said faintly, and met his eyes. 'You found her, right?'

He didn't speak at all. He traced his thumbs down the line of my chin, and there was a light in him that made me kindle in response. I kissed him, breathless with relief, and he responded so ardently I felt faintly embarrassed to be doing this in public view. The kiss was a promise, intimate and gentle, of a lot more to come. When I pulled back his hands continued to move over me, restless and frantic, silently assuring me that he knew. He *knew*.

The Wardens were all looking at Lewis. Lewis, in turn, was staring at the two of us with a stone-hard expression and dark, impenetrable eyes.

And then he smiled, and there was a trace of bitterness in it, but just a trace. The rest was pure satisfaction. 'Well, that was close,' Lewis said, and jerked his head at the other Wardens. 'Glad to be right. Back off. Give them some air.'

The Wardens clustered together, murmuring in low voices. Lewis didn't join them. He took a cell phone out of his pocket and dialled, said a few words, and sat down on a log to wait.

I focused back on David. 'You really thought that bitch was me?' He flinched. 'Oh, come *on*. You didn't.'

His hands stroked through my hair, combing out tangles and curls. It fell in a shining black silk curtain over my shoulders and his hands. 'I love your hair,' he whispered. 'Did I ever tell you that?'

'Can't remember,' I said, and smiled just a little. 'Sorry. Nothing personal. The other one's got my memories. I'm still brain-damaged.'

He sighed and rested his forehead against mine, a gesture of trust more intimate than a kiss. 'The morning after we got you to the clinic, you – went crazy. Tried to kill the staff and escape,' he said. 'We found you and restrained you, and when you woke up, you...remembered. You were all right again.' Shadows flickered in his eyes. 'Except you weren't. And it wasn't you. It was *her*.' He swallowed hard. 'But she *remembered*, Jo. She remembered *Imara*. She knew your past, she knew me – I had no reason to doubt it. She felt...'

'Real,' I supplied soberly. 'I know. It's not your fault. She knew what you wanted, what you needed, and she played right to it. I can't blame you. I wouldn't have believed me, either. She set me up good. Pretty stiff competition.'

'She's not competition,' he said, and kissed me,

fast and hard. 'She's been voted off the island.'

I didn't know why that was funny, but it was, and I felt giggles bubbling up inside me, hot and giddy. 'Speaking of islands, I'd really like to be on one. A deserted one, with sandy beaches and warm breezes and—'

'And clothing optional?' he murmured. 'I'd like that, too.'

'Well? Get to it, Magic Man.' I wasn't serious, and he wasn't taking me seriously. Man, being responsible was a huge pain in the ass. 'David – I still don't remember. What memories I have, they're borrowed, they're not mine. But my feelings...those are mine. And they're real.'

His hands went still, waiting.

'I have these feelings for you that I really can't – God. David, look, if you want to go find Joanne Number Two, go ahead. She's a ready-made girlfriend, I'm kind of a DIY project, at best.'

He gave me a slow, wicked smile. 'But I like working with my hands.'

I fought the urge to melt against him. 'What are we going to do about her?'

His eyes, which had faded to a warm human brown, flared back to bronze. 'She tried to convince me to kill you,' he said. 'I don't know what she'll do next.'

'Well, Venna had a plan—'

'Venna. I thought she'd been deceived.' David

smiled crookedly, well aware how ironic that was now. 'She was protecting you. From me.'

'I'm not so short-sighted,' Venna said, out of nowhere. I jumped. Five feet away, the air shimmered, shifted, and revealed Venna's tiny, tidy figure – spotless, composed, back in her Alice-themed dress and pinafore. She smiled slightly. Nothing innocent about it.

At her feet lay Ashan, unconscious.

'I wasn't just protecting *her*,' Venna continued, as if she'd been part of the conversation all along. 'What Ashan did caused an imbalance, and the Demon took advantage. We have to right the balance – you know that. Joanne is a means to an end.'

David's eyes were fixed on Ashan. 'What about him?'

'All locks have keys.'

'You can make duplicate keys,' David said, 'when you break one.'

To his credit, David didn't rip Ashan in half on sight. I suspected that was because of what he'd found in Sedona, and because – maybe – of what Imara had conveyed to him. He hadn't said a word about it, but there was a deep-seated peace in him that hadn't been there before. Apparently he was willing to let bygones be...

Well, maybe not. After staying still for several long seconds, David flashed across the intervening space, grabbed Ashan by the back of the neck, and dangled him off the ground like a toy. His lips were drawn back from his teeth, and those teeth were *pointed*. I remembered Rahel giving me the shark grin when we'd met after the helicopter ride; that was nothing compared to the savage expression on David's face at that moment. *Even predators can be pets*, Venna had said, but David was more like a T. rex, and I wasn't so sure he'd ever been tamed.

'If you kill him,' Venna said, tense, 'the Demon wins, and this Joanne dies. Is this what you want, David?'

I was afraid he hadn't heard her for a second, but then he threw Ashan down – hard – and crouched to converse eye-to-eye with Venna. 'What game are you playing, Venna?'

'The same as you,' she said. 'I found her here. I kept her alive. I found Ashan.'

'You *kept* Ashan from me. Didn't you?'

'Well, yes, I expected you'd try to destroy him,' she said. 'Confess. Aren't you glad I did? Really?'

'You didn't do it to help me or Joanne. You did it for your own reasons.'

She shrugged.

David looked grim, and almost angry. 'Venna, if you're thinking about standing against me, don't. I don't want a fight. Back off.'

'I can't,' she said. 'It's not my choice, David; it's just practical. You may be in charge now, but you won't be for long, because the old ones aren't listening to you, and they won't ever listen. You may be the conduit, but you're not Jonathan. They won't obey you. Somebody needs to be able to control them, and it can't be one of the New Djinn this time.' She looked down at Ashan. 'He might have been wrong, but he was right in one way: The fight's coming, whether he ends up in charge or not. You can't stay where you are, David. I'm just trying to give you a chance to consider your options and control how it occurs.'

I didn't know what she was talking about, but it sounded ominous. Worse, it sounded ominous for *David*. Personally.

'You didn't save Ashan for me or for Joanne,' David said. 'I'm not stupid enough to think you like either of us that much. You protected Ashan because he's a symbol of the Old Ones. You're trying to restore him to what he was.'

She didn't even try to deny it. 'Yes,' she said. 'He deserved punishment, and he *was* punished. But he doesn't deserve destruction.' She met his eyes. 'He's my brother, David. He's your brother, too, in a lesser way. But I wouldn't expect a human-born to understand what that means to one of us.'

David's face tightened. 'She wasn't your daughter, Venna. Joanne isn't your lover.'

'More loss doesn't balance the scales. It's enough, David. *Enough*.'

He let out a slow, unsteady breath. 'You want me to help restore his powers? And trust him?'

Venna said, quite simply, 'Yes.'

'Excuse me,' I said, and stepped forward. 'Could you speak in the kind of English that makes sense? Because it sure as hell sounds like you're planning to give Ashan back his powers, and just from what I know about him, I am *not* voting yes.'

Venna looked at me like I was a bug on her bathroom floor. 'I thought you wanted to live.'

'Venna.' David was making a real effort to keep his tone even and calm. 'It's impossible.'

Venna's stare was predator-steady. 'Oh, it's possible,' she said. 'It comes down to what you really want, David. And you don't know, do you? You want everything. You want to be Djinn and carry on Jonathan's work. You want to be human and live a human life. You want your lover; you want your daughter; you're nothing but *wants*, as infantile as any human. But *you can't have these things*. Not all of them. You're going to have to choose.'

'Shut up,' he said, and took a step towards her. Venna, small as she was, fragile as she seemed, suddenly looked much more dangerous.'

'Don't tell me what to do,' she said. 'I'm not your toy. And you're not Jonathan.' She reached down, grabbed Ashan by the collar of his shirt, and dragged him up to a sitting position. He remained limp as a puppet. 'When you decide to be sensible, let us know. Until then, he remains with me.'

'Venna, wait—'

She disappeared with a faint shimmer and a pop.

Lewis walked over, hands in the pockets of his jeans, casual and laconic as ever. 'That went well,' he said to David. David just glared at him. 'Right. Well. I tried intercepting our impostor's SUV. It was empty. We have no idea where she's going.'

I cleared my throat. 'Actually,' I said, 'I think I might be able to find that one out.'

It wasn't flattering that they both looked so damn surprised about it.

'Hang on,' Paul Giancarlo said. 'What do you mean, *this* is the real Joanne?' He gave me a look that rivalled Venna's for its ability to reduce me to the status of a small crawling thing. 'No offence, but I think you've both been smoking something. Joanne left here in the SUV with you guys, and you come back with *this* and tell me *she's* the real deal? Are you fucking crazy?'

We were in the lodge, which was a nice, woodsy sort of place, privately owned by the Wardens, halfway up the slope of a decent-sized foothill to a more-than-decent-sized mountain. Blanketed by a light covering of snow, surrounded by the fresh green towering trees, it looked like a Christmas card. There was even a fire snapping and roaring in the hearth, bathing my right side in heat where I sat on the couch. Lewis had a wing chair across from me, booted feet up on a primitive-style coffee table built out of uneven round logs. David was pacing. The other Wardens had come with us, but they'd stayed in other rooms. Reporting to HDQ, presumably, or doing whatever it was that Wardens did, generally.

The other two in the room had been waiting for us at the lodge: Marion and Paul. Marion looked tired, but I couldn't see any long-term effects from our last encounter. I was glad, because I had the feeling that damaging Marion would be a very bad move on many different levels.

Paul looked pissed. He was scary when he was pissed.

'The other one convinced all of us,' Lewis said. 'She told us what we wanted to hear, and we all bought in. But it wasn't real. *She* wasn't real. And now she's out there, and we need to stop her.'

'This is *bullshit*!' Paul spat, and stalked away, arms folded, to stare out the big picture window at the gorgeous view. I exchanged a look with Lewis, then got up and went to stand next to Paul, my hands folded on the windowsill. 'Don't try to slick me, chickie. I got zero reason to believe you, either.'

'That's true,' I said, and turned to look him right in the eyes, then jerked my head to the door.

'Can we talk in private? Please?'

He glanced at the others, suspicion grooved so deep into his face it looked like tribal tattoos. 'I got nothing to say to you.'

'Paul.' I kept watching him, then turned and walked to the door. I didn't look back, but after a few seconds of silence I heard his heavy footsteps coming after me. The next room over was a small library. No fires lit in this room; it was cool and smelt of old paper, spiced with a hint of pumpkin from a bowl of potpourri. The curtains were drawn over the single window, and I shut the door after Paul followed me inside, and leant against it with the knob digging into my back.

He folded his arms and glared. 'What? And don't even think about touching me, bitch.'

'You seem pretty angry about being fooled. Just what did she do to get you on her side?'

He went white, then mottled red. He didn't answer.

'Paul,' I said. 'Look, I don't remember you, OK? All I have is memories from a few people—'

'Yeah.' He snorted. 'Heard what you did to Marion and the folks at the clinic. Sounds like you're the menace, not the other one.'

' – and a whole lot of guesses. You and me, we were never...?' I was keeping my voice very low, although I wasn't stupid enough to assume that the rest of them couldn't hear me if they wanted to eavesdrop. Especially David.

Paul shrugged, looking extremely uncomfortable. 'None of your business.'

'I'll take that as a no. Then why am I thinking you're looking at me in a whole different way than you were the last time I met you?'

He gave me a miserable look and scrubbed his hands over his dark five-o'clock shadow. 'Jesus fucking Christ, don't go there.' His voice had dropped to an urgent whisper. I matched it.

'Did she? Go there?'

Of course she had. He looked helplessly at me, and I understood. Evil Twin had set out to win over every single person that I could count on, and Paul had an Achilles' heel...he wanted me. So...she gave him what he wanted. And somehow she'd kept David from knowing it. (Because otherwise Paul wouldn't be standing here intact and unharmed. I knew that without the benefit of any memories.)

I shook my head. 'Paul, that wasn't me. *She* wasn't me.'

'So *you* say. Sorry, but I'm not buying the next load of crap to get trucked by.' He was looking a little ill now. 'That was *you*. Joanne. Christ, I've known her – you – half your life. I'd know the difference!'

The scariest thing about it? Maybe he was right about that. Maybe the Demon really had become more me than me.

'She showed you what she wanted you to see,'

I said. 'She showed David the faithful lover. She showed each of you exactly what would get her the maximum mileage...' God, what had she shown Lewis? *One hell of a good time.* I tried hard not to even consider it. 'She wanted you on her side. Against me.'

'I repeat: I've got zero reason to believe you. And I'm not hearing anything to convince me.'

I spread my arms. 'I'm not a Demon. You can check.'

'How do you think we do that? It's not the fucking Inquisition around here.'

'Ask Marion. She'd know. She can see Demon Marks.' Which begged the question... 'Why didn't she recognise Evil Twin?' I asked it aloud, not expecting an answer, but surprisingly Paul actually had one.

'She wasn't awake,' he said. 'After you pulled your stunt that night in the clinic, she was in a coma. She came out of it this morning.'

'When the person you thought of as me left,' I said. He frowned and nodded. 'Well, that's a coincidence. Lucky E.T. didn't just kill her.'

He looked suddenly ill.

'What?'

Paul's mouth opened and closed, then opened again to say, 'Marion's breathing stopped three times in the night. If there hadn't been an Earth Warden with her...'

Evil Twin didn't dare act directly, then, not if she was trying to carry on her campaign to become the one true Joanne. That had saved Marion's life. No doubt E.T. would have been delighted to have dispatched one of the only people in the world who could see her true, unpleasant nature. But Faux Joanne probably would have managed to keep her in a coma indefinitely, until an opportunity came around to quietly shuffle her offstage.

Paul's gaze, which had unfocused to mull things over, sharpened back on me. 'How do I know you weren't behind that?'

'We could play this game all day, Paul, but the point is, I'm here, Marion's awake, and she's not pointing at me and screaming, 'Demon,' now, is she? So you're going to have to take something on faith.' My turn to fold my arms and frown. 'Paul, if I was in love with David, I'd never have slipped off with you. Not that you aren't studly, but...'

He looked deeply uncomfortable. Shuffled his feet and cleared his throat. Adjusted the limp tie at the collar of his much-rumpled business shirt, which was finely tailored but not up to the rigors of a Joanne Baldwin crisis. 'Yeah,' he mumbled to the floor. 'I guess I knew that. I've known you a long time. You're a tease, but—'

'Tease?'

'Flirt,' he amended hastily. 'Jesus. Touchy, ain't ya? Look, whatever happened, the point is, she didn't get what she wanted, right?'

I wasn't so sure of that. 'What *did* she want?' I pushed away from the door and paced a little, nervous and chilly. 'She wanted to cut me off from any support, sure, but it was more than that. She went out of her way to enlist people. She wanted to be part of the Wardens. Why?'

'Because you were?'

I shook my head. 'It wasn't just that she wanted a life. It's more than that.' I remembered the way she'd felt in the clinic when she'd been about to kill me. And even back in the forest before the helicopter rescue. She'd refined her methods, but what she wanted wasn't just to be *me*. 'Before she came after me, she took over Kevin. She wanted something, and it wasn't just about finding me, because she took him over when he was fighting the California fire – when was that?'

Paul pulled a handheld computer from his pocket and booted it up with a press of his thumb. He had big hands, but he was good with them, tapping out commands with effortless speed. 'Same day,' he said. 'Same day you disappeared in Sedona.'

I nodded. 'Then I need to talk to Kevin. Now.'

Summoning Kevin for a personal chat took about an hour, during which somebody provided lunch; I'd forgotten how good food could taste, and devoured two sandwiches without pausing for much beyond swigs of bottled water. Oh, it was good. I'd been willing to settle for some of Lewis's stale trail bars.

When he arrived Kevin wasn't alone; he screeched up the drive in a black Warden-issue SUV, the kind with the sun symbol aetherically embossed on the side, and for a second I was afraid that Evil Twin had come home for a *High Noon*-style showdown.

But when the passenger door opened, it was Cherise who got out. I was unreasonably cheered to see her, because she looked a hell of a lot better than she had – fresh, scrubbed, cute as a button in her snowflake-patterned tight sweater and blue jeans.

She had to be feeling better. Her nail polish matched the outfit.

'Jo!' Cherise was the only person I didn't need to win over; she flew across the room and hugged me like a sister. Well, from what I'd been through with Sarah, more like the sister I *wished* I had. 'God, you look like *hell*! Hygiene, honey! Look into it!'

'Been busy,' I said.

'Too busy to comb the crap out of your hair?' But she was kidding, and her grin faded fast. 'What's going on? I thought you were better.'

'Was I?' I gave her a long look as we stood at arm's length, and she slowly shook her head.

'Oh, man, that wasn't you, was it? Dammit. I knew something was wrong; I *knew*.' If she had, Cherise had been the only one. Ironic, since she was also the only one of the entire group without some superpower or other, beyond looking fabulous under difficult circumstances. 'You didn't seem like...you.'

'But I remembered you.'

'Sure.' She shrugged. 'But still. So. Evil twin?'

'Evil twin.'

'That's hot.'

'Not so much, from this side.'

'Oh, come on, I'd *kill* for an evil twin. How cool would that be?'

I reached out and put a hand on Cherise's shoulder. 'Cher, I think she's the one who hurt you. And Kevin.'

I felt her flinch, but somehow she managed to hold on to her smile. 'OK. I take it back. Wouldn't kill for an evil twin, but I might kill *her*.'

Kevin had come in sometime during our conversation, stomping snow off his heavy Doc Martens and shooting distrustful looks around the room. He wasn't judgmental about it. He didn't like anybody, except, of course, Cherise. He unzipped his black jacket – it was a Raiders down jacket, with the pirate logo on it – as if he were intending to pull out an Uzi and mow us all down, but that was just his normal urban 'tude.

'You yanked my leash?' he said to Lewis, who was sitting next to the fire with a cup of coffee. Lewis lifted his mug in my direction. 'Great. Not her again.'

I ignored his hostility. Seemed the best way to deal with him, all the way around. 'Kitchen,' I said. 'Let's do the inquisition over some lunch.'

It was a pretty strategic move, seeing as how it put me within reach of a plateful of chocolate-chip cookies someone had left behind, and Kevin was too busy shoving turkey on rye into his mouth to give me much grief. Cherise quizzed me on ingredients, natural versus processed, organic versus pesticides, and other questions that I cheerfully lied my way through to get her plate filled. She even nibbled her way through a quarter of a cookie, looking mortified the whole time that she was doing it.

'You ask us here just to feed us?' Kevin mumbled around a mashed-up mouthful of sandwich. I resisted the urge to tell him not to chew and talk.

'I need to ask you about what you remember,' I said. 'When you were taken over that day.'

He stopped chewing, swallowed, and put the sandwich down, growing fascinated by the pattern of the tablecloth. I felt for him, but I couldn't let it go this time. 'Kevin,' I said. 'She was in your head. That means you know things that can help me now.'

He shook his head. His hair looked lank and oily, and I wondered if he ever washed it. I marvelled at my urge to mother him, considering how much he disliked me. And how generally unlikable the kid was.

'She's still out there,' I said. 'She could do to other people what she did to you. For all I know she's already doing it. You can't seriously be OK with that.'

Another mute shake of his head. I didn't know what it meant, but it was at least a response.

'You don't want to remember,' I said. 'I know. I get that. But we don't have a lot of choices now. We have to find her.'

'What's this 'we'?' He looked up, and his eyes were dark with resentment. 'It's never about the 'we' with you. When you say 'we,' you just want something. And then you'll leave me behind.'

'I won't. Not this time.'

'Why should I believe you?'

'No idea. But I'm telling you the truth. If you want to go with me, I've got no issues with that. You've got more motivation than most people out there to take her down, right? I could use that.'

He frowned. 'What if Lewis says no?'

'You think Lewis is the boss of me?'

He chewed another bite of sandwich while he thought about it, then gave me a grudging nod of acceptance. 'OK. What do you want me to do?'

I took in a deep breath and looked at Cherise, who'd put down her barely nibbled cookie and was watching, wide-eyed. 'It's what I did to Cherise before. I want to look at your memories and—'

I didn't get to finish, because Kevin slammed his chair back with a screech of wood on wood, and headed for the door. I summoned a blast of wind to slam it shut in his face – too much wind, too clumsy, and I had to bleed off the resulting energy into a surge of static that made sparks flare in the light fixtures.

'Screw you! You're not touching me!' Kevin yelled, and grabbed the doorknob. Another unintended consequence of my ham-fisted use of power: It was hot enough to burn. He yelped, cradled his hand, and backed away.

I got up and took his hand in mine, palm up, and smoothed my fingers over the burn. This was easier, somehow. There was a rich, quiet flow of power coming up from my feet, channelled up from the ground, and it spilt like golden light through my body and out of my stroking fingers, to coat his wound and sink in deep.

In seconds the burn was gone.

'Shit,' Kevin said, and pulled his hand back to stare at it. Then he looked at me. 'Thought you were Weather.'

'Well, you know, I joined one of those Power-of-the-Month clubs, and it looks like I've completed the set.'

His fingers curled in over the palm, hiding it. 'I don't care what you are. I still don't want you in my head.'

Kevin had issues, with a capital I. 'I'll limit it to just what I need to know,' I said.

'And what, I'm supposed to trust you?' He gave me a scorching look of contempt. 'Please.'

'Kevin.'

'What?'

'I'm asking,' I said. 'I'm just asking. I won't force you to do it. I won't take it from you. But without you I don't know how we're going to do this; I really don't. You're important.'

I kept it simple, and straightforward, and he frowned at me, looking for the trick. For the spin.

There wasn't any. I meant exactly what I said.

He looked away, to Cherise. She was uncharacteristically quiet and sober, and she slowly nodded.

'I'll be right here,' she said. 'Right here.'

Kevin sank down in his chair, hands scrubbing his knees in agitation, and gave me one quick, jerky nod of acceptance.

I didn't wait for him to have second thoughts. Sometimes it's better to pull the Band-Aid off quickly.

I put my hand on his head and dropped into the world according to Kevin.

Chapter Fourteen

He was just a kid when his dad got married to the Evil Hag Bitch from Hell, just a kid, and she wouldn't leave him alone; she was always touching him, coming on to him; he was a kid...

I tried to pull away from the memories, but Kevin's mind was full of mines, booby traps, sinkholes of horrible things. He'd been a good kid once, or at least no worse than most boys his age, but throw in a stepmother who wasn't above teasing him, then using him, then outright molesting him...

Kevin's mind was a house of horrors. I was afraid to move; everything I did seemed to resonate through him, and there was no clear path, no direction. I tried viewing him in the map of lights that had become my guide, but his lights were grey, blood red, almost nothing clean. *Oh, Kevin.* It broke my heart how much he'd suffered, and that the memories never left him. And no matter how careful I was, things shifted, bled, broke open as I moved.

And things oozed out, whether I wanted to know them or not.

The night she finally did it, the night she turned off the lights and crawled into bed and Did It, it all got confused; it all got mixed-up; he felt horrible and wrong and excited and sick and scared and worried, and there was something wrong with him, wrong, and what would Dad think? But Dad was asleep, drunk off his ass, and that was that, this was this, and even though he didn't really want it he did; there was something sick about it he couldn't control, and –

God, stop! I yanked myself away, but the memory was like tar – it wouldn't come off. Wouldn't go away.

– after it was over she went away and he tried to sleep but there was something wrong in his head, something he couldn't start, couldn't stop, couldn't control, and it was this heat, this shimmer, and he could almost...

When he woke up, the house was on fire. His bed was on fire. And he could hear his father screaming.

And the fire didn't burn him, it dripped out of him like sweat, and his step-monster Yvette had shrieked at him to STOP, KEVIN, STOP, but he didn't know how, and whatever she did didn't help, and when he found his dad and tried to drag him out, the skin just –

I pulled free of Kevin's horrors with a yank that I felt through my entire soul, and tried to touch as little as possible while I sped through those filthy, polluted halls of memory, avoiding the traps where things whispered and beckoned, looking...

Looking for a clean path.

And I was shocked to find that it was...me.

'She's a bitch,' Kevin said to Cherise. They were sitting in the back of an airplane, rattling through turbulence, and he was staring at the back of my head a few rows farther up. 'No offence.'

'None taken,' Cherise said cheerfully. Turbulence seemed to agree with her in some strange way, or maybe it was just the extra glow she seemed to have with Kevin. Resentment was just part of who he was, but in Cherise's company it evaporated like ice in summer. 'She can be, sure. But she's a good person, Kev. Like you.'

He snorted. 'You don't know me.'

God, that was true. Kevin had done terrible things, but he'd also had even worse done *to* him. I couldn't blame him. I couldn't imagine the strength it had taken to get him through it in the first place.

'Besides,' he said, 'she's just looking for a reason to turn me in. She thinks I'm dangerous.'

I realised something important. Kevin honestly feared me, and he honestly respected me, too. He didn't like me. He'd never like me, not in the way that Cherise did, but it mattered what I said to him. What I did.

I had become an authority figure in his eyes. Kevin hated authority figures, but he needed them, too. Same for Lewis...respect, contempt, and need, all rolled up in a toxic mixture together.

'You are dangerous,' Cherise said, and winked at him. She reached out and took his hand in hers. He loved the way her small fingers wrapped over his, loved the way she smelt, the way she sounded and looked and felt. Cherise was the one thing in his life that he loved without judgment.

Without resentment.

He'd do anything for her.

God, she was pretty. Not just pretty – beautiful. And she was so...bright. Yvette had been pretty, but in a cheap kind of way, a slutty way, but Cherise...when she smiled it was like the sunshine. What the hell she was doing hanging with that stone-cold bitch Joanne...

(whom he nevertheless respected...)

...Cherise was somebody he could help. Somebody warm and soft and someone who needed him, needed him. And when he got between her and trouble, she made him feel... He was too young for her, she'd teased him, but she hadn't treated him that way, not really.

And she hadn't used him. She'd just been... amazing. Sweet and kind and funny and normal, in ways that he'd never known before. She didn't want anything except his company and his time. She wasn't looking for an advantage – hell, she had guys crawling over broken glass to ask for dates. She didn't need him.

And yet somehow she did, and that made this so much better.

And that made it so much worse, when he failed in the forest.

I'd found it. The trail turned dark again, as if Cherise's sunshine presence had gone behind a cloud, and all his internal demons had crawled out of their holes, never more than a heartbeat away.

I took a breath and sank deep into his memory.

At first it was good. Better than good. The Wardens had given him assignments, and he'd surprised himself with how good he'd been at it. Lewis had been an ass at times, but he'd shown him stuff, and Kevin had learnt, although he hadn't wanted to let on that he was paying attention. Wasn't cool to be too eager.

So when the Wardens dropped him on the front lines of the California fire near Palm Springs, he'd taken Cherise with him. Wasn't supposed to; he'd been told to leave her at the base camp, but she'd wanted to come, and he'd wanted an audience, right? Somebody to impress.

So it was all his fault.

At first it had worked just the way he'd wanted. He'd been taught how to set controlled fires to create firebreaks, and he could do it faster and better than the regular firefighters, without any risk of losing control no matter how long the fire line got. He'd done a good job, a really good job, and Cherise had kept him supplied with water and sometimes kisses of congratulations, which had been pretty great. Because she'd asked him to, he'd worked with some crotchety old bastard of an Earth Warden to save some horses who were trapped on the hills, and the light in her eyes as the small herd galloped past them, safe, had been better than any sex he'd ever had.

And then it had all gone bad right around dark. First he'd felt it as an ache in his chest, and he'd thought he'd caught some smoke, but he couldn't cough it out. There was something wrong with him, and there was something wrong with Cherise, too, and he couldn't stop it. Couldn't help her. It was like the whole world was dying around him; he could feel it slipping away, and...then it came back, and things had returned to normal for a few minutes, and he'd held Cherise and told her it was all going to be OK, and that had been a lie.

The fire jumped one of the breaks he'd set, so he went closer to try to stop it before it could leap treetops. He told Cherise to stay back, so he didn't see it happen, but when he extinguished the flames racing through the dry underbrush, he turned back and...

She was on the ground, and there was a thing, a *thing* with its hands buried in her chest.

Kevin screamed and threw himself at it, and it batted him away into a tree. He saw blood and stars and felt something wrong with his head, like he'd hit it too hard, and when he got up again Cherise was standing there like nothing had happened.

But it wasn't Cherise, and that wasn't her smile, because it wasn't the sunshine.

It was something else.

'Kevin,' she said, and came towards him. 'Honey, it's OK. It's all OK. I need you.'

Cherise had known to say that, not the thing inside, and that was what stopped him from backing away. That, and the bleak, black knowledge that nothing ever really worked right for him in the long run. Of course this had to happen.

It always did.

Oh, Kevin, I thought from that separate quiet place where I stood. *It doesn't have to. You have to have faith.*

But he wasn't listening, and anyway, this was already done, already past, and he was giving up because he just thought there wasn't any real point in trying.

So he didn't fight when Cherise reached out

and put her hands on his head – *exactly the way I'd done it when I'd entered his memories* – and the Demon began to tunnel through his head like a huge tapeworm, digesting his memories, relishing the pain and the horror and the struggles in a way that nothing human should. It learnt him, every part of him, and it learnt his body down to the cellular level.

And from that point on I wasn't in Kevin's memories anymore.

I was in *hers*.

She was cold inside. Ice-cold, all clean logic and calculation, empty of kindness or compassion. She made Eamon, messy and awful as he was, seem like Father Christmas in comparison. She wanted only one thing, and it was the iron-hard central core of who she was: *She wanted to go home.*

And she would do anything, use anyone, destroy the world to get there.

Starting with Cherise, because she'd been close and vulnerable, but really starting with Kevin, because he was what she needed. Power. Strength. Energy.

She used him like a straw, an empty vessel good for nothing but as a conduit between her and what she craved...raw aetheric energy, the stuff that powered all Wardens. She would have preferred to consume a Djinn for the sheer force of the experience, but since the Djinn had slipped their bonds to humans, it was far riskier to her. No, a Warden would do to satisfy her hunger.

She had tried the girl first, but the pathetic meat hadn't been able to deliver much of a meal; humans barely brushed the aetheric, and so were of little use. But she kept Cherise, aware of the emotions it roused in the boy; the angrier and more afraid he was, the more energy the Demon was able to draw.

It was horrible, and it was cruel, and it interested her for a long time. Too long.

She used Cherise and Kevin to stalk other Wardens. Those she did not bother to control, only to drain and slaughter, but Cherise and Kevin provided her with a self-sustaining well of anguish that she would not easily give up.

And then something happened. Something startling.

There was a shift of energy on the aetheric, titanic in its intensity. It was like some soundless explosion, and everything rippled. The Demon felt it and chased after, not even sure what she was chasing, but there was something floating there in the emptiness, something free and powerful...

She battened on to it and consumed it, mindless in her raging hunger. Back in the forest, Cherise and Kevin fell like abandoned puppets, and the Demon...changed.

She took on form and weight as what she'd eaten took hold of her.

She'd taken my memories, along with a substantial jolt of my power. She'd found the pieces Ashan had ripped away from me in the chapel in Sedona. The Demon didn't know what had happened to her, didn't have a sense of *self* in the same way that a human did. The change was painful for her, startling and – a new emotion – frightening. She no longer wanted only one thing. Memories confused her, made her want more things, made her ache for what she did not understand, had never had, and she couldn't put it out of her mind because the problem was *in* her mind.

Never to be corrected, because it had been made part of her, imprinted deep.

My memories had damaged her.

I'd woken up afraid, alone, cold and naked, without any memory of who or what I was; she knew, and she was still afraid, still cold, still naked in her own mind.

Demons could not become human, but now she craved the rest of what I'd once had, and she understood something that, as a Demon, she never could: The Wardens were a force, not individually, but as a group. They could be used. Directed.

Made to do her bidding.

She woke up Cherise and Kevin and sent them in pursuit of the remnants of Joanne Baldwin – the sole threat to her existence. She could sense me, not in an aetheric sense but in some other, primitive way that I didn't fully understand; now that I felt it, though, I knew I'd never mistake it.

I stood silently by as the Demon piloted Cherise and Kevin through the forest, hunting Lewis, hunting me, finding us, pursuing. She used them ruthlessly, but all the while she was learning.

Learning a terrifying amount about how to bend people, how to find their buttons, how to get what she wanted.

Because she knew what she wanted now, and it wasn't just being me.

She wanted to open a door between worlds and bring other Demons here to nest, feed, and grow into what she had become.

She wasn't going home.

She was bringing home *here*.

It was a memory, and I'd seen some shocking things, but a chill still zipped up my back as I saw the Demon step out from behind a tree to face Cherise and Kevin. She was me, or partly me, anyway. Her eyes were black and empty, and she was a cheap plastic doll made in my image.

She had no further use for her toys. They were a liability now, not a help, and she knew they were on the verge of failure. Their deaths didn't bother her, but she couldn't take the risk of a tool breaking at a critical moment.

She ripped her awareness out of them as brutally

as she'd put it in, and Kevin had fallen, stunned, as Cherise staggered away crying into the dark, cold world...

And Kevin hadn't been able to follow.

He'd been afraid. Too afraid.

It's useless anyway. I always lose. I lose everything.

The Demon stood over him with her cheap doll eyes and cheap doll skin and cheap doll hair, and smiled.

And then she looked up and smiled directly at me.

I took a step back. *Easy*, I told myself. *It's just a memory. It's the past. It can't hurt you.*

'Yes it can,' she said. 'I knew you'd come. I knew you'd try.'

Oh, shit.

I backed up. It felt as if I were backing into mud, into tar, into sticky spiderwebs.

'This isn't the past,' she said, and stepped *through* Kevin to come towards me. 'This isn't safety. There's no safety for you.'

I stopped. Not because I couldn't back up, but because I knew she wanted me to be afraid. To run. And I was tired of running.

'You know what?' I said. 'Works both ways, bitch. No safety for you, either. So if you want to do it, go on. I'm here.'

She stood there. The doll persona of the Demon

didn't move like a human, didn't act like one; it was just a shape, not even as lifelike as a Disney animatronic.

'Yo! Fembot! I'm talking to you!' I taunted, and took a step forward.

It took a step *back*. Around us, Kevin's memories continued to unspool like a broken movie reel, steeped in hopelessness and fury. Cherise was dying, and he was doing nothing because he knew he couldn't win.

My doppelgänger had helped create that world for him.

And I was going to fix it if it was the last thing I did.

'I'm coming,' I told her. 'I know what you're trying to do. You won't get the Wardens now. You won't be able to use them to open the rift. So what are you going to do instead?'

'Do you really think I'll tell you?'

'I think you already have. See, you think you're being original, but remember, you're just my memories pasted onto a phony doll, run by a smart but cold eating machine. You're predictable.'

It blinked slowly. It probably couldn't do expressions, or didn't want to, but the net effect was scary as hell. I tried not to let it get to me.

'What?' I demanded. 'No threats? No I'm-gonna-get-you-sucka? Come on, get your big-girl panties on already.'

'You're trying to trick me,' it said.

'Not really. I don't have to trick you. You're going to trick yourself right out of existence; you can count on that.'

'I'm going to destroy you.'

'News flash: You made me. When you consumed my memory you created an imbalance of energy, and we know that energy has to go somewhere. Right? It's all balance. And what you gave me back was a chance to survive.' I'd figured that out a while ago, but it still hurt to say it; the last thing I wanted to do was owe my existence to this creature. This land shark. 'If you want to get rid of me, you're going to have to work a hell of a lot harder.'

That pushed a button. A big, red, nuclear launch button. 'I *will*!' it screamed, and there was nothing human about that sound, or about the raw will behind it.

I rolled my eyes. 'Whatever. Is that why you keep using people to do your dirty work? Kevin? Cherise? *David?* And believe me, you're going to pay for putting your dirty little hands on David. Big-time.' I made a show of checking a watch I didn't actually have on my wrist. 'You know what? Drama period's over. See you around the schoolyard, E.T.'

It was a risk, but I thought I could do it, and I did... I turned around and zipped along the path of lights, through the dilapidated, sad halls of Kevin's mind, all the way to the light at the end of the tunnel.

Out.

When I opened my eyes, I was standing right where I'd been, and Kevin had his head down on the table. He was breathing, but unconscious.

I put my hand on his head again, this time just to gently stroke his greasy, matted hair. 'Not everything is a tragedy, Kev,' I said. 'Come on. Wake up now. Nightmare's over.'

He did, lifting his head and blinking like a kid coming out of a long, difficult sleep. He stared blankly for a few seconds, then focused on my face.

'Did you get it?' he asked. He didn't seem bothered by the fact that I was stroking his hair. I didn't stop.

'Got it,' I said. 'Good job, man. Thank you.'

He ducked his head, and I saw a dull flush build in his sallow cheeks.

'Kevin,' I said. 'What happened to Cherise wasn't your fault.'

Cherise looked startled, and mouthed, *Me?*

She didn't remember.

Ah, the beauty of the human mind; I wasn't sure if that was her own doing or Lewis's; maybe he'd taken the bad memories away. Either way, I was glad.

'You know what I remember?' I asked. 'I remember

you going after the first enemy you found back in the forest. I remember you risking your life to even the score when you thought Cherise was dead, and Lewis and I had killed her. I remember the look on your face when you realised she was still alive.' I looked straight at Cherise, who was a little flushed now, too. 'He needs you,' I said. 'And you need him, too, right?' She nodded. 'Better tell him, then,' I said. 'And Kevin? In case you're wondering, that's the reason you're going to want to live through this.'

I pushed through the kitchen door and went through the empty library, back into the large common room where the fire blazed. My own reasons for living were gathered near the warmth. David looked up, smiling. Lewis raised the coffee cup to his lips without comment. The rest of them, including Paul, waited for me to speak.

'The Demon wants to go home, or at least *reach* home,' I said. 'Lewis. If I were going to choose a place where the veil that separates our world from hers is the thinnest, where would I go?'

He put his coffee down, leant forward, and thought about it for a second. He exchanged a look with David, who frowned, and together they both said, 'Seacasket.'

I blinked. 'You've got to be kidding.'

If I'd hated the helicopter flight, I *loathed* the plane ride cross-country. But, given the time ticking away, not to mention the stakes, I thought I'd better suck it up, take the Dramamine, and try to avoid wincing every time the plane hit a wind shear, which was about, oh, every thirty seconds, give or take.

The Wardens had a corporate jet. Who knew? Apparently I now had the authority to commandeer it, or so Lewis told me once we were strapped in. 'Shouldn't there be, like, paperwork?' I asked, and snugged my seat belt tight. 'At least a signature card for that sort of thing? For security?'

Lewis had his eyes shut even before takeoff. 'Trust me. If we live through this, you'll have enough paperwork to keep you in ink stains for the rest of your life.' He paused for a few seconds, then said, 'How sure are you about this?'

'Any of it? On a scale of one to ten? About a three.' That was probably more honesty than he was looking for, I was guessing, from the pained expression that flickered over his face. 'Look, when I was taking on Kevin's memories, I took on some of hers, too. More than that, I felt her...well, I can't really call them emotions. But there's a sense to it I really can't describe. I know that in the beginning her only goal was to go home – it's almost like a spawning thing for them. Even though her motivations have got more complicated, she still has that instinct.'

'Then why do you think she was wasting her

time with trying to take over your life?' he asked, and then looked instantly sorry he'd said that. 'Not that your life isn't important or valuable...'

'Yeah, nice save. The thing is, I don't think becoming *me* was an end in itself. It was all about the Wardens. Think about it: Get enough Wardens together, set them to one common task, and you can get a massive build-up of power. Something she could use to rip a hole from this world into her own.'

He looked ill, and I didn't think it was airsickness. 'I would have helped her do it,' he said. 'We were talking about ways to reorganise the Wardens, concentrate their power. Nobody would have questioned her.'

'It's not your fault.'

'Sure it is,' Lewis said, and closed his eyes. 'I'm going to take a nap while I still can.'

'How can you possibly sleep while...'

He switched himself off, pretty much just like that. I stayed put through the teeth-rattling jounces, and tried to pretend that I didn't hate flying at a cellular level. Lewis really was asleep. I hated him.

Now that we were safely in the air – if that was the right term – we were free to take our lives in our hands and move about the cabin. I unbuckled and made my way through the small, cramped area towards the back. Kevin and Cherise were sitting together, heads close, whispering; they looked up at me, and Cherise winked and offered a thumbs-up. I weakly returned it, crushing the back of Paul's seat in a death grip as the plane dipped and dropped unexpectedly, and he broke off his conversation with Marion to ask me if I was all right. I decided it was better not to lie, so I just smiled palely and kept going.

David was sitting alone at the back of the plane. He hadn't bothered with anything so superfluous as a seat belt, of course. He, like Lewis, seemed perfectly calm, and he was reading a paperback novel, one that looked vaguely familiar to me. *Lonesome Dove*. Larry McMurtry.

I dropped into the seat beside him and whimpered under my breath as our fragile flying machine sledded from one punishing draft to another. He closed his book and took my hand.

'Have we done this before?' I asked.

'Flown in a plane together? No. Mostly we drive.'

'Mostly I understand why.' I gulped and tried to relax. 'So, you want to tell me about Seacasket?'

'Is that why you came back here?' He was staring at the cover of his book. He was wearing round little spectacles, and they softened the lines of his face and made him seem gentle and bookish. And hot, though the hot part was pretty much a given. 'Information?'

'Thought it would be important.'

'Information won't take up much time. It's a long flight.'

Not a pleasant thought *at all*. It was already too long, as far as I was concerned. I wanted my feet on the ground – or at least, my butt in the driver's seat of a car. Now *that* was transportation.

'I need to keep my mind off of this,' I said, and gestured a little wildly at the clanking, shuddering aircraft we were trapped in for the next eternity.

'Be careful,' David murmured. His voice had drifted lower in tone as well as volume, and his eyes were half-closed, still focused on the book cover. 'There are all kinds of ways to take your mind off of it.'

Even in the midst of ongoing panic, that sounded...interesting. More than a little. 'Mmmmm?' That was noncommittal, yet expressed...

David put the book aside, flipped up the armrest that separated us, and shifted to face me. 'I want to try to give you some of my memories.'

Whoa, that was *not* where I'd thought we were going. I'd been in a warm, happy place for a second, and now I was falling right back into Anxiety Alley. 'Um...Venna said it wasn't possible for a Djinn to—'

'You might have noticed that we all have... specialties,' he said. 'Venna's the only Djinn I've ever met who can – sometimes – transport humans through the aetheric without damaging them, and she's got other skills that the rest of us have to only a lesser degree. Doesn't make her more powerful, necessarily, because she's deficient in other areas. Like controlling what you'd term Earth powers.'

'Which you're stronger in.'

He nodded slowly. Light flickered across the surface of his glasses. I wondered why the hell he was wearing them; was there such a thing as a physically imperfect Djinn? Was it just a comfort thing, like a favourite shirt or pair of shoes for a human being? Like his coat... 'What's the deal with the coat?' I asked. I knew it was a non sequitur, but it gave me a chance to consider what he was saying, and how scary it could be to let David in my head. Or me in his, as might be the case.

He blinked. 'My coat?' He wasn't wearing it at the moment, but it was draped over the back of his seat. Olive-drab, vaguely military from an era about a hundred years ago.

'Yeah. You don't even need a coat, right? You don't get cold. And it's very...specific.'

His eyes widened this time. 'Let me understand. We're on our way to stop a Demon wearing your skin from ripping a hole through this world to hers, possibly allowing other Demons to pour through, and you want to talk about my fashion choices?' He paused for a second. 'Wait, coming from you, that actually might make sense.'

I didn't answer. The plane rattled its way through another set of bounces, and I didn't have enough breath in my lungs to curse, because my diaphragm didn't want to function. Maybe, if I held my breath long enough, I'd just pass out. That would get my mind off of the flight.

'The coat was given to me,' he said. 'By someone I cared about.'

'Yeah? What was her name?' Shot in the dark, but not much of one, and I had a fifty-fifty chance of being right, even at the Djinn level.

'Helen,' he said. 'The coat belonged to her son. She lost him in the war.' *Oh*. I searched for a way to get him to tell me the rest, but he shook his head. 'Wardrobe choices aside, Jo, while Venna might not have thought it was possible to share a Djinn's memories with you, I think it might be, if I'm careful and limit the scope of what we're doing. But you have to promise to let me lead.'

Which took me down another path altogether. 'You dance?'

That got a definitely odd look. 'Of course I dance.'

'Have we ever danced?'

He braced himself against the bulkhead, turned sideways in the seat towards me, and extended both his hands. 'Find out,' he said.

I didn't move. 'I'm not sure if this is a good idea.'

'Why not?'

'Because...it just feels – it feels wrong. I don't want an info-dump of how I feel about you.'

He lowered his hands to rest on his thighs as he considered that. 'You're not sure how you feel.'

'Yes – no. No, I am, I just – look, I want to build memories, not just stuff myself full of how other people see me. It's confusing. And it's kind of painful.' I met his eyes directly. 'And it would be cheating for you to show me how deep this goes for you right now. It could scare me off. I don't want to be scared off.'

I bit my lip in agitation as the plane's engines shifted to a deeper thrum. We hit a patch of slick-as-glass air, then steadied out. For the moment.

He didn't seem to have a response to any of that. I pulled in a deep breath and said, in a rush, 'Did you, sleep with her?'

'Who?' His expression went from blank to shocked. 'You mean Helen?'

'No! No, I – wait, did you?'

He ignored that, finally getting my point. 'You mean, did I sleep with the other you. The Demon.'

I nodded. For a few long seconds, there was nothing but the sound of the aircraft, the distant buzz of what other people were saying, and the pounding of my heart.

'Even if I did,' he said carefully, 'it was because I thought she was you.'

'And you didn't know the *difference*?'

He had the grace to look ashamed, and a little sick. 'I didn't have a lot of time to think it through. And to be honest, I don't think I wanted to question it. Not when...'

'Not when you'd been bracing yourself to lose me for ever,' I said. 'Right?'

'Right.'

I felt my lips curve into a smile I couldn't control. 'You sure you've got the right one now?'

His eyebrows slowly rose. 'Fairly sure.'

'Maybe soon we can upgrade that to completely sure.'

'Maybe?'

'Well,' I said, 'privacy's an issue.'

He gave me a slow, wicked smile. 'It really isn't,' he said, 'if that's all that's stopping you. I'm fully capable of giving us all the privacy we want. Right here. Right now.'

I had to admit that kick-started my heart into a whole different speed. I looked around at the cabin mutely. 'They're Wardens,' I pointed out. 'Well, except for Cherise.'

'So they are.' He didn't seem much concerned. 'Trust me. They wouldn't notice a thing.'

'Really?'

'Really.'

He looked very seductive all of a sudden – it was indefinable, how he shifted from business to pleasure, but it was a definite and unmistakable change in his body language. All of a sudden I was hyperaware of the clean, cool lines of him, the way his black T-shirt hugged his chest...the full, rich softness of his mouth.

'You're doing this,' I murmured. 'No fair.'

'Doing what?'

My attention fixed on his lips. I wetted my own lips with my tongue, suddenly remembering a ghostly echo of how he tasted. Half-remembering, anyway. I definitely needed a reminder. 'Djinn charisma,' I said. 'You'd better have a good excuse.'

'Oh, I promise you, it'll be good,' he said. *Bastard*. I caught myself leaning forward and thought about stopping myself, but there didn't seem to be all that much reason, and deep down, I didn't want to even try.

So, I kissed him.

He tasted rich and warm and real. His lips were damp and firm, smooth as silk, warm as sunlight, and I sank against him with a moan. I'd missed this. My body had missed it, not just my mind, and my body stuck my mind in the backseat, bound and gagged it, and took the wheel.

David's kiss filled me with an exhilaration and heat that my skin could only barely contain, and when I opened my mouth to the gentle stroke of his tongue on my lips, he bent me back, cupped my head in his large hand, and got down to business.

The boy knew what he was doing, and French was definitely something in which he was fluent. The warmth in me coalesced into specific aching places.

I don't know exactly how it happened, but I was on his lap by that time, feeling thoroughly and satisfyingly ravished, and his hands started to roam. Innocently at first, fingers dragging down the line of my throat to my collarbone, tracing curves and lines. Then down. As he felt the resistance of each button on my shirt, it gave without a whimper of friction.

Had I ever been magically undressed before? If I had, it was a memory worth keeping. There was a breathtaking sense of being out of control, but utterly safe in his hands. By the time he'd worked his way down to my waist, the shirt was open and loose, and my bra underneath seemed more like a display case than a cover.

Because he'd made it transparent.

'Um...' I pulled back, cheeks flaming. I could still hear the other Wardens talking, moving around, coughing. Somebody was playing a personal stereo at high volume to be heard over the turbulence and engine noise.

Surely *someone* – probably Lewis, with my luck – was going to look back and get the topless show. Not that I minded making extra money, but it seemed excessive. Not to mention unprofessional, if I had to work with these people later.

'They can't see or hear us,' David said. 'What they'll see, if they actually do look, is the two of us talking. It's what they expect to see.'

Maybe, but still...I found myself gathering up the gaping halves of my shirt and pulling it together. 'Sorry,' I said. 'But this is just too strange. It's not that they might see me; it's that I can see them. It's distracting.'

'Oh.' David looked briefly chagrined. 'Sorry. I didn't think about it. You always—' He broke off before uttering whatever sordid bit of my personality he was about to disclose, and instead vaguely nodded towards the rest of the plane.

Which disappeared behind a milky white wall. I reached out and touched it, and my fingers registered a cool surface, not quite solid.

'Soundproofed,' he said. 'But if you want out, all you have to do is push.'

I took my hand away and looked at him. 'I don't want out,' I said. I meant that in so many ways. 'Any chance these seats fold out into a bed?'

'There is now,' he said, and his eyes sparked to a hot, swirling bronze.

He put his hands behind my back and lowered me. Slowly. The seats dissolved into a soft, firm expanse of what felt like a real bed. My head encountered the airy softness of a feather pillow, and I couldn't help but sigh in true happiness.

David was watching me, his eyes half-closed.

Braced above me on stiffened arms.

Not touching me in any way. Not yet.

My breath caught helplessly in my throat as his elbows bent, as his shoulders flexed and the muscles slid under that smooth, matte-velvet skin. I bit my lip as I felt his lips touch my trembling midsection. A burst of warmth zipped up my spine from down low, then exploded outward and inward like an echo. *Oh.*

His lips travelled down, and his tongue trailed gently over the inward slope of my belly button. My bitten lip started to hurt, but when I let go, I moaned. I couldn't help it. I couldn't help my body from lifting towards him, either.

He put one large, warm hand just under my breasts and pushed me back down. 'Not yet,' he murmured, with his lips brushing my skin. His gaze was dark and wicked and intensely sexual. 'We have a long, long way to go. Can't have you going off just yet.'

'Then you'd better stop touching me,' I said breathlessly. 'Because if you don't, I'm going to go off like a Roman candle any second.'

His eyebrows canted upward. He dragged his fingertips over the centre of the thin fabric of my bra, and it just...dissolved. Then he folded the two halves back from my body, along with my shirt. 'Then I'd better make it worth your while,' he said, and moved up to trail his tongue over my right nipple.

His hair was warm and silky under my fingers, and for a while I just whited out, flying on sensation. When he touched the waistband of my pants, and I felt the button and zippers giving up to him, I knew I was lost. Deliriously, deliciously, wonderfully lost.

I didn't lie to him. I did come like a Roman candle, bursting into waves of light and shuddering pleasure, striving against his hands and his lips, long before we got to the main course.

That didn't mean I was finished, though.

And he'd known that all along.

Chapter Fifteen

It felt like too short a flight, since we spent it horizontal, naked, and blissful under silken covers, protected and secluded by a swirling bubble of opal energy. David's body fitted perfectly under my hands, as though it had been made to match me. In theory I was a virgin, but in practice, memory wasn't a barrier to this at all. There wasn't any pain, there wasn't any hesitation, and there was certainly no trace of shame, no matter what I felt moved to do with him, or for him. It felt like the world had opened up to me for the first time, channelled through his lips, his hands, his firm, warm skin, the urgent and careful strength he used in every touch. There was a kind of fever-dream delirium to it, because surely real life wasn't like this. Couldn't be like this. If it was, how had I ever got out of his bed?

If he was using any kind of Djinn magic, I was all for the practice. Practice, practice, practice.

As we lay in a dreamy, dishevelled state of

paradise, twisted together in the sheets, I traced letters on his chest like a lovesick kid. 'Do you know what I'm writing?' I asked, and had a sudden dizzying idea that he'd seen lovers play that game back when writing was still in hieroglyphics. Or cuneiform.

'Tell me,' he whispered, and pressed his lips to a particularly sensitive spot at my temple. I shivered.

'I...L...O...V...E...'

'Chocolate,' he said. 'Fast cars. Dangerously expensive shoes.'

I drew a single letter – U.

He didn't speak. He traced with one warm finger the spot on my temple he'd kissed, drawing something that was more abstract than letters, more direct.

'You don't have to stay with me,' he said. 'It's true that once Djinn let ourselves...feel things like this, we can't turn it off. But we *can* turn away. And I would. If you asked.'

I put my head down on his chest. He might not have been human, but his body felt that way. His heart thumped gently under my hand, and I felt the elastic movement of his lungs. His arms went around me and cradled me there.

'Venna said this makes you weak,' I said. 'Does it?'

'Don't worry about me.'

'I do. I will. Does it?'

I felt his sigh stir the damp hair around my forehead. 'I think the more connection the Djinn have to the human world, the better off we all are,' he said. 'Personally. Politically. In every way. So, no. It's a different kind of strength; that's all. I just have to make them believe it.'

'But the Old Ones won't. Like Venna.'

'Not your problem,' he said in a gentle but subject-is-closed kind of way. 'Life over on the Djinn side of things isn't any more predictable than it is on the human side. We only seem stable because we don't let the kids see the grown-ups fight.'

I laughed, then fell silent. I never wanted to move. Never wanted to arrive. I wanted this breathlessly perfect time to simply freeze.

But I heard the engines change pitch, and David's hand stroked gently down my spine. 'We're descending,' he said.

'If you mean we're going down, I could make some jokes.'

'Stop.' There was a bright edge of laughter in the word, though. I'd made a Djinn laugh. That was... an accomplishment. 'Time to get serious.'

'This isn't serious? Because I kind of thought—'

'Stop,' he said again, this time more soberly. 'You need to know what's going to happen when we land.'

I acknowledged that with a single nod, not raising my head.

'We'll be met by another Djinn. Rahel. She's already waiting. She'll meet you there and guide you to Seacasket. She's been watching, but she says there's no sign of the Demon yet. We may have guessed wrong.'

I closed my eyes and reached for that strange vibration I'd felt when I'd been in Kevin's mind. It was still there, and getting stronger. 'No, I don't think so. I think she's there, or she's close. David – what the hell is in Seacasket?'

And he told me about the Fire Oracle. Like Imara, in Sedona, it was a higher order of Djinn, a kind of living embodiment of one of the three major powers. The Djinn revered it, though few of them could actually communicate with it.

By the time he was finished, he'd silently urged me to sit up, and he'd handed me my clothes. They felt wrong, awkward against my skin. It occurred to me, as I fastened the last button on my shirt, that dressing must be a lot faster as a Djinn. I hadn't even seen him put on his pants, but he was fully clothed.

'You expecting trouble with the Oracle?' I asked.

'No.'

'Well, you sent for Rahel as back-up...'

'About that.' He took in a breath and let it out slowly. 'I'm not going with you.'

That set up a cold, liquid sensation in my stomach. 'You're...what?'

'There's something I have to do,' he said. 'It's

important. I'll join you when I can. Rahel won't abandon you.'

'Venna did. And you're about to.' That was blunt, but I was feeling a little bit peeved. You didn't do the things we'd done together and just split up, did you? I wanted him with me.

Always.

'Jo.' He squeezed my hand. 'Trust me.'

Couldn't argue with that, although I wanted to.

The pilot's cheerful voice came on to tell us to put our tray tables and flight attendants in the upright position, and the opal shield faded around us. The bed became seats, and we were back to reality. It hadn't been a dream. My whole body was relaxed, languorous with warmth, deliciously sore.

'I love you,' David said. He said it quietly, without any drama, as if it were part of normal conversation. Which maybe it was, for us. Or could be. 'No matter how this goes, that doesn't change.'

I closed my eyes as the plane began a terrifying, jerky descent towards New Jersey.

He stayed with me until we touched down on the tarmac, but by the time I opened my eyes again, my hand was empty of his, and David's seat was vacant.

He was gone. We were on our own.

The Demon was in Seacasket. Somewhere. I could feel that noise in my head, like subtle static on a channel I'd never known my radio had received before.

The process of shuttling my little raiding party from planeside to Seacasket wasn't short, but it was fairly efficient; the Wardens, it seemed, excelled in logistics. That meant a passenger van, complete with communications gear and a hotline that Lewis immediately used to chat with somebody in an office. He hadn't commented on David's disappearance, which seemed odd to me until I realised that he probably knew where David had gone, and why.

Or maybe he was just distracted by Rahel, who'd shown up in the van without preamble or introduction, scaring the holy crap out of at least some of the Wardens, including Paul, who'd nearly jumped out of his seat. 'Post-traumatic fucking stress,' he'd growled at me, and thumped down hard. 'Last time a Djinn popped in on me like that, she was trying to rip my head off.'

Rahel raised one sharp eyebrow, elegant and amused. 'I can't imagine why,' she said coolly. She was in neon orange today, a beautifully tailored pantsuit with a tangerine sheer top layered over neon yellow. Matching fingernails that looked sharp enough to slice paper. She'd jazzed up her multitude of black braids with tiny gold bells and glowing orange beads, and she gave off a very faint chime when she moved. 'You've treated the Djinn so well during your partnership with us, Warden.'

'Hey. This particular Djinn wasn't trying to kill the *institution*.'

They exchanged the kind of look reserved for respected adversaries, and went to their separate corners, metaphorically. In actuality, the van wasn't that big.

'I should help the driver,' Rahel said, and moved up a row to lean over to touch him on the shoulder. She didn't speak, though, that I could see. I wondered what kind of 'help' she was providing, and decided that maybe sometimes it was just better not to ask.

'It's the town,' Lewis said, following my gaze. 'I've tried to send Wardens here for more than six months. They never make it within twenty miles before they turn around.'

'That bad?' I asked.

'No. They just forget where they're going. It's part of the protections the Djinn put in place ages ago.' He nodded towards Rahel. 'She's navigating for him.'

The closer we got, the stranger the weather seemed. It had been cold and windy in Newark, with that chilly, damp edge that could only mean snow on the way. But as we moved towards Seacasket, everything went quiet, smooth as glass. Like weather simply didn't exist, or was artificially flattened out to some even balance.

I put my hand up against the van's window. Cool, but not frigid outside. The clouds had swirled away, and the sunshine seemed brighter than it should. The fall colours were gorgeous, and the leaves fluttered in a very slight, decorative breeze.

We passed a sign that announced we were entering the historic town of Seacasket, and I felt a shudder go through every one of us – not a reaction to what we were reading, but something else. Some force dragging over us like a curtain.

Rahel continued to sit quietly, communing with the van driver, as we drove through town. I stared out at what looked like a normal place, normal buildings, normal people. It looked *too* normal, in fact; a Norman Rockwell perfection that existed all too rarely in reality. Kids in this town would be happy and well-adjusted, with just enough spice of harmless rebellion for flavour. Adults would be content and well-grounded, going about their productive and busy lives. Crime would be low. Lawns would be perennially neat.

Too good to be true, although it *was* true at the level most people lived.

But up on the aetheric, it was different. There was a kind of illumination to everything that spun it just slightly towards the positive, and it was easier here than anywhere I'd ever been to move from the real world into Oversight – it happened in an effortless slide.

The veils were definitely thin here.

We parked on a main street next to what looked like the most picturesque town graveyard I'd ever seen, all gracefully sculpted willow trees, manicured grass, artfully aged tombstones. Ethereal. If I had to pick any place to get my bones planted, well, I could certainly do worse.

I tried not to think that it could happen sooner than I thought.

We filed out of the van onto the sidewalk, moved around in the Brownian motion of people who didn't have any idea where they were going, and Rahel emerged last. She swept us with a look that clearly said, *Hopeless*, and turned to Lewis. 'Perhaps you'd like to deploy them,' she said. 'Unless you think they look less suspicious this way.'

I covered a snort of laughter with a cough.

'It's Joanne's show,' he said, which made the laugh on me. 'We're here for muscle, not brains.'

I smiled thinly. He smiled back in a way that made me paranoid about just how solid David's privacy bubble had been on the plane. Surely I was imagining things.

Dear God, let me be imagining things.

'Spread out,' I said. 'Rahel, Lewis, maybe you should each take a corner. The rest of you, find someplace to blend.'

There was a general shuffle, and then people

broke up to assume their chosen locations. Except for Lewis, who was waiting for something else from me, and Rahel, who just wasn't going to be given orders by some mere human anyway.

'Where are you going?' Lewis asked. I nodded at the open gates of the cemetery.

'I need to go in there,' I said. 'Right?'

He exchanged a glance with Rahel, who inclined her head silently.

'I've been here before,' I said. 'The other me, she remembers everything, including how to reach the Oracle.'

That made some fierce golden fire light up in Rahel's eyes, and she looked hard all of a sudden. Cutting edges and slicing angles.

'Is the Demon here?' she asked. 'Inside?'

I shook my head. 'Not yet. At least, I don't think so. It doesn't feel that specific. But she's got to be close.'

My own voice said, from right behind me, 'She is close,' and something hit me with stunning force. I was tossed forward and collided with the stately brick wall. I somehow managed to get my arms in front of me, which resulted in some bad bruises but no broken bones, and tried to summon powers to fight.

I had nothing. It was the same eerie, dead flatness, so far as access to power went, that I'd experienced in Sedona when I'd tried to fight

Ashan. *Oh, boy.* Not so good, because although *my* powers were on the wane, my evil twin's supernatural abilities weren't.

Because, of course, she *was* supernatural. Like the Djinn. It was in whatever passed for her DNA.

Well, one thing she wasn't, was immune to a punch.

Lewis stepped up and gave her a solid right cross, snapping her head back with real violence. But even as she staggered backward, I heard Rahel scream, 'Lewis, *no!*' and saw that Evil Twin, who looked more like me than I did with her glossy, sleek hair and vibrant, glittering eyes and perfect skin, had grabbed hold of his wrist.

She yanked him forward, body-to-body, and met his eyes with hers, staring deep.

Rahel paused in the act of moving towards them. I shook the stars and explosions out of my head, trying to see what the hell was happening, and felt Lewis doing the impossible: pulling power in a place where power was locked off tight. Seacasket was a town in the aetheric equivalent of an airless, vacuum-sealed iron vault.

And he was ripping the vault door off its metaphorical hinges, as if it were *nothing*.

I'd never fully appreciated what Lewis was, and what he could do, until that moment. He wanted her to let him go, and she was either going to do it or be blasted into so many tiny pieces that even a

Demon would have a hard time surviving it.

And then I realised why he was reacting so violently. Granted, he wouldn't want her hands on him, but what he was doing was far, far beyond merely trying to get loose from her hold. No, he was fighting to save himself, because she was *trying to take him over*, the way she'd grabbed Cherise and Kevin and cored them out to insert her own will, power, and thoughts.

If she could do that to *Lewis*...

Rahel understood what was happening, but she didn't act. Perhaps she couldn't here in this place. The power that Lewis was pulling into himself, using as a shield, was absolutely stunning in its intensity, as if the entire Earth were rising up through him in his defence.

And still the Demon was eating right through.

There was a slipping sensation under my feet. I can't describe it any more accurately; it wasn't an earthquake, because the ground itself didn't shift. Not a tremor. Not a shudder of any kind.

And yet, something *moved*.

'No,' Rahel breathed, stricken, and I saw her make some kind of decision.

She broke out of her paralysis, crossed the few steps, and grabbed E.T. by her shiny supernatural hair. For her part, my evil twin wasn't going down easy; she snarled and twisted around to backhand Rahel, but she didn't let go of Lewis to do it. His eyes were closed, his face unnaturally still, as if he were in tranquil meditation. I'd seen this before. I could almost remember...

When Rahel lunged for her again, my doppelgänger did something that blurred in this reality, blazed up in the aetheric, and slammed the heel of her palm into Rahel's chest.

Her hand kept going deep into Rahel's flesh and bone, and I saw a flood of what looked like blue sparks shoot down the Demon's arm disappearing within Rahel's body. Rahel's mouth opened in a soundless scream, and I saw the shadowy presence of her on the aetheric turn smoke grey, then a poisonous shade of pale blue.

Could she possess *Rahel*?

As the Demon pulled her hand out of Rahel's chest, a flood of tiny blue sparkles followed, foaming over Rahel's body in a matter of seconds.

She convulsed and went down. It looked...Oh, God. It looked as if she were *melting*.

Lewis was still fighting, but whatever power he was using was dangerous in the extreme. I could feel that in the unsteady pitch and wave of the ground – no, not the *ground*, I realised, because the actual soil wasn't moving. This was something else.

A stray metal button on the sidewalk rattled, rolled, and suddenly flew straight up in the air to impact a metal street sign. Which was bending as if an invisible wind were pulling at it.

Something was going badly wrong with the Earth's magnetic field. Whatever power Lewis was using was unbalancing it, and although I had no idea what that meant, it just could *not* be good.

The other Wardens were converging on the spot, but nobody could do much – I saw Paul running to grab Lewis and bodychecked him on the way. 'No!' I yelled. 'She'll take you! Don't touch either one of them!'

'We can't just *stand* here!' he screamed back at me. I heard the wail of police cars a few blocks over, and realised with a cold start that the rest of Seacasket, this Norman Rockwell town with a touch of the Gothic, would have just seen a bunch of strangers pile out of a van and some kind of fight. They couldn't see or feel what was happening all around them, unless they knew where to look.

The Wardens knew, but we couldn't *act*.

I felt a displacement of air, heard a faint *pop*, and looked around to see Venna standing there. She didn't even glance towards me; she ran to Rahel, scooped her up, and vanished mid-step. Taking her somewhere she could be helped, I hoped, but I couldn't know.

'Now would be a really good time,' I muttered in the general direction of David, hoping he could hear me, but no miracles arrived to scoop *me* up.

I was going to have to make my miracles myself.

'Hey,' I said. I kept my voice as normal as

possible as I stepped away from Paul and began moving towards the Demon and Lewis. 'Hey, you. Bitch. You don't really want him, do you? You just want a big hole ripped open so you can get home. Or bring in a few friends. Whichever.'

She glanced sharply at me, and as our eyes locked I felt that balance under my feet shift again. Violently. *Oh, man.* It wasn't just Lewis who was causing this.

It was me. Both of me. We were a destabilising influence here.

'I'll do it,' I said. 'One tunnel into the void, coming up. Just back off and let him go.'

'Why should I?' she asked. Reasonable question, delivered in the same reasonable tone I was using. 'This way he can't act against me.'

'This way the two of you will end up ripping the place in *half*, not opening up a doorway. Not good for either one of you. Come on. I know you like this planet. It'd be a shame to ruin it for everybody.'

She laughed. My laugh. 'If you want him, I'll trade,' she said. 'Come here.'

The last thing in the world I wanted was to do it, but I didn't see much of an alternative. Of course, she might be lying, but I wasn't a pushover, and if she wanted to hollow me out or kill me, I'd demand a lot of her attention.

And Lewis would break free.

'Don't you do it,' Paul was muttering at me.

'Don't you fucking dare. I'll kill you.'

'Line forms to the right.' I smiled at him, just a little, and then walked over to my evil twin.

The static in my head was now white noise, blotting out thought, erasing everything but instinct.

I put my hand over hers, where it held Lewis, and pulled it away.

The second the contact broke, Lewis collapsed. Paul, Kevin, and the other Wardens dashed in and did a combat-style drag on him, all the way to the corner, where the van pulled up. Paul threw Lewis inside, slapped the side of the van, and it sped away.

Clearly Paul wasn't taking any chances.

Blackness smothered me, thick and more painfully intense than ever before. I barely even noticed, though, because now that I was holding her hand, I saw a network of lights flaring inside of her, rich and complex, like a bright snarled ball that sparked in millions of colours.

Oh.

That was *mine*. My memories. My lost experience. My *past*.

And I reached in and took it. Or tried to. I grabbed one end of the memory chain, the Demon grabbed the other, and the race was on.

Light and shadow. Infant memories, indefinite and barely there. Faces. Noise. Colours. Perceptions sharpening as I aged. I sped through it, imprinting it on the area that was dark inside of my own head. I didn't need training for this; there was only one place this stuff could go, and in only one order. Memory, for me, was a spool, and I unwound it faster and faster, flickering images and impressions that I could examine later, when I got time... *My mother crying. Sarah. Disneyland. A storm building, breaking, finding its perfect mate inside of me.*

Childhood, so many rich moments, so many terrible things. I aged, changed; the world shifted with me and around me. Boys. Boyfriends. Heartbreak. Always the weather, my perfect enemy, hunting an opportunity to betray and destroy.

Power. Purpose. Training. Princeton.

A younger Lewis taking off my clothes in a basement laboratory, introducing me to a whole new level of pleasure and intensity.

Glass shattering with the force of our power combining as our bodies did.

Lewis gone, spirited away. My life consumed with work, achievement, ambition.

Bad Bob. A Djinn holding me down, choking me with a Demon Mark, forcing me to face my own fears and mortality at the same time. Bad Bob died; I lived, crawling away from the wreckage of the fight.

A shattered Djinn bottle. Bad Bob's slave freed. My quest for Lewis. Meeting a stranger on the road, a vagabond named David I couldn't quite resist.

A blur of events that I couldn't even separate, ending in more destruction, more death, my own transformations.

Blue sparkles. A hole in the aetheric. Demons. The fate of the world, again, on our shoulders.

Human again. Faces flashed by at an increasing rate, because I could feel the tension of the Demon on the end of the memory chain, pulling back, and I couldn't stop now to even try to comprehend what I was seeing.

A glimpse of Jonathan, ageless and cynical and passionate about what he loved.

Fighting for my survival in a flood, and rising in the arms of my lover above the foaming, deadly currents.

The Mother of Storms taking notice, at last, and coming to end the cycle of violence.

Imara conceived. Imara born. Imara –

The memory chain shattered into a million crystalline fragments, and I lost my hold.

It all started to go away. I was losing it. *No!*

The Demon didn't waste time with my trauma. She cut to the chase and plunged her hand into my chest, just like she'd done with Rahel.

If she couldn't *be* me, then she was going to

damn sure make sure I wouldn't be, either.

The sensation that raced through me was horrifying. I'd been through bad stuff; this was *beyond*. I'd felt it through Kevin's memories, and it was even worse this time, because there was no escape.

She simply bored her way through me, ripping apart whatever she didn't need, and I felt my connection to the aetheric suddenly cutting off. It was like the sun disappearing during a total eclipse, and something in me screamed, trapped and terrified and suffering.

It couldn't live that way for long. *I* couldn't.

Although I felt like there was less and less of an *I*. It was draining away from me, like sand out of a broken glass, slow but inexorable. I was losing my childhood again. My mother's face was fading away. I lost the memory of my first date, and the nervous excitement of buying my prom dress, and the scratchy elegance of the corsage my date had bought me. I lost the memory of his name, too.

Evil Twin didn't care about my troubles. She let go of me, but I didn't move. Didn't speak. Hair blew across my face, obscuring my view of her, but it didn't matter. She could see. I didn't need to, because now I was fully, completely under her control. I couldn't fight, because I needed every ounce of strength to slow down the steady erosion of my past.

She was simply going to drain me dry, and then I'd be gone. Erased. *Finito*.

The Wardens were circling us, trying to decide which one was the good Joanne, which the bad; the problem was that the deck was now stacked, and they were screwed no matter what choice they made. Kevin and Cherise were hanging back, watching with identical expressions of sick horror; more than anyone else, they understood what was happening to me. Not that they could help me.

Not that anyone could.

The Demon accessed my Warden powers, blew a hole through the peaceful, artificial shield of Seacasket, and accessed a huge draw of power from the aetheric. She used me to do it. My control shattered, and the memories dissolved faster.

I lost my college years. I lost Lewis, swept away in a tide of oncoming darkness.

I felt the clouds gathering overhead, a soft grey pressure turning rapidly dark, and under the Demon's direction I rubbed air molecules together, creating friction, heat, driving the engine of a tiny but incredibly concentrated storm. Not my choice, but definitely my fault. The storm broke with a snap of lightning, and drenched a square-block area of sidewalk, catching nearly every Warden in its path.

As soon as they were standing in a thin layer of water, she forced me to slam a lightning bolt down and electrified the whole block.

The Wardens went down like ten pins in a bowling alley, many stunned, a few maybe even dead. I wanted to stop. I wanted to scream.

Instead I turned and walked, under the Demon's control, into the gates of the Seacasket cemetery.

'There used to be guards here,' E.T. said, as if we hadn't just lashed out against everything I knew and loved. As if I weren't dying as quickly as she was coming alive. We were strolling along the path like two sisters, hand in hand. 'There were Djinn guards. You remember?'

It was a new memory, not yet pulled apart by the ongoing destruction. I remembered. They'd nearly killed me and Imara. Ashan had been here, too.

'I won't let you win,' I said. I couldn't stop her, and she knew it, but she at least allowed me the fantasy of saying it. 'You don't have to do it this way. If you want to go home, we'll find a way to send you home. But you're not killing the Oracle. You're not ripping open any doorways. If I don't stop you, the Wardens will. The Djinn will.'

'And yet,' she said, with the same cockeyed smile I'd felt on my own face so often, 'that's *exactly* what I'm going to do. And you're going to help me, until I don't need you anymore.'

Gravel crunched under my shoes. Part of me was shrieking in agony, battering at the container that she'd stuffed it into. 'I'm fading,' I said. I couldn't even work up emotion about it, because she controlled my body, even down to the endocrine level. 'No good to you if I'm dead. Slow down.'

'You'll last long enough.' She shrugged. 'I need you, because I won't be able to open the door, not alone – the Oracle will know me for what I really am. I could have used the combined power of the Wardens to blast it open, but you've ruined that for me. Now only a Djinn will do – or someone who's been one before. You.'

We passed some leaning, picturesque headstones. A cracked marble bench. A tree that showed evidence of having sustained some fight damage in the past.

And we arrived at the mausoleum.

'No,' I said. My body couldn't hear me. It was following a completely different set of instructions as my arm lifted, touched the marble door, and then reached for the inset metal knob. 'No. No, no, *no*!' Memories flared, burnt, and dissolved. Bad Bob. Storms. My car spinning out on the road. The Djinn-hot flash of David's eyes. Lying in his arms, gasping.

My time was running out.

I traced the roots of my power to where E.T. had placed a black stranglehold on them. I couldn't free myself – no chance in hell – but I *could* focus on one tiny opening. It was like breaking the pinkie finger of someone choking you – possible, but of doubtful use.

I did it anyway. I focused everything I had, all three forms of power, through the lens of my desperation, and came out with a white-hot stream of pure energy that burnt a hole straight through the black cage holding me prisoner.

Something reached through to me. It came in a slow, warm flood, like syrup...the thick, condensed power of the Earth. It was trying to reach me.

Not enough. I couldn't use it; the opening was too narrow, the cage too confining. No leverage. I screamed inside, trying to cling to the last memories as my hand turned the doorknob, and I fell into another place, one with no up, no down, just stone and an ever-blazing fire too hot and brilliant to approach...

And E.T. was able to come through, too, because she was holding my hand, and physically she was identical.

Part of the cage in my mind cracked. I ripped at it with everything I had, frantically widening the gap, and the power poured in like water through a hole below the waterline. Filling me up.

She felt the change, and she tried to pull away, but I had control of at least part of myself now, and I body-slammed her down on the rocks with one hand around her throat.

'No,' I gritted out. 'No, you *don't. You can't have my life!*'

Heat rose up through my body. A wave of fast,

tingling fire, a cooling whisper of air and water, then the slow, whispering power of the Earth, the gift of my daughter, Imara. I sensed her now, calm and utterly focused. *It's OK, Mom*, she whispered to me. *We can do this. The three of us. Just hold her still. That's all you have to do.*

The *three* of us? Was she counting Evil Twin?

No. She wasn't. I blinked sweat out of my eyes and looked up as the door opened again, and a Djinn formed out of the darkness, moving fast. His olive-drab coat swirled around him, and he blazed like new morning here. Djinn were children of fire, more than any other element, and he burnt – oh, God – he burnt so magnificently bright.

David took a bottle out of his coat pocket – a thick, ancient, cloudy thing, sealed thickly with wax and dust. A complicated knot of ribbons and more wax dangled from the neck of it. I recognised it. He'd nearly popped the cap on that thing back in the forest, when he'd thought I was the Demon.

There were more Djinn with him, stepping out of the walls all around us. Silent, powerful, angry. Merciless.

With the last core of my being, I recognised one of the newcomers standing near me – pale, silver hair, eyes as vicious as a wolverine's. Oh, he hated me. Not the Demon...me.

Ashan. Still human.

A little girl in a blue dress and white pinafore

stood next to him, her hands folded primly in front of her. Blue eyes shimmering with ageless power.

'Hurry,' she said to David. 'If you want to save her, yield.'

David faced Ashan. I was caught between the two of them, with the Demon writhing around and trying like hell to get me off of her. Luckily, her ability didn't include superstrength, and she'd lost her hold over me. Still, all she had to do was wait. I was losing myself fast. She was draining it all away...

David said, 'I yield.' He said it to Venna. To Ashan.

And then I saw a swirl of fire erupt out of the pit, wrap around him, and I heard him scream.

'David!' I couldn't let go. If I did, the Demon would destroy us. 'David, no!'

Whatever was happening, it was ripping him apart. I could hear the agony, feel it resonating in the stone all around me. I could hear a distant groan, as if the whole world had felt it, too.

And then the flames leapt from David over my head to engulf Ashan.

And he burnt. Venna didn't move, even as he shrieked in agony, but I saw perfect crystal tears trickling slowly down her cheeks.

'What are you doing?' I screamed at her. She was watching Ashan, watching the tornado of fire that he'd become.

I felt some fundamental balance shift, and in an instant the flames just...went out.

David went to his knees, gasping. Ashan...

Ashan was perfect. Hard as alabaster, inhuman and burning with power.

Oh, my God. What had David done?

He looked up, eyes burning copper-bright. 'What are you waiting for?' David gasped. He was fire to Ashan's cold, frozen steel, and the two of them looked inhumanly strong as they glared at each other. I could feel the violence gathering in the air. 'You've got what you wanted. Keep your promise, you bastard.'

Ashan's smile was as thin as a paper cut. 'Perhaps I'll wait a bit.'

David's voice dropped almost to a whisper. 'Now,' he said. 'You've cost me enough. We have a truce. Don't test me.'

Ashan's smile disappeared, not that it was ever real to begin with, and the two of them locked stares in that hot, airless place, with the eternal pale fire burning just steps away. This was a place of power, and it was full of very scary Djinn. I didn't know what could happen, but it wouldn't be good.

Venna said mildly, 'Ashan. You did promise.' She said it with no particular emphasis, but it sent shivers down my spine. Venna – was that her name? I no longer knew her, or the black-skinned

Djinn with cornrowed hair, staring at me with burning golden eyes. Or the well-dressed one with the chestnut brown hair, cold and elegant. There were dozens of them, and they were all riveted on me, on the Demon, or on Ashan and David.

Ashan abruptly reached out and put his hand on the back of my neck. I yelped at the cold shock against my sweating, hot skin, and then felt the ice sink in like winter.

'This will hurt,' he said. That wasn't a warning. That was a promise.

And then I came apart, screaming, in a red haze, and he *rebuilt* me, cell by cell, neuron by neuron, in a brutal, fast, cruel process, and I felt every single nanosecond of it like an eternity.

My memories returned with it.

Every one.

I heard the Demon cry out and knew that what she'd stolen was being ripped away, leaving *her* the shell, making *her* the excess baggage of the universe, and even though I hated her for what she'd done (and tried to do), I couldn't help but hate Ashan more.

Because he was enjoying it.

He let go and stepped away, wiping his hand fastidiously against his grey coat. 'That fulfils our bargain,' he said, and met David's eyes with absolute menace. 'Finish this, or I'll finish you.'

And then he just...left. And half the Djinn

disappeared with him. The ones who were left seemed to take a collective breath, as if they'd been dreading the outcome of all that, and even David looked a little relieved. Just for a second.

Then he crouched down to eye level with me and touched my face. 'Trust me?'

I nodded, but I really didn't have a choice. And if he had to destroy me to end this, well...then I knew he'd do whatever was necessary. Because David had responsibilities that were greater than his love for me.

I love you. No matter how this goes, that doesn't change. His words to me on the plane, and they were echoing in the stark, primitive confines of this place. I couldn't stay here much longer; the heat was suffocating, and the flames blazed hotter every moment, sucking moisture out of my fragile human body, flirting with igniting my hair into a fireball. I didn't have the time or concentration to spare to protect myself, and I wasn't sure, with *this* fire, that I'd be able to in any case.

I blinked sweat from my eyes and managed a smile. 'Of course I trust you,' I said. 'Do whatever you have to, but she can't leave here. She can't live.'

Evil Twin's eyes widened, and she said in a surprisingly soft, vulnerable voice, 'David, no. Please, no.' He hesitated for just a second. Long enough for her to continue. 'I'll leave if you'll send me home. But please don't kill me. I'm not like the other Demons you've destroyed – they didn't know; they didn't understand. I know what's going to happen. Please, you can't torture me like this!'

'You want me to send you home,' he repeated without inflection. And tears rolled out of her eyes, vanishing into steam in the superheated air. My skin was agonisingly painful, already beginning to cook.

'Please,' she said. 'With this many Djinn you could do it. Open up a portal, then seal it. Then my blood won't be on your hands.'

'No,' he agreed. 'What *would* be on my hands would be the risk that you would come back, and this time you'd lead an army. That's exactly what you're planning, isn't it?'

The tears cut off instantly, and the Demon's voice hardened. 'You'd do the same.'

'Trust me,' David said, 'I've done far worse. And I've done it to people I loved.'

And he broke the seal from the bottle, opened it, pressed the heel of his hand to her jaw to pry apart her lips...and fed her a Demon.

I let go. It wasn't conscious, just instinct; I felt the raw menace of the thing as it snaked its way out of the bottle, and I just had to get away from it in an awkward scramble. David's face was like cast metal, no softness there, and no mercy. My doppelgänger was screaming, but it was too late; he held her down, slammed her mouth shut to lock the thing inside, and I watched as the Demon shed her human disguise in the extremity of her fear and rage.

The skin simply shredded into a mist of blood and tissue, and underneath red muscle hardened into black, crystalline shell. Insectile and unsettling.

Her eyes stayed blue. *My* eyes, and she defiantly focused them on me as she struggled to throw off David's hold and expel the poison he'd just forced down her throat.

But not even the strongest Demon could fight Mother Nature – *their* Mother Nature, not mine. Theirs dictated that they hunted by territory, and they'd hunt each other if forced together, to the exclusion of other prey.

Two Demons, one body.

I watched them rip each other apart, screaming, into a black shredded mist, and didn't realise I'd fallen down until David cradled me in his arms, partly shielding me from the heat. I was shaking all over, partly from dehydration, partly from the horror of what I'd seen. Partly from realising that she'd just been destroyed by the same thing that had once killed me, and my mind had blocked out the details until Ashan had brought it all back.

A stream of blue fog poured from the mouth of the open bottle, and a Djinn formed out of the air and collapsed on his side on the floor, trembling.

Wounded, haunted, hurt – but alive. The others closed protectively around and helped him rise.

David didn't speak. He tossed the bottle to another Djinn – a tall, dark-skinned guy dressed in classic *Arabian Nights* costume, whose legs misted into fog about mid-thigh. I recognised him, complete to the one gold hoop earring. He'd once guarded Lewis's house in Westchester. The Djinn set the open bottle on the floor and stepped away, and the black mist swirling above the remains of the Demon formed a vortex about the bottle.

It fought hard to stay out, but gradually it was pulled in, a steady stream of black fog condensing and rushing into the open mouth.

As soon as the last of it had vanished, the Djinn slammed the wax stopper back into the opening, tied the ribbons, and nodded to David. Who nodded back gravely.

The Djinn vanished, along with the bottle.

'Where's he taking it?' I asked. My lips were dry and cracked, and my tongue felt like old paper. I didn't recognise my own voice.

'Someplace safe,' David said, and frowned at me. 'Let's get you out of here.'

But when he opened the door of the mausoleum and we stepped out into the cool, soft air, we had a surprise.

The graveyard was full of Djinn. My first thought was, *Wow, when he calls for back-up, he calls for* back-up*!* But then I realised, with a sick twisting sensation in my guts, that David looked just as surprised as I did.

And then his gaze focused on something in the midst of that crowd of several hundred, and a path formed to let two people walk out of the centre.

Venna, in her Alice costume.

And, holding her hand like a father taking his favoured child for a stroll, Ashan.

David didn't speak. Neither did Ashan nor Venna. I shifted my gaze back and forth, worried, because I could feel the battling tides of power and purpose all around us.

Finally David shook his head. 'Let her leave,' he said. 'She's got no part in this.'

'But she does,' Venna said, and her hot blue eyes locked on mine. 'It should never have got this far, David. You put the Oracle at risk.'

'Not the first time that's happened, Ashan. Is it?' David was growing brighter, more Djinn-like, less human. I let go of his hand and took a step back. 'Don't pretend you're the saviour of the Djinn now. You were more than willing to destroy half of us and *all* of humanity to go back to being the favoured of the Mother. Who gave you the right, you cold bastard? Just because you're *older*?'

Ashan's eyes had turned silver, and they looked like cold pools of mercury, still and uncaring. 'Yes. Because I'm older,' he said. His voice resonated with assurance and cool, still energy. If other Djinn were fire, Ashan was pure air and water... nothing hot about him at all. You could drown in his deadly calm. 'The Mother makes her own rules, but we choose how to obey them. I have a message for you, David.'

'*You* have a message.' David looked wary. Worried.

'Through the Air Oracle,' Ashan replied. 'We will no longer be one. You may have the New Djinn, but I will command the Old Ones. Two conduits.'

David's glow cooled. It was a slow process, but definite, and when it was over he stood there looking at Ashan with an odd, vulnerable intensity I didn't really understand.

'I see,' he said. 'You mean to destroy us.'

'No. I merely mean to protect those of my own kind,' Ashan said. 'We will not fight you, nor the humans, unless attacked. If the Mother asks, we will answer. But we will have nothing to do with mortals. If you and yours choose to do so, that's your affair, but no agreements you make will bind us.'

'You're leaving,' David said, and frowned.

'Not quite yet,' Ashan said, and looked down at his feet. No, at the ground. And I felt that strange slip-sliding again, the rapid movement of the planet's magnetic force. I heard a distant hum of metal trembling, and felt the metal parts on my clothing, like zippers, pull just slightly away from me. 'The magnetic field is shifting.'

'It can't be. It's not time,' David said, but like Ashan he was staring down, and I sensed it was more of a pro forma objection than a real argument. 'Jonathan had plans for handling this.'

'Yes,' Ashan said. 'And we will need all of our strength to carry them out. Get the New Djinn. Gather the Wardens and the Ma'at. Get them here soon.'

'Here?' David asked. They were suddenly talking reasonably, two professionals approaching a problem. They'd blown past the personal – that Ashan was a conniving, evil bastard who'd killed my child and tried to kill me – and gone straight to the job at hand with dizzying speed. I couldn't keep up with the shifting currents.

Venna sent me a pitying look that indicated she knew that feeling all too well.

'It should be here. Sacred space.' Ashan said, and tugged on Venna's hand. She looked up at him and smiled, and that smile was pure pleasure. 'This will be our place. Held by the Old Ones.'

'*Here* won't work unless you release the shields that keep us from touching the aetheric,' I pointed out. 'And…unless you're willing to let us mere mortals enter.'

I got a glare. Ashan was angry at the reminder.

Wardens weren't meant to be here. It was, for him, an offence that one had ever stepped onto the sacred ground.

He wasn't the only one, I sensed. There was a definite energy coming from the crowd, and it wasn't good, and most of it was directed towards me. I suspected a lecture on tolerance and the evils of bigotry wasn't really going to be all that well received, so I kept my mouth shut and let Ashan think about it.

'Yes,' he finally said. 'We'll lower them. Bring them here. Bring everyone here.'

David nodded, took my hand, and walked me through the crowd of Djinn – who silently moved aside, although some of them, staring at me, looked like they were holding ancient grudges. I was the Wardens personified, at the moment, and burning in effigy was a tradition going back to when my people were just a gleam in Mother Earth's eye.

I held my silence until we reached the cemetery gates. Miraculously, the Djinn held their peace. I couldn't tell that David was worried until we reached the relative safety outside on the sidewalk, where the other Wardens were clustered around, some still shaking off the stun effects, and then he let out a breath that told me everything about how he'd been feeling.

'What the hell was *that*?' I asked. He didn't meet my eyes.

'That was a coup,' he said, 'and Ashan has effectively been declared the leader of more than half of the Djinn. The Old Ones outnumber my...I guess you'd call it my generation – and they're more powerful. When Jonathan was in charge that balance of power evened out, but I'm not Jonathan.' He shook his head slowly. 'Not even close. I don't know what it will mean.'

I wanted to ask him harder questions, but the Wardens weren't letting us have a moment; everybody was talking at once. Paul had grabbed my arm and was trying to hustle me to the van, Kevin and Cherise were blabbing at us, someone was urgently talking on the cell phone, and David...well, David clearly was willing to let me get dragged off if it meant he didn't have to undergo twenty questions.

I felt the slippery sensation again, heard Paul saying something about magnetic surges as polarities threatened to shift, and the cell phone that the Warden – I knew him now, his name was Otombo; he was a Fire Warden out of Arkansas – the cell phone suddenly let out an ear-splitting shriek and exploded into sparks. Otombo winced and dropped the useless piece of equipment. It let out a thin, whiny sound of electronic distress, and a tiny wisp of smoke curled up from the speaker.

'Cell phones off! *Off*! Paul bellowed. He was right; it was the only way to save them. People patted their pockets, a couple of women pawed through purses, and most got their phones shut off before anything happened. I heard the electronic wail from another quarter, and a French-Canadian curse. *Oops.*

'What the *hell* is going on around here?' Paul demanded – from me, of course. I looked over my shoulder at David. He was staring back at the cemetery, no particular expression on his face.

I started to repeat the question – there had been a lot of cross talk, with the other Wardens all basically asking each other the same thing – but there was no need. David said, 'How much do you know about magnetism?'

'Well, if you bang an iron tie-rod on a metal grate, you can make it a magnet,' I said. 'I saw it on *MacGyver*.' And I was ridiculously pleased to be remembering it.

He spared me a glance. Not a patient one. 'The magnetic field surrounding the Earth is moving,' he said. 'Breaking into islands of polarity.'

Sam Otombo nodded. 'Yes,' he agreed; He had a faint tropical accent, and his long, clever face was very serious. 'The field has been concentrated as we know it, at the poles, for perhaps three quarters of a million years. But there is evidence that it has shifted before, completely flipped from north to south, and this begins with islands of magnetic polarity shift.' He nudged the remains of his cell phone with his foot. 'There was speculation that it could affect some types of communications, global positioning satellites...'

'Wait a minute,' I said. 'You mean north is now *south*?'

'In some places, yes. I mean that if you looked at a compass needle right now, in this place, you probably wouldn't see north,' Otombo corrected. 'Anything but. The magnetic field is moving, but it may take hundreds, even thousands of years for it to settle again.'

I was completely lost. They hadn't really covered this in weather school. 'Is it dangerous?'

'Long-term, perhaps. We could have increased cosmic radiation. The magnetic field shields us from that at all but the most remote places on Earth.'

David nodded. 'You're right that it has happened before, sometimes as often as every few thousand years. But the Djinn and the Wardens have kept the system stable for millennia.'

'Until now,' I said. 'Because we're no longer working together to hold it. Right?'

'That's why you have to bring them here, Jo,' he said. 'Bring the Wardens. Bring the Ma'at. And hurry.'

Chapter Sixteen

Funny, most people wouldn't even know it was a crisis. It didn't have any of the usual signs – no menacing clouds, no tremors in the ground, no forest fires charring acres of homes. This was the quietest, most subtle disaster I'd ever seen. Except for a few cell phones squealing their last, and some random weird magnetic effects, it seemed to go almost unnoticed.

'Yeah, it's definitely weird,' Paul said when I pointed it out as we made phone calls not from mobiles, or from the tricked-out communications van (which had been hastily shut down, just in case), but the old-fashioned way, from a bank of phone booths in a hotel lobby. David had quietly disappeared, I supposed to go try to persuade his fellow Nouveau Djinn to participate. Did even *they* take orders from him these days? Had I really seen him lose his place in the world there in the cemetery?

I hadn't asked him, but surely he was still the

conduit of energy for the New Djinn. Through him they were connected to the Mother – that gave him some security.

I hoped.

The list of numbers Paul had handed me included names I recognised, a marvel that I didn't think was going to get old anytime soon. I *liked* recognising and remembering. It was a real thrill.

Talking to the Ma'at, well, not so much. Charles Spenser Ashworth II, in particular, was a great big pain in the ass. 'We're well aware of the magnetic instability,' he told me, in that waspish, precise way he'd once commanded me to tell him the circumstances of his son's death. He'd tortured me when I'd refused to tell him. OK, that was a memory I could have safely kept buried. 'There's nothing to be done about it. The Ma'at don't interfere in the natural order, Ms. Baldwin; you know that to be our guiding principle. If you want to twist nature to your will, then perhaps you should call upon your friends in the Wardens.'

'News flash, Charles: I'm standing with them right now. And we're asking you to help.' I tapped my fingernails on the chromed surface of the pay phone in frustration. 'Come on. Come out of the shadows. The Ma'at have a different take on this, and I for one think they ought to be heard before the Wardens and the Djinn decide what to do. Don't you? Don't you want a seat at the big table?'

I'd played directly to his vanity, shamelessly. Ashworth was rich, white, old, and patrician, and he'd never had *anything* but a seat at the big table. Usually red leather, handcrafted. On his own he hadn't manifested enough power to qualify for the Wardens – there were thousands of people every year who were either borderline talented, or just below the line, who were left to go about their lives without Warden interference. Most of them never even knew what they had, or what they could do, and those who did couldn't do much with it. Maybe light some candles without matches, if they were Fire; maybe grow out-of-season plants, if they were Earth. A weak, brief rainstorm, if Weather.

But put those marginal talents together with Djinn who willingly helped channel it, connect it into a series, you got additive power of a unique kind. The Ma'at had been focused on undoing the excesses of the Wardens; they rarely influenced things directly unless forced to it, mostly out of self-defence.

But then, they'd never been asked to step up on the front lines, really. Not until now.

'What do you want?' Ashworth asked.

'I want you, Lazlo, and everybody else in the Ma'at you can pull to get on a plane and come to Seacasket, New Jersey. The Wardens will meet you and bring you in from the airport. Call the Crisis Centre number' – I gave it to him from memory, another thrill – 'and tell them who you are and when you're arriving. They'll coordinate.'

Ashworth was silent for a few long seconds, and then said, 'We won't do anything contrary to the best interests of the planet. You understand that.'

'Believe me, I wouldn't ask you to. Get moving.'

When I hung up, Paul was hanging up as well. He offered up a big, square hand, and I high-fived it. 'Right,' he said. 'We got ourselves a party. Before nightfall, there should be about five hundred Wardens here, and however many Ma'at. Throw in the Djinn, and...'

'And you've got a real recipe for disaster,' I said, not feeling so high-five-ish anymore. 'This could turn bad so easily.'

'But it won't,' Paul said.

'How do you know?'

He grinned. 'Because I'm putting you in charge of it, kiddo.'

We took over the Seacasket Civic Centre, and we did that mainly with bags of cash, toted in by Warden security representatives in their blazers, shoulder holsters, and intimidating sunglasses. Whatever functions were going on there, we got them postponed, cancelled, or moved.

Even though that was the biggest indoor space in town, it wasn't exactly spacious. I'd have rather gathered everybody in the cemetery itself, but Ashan wasn't letting us grubby humans wander around on his sacred ground for longer than he had to.

It was late, I was tired, there wasn't enough coffee, and even the Djinn were crabby. Not a recipe for smooth interspecies relations.

It blew up in amazingly short order, over some dispute over seating arrangements.

I tried to get everyone's attention. It wasn't easy, because there was a whole lot of shouting going on, quite a bit of cursing, and I strongly suspected some hair pulling was involved, over where the Wardens and a few of the Ma'at had got in one another's faces to make their points more forcefully.

David had found the time, somehow, to get me a car – a vintage Mustang, unbelievably enough, a cherry red honey of a car that made me practically orgasm with delight at the sight of it – and, of course, a change of clothing. He knew what I liked: a sleek black pantsuit with a close-fitting purple silk shirt. And a fabulous pair of elegant three-inch Manolo Blahnik heels that fitted like they'd been made for my feet. (Knowing the Djinn...maybe they had. Maybe Manolo was supernatural. Having worn the shoes, I'd have believed it.)

I slipped the Manolo off of my right foot, stood up, and banged it loudly on the table in front of me. It was a cheap folding table, covered with the ubiquitous white hotel cloth, and it made a nice, satisfying racket.

That didn't do the job. Apparently, Nikita Khrushchev had either had bigger feet or heavier shoes than I did, back when he'd used the same tactic at the UN. I transferred the shoe to assaulting the microphone instead.

In the ensuing silence, as the electronic squealing died down, Lewis, poker-faced, stage-whispered, 'You must be desperate to do that to designer shoes.'

'Sit down,' I said to the room at large, 'and shut the hell up. Now.' I gave Lewis a look that included him, too. He was unmoved, except for having a very slight crinkle at the corner of his mouth. He thought I was cute when I was mad. David, who had seen me at my worst, was watching me from the other side with much more perspective on the subject, and was consequently less impressed.

The Wardens more or less obeyed, sinking slowly into the folding chairs that had been provided. The Ma'at made a point of *not*, until they got the nod from the head table by Myron Lazlo, who was – along with Charles Spenser Ashworth II, and two or three other really old guys – in charge of that organisation. Myron sat on the other side of David, who was at my right elbow, not quite touching. Counting Lewis, and Paul next to him, there were just the five of us at the head table. One step below us, down on the floor, there were round tables draped with well-used cloths, around which sat small groups of the most powerful beings in the world, all keeping to themselves. Tempers were high particularly between the Ma'at, who felt vindicated by being summoned to the meeting, and the Wardens, who felt betrayed by everything they'd ever known. Not to mention that the Wardens were terrified to be trapped in the same room with the Djinn.

The Djinn had taken over the back half of the room, standing in two separate, distinct groups. One group held the New Djinn, like Rahel, Prada, and dozens of others I'd come into contact with over the past couple of years. Marion's tall American Indian Djinn was among them, and he gave me a small nod of acknowledgment when my eyes met his.

The Old Ones, on the other hand, held Djinn like Venna and Ashan, and dozens of badass ancients I didn't recognise at all. They didn't mingle.

'Right,' I said, as chairs scraped on the floors and people settled back in their appropriate armed encampments, metaphorically speaking – or neutral corners, not that I believed for a second that there was such a thing as neutral. 'Let's just get through this with a minimum of bloodshed, if possible.'

Myron Lazlo took the microphone, frowned at the dent from my shoe, and cleared his throat. He was old enough to have been running a speakeasy during Prohibition, and he liked formality. He did not, therefore, like me all that much. He was wearing a blue suit, a crisp white shirt, and a nice brocade silk tie that looked a little too daring for a dyed-in-the-wool CPA type. Probably a gift from a great-grandchild.

'Before we begin,' he said, 'the Ma'at want assurances that this effort is at all necessary.'

'Assurances from whom, exactly?' one of the Wardens on the floor asked in a plummy British accent. 'And who the hell are you that we have to explain ourselves to you, mate?'

A growl of agreement swept through the Wardens' side of the room. Lewis gestured for the mike, and Myron passed it back to me. Lewis had recovered from my evil twin's attempt to take him over, but he was well aware that in defending himself, he'd precipitated, or at least hastened, this whole mess. He looked tired, his haircut was at least a month past its expiration date, and he had a wicked five-o'clock shadow thing going. Slumped down in his chair, he was still at least six inches taller than everybody else at the table, including me.

The room went still, waiting to hear Lewis fire back at Myron and defend the Wardens.

It didn't come to me as any surprise when he didn't.

'Myron's right,' Lewis said. His slightly raspy

voice was level and calm, and it took away at least half of the impact of what he was saying, so the uproar was mostly confused, shocked whispers rather than full-volume outrage. 'Let's ask ourselves first *if* this has to be done, not just *how.*'

The Wardens, in particular, exploded into protest. I used the shoe again, to good effect this time, and made an after-you gesture to Lewis when things had subsided to mutters again. He gave me an entirely insincere gee-thanks look in response. We knew each other so well we could be sarcastic without even speaking.

'I think we should ask the Djinn,' he said. 'David? Ashan?'

Diplomatic of him to include them both. David looked across at Ashan and made a very polite nod that I was sure cost him some pride. Ashan lifted his chin to its maximum angle of arrogance.

'In normal course, this could be allowed to happen,' he said. 'But it was not triggered by natural forces, and so it should be corrected before so much of the field is broken that the change is inevitable. It causes the Mother discomfort if the change happens too quickly.'

He hated talking to us. Hated the whole idea that we would have any part in this at all. Which, hey, I didn't much like the thought of working side by side with him, either. I had no idea what it was really costing David to do it, but I knew it wasn't easy.

'Why aren't we sticking these freaks in bottles?' one of the less intelligent Wardens yelled from somewhere in the back. 'Murdering bastards!'

Lewis didn't let anger slip free very often – he was mostly of the 'irony is the best policy' school of thought – but there was no mistaking the steel in his voice this time. 'Shut up, or you're dealing with me,' he snapped. The silence that fell afterward stretched for long enough to make his point before he continued. 'Let me get something completely clear. The Djinn aren't our slaves, and they aren't our pets. They're our partners in this, and they ought to be our partners in everything we do. If they struck out at us in a rage, they were acting in defence of themselves and the Earth.' Well, not quite. Ashan had also been conducting his own campaign against David for control of the Djinn, but Lewis was right, in the main. 'We oppressed them for thousands of years. We forced them to do things that none of us wants to think about or acknowledge. We sealed them in bottles with *Demons*. Think about it. They came after us, and we damn well deserved it.'

Another uproar, this one composed of a whole lot of variations of oh-no-you-don'ts. Lewis waited it out, stone-faced, arms folded. Yeah, that had gone over well.

Two of the Wardens got up and tried to storm out of the room. *I don't think so*, I thought furiously, and created an invisible shield of hardened air around the door. The first rebel hit it and bounced off...an Earth Warden, big and burly in a lumberjack kind of way. The second, however, was a Weather Warden. Sarah Crossman, from Iowa. Decent enough person, but hidebound. She lost her temper and tried to pry at the hold I had over it.

And the fragile, highly undependable hold I had over my own temper broke. It sounded like shattering glass, which made sense, because somehow the air pressure in the room had dropped, along with the temperature, and the cloudy windows way up at the top of the room (because the other, alternative use for this place was basketball) blew out in a spray of powdered glass. People screamed, and wind whipped in uncontrollable currents.

And then everything went very, very still as Lewis grabbed hold of the air and took control from me. The door that Sarah Crossman was pulling on suddenly opened, smacking her in the face and sending her reeling backward.

Lewis said, 'If you want to go, go. But if you leave this room, you're out of the Wardens. And I'll see to it that your powers will be neutered.'

There was an audible gasp from the Warden side of the room, and both of the groups of Djinn smiled ever so slowly. The Ma'at exchanged uneasy glances.

'You can't do that!' Ah, it was my old friend Emily, from Maine; I hadn't seen her since Eamon had drugged her and abducted me out of the cab of her truck. Good times. She was a solid, blocky woman, prone to clunky shoes and flannel shirts and mulish expressions. 'You can't force us to agree with you!'

'It ain't a democracy, Auntie Em,' Paul noted dryly. 'I think he can. You don't like it, just let me know what time's good for that clinic appointment.'

'Don't you threaten—'

I slammed the Manolo down hard on the table, 'Emily! I will personally make sure you end up strapped to a gurney. And I won't be nearly as nice about it as Lewis; you can bet your ass on that! Now *sit down*!'

Silence. Most people in the room knew pieces and hints of what had happened to me in the last week, and more than a few had heard some version of a story that I'd had a daughter, and lost her in a Djinn attack. It wasn't wrong in the main, just fuzzy in the particulars.

The thing was, I wasn't seen as entirely sane, so nobody really wanted to cross me. I could only imagine that I looked just as ragged-edged as the stories indicated. That, combined with such a spectacular loss of control, suggested that a certain amount of caution might be in order.

Things were very, very still. Lewis was looking at me. So was everyone else.

'Jo.' David's very quiet voice next to me. I felt the pressure of his hand on my shoulder, then the friction of his fingertips stroking my hair. He wasn't using magic of any kind, except the whisper that was always present between us. 'Easy.'

He was right. There was emotion boiling up in me, and I couldn't afford it, not here. Not now. I pulled myself sharply back with a flinch that I was sure was visible.

David slowly settled back in his chair, still watching me with total, gentle attention.

Lewis had started talking again. 'I think we're agreed that since this isn't the natural time for this magnetic flip to begin, we should counter it while we still have the chance. Now, the Ma'at have developed a whole new way of looking at the manipulation of power on the aetheric plane, and there's a lot we can—'

'Who are these people? Why were they operating in secret?' demanded a Warden from the floor, who was too angry to let a little thing like my mood swings stop him.

'They were formed to try to undo some of the damage the Wardens were doing to the environment,' Lewis said. 'They never interfered directly with us.'

'No, but they were undermining us! No wonder

our success rate kept getting worse! Lives were lost!'

Lewis kept the microphone, despite impatient waves from Myron to pass it back. 'The Wardens' success rate was getting worse because we were undermining *one another*,' he said. 'Amongst other things. You know there were a lot of things wrong in the organisation, including Wardens selling out innocent people for profit.' He wasn't pulling any punches. So far as I knew, nobody had *ever* put it that baldly, at least outside of very private, hush-hush conversations at the highest levels. 'Demon Marks have subverted key members. Senior Wardens have taken kickbacks from criminal organisations. Wardens at all levels are guilty of outright murder. So let's not pretend that anybody in this room has a monopoly on being right.'

That last word fell into a vast, ringing silence. Somebody shifted uneasily in a folding chair, waking a squeal of metal like worn-out brakes.

'I'm not making accusations,' Lewis said. 'I'm stating facts. These things happened. And they're not going to happen anymore.'

'Or?' someone stage-muttered. It might have even been from the Ma'at.

Lewis smiled slowly. I wouldn't have wanted to be on the receiving end of that one. 'They're not... going...to happen...anymore,' he repeated very softly, and held the entire room's stare. The place had gone very quiet, and the air was crackling with potential energy. 'We're not going to be the bad guys. The Ma'at have things to teach us. We probably have a few things to teach them, too. Now. Everybody choose.'

One Warden stood up and walked out, not bothering to mitigate the shriek of metal chair over bare floor. We all winced, even the Djinn. The door banged shut behind his grand exit.

I didn't try to stop him. Besides, I'd already blown out the windows. Not much of a big gesture left to make.

'One down,' Lewis said, unruffled. 'Anybody else want to join him and stop wasting our time?'

The rest of them exchanged glances and settled back more comfortably into their places.

I reclaimed the microphone and nervously clutched it in both hands. 'We worked out that we should have three teams: Fire, Earth, and Weather, with Ma'at and Djinn equally distributed among them. The Djinn will interface us directly with the Oracles of each of the three types to ground us.'

Someone out there gave a disbelieving snort. 'It'll never work.'

'Maybe not. But I'd take it as a personal favour if you could try.'

That caused a stir, albeit a discreet one. Nobody knew quite what to make of me, really, but the rumour had already flown like lightning through the ranks of the Wardens – and no doubt the Ma'at as well – that I was falling into the more-than-human category. They didn't know I, like Lewis, was now a triple threat...that I controlled all three elements. I wasn't too comfortable with anyone knowing quite yet.

I wasn't sure what it meant, either personally or professionally. Or even if, long-term, I planned to stay a professional Warden. I was kind of interested in what the Ma'at had to say, although I still didn't much like their leadership.

Half of the Djinn were looking at David, half at Ashan. What a scary bunch they were – all packaged up nicely in human form, but with a slight edge to them that let everyone around know not to get too comfortable. It was going to be quite an adjustment between the Wardens and the Djinn. Wardens had lorded it over the Djinn for thousands of years. Djinn had worked as slaves, handed off from one master to another, their will subjugated to the needs of the moment or their masters' whims. That kind of thing doesn't just stop because somebody waves a magic wand, not even in our world. Too many of those Djinn had been abused, and all of them were wary of it ever happening again.

Ashan nodded, after keeping David in suspense for long enough to make his point. David said, 'The Djinn will cooperate in this. All of us.'

Lazlo cleared his throat. 'The Ma'at will of course help any way we can,' he said stiffly. 'We'll be happy to demonstrate our way of channelling forces. It might be helpful for this. Of course, we're shorthanded, and the Ma'at were never as widespread or powerful as the Wardens...' He was back-pedalling so fast that if he didn't watch it, he'd fall under the wheels.

The Djinn suddenly transferred their attention as a unit from David to Lazlo. It was like being hit with a truck, and then being knocked into a black hole. I watched his throat work, pale, wrinkled skin trembling as he struggled to stay calm.

'But of course,' he amended, 'we will give our full support.'

The Ma'at had never participated in the slavery of the Djinn. The Djinn that helped them – Rahel among them – were always free to come, go, or stay. It was an easy and practical arrangement, and the Djinn had a level of trust in the Ma'at that they did not have – and might not ever have – in the Wardens.

But the Ma'at had no illusions about the Djinn, as the Wardens had... We'd been lulled into a false sense of security over the millennia of ordering around creatures far more powerful than we could ever hope to be. We thought that if a predator took orders, it was no longer a predator.

We'd learnt better these past few weeks.

We got down to the operational details. I let Lewis and Lazlo handle the fierce debate. I was mainly there to act as a moderator, and to wield a mean shoe when necessary. And terrify anybody who got out of line, of course.

David was still holding my hand. I looked sideways at him without turning my head, and saw he was openly watching me.

He leant closer, put his mouth to my ear, and said, 'What do you think? Can we do this? Together?'

'It's day one of the new world,' I said. 'These things take time. But yeah, I think we probably can. It'll be messy and bumpy, but we'll get through it. And next time it'll be a little better.' I turned to look at him, and our eyes met. I felt that warm shiver go through me again, as if we were still connected in some odd, unexplained way, although the bond of master and slave-Djinn was long dissolved. 'David. Are you going to be all right?' I meant in this thing with Ashan.

He shrugged. 'It's complicated.'

'What, and *this* isn't?' I raised an eyebrow at the debate, which was rising in volume. 'Spill.'

His eyebrows climbed, too. 'Why?'

'It might have escaped you, but what affects the Djinn pretty much seems to roll downhill to humanity. So I'd like to know now, instead of later, when I'm fighting for my life. Also, I love you, and

I'll kick his fine Djinn ass if he hurts you.'

He glanced around the room, looking innocent. Entirely false. I had reason to know. 'You really want to talk about it here?'

'No,' I said. 'I want to talk about it someplace a lot quieter than this, with a hot tub, but if we leave, things are going to slide downhill without us, and you know it.'

He nodded slowly. 'This had to happen, Jo. The Old Ones weren't going to endure having someone like me as their conduit. I'm not like Jonathan. I can't...step away from the world and take the long view.'

'Too close to humans,' I said, remembering what Venna had said. 'Too close to me. *I* caused this.'

'No,' he said. 'And change isn't destruction. It's just change. Maybe we're adapting into two species – the Old Ones as pure Djinn, the rest of us into something that can – and should – remain closer to you. To help.' He glanced over towards Ashan, who was watching us with eerie concentration. So was Venna, frowning slightly. 'When they're finished today they'll go, and they won't interact with humans unless they have to, for the good of the Djinn or the good of the Mother. But my people will. We'll stay with the Ma'at. We'll stay with the Wardens. We'll stay part of everything.' He lifted my hand to his lips. 'Everything.'

My heart rate picked up a few dozen beats per

minute. The debate was slowing down, Lewis was making notes on a big wipe-board with names and procedures, and already there was a sense of purpose in the room. A sense, strangely, of excitement.

It was day one, and we were going to change.

And change wasn't a bad thing.

'Well,' I said, 'when this is over, you're mine, David. I expect to have your full, undivided attention for at least twenty-four hours. Maybe longer.'

He kissed my hand. There went the heart rate, edging up again.

'You have it,' he said, 'for the rest of your life. When this is over, we can go for a drive. I understand the seats recline in the Mustang.'

I closed my eyes and soaked that in, and then I stood up.

I addressed the entire room. 'Let's go save the world.'

Because from this day forward, that was officially our job.

Sound Track

Once again, music saves my sanity. Enjoy this track list on your iPod...I sure did!

'Ain't No Sunshine' .... Bill Withers
'Ballroom Blitz' .... Sweet
'The Bitter End' .... Placebo
'Black Horse and the Cherry Tree' .... K. T. Tunstall
'Blockbuster' .... Sweet
'Bother' .... Stone Sour
'Boulevard of Broken Dreams' .... Green Day
'Bridge to Better Days' .... Joe Bonamassa
'Calling Card' .... Rory Gallagher
'Coming Undone' .... Korn
'Crazy' .... Gnarls Barkley
'Cry' .... James Blunt
'Dani California' .... Red Hot Chili Peppers
'The Denial Twist' .... The White Stripes
'Face Down' .... Red Jumpsuit Apparatus
'Give Me Your Love' .... Reef
'God Is a Bullet' .... Concrete Blonde
'Going to My Hometown' .... Rory Gallagher
'Gone Daddy Gone' .... Gnarls Barkley
'I'm Still Awake' .... Hybrid
'Inertia Creeps' .... Massive Attack
'The Jean Genie' .... David Bowie
'Jenny Was a Friend of Mine' .... The Killers
'Judith' .... A Perfect Circle
'Just Another Day' .... Oingo Boingo
'Killing in the Name' .... Rage Against the Machine
'Ladyfingers' .... Luscious Jackson
'Last Resort' .... Papa Roach
'Look After You' .... The Fray

'Maybe Tomorrow' .... Stereophonies
'Original Fire' .... Audioslave
'Private Idaho' .... The B-52s
'Pump It Up' .... Elvis Costello
'Punish Me with Kisses' .... Bird York
'Rock Lobster' .... The B-52s
'Steady as She Goes' .... The Raconteurs
'Stuck in the Middle with You' .... Stealers Wheel
'Take a Number' .... Stone Sour
'Tear You Apart' .... She Wants Revenge
'Temperature' .... Sean Paul
'Through Glass' .... Stone Sour
'...To Be Loved' .... Papa Roach
'Tubthumping' .... Chumbawamba
'Venus' .... Bananarama
'Voodoo Light' .... Jim Suhler and Monkey Beat
'We Used To Be Friends' .... The Dandy Warhols
'When I'm Gone' .... 3 Doors Down
'Wichita Lineman' .... Glenn Campbell
'Worry About You' .... Ivy

HIGHLY RECOMMENDED: Joe Bonamassa's new album, *You & Me*!

Want to make track list suggestions? Send them to Rachel@rachelcaine.com!

Also by Rachel Caine

The Morganville Vampires series

Check out our website for free tasters and exclusive
discounts, competitions and giveaways, and sign up to
our monthly newsletter to keep up-to-date on our latest
releases, news and upcoming events.
www.allisonandbusby.com